Leoshine

Princess Oracle

Book 1

N. M^{ac}Cameron

Dear Heather,

Thank you for your support and patience as Leoshine was developed. I hope you enjoy this introduction to her story.

Love
[signature]

Siretona
CREATIVE

Published by Siretona Creative. www.siretona.com

Printed in Canada by BlitzPrint, Calgary, AB.

Distributed to the trade by The Ingram Book Company.

Cover design begun by 100 Covers with direction by Margarita Felix; completed by Travis Williams and Colleen McCubbin of Siretona Creative.

Cover painting by Anna Pederson https://graceartistry.com

Tassanara font designed by Travis Williams https://www.booksbytravis.com

Map design by Rachael Ward; map editing by Nathan Ledbetter and Travis Williams.

Cover titling fonts: Avenir, Palatino, and Tassanara

Interior titling fonts: Garamond and Tassanara

ISBN 978-1-988983-18-9 paperback
ISBN 978-1-988983-20-2 electronic book
ISBN 978-1-988983-21-9 audiobook

Dedication

To Third Culture Kids (TCKs) everywhere,
especially my elder brother:
Willem Bosch 1966-2010

LEGEND

	1 DAY
	RIDE

▭▭▭▭▭▭▭ UNDERGROUND RIVER

············· ROAD / BOUNDARY MARKER

4

GAVIN'S TOWN

EQUINE PASTURES

TVH

THE CATHEDRAL

ILIANA'S PALACE

GAVIN'S PALACE

PALACE GARDENS

THE BATH HOUSE

THE ARENA

THE WATCH TOWER

THE ORCHARDS

Contents

ao Kenan Leoshine's Guide to Myxolidia

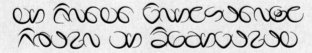

In the far distant future, those who read this history of Myxolidia, as well as those who visit, may wish to know the meaning of some terms and place names familiar to the Myxolidian people.

Here I, ao Kenan Leoshine, Co-Regent of Myxolidia, offer a humble assortment of definitions and pronunciations to you in hopes that you will feel at home among us.

Characters

Leoshine – The youngest child of Curtstas. Mediary between the Aeolians and her own people of Myxolidia.

Avram – Also known as ao Kevath. Chosen leader of the Aeolian mission to regenerate the atmosphere of Myxolidia.

Resham – Valet to Avram. Also chief cultural advisor, bodyguard, priest, and physician. Taken from Myxolidia to Aeolia as a child and adopted by ao Kenan Iliana as a son and brother to Avram.

Ao Kevad – High King of Aeolia and Myxolidia. Instigator of the rescue mission.

Curtstas – Leoshine's father. Mayor of the only pre-Aeolian town under the Myxolidian Dome. Studied the Dome and invented a system to record its deterioration. Taken to Aeolia to experience and recognise the benefit of re-establishing connection with our progenitors' descendants.

Mother – Leoshine's mother, keeper of traditions. Wifeholder of Curtstas' compound and weaver of fine linen.

Iliana – Avram's mother. Priestess, physician, and teacher. Daughter of a past Overlord of Aeolia.

Georg – Leoshine's oldest brother. Trained to lead. Brave, trustworthy, and dead.

Giffshine – Leoshine's oldest sister. Deranged by several failed Rites of Womanhood. She did not give birth to a live child. A rebel against the Aeolians.

Hillashine – Leoshine's middle sister. Initiated through the Rite of Womanhood, she is pregnant at the beginning of this history.

Wol – Leoshine's nearest sibling in age. His rebellion against Father transfers to Avram. Leader of the Woltreaders. Intelligent, arrogant, favourite of Mother.

Gavin – Avram's city general. Giant, gentle, and observant. His wife Heien (Iliana's niece) and five children arrive with Iliana.

Uly – Avram's general. Spokesman for the generals. He had a wife who died early in their marriage. Expert in transportation.

Dorim – Avram's general. He had a wife who refused to come to Myxolidia. Expert with energy forces.

Kirim – Avram's general. Brother of Dorim. They were abandoned to Iliana's orphanages on Aeolia. Loves swimming and boating.

Lantro – Avram's general. Quick with the sword. All the generals grew up with Avram, schooled together, trained as soldiers together.

Alan – Avram's general. Tall and hawk-like. Most cynical and prejudiced of the generals.

Zolous – Gavin's second in command.

Rasset – The chief scientist responsible for the regeneration of the Dome. He would have been called a Trickixim or "guardian of the Dome" in pre-schism days. Post-schism they became an order of priests.

Paulos – Avram's stallion. Imprinted on Avram and trained for war.

Gorphiline – Leoshine's Rellogat servant before Avram arrives.

Geography

The Dome of Myxolidia – A generated atmosphere first established on a planetine by the Aeolians 1000 years before Avram's arrival. Her people suffered a tragic schism that led to the Dome's neglect and deterioration.

Gavin's Town – Used to be Curtstas' Town. The only pre-Aeolian town under the Dome and the seat of government. Avram rebuilds the wooden structures with stone quarried from freeing the underground rivers. None of the streets run very far in one direction.

Leoshine's Family Compound – The home where Leoshine grew up. The women's quarters are segregated from the men's quarters. Curtstas' governing council chambers lie within the compound walls. The only source of water for the town, the only well kept alive from pre-schism days, lies under its foundation.

The Watch Tower – The tallest building located in the centre of the town. Used to scout for Oxikobh attackers. Leoshine's childhood favourite place to escape.

The Bathhouse – Built by Curtstas when he returns from Aeolia. Only Leoshine takes up this new custom.

The Arena – Built by Alan shortly after the invasion. Used for Avram's contests with his soldiers and generals.

The Cathedral – The worship house. Built by Avram to honour Ao Kevad.

Iliana's Palace – Built by Avram to house his mother when she arrives. A copy of her home in Aeolia. Home of Iliana's chapel where Ao Kevad's portrait hangs. Home of Iliana's workshop where she manufactures medicines and has hospital equipment.

Gavin's Palace – Built by Avram to house his city general and family.

TVH (Transport Vehicle Hanger) – The storage facility for the only Aeolian transport under the Myxolidian Dome. The pilot quarters here.

Equine Pastures – Curtstas and his sons trained horses here and taught Leoshine to ride. Horses were a status symbol in his government.

The Orchards – Planted by Curtstas after his return from Aeolia. He took wild stock from the forest. This wild stock had been cultivated before the schism.

Dome Engines 1-4 – Built by the original Trickixim to generate and sustain the atmosphere that is called the Dome. Self-sustaining for many generations.

Kaaiput Mountains – Mountains far distant from the town where Oxikobh try to mislead Aeolians.

Elego's Compound – The Oxikobh compound where wife-holders and children have gathered to wait the return of their men.

Landing Site – Ancient touchdown site for Interdomiary Vessels (IDV). The *Talon* IDV is a shuttle that goes between Aeolia and Myxolidia on an approximately three-month schedule.

Resham's Workshop – Jail, prisoner of war camp, torture chamber.

North Gorge – Far distant from the town where Oxikobh try to mislead Aeolians.

Wol's Camp – Wol's headquarters.

Dictionary

Military Manoeuvres

Bertrae Bair-trāy – A strategy for protecting the town. Four generals are posted to the four points of the compass. Gavin remains in town. The sixth general is available to support wherever he is needed.

Cortransa Cor-trăn-să – When two large bodies of soldiers meet outside the town, this manoeuver allows them to mix without accident. The leader of each body swings it around behind him and then converges on the other leader.

Equipment

Teshaddar Tĕ-shĕ-ddahr – An electronic shield that secures Leoshine into her saddle.

Endearments
Aeolian

Obenici Ō-bĕn-ēssē – Oracle

Ephitide Ĕff-ĭ-tyd – Treasure

Whips-tarn Whĭsp-taarn – An Aeolian sprite - character in a fairytale. **Tassanara** Tă-ssă-nă-ră – Princess

Myxolidian

Epiphrondite Ĕp-ĭ-frŏnd-yte – Darling

Sassnigor Săss-nĭ-gor – Someone who lags behind

Tobera TŌ-bear-ă – Diminutive Slave

Babim Bă-bim – Infant Darling

Snoriginund Snor-ĭ-ghĭ-nund – Sleepy Head

Norfinoof Nor-fĭn-oof – Ninny

Torpvehr Torp-fair – Beauty

Flora and Fauna
Aeolian

Asced Āth-sĕd – Plant Species

Pulimeit Pŭl-ĭ-mēt – Plant Species

Planetine Plă-nĕt-ēn – The perfect chunk of rock for building generated atmospheres

Myxolidian

Aeok'n – the Myxolidian name for the generated atmosphere.

Chackwood Chăck-wude – Twigs of a shrub that taste sweet and are good for cleaning teeth. "To suck on chackwood" is to be part of the family.

Coeval Cō-ēvaal – A stream

Gallalla Ghă-lă-ăh-lă – Tiny, fierce bird that hides its nest in hedges.

Insults
Aeolian

Codmockers Cŏd-mŏkk-ers

Myxolidian

Barskatrafing Squallywalker Bår-skătrā-fŋ Skwållē-wå-ker

Oxikobh Ŏx-ĭ-cŏb – Savages in the Myxolidian Forest

Servants and Slaves

Rachnorgat Raɣ-nor-găt – Victim of the Mercy Plea

Rellogat Rĕl-lŏ-găt – More like a servant than a slave. A trusted member of the household who does menial work in exchange for food and shelter.

Omaeulenen Ō-mæ-ü-lĕ-nĕn – Handmaid to Iliana (Plural: **Omaeuli** Ō-mæ-ü-lē)

Cooking and Food
Eqipgn Oil Ĕkwĭ-pĭdgeon – Oil, cooking oil

Units of Measurement

Rihg Reeg – Paces

Lort Lort – Kilometres

Titles of address
ao Kevath eye-0h Kĕ-văth – my lord

ao Kenan eye-0h Kĕ-naan – my lady

Dsxano'i – Princess in Myxolidian. Used to refer to the Dome Aeo'kn.

Concepts, Rituals and Protocols

Mercy Plea — When one Myxolidian wrongs another, they pay with their life, unless, they call "Mercy." At that point they become a Rachnorgat — the lowest form of slave. They are kept in animal-like conditions, fed minimally. But at least they are alive. The wronged party becomes the Rachnorgain or 'master.'

Rite of Womanhood — Myxolidian Initiation for girls into childbearing. Her parents choose a man for her. She must fall pregnant during the ritual. After that, she must give birth to a live child before she is allowed to join her man as a primary wife. If she fails to give birth to a live child, she either stays with her parents, or becomes a secondary wife to any man who will support her. He must protect and feed her. In return she gives him sexual rites without fear of feeding children. (Note: From her place of privilege, Leoshine's oldest sister, Giffshine was given several "Initiations" before her father returned from Aeolia and stopped the practice.)

This Guide is dedicated to
a wonderful young woman named Emily,
who has contributed a powerful amount
of information and advice to Leoshine's creation.

*This is a condensed version with matter specific to Book One.
For ao Kenan Leoshine's full guide please visit
http://www.tassanara.com/resources/2/#Guide/

In the Beginning

Leoshine reveled in the warm embrace of her bathwater, submerging her chin and drawing it up until the surface tension broke and set her free.

She drew a deep breath. The water molded to her lithe form and allowed her ribs to expand to their fullest. Steam swirled in little eddies and moisture collected on the fine hairs of her upper lip and eyebrows.

Father, the builder of the bathhouse just outside the women's compound, had disappeared late in her childhood, no one knew where. Mother was just finishing her widowhood rites when Father reappeared one day, reclaiming his position as Mayor of the only town under the Dome of Myxolidia.

He implemented all manner of new ideas. Leoshine glanced at the rigid chest brace that lay on top of her clothes. She had worn the hard plate strapped to her chest since the day after he returned. She inhaled again, dreading leaving her warm womb and strapping that "new idea" to her breast.

While he was away, all her aunts' daughters had been initiated into their men's houses. Even Gorphiline, the Rellogat servant who waited outside to bind Leoshine up again, had recently birthed a live child to prove her womanhood. Mother railed almost every day at Father. "Curtstas, what are you doing to your daughter?" Leoshine glanced down at her chest. She didn't think she'd have trouble nursing babies if she ever had to.

Mother railed about other things too. She feared the Rachnorgat slaves that father freed and elevated to Rellogat status when he returned.

The walls of the bathhouse exhaled steam, enough to muffle the voice of Giffshine, Curtstas' eldest daughter. "Leoshine, Leoshine!"

Leoshine rolled her eyes to the dripping struts of the roof and sank up to her earlobes.

"Where is that vagrant?"

Wol, their brother answered. "She's in Father's water tub again."

Hillashine, the middle sister sneered. "Bent on destruction."

Wol raised his voice. "I'll tell you what I'll do. I'll get a bucket of worms ..."

Leoshine jumped when Giffshine banged on the bathhouse door. "Leoshine. Mother wants you. Now!"

Gorphiline slipped into the moist bath chamber and placed her baby on the floor. Without a word she held a towel with her arms stretched out straight and jerked her head at the door.

The water cascaded off Leoshine as she left the bath. As the water music lapped at the tub walls, and the ripples interlaced and grew quiet, she toweled herself and dressed her long golden-brown hair.

Gorphiline held the brace. "Turn around."

"Why do I have to?" Leoshine asked for the first time in a long time. "You lost your teeth at the same time as me." She turned her back to her personal attendant and lifted her arms. Losing teeth was a mark of age, like hair length. Gorphiline used to be the same as her. Now she wore the woman's more ornate robe, an infant on her hip, and one in her belly.

The servant wrapped the brace under Leoshine's arms and pulled. "Your father said so."

Leoshine groaned. The ties at the back drew the hard part of the structure into her chest from her collar bone to the bottom of her ribcage until her breath caught. Since he returned, Father kept telling her she was special. He allowed her to see where he and the other men worked. He told her secrets about Aeok'n, the Dome Dsxano'i.

"Not so tight!"

The servant grunted, threw a simple tunic at her, scooped up the baby, and left.

Leoshine wriggled into the dress that was undecorated and perfect for an uninitiated girl. She peeked out the door, and listened. More than once she had emerged from the bathhouse to be pelted by rocks, mudcakes, and eggs.

Her soft soled boots hardly bruised the grass as she trotted across the lawn toward the women's compound in her father's low-built, rambling palace.

Wol's rabble, bullies of anyone who followed Father's "new ideas," rounded the corner. Leoshine slammed the women's gate behind her.

The rhythm of looms welcomed her to her mother's workroom.

"Leotjie!" Mother exhaled in a gust. In one gesture she swept her daughter onto a stool and threw an avalanche of wool challis dyed with orpher berries over her head. "Stand still."

Leoshine poked her head through the neck hole and gazed out over the vegetable garden. The Rellogat girl picking peas plucked a weed by the roots and flung it at the girl picking beans. A chicken pecked at the new dirt.

In the orchard, planted in the shadow of the town wall, the men would be harvesting apples while the women put the flax stalks into tubs for retting. Behind Leoshine, five strong women shuttled and cocked new stretches of Mother's fine linen on five clacking looms.

Leoshine's shoulders sagged under the weight of her new gown. She tipped her head back. Mother had hung tapestries over the roughhewn walls to block the draft. Not so the rafters. Blood pooled in Leoshine's lax fingertips. Mother muttered below, buried in the folds.

Footsteps hammered down the hall. Hillashine stormed in. "Leoshine! Where's my lace collar?"

Mother fought her way free of the hem, and Leoshine turned toward the doorway.

"I said, where is it? I gave it to you to wash."

"Why didn't you give it to Reanour?" Mother cocked a questioning eye at Leoshine.

"On the window sill. Drying in the kitchen." Leoshine frowned. Mother chose too often to ignore Hillashine's petty rivalry with the Rellogat servants.

"You slow batraworsk hog! You only just did it, didn't you? You lazy …"

Leoshine's fingertips curled and her shoulders gathered up to her ears.

Hillashine stomped away. Mother sighed amid her work in the folds.

"She didn't need to talk that way," Leoshine complained.

"You could have done it sooner." As she disappeared under the hem, Mother muttered, "Everything's changing again."

Leoshine closed her eyes. The clack of the looms droned on. The girls finished their harvesting and left the garden to tend to Mother's bees.

The moment Mother set Leoshine free, she ran all the way to the top of Father's palace, the highest watchtower under the Dome, or "Aeok'n," the mother atmosphere that stretched above her, uniformly grey and predictable. She looked out over the tree tops and inhaled their breath as her own.

Father claimed town and forest as his kingdom. Myxolidia, he called it. The compound lay at her feet, the women's quarters separated by a wall from the men's chambers, where Father ruled the council. The spring that bubbled up beneath the kitchen made the palace the most important land under the drought-stricken Dome. Laid at her feet, she saw the rooftops of the citizens who remembered and honoured Father's ideas.

Leoshine shivered. Stories about the horrors the Oxikobh, people who rejected Father's authority did to each other and town folk outside the protective wooden barricade, throughout the forest, were often whispered around her.

Once a cycle Father braved the threat to take care of Aeok'n. He ventured to the barrier lands, sacrificed at what he called "engines" and showed strange markings on parchment to her when he returned. She understood a little more each time. As his daughter she was supposed to stay within the women's quarters. She certainly wasn't supposed to venture into the wilderness.

Leoshine smiled to herself. She was different. High above the squabbles and laws, far from prying eyes, she gazed upon Myxolidia and wondered, *Where shall I explore? And what are those changes Mother talked about?*

Capture

"Mine own!"

Mother's wail rippled through Leoshine.

Tears glued her sisters' greasy hair to her face. Giffshine and Hillashine's bodies, tight against her own, convulsed with sobs. Mother's hands stroked and pulled them closer into her embrace, which squeezed Leoshine's already constricted breathing.

For two nights they had staggered through the forest with the main group that had fled the town, and later, after Mother collapsed yet again, as a forlorn huddle of four with no food and only mouthfuls of cursed water from the wild creeks in Oxikobh territory.

Today at dawn a knot of filthy Oxikobh had ambushed them and dumped them into this dark hole in the side of a low bank.

Giffshine moved to disengage from the embrace. Leoshine heard straw rustle beneath them. Her hand clenched on Mother's neckline, drawing the coarse weave to her lips.

It smelled of home—the fatty suds of Mother up to her elbows in raw, wet fleece, the stench of retting, rotten flax, and the lint of a lifetime of weft. Mother secured the strands of the entire family compound.

Voices outside warned them a moment before the hingeless lid of the cave ripped open. Grotesque shadows rushed up the rough rock walls like an advancing ghoul army.

The reek of sweat and breath from the slinking Oxikobh filled the cave. Their grunts and leering laughs drew curses from Mother.

Hillashine hurled insults in the dagger-tongued language

of the Oxikobh. Giffshine had taught her the words after they thought their little sister slept. Leoshine shrank deeper into the straw. Her brace dug into her armpits. She hugged it closer. If they took it off they would see how ready she was for the initiation.

Giffshine seemed to melt into the rock wall.

The first captor to reach them fastened his sausage-like fingers around Hillashine's wrists. She screamed louder and Mother swung her fist. Another man grabbed Hillashine's waist and swung her toward the door. Mother rose and rushed at them. Another savage shoved her backward and Leoshine felt the crushing weight of Mother's bulk on her leg and hip as she tried to scramble clear.

Giffshine emerged from the shadows, grabbed the wrists of Hillashine's captor, and stared into his eyes. "Take me," she commanded.

Another Oxikobh kicked the man who towed Hillashine's ankles and both her captors dropped her. Giffshine disappeared out the hole, with the Oxikobh licking their lips behind her.

The halo of light around the hole lid burned into Leoshine's retinas. She ached to pull her knees into her chest.

Straw rustled as Mother shifted. Leoshine's forehead grated against Hillashine's as Mother gathered them onto her clammy bosom. Hillashine's breath stank.

Only last week Leoshine had lounged in the bathhouse in the women's compound. A tear on her lip reminded her of how the water had tickled the hairs on her half-submerged chin. She shifted to free her head and clear clingy hair strands from her face.

Convulsions seized Hillashine. Mother's voice joined her thin wail. They knew she would be next.

What will this outrage mean to Hillashine's hope? Leoshine's tongue melded with the roof of her mouth. Her sister had recently been through the Rite of Womanhood. It was too early to know if she had succeeded. She had to give birth to a live child before she could be joined to her man.

Where is Father? They wouldn't dare touch the town mayor's women if he was here. He had proven his authority as mayor by killing Oxikobh.

She remembered standing with him, surrounded by his councillors, near the gate in the pole barricade surrounding the town. His eyes had beamed. His teeth had flashed in his beard when a towering stranger in Oxikobh clothes, wearing their long, razor-wire sword, had pushed through the guard at the gate and addressed him in unaccented town Myxolidian. He didn't even touch the hilt of his own short, broadsword hanging amid the furs from his belt.

Leoshine remembered tucking behind his arm, inhaling his scent in his sleeve. The giant Oxikobh had not bowed or shown any sign of respect to Father, who had answered with strange sounds. As he and the stranger stepped out through the gate, Father had leaned down to whisper in her ear. "These are friends, Leotjie."

Did the giant hurt Father after we left? Georg, her oldest brother, helping Father defend the town, would keep him safe, even if Wol ran away.

The lid of the cave wrenched open. Gruesome shadows rushed across the floor. Mother tucked Leoshine between herself and the rock wall behind her and stuffed straw over Leoshine's slippered foot.

The gang of leering monsters skulked toward them.

Leoshine wriggled to relieve the pressure on her lungs and gasped as Mother's elbow secured her even tighter.

Giffshine's willowy figure staggered forward. Mother flung Hillashine off her lap and lurched up to catch Giffshine.

Fingers curled around Leoshine's ankle.

She screamed and kicked with both legs. As she slid across the straw, she strained forward against the binder bruising her abdomen and pried her fingers into the grip on her ankle. She sank her teeth into the Oxikobh's wrist. Her lips curled away from the acrid taste of his skin.

From behind, someone lifted her under her arms. Mother screamed and Leoshine felt her captor cringe under Mother's blows.

"She's not initiated," Mother screeched. "A curse is a curse on Townsman or Oxikobh for taking a girl not initiated."

Leoshine twisted her torso and her arms and legs in all directions against the binding hands. Her teeth found leverage before her legs were yanked up and her head scraped along the floor. Her dress fell over her face. She was lifted and suddenly the hands released her.

She rolled to stand and tumbled as the floor moved. The light filtered through a course weave. *A sack.* Her hands filled with the cloth. *I'm inside a sack.* She pulled one side of her prison up and tumbled as the other side wrenched from under her feet.

In the next instant her arms flailed and her body collided with bone and muscle.

Mother and Hillashine's screams grew fainter. Leoshine swayed and thudded amid sounds of feet shuffling through dead leaves. The last she heard was a mournful howl.

"Mine own!"

She fought to get her feet under her. Once, twice she bounded up and down while pummeling her elbows into the back of the man carrying her. A fist grazed her head and landed with a thump on the shoulder behind her. She cringed in murky darkness.

Leoshine struggled to draw breath in the musty sack. Her sweat-damped brace-ties and dress chafed wherever she touched the back of the man carrying her.

The sway mingled with dizziness, hunger and drowsiness. She had heard them drinking and eating at a rest-stop. She tried to swallow past her swollen tongue.

Where are they taking me? Mother cursed them. Do they care?

They have something worse for me. She allowed her tears to fall unhindered. Her lower lip cracked and bled when it rose under her upper lip.

They had wandered for three days in Oxikobh territory before being captured. How far did they wander from the town?

As a little girl, before Father returned and changed everything, she used to stretch her arms above her head, even stand on her tiptoes, and imagine her fingers wiggling in the 'ether' of the Dome far, far above her head.

Leoshine huddled her head deeper into her shoulders. *I'm different, I went into the council chambers. I climbed the tower to look at Myxolidia.*

At the gate, only three days ago, after almost banishing her in his haste, Father had followed the giant Oxikobh outside the walls, and returned, dancing with victory.

"These are friends, Leotjie," Father had whispered. "These are they who took me and taught me; now I can say their name." He had puckered his lips, wet them with his tongue, and mouthed a foreign syllable: "Aeolian, my dearest child. These are the Aeolians who will bring greatness to our Dome. Abundance. Food that you can't dream of, soft cloth like your mother would sell her soul for." He had kissed his fingers to the air.

Mother didn't believe him. She had gathered her women and their daughters and run, cursing him for the danger he courted. Leoshine had tried to stay, but Mother promised she knew a safe place for her women to hide.

Noises of combat had followed them through the forest. They had stumbled on a man lying prone with blood on his neck. Before Leoshine could see more, Mother had covered her eyes and dragged her away.

After three nights of hiding in the undergrowth and two days of trudging, Mother had collapsed, moaning, "Disaster, disaster."

Leoshine opened her eyes. Through the coarse woven sack wall, she could see the hunched Oxikobh trudging behind the one who carried her.

By her knee she noticed a small beam of light. She set her fingers to enlarge the hole. *Not too big*, she cautioned, *just enough to see*. In a short time, she pushed both sets of her fingers through.

Her eye neared the hole. Suddenly a slimy tongue and lips fastened on her fingers and forced themselves through the hole. She screamed and kicked her feet out to shove the sack wall as far away as possible.

Laughter outside reminded her of Giffshine telling how Oxikobh licked the skin off townswomen. Her skin prickled and perspiration ran down her temples.

Their speech grated all around her. "Lively." She recognised. "Gift."

I'm being given to someone. Her heart beat in her ears. *Lively, gift. Lively, gift.* She covered her mouth and nose. With closed eyes she forced her ribs against the brace and drew breath.

Who leads the Oxikobh? Who will receive me? Someone with more imagination than those who took my sisters. She gulped air and shuddered.

The hole remained. Many times she dared herself to peek.

The light suddenly strengthened. Voices sounded on all sides. She heard the steady slap, slap of her captor's leather soles on a hard surface.

Wriggling down, Leoshine peered through the hole in the sack. She gasped. Leveled stones stretched across a treeless expanse all the way to the forest they had just come from.

Father had cleared a space around the town to prevent an ambush by the savages. He had paved the dirt in front of the town gate after he came back from … *Aeolia?*

A voice nearby spoke a few words in Town Myxolidian. Leoshine stiffened inside the sack.

The Oxikobh passed unhindered into the town.

She caught glimpses of figures standing by the gate. They had smooth black, red, and silver striped torsos, legs and arms. Deep voices echoed from their faceless heads. *What are they?*

Leoshine gasped and pulled away, and immediately renewed her vigil. She recognised the street leading to her father's compound.

They are taking me home. She could not piece together the meaning as they carried her through the family compound entrance.

Black and red figures filled the court, the porches, and the halls. They moved like men, yet they did not resemble any people Leoshine knew of. They paid no attention to the group of Oxikobh carrying the Mayor's daughter in a sack. Leoshine's cry clung to her swollen tongue. *They are taking me to Father.*

Why does Father allow Oxikobh in his house?

She choked on the bile rising from her empty stomach. Soon she glimpsed the tapestry Mother had woven to keep the drafts from her husband's sleeping chamber. His private porch roof sloped to the open courtyard.

Leoshine pulled back into the darkness of the sack with wide and unseeing eyes. She felt herself lifted off the back she had almost become ingrained into. Upended, she tumbled to the board floor. A pair of boots so smooth they might have been made from human skin filled her vision as she tucked her knees under her and covered her head with her arms.

Father's own chamber, she repeated to herself. Mother lined her children up once a year on the porch to sing a song declaring that they would never enter here. Her skin blistered with gooseflesh. *Father will kill me!*

Hands gripped her. Her instinct shivered at the meaning of the men's laughter. A mattress absorbed her body, like liquid into a sponge.

She lay as though the sponge had frozen, breathing through her fingers.

Colours blazed in her eyes. Loud voices and a slamming door jarred her nerves. Oversized, warm hands smoothed back her hair from her cheek and raised her shoulders until they almost touched her bent knees.

The pores of a man's nose filled her vision as he wiped her hands and face with a cloth softer than Mother could weave, soaked in water warmer than tears.

His eyes blinked green and hazel with many black specks below lowered brows. His mouth twisted up on the right side. A black, red, and silver shell encased his neck and chest.

For a moment Leoshine's senses groped in an empty space.

Before she could think further, the hazel eyes returned with a voice like underground caverns opening. "Drink."

Leoshine's eyes widened as the man placed a steaming cup in her hands. Her tongue demanded the liquid as she blinked.

He turned his head. Sounds unlike speech came from his full, hairless lips. Leoshine's instinct curled against another presence in the room that seemed to answer.

He turned back and lifted the cup that warmed her hands. His other hand reached behind her head. Before he touched her, she tipped the rim to her cracked lips. Herbs and vegetables danced in her nose and in no time her hunger lay in ruins.

The man lost his edges in the swelling fog. She felt his hands moving her limbs and body to lie down, then covering her.

Blanket. The word teased from a far distance. Listless, weightless, she drifted beyond her fear.

The Maiden Awakes

ᴏᴝ ᴀᴏᴏᴢᴧᴇ ᴏᴏᴏᴍᴇ

Leoshine sprang from the nest of downy luxury like it was infested straw in the Oxikobh hole.

How long ago? Where am I? Her feet shifted in the mattress and she pressed her spine and hands flat against the wall plaster. Her chest brace hung lopsided. She'd never slept in it before.

Father's private chamber. She crushed her lips together.

The largest man she had ever seen with the baldest face, exposing an unmarred complexion, lounged on the other side of a table in one of eight carved wooden chairs. He wore the hard shell on his chest that she had seen on the figures by the gate.

If he was a man, those tight o's on his head were golden and red hair with darker shades intermingled. Behind him the blood red canopy of a curtained bed seemed to fight with Father's embossed mayoral medallions hanging on the ceiling beams.

The low-slung frame that held her mattress lost all significance next to it.

Leoshine glanced from the door at her left and back to the table where a cylinder illuminated half the giant man's face. His eyes drilled through her.

Fierce? Dangerous? Her mother's hysterical warning resounded in her ears as when it had pierced the fetid air. "Don't let them do anything."

How do I stop them?

The giant man moved to rise and approach. Leoshine cowered flatter against the wall.

He eased his limbs back to the edge of his seat with his elbow on the table.

They shared the chamber. His bed lay so close. *He watched me sleep.* Sickness rioted. What else had he done while she slept?

Father will kill us. Being his favourite would not save her.

The giant's mouth yawned. A sound like water over pebbles came to Leoshine's ears.

He gained his feet like a hunter wary to disturb his prey and strode to the door.

The figures she remembered at the gate did not seem human. Bareheaded and divided, this one purred and gestured toward her and approached, hesitated, retreated, commanded at the door, and now paced with his shoulders hunched to avoid the room's timber trusses.

The light on the table expanded and followed him. When she moved, it swallowed her too. *Is the Dome dark for night?* Or worse, had the aliens destroyed Aeok'n as Mother prophesied?

He paced away. She dragged her fingers through the burrs and sticks deeply entangled in her hair. She examined her scratched hands, her arms caked with blood and mud, her torn clothes.

Lately, Father had insisted upon clean clothes and tidy hair more than usual. He had built tubs of water all over town and had given rewards to the folk who used them.

Father. She cried in agony. "Father?"

The man paced one stride toward her. She fled into the pillows. Her eyes followed his movements over a blanket she held to her nose.

The man uttered a curt noise and fretted his brow with the side of his finger.

A knock swiveled both their heads to the door. Another shelled giant strode toward the table. He placed a tray full of shiny rattling domes in front of the first giant's chair.

The new arrival did not hesitate. He placed his heavy hand on her shoulder. "Go, empty yourself." He spoke perfect Myxolidian and pointed to a small door beside the canopy bed.

His fingertips on the top front and back of her brace compelled her off the cot. She shot a pained glance into his hazel eyes. Their black flecks stirred her memory.

She slunk round the table with her eyes riveted on both men until she disappeared into the dark chamber.

She hesitated but the need was overpowering. She reached for the rope handle when she finished and paused. Voices in the main room piqued her curiosity.

She peeped out. A haggard-looking older man with a beard and furs falling down his chest stood at the foot of her cot.

"Father."

She rushed across the floor. He reached to his belt.

The giant who brought the tray stepped into her path. The sitting giant barked a command.

Father's hand came away from his knife and the giant stepped to the side.

Leoshine fell at Father's feet and wrapped her arms tight around his knees. She buried her face in his leggings and felt the same extravagant softness as her bedding.

"You're alive." She peered at him. "Mother said they would kill you. Mother? Is she alive? Georg? Wol? Oh Father, I saw them killing." She buried her face again and wiped tears in the folds of his breeches.

Father rubbed the top of her head. "Leoshine, Obenici. You must be brave." He grasped her elbow and pulled her upward. "Trust me that this is for the best. I have never done anything without thinking of your future and I know you will be happy here." His eyes darted between the strangers, down at her, and back at the sitting one. His lips moved rapidly. "The Overlord has shown you special consideration and does our family great honour to take you into his personal household. You won't disappoint me? Obey and be quick to learn as I have always known you to be."

Once more hands guided her shoulders. *Father's hands. More gentle than the Oxikobh, more trusted than the giant servant.*

"Leoshine, daughter, kneel with me and show the Overlord your gentleness."

Leoshine choked and stared hard at her father. *Overlord? Bow?*

Father's eyes crinkled. The corners of his mouth bared his teeth and then covered them, bared and covered, while the crinkle between his eyes pleaded.

The Overlord at the table smiled back. He extended his hand. His eyelids drooped and his lips curled just a fraction. He glanced at the other giant standing at his side.

Father knelt and touched his forehead to the tips of the draping fingers. To Leoshine, the hand made no token, no sign that the

Overlord welcomed a similar action from her.

'Special consideration'? Her mind rioted. *'Personal household'? Show the Overlord my what? He stopped Father from killing me. Father obeys him.*

"Come. Sit. The food will be good."

Leoshine whipped her head around to catch the Overlord's lips moving. Father replied to him with alien noises. Leoshine looked up, watching his mouth.

The serving giant removed the covers from the dishes, then stood behind the Overlord. Father assumed one of the carved chairs at the table.

Waves of hunger urged her forward. Her head swam in the aroma of the hot food and she almost choked on the water in her mouth.

The Overlord gestured toward her and the plate that lay in front of an empty chair.

The serving one muttered. Father nodded and looked at her.

The Overlord commanded again in Myxolidian, her language. "Sit. Eat. I say so."

Her father flapped his hand over the seat and she slithered into the chair.

The food that Mother supervised in the great household kitchen, that fed Father's family and all the Rellogat and their families and guests at banquets, the only food she knew before this, came in neat mouthfuls wrapped and ready to be conveyed to her mouth without messing her hands. She looked at her fingers.

The Overlord shot a glance at her and poked at a heap of loose grains with a metal-pronged instrument. He lifted a scoop. His lips wiped the grains from the utensil which he rested over the plate. The stones in his throat pumped up and down. "Eat. I say so." He nodded to her plate and then attacked his food again.

She remembered cuddling her hand under Father's abundant beard and feeling those stones in his throat. She had been too young to see Georg's before his beard developed. She remembered the beginning of Wol's and the fuss Mother made of him. They were hidden by all men, Giffshine had told her. Sacks of mysterious treasure that uninitiated sisters were not allowed to know about.

How old was this man if his were exposed? His skin was smooth, but not downy like Wol's at that early age of manhood. Wrinkles around his eyes and the growl of his voice belied the hypnotic vision of them ferrying food down his gullet.

Father tested a pronged utensil and began speaking. "This is your master, Leotjie. You didn't have a master before, though you were pleased to obey me. Now you must learn to obey him absolutely to the finest detail."

Leoshine looked into his eyes and felt a chill creep across her shoulders.

"I don't know why you have gained such favour in his eyes. But, yes, even though I cannot assure you he will ask no evil, I don't think you will suffer any harm from him or Resham, his servant."

The master interrupted, gesturing toward her. Father grinned and ducked his shoulders. The servant grunted.

"Leotjie, he really desires you to eat. Doesn't that speak of his concern for you? I beg you to lift this tool, called a fork, and taste a morsel. Yes, it is not our food and it is not our custom for men and women to eat at the same table but …"

Leoshine flapped her hand over her plate. "I don't care about the food. It is the"—she gulped at the thought of the Oxikobh's touch—"the killing." She tucked her hands into her lap. "I will not eat with one who brings killing." She shuddered.

Father scooped a fork full and pressed his shoulders against the back of the chair. "Leotjie, don't be stubborn. Aren't you hungry? Eat a little while I tell you the story. Since you were a little girl, I have told you how our Dome was built."

Why does he speak to me as if I were a man and part of his council?

"Clever people from far away built Aeok'n to give us air to breathe and moisture and temperature perfect for all the plants and animals that they brought to live here. Then people arrived to live here, your father's fathers and your mother's mothers. Do you understand?"

Father looked around the table and inflated his chest. "Your forefathers grew lazy and fractious, my child. Harmony and plenty have been wasted, until now the town folk fear the forest folk, violence is common outside the walls of my city, and the law and custom that gave us peace is ridiculed. We were made so comfortable by the Dome that some minds gave up searching and seeking, exploring and working to be better. We would not have the Dome unless the Ancient Ones sought a place and worked and used their minds to establish us."

Leoshine peeked through her lashes at her father's real audience. "That's not what I learned from Mother."

Father hurried on. "You will remember that I routinely inspected the barrier lands where our atmosphere ends." He rubbed his palm over his fist. "I have shown you that the Dome does not cover the whole land mass. In their wisdom, the Ancient Ones plotted the proper amount of space for our needs. During one particular tour I was, er ..." The old politician glanced around the table, easing a lump of food around his throat stones. His face brightened. "The Overlord, in his magnificent wisdom, sent envoys to our land to choose a representative, and the honour fell to me"—he lowered his eyes and held his fist against his chest— "to cross the barrier and make contact between our worlds. They asked me to inform them about my people and act diplomatically on their behalf. To prepare the way before they arrived. You know, and share the vision of hope I have held for my people, to raise them above the squalor and lawlessness that plagues them. The wondrous devices and machines available in the other world will do that." Father's eyes sparkled. "They have some here in this room, to make light and talk beyond these walls."

The Overlord tapped his fork handle on the table. A twisted smile slithered in the servant's eye.

"This man, Resham"—Father indicated with a sweep of his hand—"delivered me to the Overlord. He said he had watched me for a long time because I had not lost the spirit of searching and seeking." He glanced at Resham's strengthening glint and swallowed. "I remember your questions when I returned. Such questions from a girl. You, more than any other, hungered for the ideas and innovations that I implemented upon my return. How I longed to open fully to you the experience of interdomiary voyages, flying outside the Dome to another Dome. Of meeting the elegant people of the Overlord's world. Of learning his language and how to operate, work, the"—his words stuttered—"the things they have.

"Machines for everything. Their buildings are so mathematically precise they reach high enough to touch their Dome. And so ornately designed. Decorations. Colours. They have ... oh, Leoshine. Our words are too primitive to explain. They understand the force that propels the Dome. Our desperate ignorance and neglect have brought drought and disease and famine. Our Dome is sick, but they have arrived to help us heal her. In the future we shall produce the quantities and qualities of food that were originally intended by the Ancient Ones for our Dome.

"And there are medicines to cure every ill. I wanted to bring some with me but restrained myself to maintain the strict secrecy they required. Now perhaps I shall show you. I quickly understood the benefit of their offered allegiance and I pledged to give whatever aid in my power to bring them safely to us."

Leoshine watched her beloved mentor's face. Before his disappearance, he had believed the old ways as much as Mother did. These strangers must have weaned him from the legends of the Trickixim, the priests of Aeok'n, into a new "Mystery of the Dome."

While Father spoke, she had toyed with a scrap of something on her fork. The next time she looked at the Overlord, she saw sparkling amusement in his eyes and realised she had put some food into her mouth.

Father continued. "I was sworn to secrecy. Then they told me of their plan for us. They have watched us and now their High King commands their return. Yes, my clever girl, you have guessed."

Leoshine blinked up at him. *Guessed what?*

"They are the sons of our father's fathers. Yes, it was very difficult to keep the secret, especially from you because you are so bright and the spirit of seeking and searching is so alive in you. The gracious Overlord gave me the honour of opening the secret to you myself. I have brought the future to the people. The vision of hope is here." He waved his hand over his head and rose up in his chair. The next instant, he slumped down, glancing under his brows at the strangers.

Leoshine's question seared through his illusion. "Did you know the killing would come with it?"

The Resham man glanced at the Overlord. The Overlord inclined his head toward Father.

He honours my question. He expects an answer.

Father shrugged. "I knew it could not come without pain. I knew that it would come no matter what I did and that the enlightened people called upon me to reduce and, with sincere hope, to eliminate the pain. I hoped, and Leotjie, I want you to remember, ao Kevath here hoped it would be smoother. Some elements have created resistance where none is needed." He glanced at Resham. "No one desired the blood to be spilled. Leotjie, you must believe that."

Leoshine straightened in her chair and addressed the Overlord, emboldened by his twinkling eyes. "When can I go to this place that you come from?"

"I bring here." The Overlord's ice-and-innocence eyes sparkled.

She blinked and swallowed an errant morsel. *See his world here?*

His lips moved again.

Leoshine prodded Father. "What does he say?"

"Be a good girl, Leotjie, and an attentive student in his care, and you may live to see his land."

"How is it you understand and speak to him, Father? I have never heard such sounds."

"Your new master's people taught me while I lived among them. You will learn too while you attend here. It is the best way to limit and stop the killing that you have in your little power."

Leoshine again sought the true authority in the room. "How?"

The Overlord's pupils dilated and shrank, hypnotising. Her gaze dropped to her empty plate.

A long utterance followed.

Father translated. "You will be his special attendant, Leoshine. You will serve his food and wash his clothes like your mother taught you." His eyes bore deeply into her soul, begging her not to fail, perhaps regretting pulling her away from Mother's attempts to teach her domestic chores. "He will teach you his language, yes, and to read and write. In his world the women do that. I have shown you some, but with him you must do better."

The Overlord gesticulated with his hands, even rapping the table with his knuckles. He leapt from his chair and circled the table. Father shrank down in his chair.

Just as suddenly, her new master sat with his long legs stretched across the room, his eyes hooded, and the perfect lines of his mouth stilled.

"Obedience is everything, Leotjie." Father licked his dry lips and glanced even more restively between the strangers. "You will be safe here, safer than outside where everything is changing. It is the highest honour. I told him you are a good girl, clever and quick with your mind."

The Resham man cleared the plates and muttered beneath his breath. He and the Overlord appeared to be conversing behind Father's strictures.

Leoshine leaned toward Father. "You want me to sleep here?"

"It is the only way, Leotjie. He has promised not to hurt you. He is a man of great honour." He darted a glance at the pile of blankets where she had rested. "This is his servant's bed. He has turned him out to make you comfortable. You have no power to refuse now. But wait." This last Father spoke without sound and with the least twitch of the corner of his eye.

A thunderous pounding shivered the door. Terror seized Leoshine and propelled her behind her father's chair with a pronged fork in her hand. Father looked as a dog does toward his master.

Resham opened the door and the room flooded with enormous, armour-clad warriors. The air rang with their laughter, and they slapped both the Overlord and Resham on the shoulder.

In the chaos Father beckoned and Leoshine slipped under his arm.

She whispered in his ear. "Who are these?"

Father's eyes shone, and he bowed to them though they gave no notice. "The master's generals. They came to rule with him." With each dip he shuffled her closer to the door.

Leoshine saw the porch railing outside the door. The next instant, Resham's voice boomed out. He seized the back of her neck and Father's shoulder, separating her terror-stricken body from the folds of his cloak.

The generals answered with laughs and sneers. All eyes searched the seated Overlord for direction.

In the silence his voice rang clear, gently mocking, Leoshine wasn't sure whom.

The generals assumed seats, exchanging questioning glances and wry smiles.

All she knew was swallowed by the bulk of the Resham man. Sharp pains stabbed her neck and jaw where his fingers gripped.

Resham pointed to her cot. "Go."

The door had closed. She couldn't see Father anymore.

Her body stiffened. Her head shook slowly. "No." Her lungs closed over. "No, I go." Her arm lifted, heavy and tired, to point to where Father must be waiting for her, behind the door.

Her master's voice purred. The servant relaxed his guarded stance. The generals frowned and shuffled their feet under the table.

"Please." Her body crumbled to the feet of the servant. She would have embraced his knees. She would have entwined herself around the Overlord's knees, but that might be mistaken for an attack. "Please." Tears and the recently eaten food tormented her. "I am no use to you. I can't … I never learned …"

A longer conversation ensued. Her ears caught one word. "Leoshine."

They know my name.

Time stretched, and her legs cramped. The group at the table turned their backs and spread tools on the table.

The servant bent and picked her up under the arms. He strode a step and deposited her in the cot.

"You stay there until I think what to do with you."

Leoshine clutched at his words. "You didn't know I was coming. You don't know what to do with me."

With a raised open hand, he approached. "I know what I want to do with you."

She plunged deep into the pillows, shivering.

No blow came.

Tears seared behind her eyes. They refused birth.

She recognised him now. He had come to Father at the beginning of this disaster as a monstrous, Oxikobh-garbed warrior at the gate. No, he wasn't an Oxikobh. No savage of the forest towered above Father like this man did.

How Long 'til Landing?

Avram, son of Avram and ao Kenan Iliana, ao Kevath to the rest of the world, scuffed weary feet across the threshold of his new headquarters and inhaled. Through the scent of his predecessor in the room, he detected the new member of his household.

He turned his stooped head in time to catch two wide orbs sinking into the blankets on the cot. On the door side of his bed, he extended his arms at his sides and his personal servant began unbuckling his armour. Resham's head joined his between the rafters. Even there, both of them inclined their necks.

Resham peeled the breastplate off and placed it in the cleaning cupboard.

Avram paced a circle and shook out his arms. He moaned as he sank on the edge of his bed. His tunic and blouse came over his head into Resham's hands. "Oh, brother who serves me so well. For what we are about to receive …"

His servant brother unfastened his boot and tugged until his joints complained.

Avram mentioned the place-name he had visited.

Resham spoke the Myxolidian name as he ran the cleaning comb through Avram's curls.

Avram grimaced. "Why are our languages so different?" He held up his right hand as Resham opened his mouth. "Don't tell me! I don't need a history lesson. If those sons of their fathers' sins show up against me, I'll teach them to tamper with languages."

Avram reveled in the cloth of warm water wiping his face

and neck and front. "Went there to give the *Talon* something to report back home." The interdomiary vessel that had brought him to Myxolidia would shuttle between the Domes every cycle, bringing supplies and settlers. "Folk are in shock. Inside town walls they seem to be listening to Curtstas, waiting until we do something wrong. Outside, only deserted compounds. Saw some shadows in the trees. Left food at the compounds, hanging from the fence posts. Might change their minds."

Resham grunted.

Avram lay back and freed his legs from the breeches. "Rasset's itching to get into the Dome chemicals." He rolled onto his front and submitted to a light scrub. For a while he only moaned as Resham stuck his elbows and knuckles into knotted muscles on his back. At Resham's tap he turned over and allowed himself to be draped in a fresh blouse and hose.

He gestured toward a wooden chest carved to match his bed and the table and chairs. The *Talon* crew had delivered it while he rode out. "You think I'd sleep with that in my room?" He waved Resham away from anointing his feet and flung himself into his favourite chair. "Open it! Let's hear what she says."

From the box, Resham brought forth clothing and food and a rectangular, grey object. Both men stared at its screen until the image of an older, silver haired woman with stately carriage and dancing eyes appeared.

Smile-wrinkles played about her mouth. "My dearest boys, I miss you terribly, even though you only set off two days ago."

Two days and three months ago, Avram calculated. The captain of the *Talon* captured this message at the extremes of contact with Aeolia. *We've been here three days.*

The warm voice continued. "Everything is so deathly still and silent. You have taken all the jolly people with you and life has grown dull. Oh, how I miss your great big boots, all my boys' boots, banging in the halls. Your voices too. The whole Dome is mad with the news of your departure and mission. Friends that I have never met call to hear about you. They ask the silliest questions! I don't answer anymore but leave them to Jiine.

"Ao Kevad Himself called to be sure I knew of the *Talon's* departure. Wasn't that thoughtful of Him? He gave me a message personally for you, my son, from His beloved self. He wishes you every blessing. He said there would be all kinds of other official proclamations, but He wanted to send something more personal.

"Now, Avram! Send word back directly that I may come to join you. I can't wait to see the new kingdom! I have been studying the language very diligently, though I miss my tutor, Resham. Just to impress you, I have included a message from myself to your new subjects in their own words. Please tell me I am clever.

"Love you. See you soon!"

The screen blanked and the "boys" stared as figures and lists scrolled by.

Avram indicated an icon. "Here, play this one. I won't understand a word but at least I can see her."

The motherly voice enunciated raw Myxolidian syllables. "Greetings to you, my fellows. My name is Iliana. I greet you from my home. Soon I will greet you from your home. Please make place of … for me in your heart."

This time they stared much longer at the blank screen.

"So short? Well, at least I could understand it. That should please her. Are you pleased with your student, Resham?"

"Yes, ao Kevath. She has learned the harsh syllables of Myxolidian. She corrected her grammar on her own."

Avram sank down in his chair and placed his index finger along his lips. "If all of them spoke like that, I would have an easier time. Perhaps I'll make Mother the interpreter." His eyes rested on the figure on the cot. Dark hair with flaxen lights interlaced with her fine-boned fingers sprawled over the pillow. A scratch marred her smudged cheek. *How many other fair children are hiding in the woods? Why are they afraid of me? Why are their men making war?*

"What do you know?"

"The mayor is a double-edged sword whose blade has cut for us up to this point. Now he counts the cost. His eldest son is dead, his women are captives, and Wol, the younger son, fights openly against his father's alliance with you." Resham paused and tilted his head at Avram's slouching form in the chair. "Does ao Kevath remain here tonight?"

"Openly? Did he …?"

"Wol did not know about you, no. As a 'second son' he would have fought his father whether you came or not. The opportunity he thinks you provided, routed him. He will die." Resham placed a cup of steaming brew in front of his master and tilted his head again.

Avram nodded at the cot. "What of the girl?"

"Leoshine. The youngest and most precocious of the three daughters. Privileged, spoiled by the father, sharply intelligent. You will have no difficulty teaching her. She has already adopted the bath and knew by intuition at least some of her father's secrets."

Avram sprang from the chair to pace the floor. "So you agree with me! A useful instrument. Oh, but I wish Iliana were here! What does one do with girls? Now if she were a boy ..."

"The women are strictly segregated, ao Kevath."

"So she will struggle with us. Out of two metals comes a stronger alloy, no?" Avram sat on the front edge of his chair, leaning his forearms on the table and manipulating the communicator screen. The faces of all who landed with the *Talon* appeared with their curriculum vitae.

After a long silence Avram looked up. "Did you drug her?" The girl had taken Resham's bed. "What about you?"

The telltale patch behind Resham's ear flared. "At least I sleep, ao Kevath."

Avram grimaced. Ever since his initiation when Iliana gave him his grandfather's great poster-bed, Resham had slept like the girl did now, soundly and at its foot.

Resham eased into a chair beside his master. "As for her, sleep is the best medicine. Relief from the terrors of the day." He nodded at the communicator. "What of the instructions, ao Kevath?"

Avram tossed his hand and Resham read out the scientific mandate. Over the next hour they discussed the details until Rasset's regulations lay in figurative heaps in the communicator.

Avram stretched. "What of the mayor's sons?"

Resham's mouth twisted into a hard line.

Avram stiffened. "Dead in battle?"

"Fratricide."

Avram gripped the edge of the table. "You have witnesses? There will be an Aeolian trial." *Myxolidian justice would serve me better.* He glanced at the one he valued as a brother. "What will you tell their sister?"

Resham rose from the table. "I'll tell her what will keep her obedient." He strapped on his sword. "I go to bring the rebel in. The traps are set."

I Go to My Room

ᗝ ᑎᐯ ᑌᗝ ᘔᗢ ᑎᐯᗱᗝ

"I go to my room?" Leoshine stood from her cot and offered to Resham the Myxolidian gesture of request, touching her right hand to both shoulders, then holding her fist against her chest while her left hand gripped her wrist.

The garment Resham attended on the table stilled in his hands. He did not look up.

"There are clothes and"—she paused, imagining her room in the women's quarters—"things I could use." Hair brush and clips came to mind.

Resham resumed his regular motion.

What does he do with that cloth?

She repeated her gesture, more urgently. Did he recognise the appeal in her eyes? He would not see the appeal unless he looked at her.

Silence.

She enunciated and exaggerated her charade. "I go to my room."

His hands stilled again. He drew breath and rolled his eyes, growled in unaccented Myxolidian—"Nothing there for you"— and immediately returned to his work.

"There's clothes! I can't wear this anymore!" She held out the torn skirt draping her legs. She needed someone to retie the brace on her chest. She could breathe, but having it slip made her nervous.

Resham folded the garment and began polishing shiny fastenings on another. "You're well provided for by your master."

Leoshine plopped down. *Attack him? Shout and scream like*

Mother? Pout? Cry? She burned her gaze into the side of his face. *What does he do with those shiny things? No one would wear such material close to the skin.*

She counted to sixteen twice, the number of bright fasteners on either side of the garment opening, before Resham rose to retrieve a brush from the wardrobe. Long and lovingly he stroked, dampening the nap of the fabric, more meticulous than Mother with her fleece.

A voice spoke from out of the air.

Leoshine jumped and clutched her hand to her chest. Resham spoke back, his hands suspended over his work. Words dripped off his tongue completely devoid of emotion. She could not tell whether the other voice was his superior or inferior. When the voice thrower fell silent, he hung the garment in the wardrobe and returned with a grey cube that seemed small in his hands.

He sat before the cube and seemed utterly absorbed by the light that washed his face to a colour as unnatural as his silence.

Leoshine's eyes rounded and grew watery. Her lower lip swelled and rose against the other. People lived beyond this room! *Their voices visit. Can't I speak to my mother? Or did the Oxikobh ...?*

The light from the windows changed, leaning on toward darkness. One full day she had sat unoccupied, unwanted, unnoticed.

Abruptly, Resham folded his box work and strode to the door.

Leoshine jumped up to follow.

"No."

His denial slapped her in the face.

"You don't understand! Let me go! I'll come back. I know the way."

He opened the door.

"You understand, you just don't care!"

He re-entered the room to respond. "I am the most caring person you will meet."

Heavy as a wall falling on her, she felt the doom of the closed door.

Casting her head among the pillows Leoshine wailed until her voice failed. Her tears ran into the blanket folds until a veil of slumber smudged her grief, soothing the separation from her family and everything she had ever known, strengthening her to fight, tomorrow.

Bright Domelight from the solitary window and the sound of tramping feet sent Leoshine into a terror-filled huddle against the wall.

Before she fully gained her bearings, the Overlord's servant tied a light cord around her wrist and opened the door. He motioned without pulling the tether, waiting for her to follow in his wake.

She trotted at his heels, glancing at the walls, Mother's tapestries, the tall, armoured figures standing erect and motionless as she passed. Were they men?

At the entrance of the women's hall her hope soared. He had heard. He had understood and honoured her request.

There were no women around. He led her straight to the door of her closet in the larger chamber where she and her sisters had lived and slept and played.

A tall, cleanshaven man—one of the invaders—stood within. An unnaturally bright light sterilized the bare walls. An acrid, burnt smell hung in the air.

Would her heart ever beat again? All her memories, trinkets, presents from Father from his missions without the walls had been stripped away—by a man. The sudden death of capture gripped her again.

"Nothing here for you." Did Resham speak or did her memory provide his explanation?

She gaped at him. What would she wear? How would she look after her hair and skin and nails?

With firm hold of her shoulders, he turned her and led her away.

She stumbled forward, completely at his mercy, vaguely aware of leaving the aliens behind to walk amid a green space. He could lead her to oblivion. Had he not already?

Among bushes and flowers, she began to recognise her surroundings again. Resham stopped outside the bathhouse. After releasing her wrist tether, he swung the door in and nodded.

She crossed the threshold and looked behind, fearful he would follow. He closed the door from the outside.

A stick-light hung beside the door. Leoshine put her face right up to it. No heat or sound came from it. The lantern Father had made hissed and burned her hair if she came too close. She touched the tip of her finger to the smooth surface. *I can touch light.*

Steam tickled the surface of the bath. Now she knew where Father got his ideas from. How long ago? Seven or eight cycles since he'd re-established his authority over the town and begun the changes. *Changes,* he had whispered, *improvements for now, bigger things to come.* Always he promised bigger things to come.

A glistening wooden bench lined the other walls. Rafters dripped with condensed steam. She opened a small cupboard door where she remembered hiding hair ribbons and undergarments. An ornate set of brushes and cloths of vibrant alien colours stared back. Her shoulders slumped. She tried to grasp the total invasion of her world by these smooth-tongued strangers.

A pebble plunked on the wooden wall. Her skin contracted quickly enough to stab her heart.

Resham spoke through the walls. "Capture and adoption of a slave was not calculated in the Aeolian mission, Torbera."

Leoshine frowned. How could he use the word "slave" and the endearment "Torbera" in the same sentence?

His voice kept on. "Don't have any women with us. We don't have any suitable clothes for you." Another pebble struck the wall and fell with a thud to the dirt. "What you see there is mine, a simple blouse and a long scarf to serve as a belt."

Yet again a pebble punctuated his speech.

On the bench she saw a clear-sided box containing pale yellow cloth and a red sash.

On this tour of her familiar places, he wore a high-necked jacket buckled at the throat with an ornate jewel. In the room, she remembered, he wore either the red and black shell or a sleeveless tunic with a voluminous blouse underneath. She rubbed the cloth between her fingers. *Just like this one.*

The water called. Her skin itched and her hair hung limp. With a stone wedging the door, she stripped and sank into the sooth-ing pool amid gurgling, splashing and echo-drips. Frothy islands floated around her. She rinsed her hair and scrubbed her limbs. Scratches and cuts stung.

Thump, thump, thud, the pebble percussion continued. In a little while the water music calmed.

"Don't think to escape, my Torbera."

Sharp, tingling pain in Leoshine's spine radiated to her skull.

"I know who you are. I'm surprised you don't know me, but then I was in disguise."

She clenched her fists against the spreading shivers despite the hot water wrapping her round.

"You were out with your brothers, meeting with the Oxikobh. Telling them who was really in charge and how old feuds could end."

Leoshine listened with her teeth clenched. What did he know about Georg and Wol?

"Your father thought you were all safe in the palace. Did he ever find out your betrayal, my sweet?"

Thump, thump, thud. He did not throw stones while he spoke.

Leoshine remained hidden and still, submerged to her chin.

Georg loved Father; he always showed her how to obey and respect him. Wol on the other hand, would be out in the wilderness for days. He would visit Mother's chambers, choosing times to be alone with her, mysterious together. He beguiled his little sister with fantastic stories of the people living outside the town walls. The prospect of adventures kept her quiet when Wol's insolent side glances at Father confused her loyalties.

Resham continued. "Your horse ran away. My master and I caught you and returned you to your brothers, do you remember? You disrupted our plans then, too."

Sometimes her brothers placed her on a fresh mare that took all her skill to ride and took her into Oxikobh territory. Brave Georg loved conquest. Wol loved to defy Father's commands.

She remembered a wild ride, crashing through vines and dodging trees. Riders had appeared on either side and caught the bridle of her beast. Fear had struck deeper into her heart when they did not immediately stop and she realised they were not her brothers.

Plunk, plunk, thud.

"We've been scouting here twice before now. We only saw you once, but we saw your brothers many, yes, many times."

Bubbles frizzled on the surface. No other sound broke the silence.

Resham's voice rumbled through the wet walls. "No harm came to you then and none will come to you now if you obey like your father told you."

Leoshine plunged into the air and left the water swirling behind. She toweled herself dry with sharp hard movements and picked up her brace and ragged dress, loath to put on her enemy's clothes. With tears running down her cheeks and her teeth digging into her lower lip, she contorted her body and managed to apply the brace to her chest. Not as tight as Gorphiline did, but better than before she bathed.

Finally, she flung the soiled cloth on the bench and dressed in the blouse, shivering at the caress of his fine fabric on her arms, and tied the scarf severely five times around her waist.

Her hands shook. She struggled without strings and ribbons to make a simple knot with her thick, wet hair.

Resham's voice sounded much nearer. "Do you need me to come for you?" She imagined his hand on the door handle.

Her hands scrabbled to drag the stone from the door. One step stood her on the threshold.

Resham tilted his head one way then another and his sinister lip mellowed with approval. "It will do 'til we order something more suitable for you from home. Go back and put a towel over your shoulders until your hair dries."

Leoshine stared at him for a moment, then obeyed. "What do you mean, home? This is home. And don't talk about Georg unless you tell me where he is. He was protecting us! From you!"

Resham's lip lifted at one corner. Looking toward the palace, his eyes seemed to soften and narrow at the same time. "Nay, my pretty, don't be deceived any longer. He rode out to kill your father, but our troops killed him first."

Georg dead? The leader she had trusted and the brave brother she loved? Her lips formed the word. "No."

A bird flew into a bush bordering the bathhouse. She dove toward the gap.

A punishing hand grabbed her arm. She screamed and writhed. Resham lifted her off the ground by her upper arms squeezed against her body. Her face came level with his smirking grin. Low chortles erupted from his chest.

"Evil, cruel fiend!" Leoshine struck at the air between them with her knees. "What do you know about anything?"

The chortle ceased suddenly and his brow furrowed. "Life has changed, Tassanara." He placed her back on the ground and held her with one draping hand on the top of her head while he twitched the towel back over her shoulders. "Remember I said no harm will come to you? Meek and mild, do you understand?"

For a long moment he stared into her eyes.

He bent to tug her hem straight and her knees gave out. His clamp-like fingers gripped her temples and jaw from above, leaving her dangling like a puppet.

Dizziness blurred her impressions of him.

He swung his free hand in circles, unwinding the tether from his wrist. "You are good to defend your brothers. ao Kevath admires that. I only wish they thought as well of you."

"Come." Resham set her down lightly and tugged at the tether suddenly retied. "ao Kevath needs me. Ah!" He bent to look first in one of her eyes, then the other. "You want to know who ao Kevath is!"

Leoshine wrinkled her nose and looked away. He invaded even her thoughts. Her body froze in place.

Resham lifted the tether tied to his wrist, pulled so the other end lifted her arm and raised a questioning eyebrow. "No? Your tongue must work out a way to say that while your brain teases out the riddle."

Leoshine bit her lip. To the gentle pressure at her wrist, she stepped forward and stopped. The pressure continued. Resham stood close and stepped when she stepped, leading to the prison.

A long moment passed. She stared at the ground, fighting tears and a cloudy vapour. The bird in the bush flew away and numbness stole her joy at the rare sight.

The tall, unpredictable man at the other end of the rope was giving her time. She appreciated that. He did not force her with violence now that fatigue had broken her spirit. Later, she promised herself, she would fight again.

The tug on her wrist moved her forward and soon she was standing outside the chamber. The red and black statue beside the door moved and she jumped. A sentry, she realised, an armour-clad soldier who opened the door to reveal ao Kevath. *Yes, I know my master's name.* She answered Resham's deriding riddle in her mind.

He lay prone on the small servant's cot.

With gentle movements Resham tugged his master's legs further onto the mattress and covered him with a light blanket. He motioned Leoshine into a chair half facing the door and tied his end of the tether to the arm.

While Resham glided in the background, attending to some duty or another, Leoshine climbed into the over-sized chair, tucked her knees under her chin, wrapped her arms around her legs and secured her toes under the opposite arm. Pressing the breath out of her lungs forced the tears away. Every twenty heartbeats she gasped and sobbed and tried again.

What was he doing in her bed? Not even that borrowed space was safe from his invasion. What was he doing in her father's room? Where did he come from anyway?

Leoshine picked at the tether strap around her wrist with her fingers and wet it with her teeth when she thought Resham wasn't looking. She squinted at it. There was no loose end to pull through the knots and her biting made no impression.

What has happened to Mother and Giffshine and Hillashine? Leoshine crushed her lip on her knee and longed to be folded in the safe, soft, warm, tallow-scented arms of Mother. Father bowed, Georg died. She had forgotten to ask Resham if he killed Wol as well.

The plans of escape she had formed all involved her virtuous, strong brother. Maybe Wol was her only hope, unpredictable Wol, who never helped without a reason.

What would he do? He had friends among the Oxikobh and a gang of the councillors' sons who rebelled against "new ideas."

The wooden arm of the chair bit into the brace knots on her shoulder blades. She tried not to care. What was one more misery? She did not want to sit like *him*, against the knobbly carvings on the back. Her feet wouldn't reach the ground while his splayed out long and far under the table. She twisted and set her spine against the flat edge of the arm.

Who am I now? She rubbed the bonds of her wrist on her forehead. Why did Resham tie her down in the room? How did he expect her to escape with two men watching and living statues outside?

Who was I before they changed everything? A privileged nothingness, as Resham intimated? Who made the change? When? No, the change was still happening. Should she allow it? Did anyone care what she wanted? Would anyone stop to ask?

She thought of Father. His cringing before the nonchalant master warned better than his words to obey the Invader, embrace the new food, the new customs. Learning new ways from Father made her different from her siblings.

Who was this man sleeping unaware before her? What did he mean to her?

He rolled to face her. She blinked at him with her mouth open.

His eyes bored into her like a crystal of light—deep, fascinating eyes of intrigue and invitation and … what?

He wasn't sleeping. He knows I was thinking about him.

The mysterious grey cube on the table gave voice and she jumped, sitting on the edge of the chair, holding the ends of the arms for support.

ao Kevath blinked and moved to sit with his head in his hands, knees cradling his elbows.

Resham touched the grey speaking cube and answered with a quiet tremour of excitement, using those syllables she feared would sprain her tongue. At the cot he covered his master's shoulders with a shawl. For a few moments he was busy by the cupboard, until he placed a steaming cup of broth on the table in front of the chair nearest the bed, opposite Leoshine.

ao Kevath rose and moved toward the table. "Sit … bed." He pointed to the rumpled blankets, his mouth twisted as though soured by a bad taste.

She stood with downcast eyes and almost reached the end of the tether before Resham caught her. In the midst of a conversation between the speaking box and his master, his fingers jerked at the knot on the chair while she stood with her wrist extended, pleading with her eyes.

Released and dismissed, she climbed into a corner of the cot, avoiding the warm places where ao Kevath lay just moments ago. In her world, men and women didn't share those kinds of spaces. She took an end of her hair in her hand. At least it was dry, and she didn't have to wear the towel anymore.

On one of his swings round the room, Resham placed a steaming cup in her hands. She tasted the broth, comforted that ao Kevath also drank it.

Her limbs grew heavy. *Why am I so …?* Her head sagged on her chest. She watched the cup tumble and felt no impulse to catch it.

The Overlord of Myxolidia settled into the armed dining chair. He glanced up from the grey-screened communicator on the table and sipped the cup of steaming broth his servant had prepared.

"Sufficient unto the day," Resham whispered and caught the cup that tumbled from the new slave's knees. With practiced hands, he stretched the girl out and wrapped her in the blankets.

"How long 'til landing?"

Resham glanced at the girl. "You mean her, ao Kevath?"

"Please, brother."

Resham approached the table and enunciated. "She'll miss the banquet, ao Kevath Avram."

"Drop the 'ao Kevath'." Avram returned his attention to the screen. "You made her sleep too long, Resham."

"There is much sleep to make up." Resham pocketed the tether that had been on the girl's wrist.

Avram's brows twitched together. "Where could she go?"

Resham rooted in the wardrobe beside the bed. "I create an impression. The tether says, *I don't trust you*. It disappears and she thinks I trust her and works to keep it away."

Avram shrugged mentally. Mind games proved Resham's subtlety. "Were those your people who brought her?"

"ao Kevath." Resham slammed the cupboard door. "Those were the lowest scum among your new subjects." He emphasised the 'your.' "They curry favour with the pleasures of a virgin."

"Ao Kevad forbid."

"Ao Kevad has forbidden." Resham returned the customary answer while he shook out the Overlord's regalia.

"Already?" Avram rose in answer to Resham's tap on his shoulder. "I thought the banquet was later." He paced while Resham dragged behind, fitting a jeweled jacket one sleeve at a time. "You call her slave?"

"Slavery is common in Myxolidia." Resham's eyelids lowered. The telltale behind his ear remained quiet. "There are levels of servitude ranging from the Rellogats who are like trusted family members to the Rachnorgat who is little more than a beast in the outer yard."

Avram sank his feet into his boots. Resham fastened them around his calves. Aeolians tolerated only one form of slavery: to Ao Kevad the High King. "I am His Rashmo …"

"Rachnorgat." Resham spat the syllables without emotion.

Avram waved his hand dismissively. "I surrender to His will. Every aspect of my life is surrendered to Him. He lowers Himself to interact with me and raises me by His presence."

Avram closed his eyes and remembered the moment he became Ao Kevad's slave. Not once, though there had been a ceremony at some point. Iliana made sure of that. Over and over he had realised how much like a beast he must seem to such an exalted being like the High King. Each time he reached out he felt the spirit-tingle of being raised up from that degraded existence.

"So you lower yourself to interact with her."

The light suddenly beamed on Avram's mind from Resham's words. "Until she knows Ao Kevad. He will raise her."

Raising the girl into Ao Kevad's will would take great subtlety. Impossible without constant submission. *Ao Kevad! I am still only a human beast!*

Her people would follow her into the Exalted presence. Ao Kevad had commissioned him, Avram son of Avram, to lead the Myxolidians into His will. He put His people to work this way, giving them every advantage to meet the challenge.

Resham put his hands on Avram's shoulders and captured his eyes. "With Ao Kevad it may not be slavery, ao Kevath. It may be expansive mutuality."

Avram pulled back. He was a military man. Slavery was a practical concept he would pin to the wall. He would leave expansive mutual-what's-it to his priest.

Family

The lone window above her master's bed drenched Leoshine in light. A fire crackled outside and men's voices drifted in. The Overlord's hard-shelled soldiers probably used the firepit in the inner courtyard. She tested the air for smoke and instead smelled the acidic tang of aliens.

Emptiness reigned. No Resham moving on velvet paws. No Overlord brooding in the chair. The grey cube that threw voices around the room sat still and empty on the table.

The floor covering oozed between her toes and she wrenched her feet back. Mother covered floors with tapestry, but this cushion felt like animal fur. Did they have beasts with such colourfully-patterned fur in the other world?

At the table she discovered a bowl of steaming water. She dipped her finger. A towel even softer and more vibrant than the floor covering lay to the side.

Beside the bowl stood a plate of bread, cheese, and fruit covered by a see-through dome. Her stomach growled.

Beside the plate a book lay open. She eased her body into the chair while her mind devoured the picture that filled the open page. A border of intricate and intriguing patterns framed a picture of a mother holding a child. A strange light appeared around their heads. Fluffy animals surrounded them and appeared to be honouring or even worshiping the central figures. The mother's face wore a soft, adoring expression as she gazed at the half-naked babe. He looked alert and eager to climb off her lap to play with the pets in fluffy coats.

Leoshine's finger caressed the page, comparing the smooth texture to those Father used to assemble his Dome measurements. He kept ancient books in a case in the counsel hall and showed them to her as a reward if she obeyed Mother. *What would Father think of these colours? The people look so real.*

Symbols covered the other page. Aeolian script, she guessed. She felt a familiar burning in her heart to decipher the code.

Her eyes leapt about the page. She reached out and uncovered the food. Juice from a block of fruit dripped down her chin. The bread tasted fresh and filled her empty spaces.

On other pages, warriors and beasts and carriages to transport people paraded before her in costumes and attitudes she had never before thought possible.

A horse whinnied outside. A few pages on she saw a picture of a chariot pulled by horses. The artist drew the ground at an impossible distance from their feet. Did horses fly in Aeolia?

Father's horses ran on the solid ground in the field along the inside foot of the town fence. She and her brothers learned to ride there. Father said personality controlled the beast, not strength, and he had taught her to command her mount with her will. Horses had given Georg and Wol status and influence when Father disappeared and other men tried to take his place as leader.

Father would have been very angry that Georg and Wol had allowed her horse to bolt. Now she knew he would have recognised those two bearded strangers who led her back. She glanced at the door, but no footsteps approached. The strangers had not spoken or she might have remembered their voices.

The last page fluttered closed beneath the hard cover and she looked up to see the water still steaming. She stepped over to dip her finger again. What kept it warm? She lifted the bowl and peered underneath. The weight suggested that something in the base generated heat. She immersed both hands and watched the bubbles form on her skin. Then she rubbed her face with her wet hands and dried all on the luxurious towel. In a moment she had repositioned her chest brace and smoothed some wrinkles from Resham's blouse.

She put her ear to the door. Voices rumbled very near. Where could she go? The alien soldiers had been everywhere she looked when she came in in the sack.

She looked around. Cupboards covered the walls on both sides of the canopy bed. She opened the doors and gazed at all the shirts and leggings neatly folded on the shelves. Rich green shirts with intricate patterns would make the wearer look like one of those paintings in the book. When did ao Kevath wear such things? Would she ever see him in the dark blue coat? She shuddered at herself for even looking at a man's wardrobe.

A loud bang outside froze her in place. She held her breath. Nothing moved. Her eyes roved again to the tools on the shelves.

In a case with an opened lock, she found a gold collar, every broad link studded with a multitude of gems that glittered like her eyes. When would they use such a heavy chain covered with symbols and filigree? She held up to her eye a glass ball, cradled in a gold-filigree ring that would fit around the base of Father's thumb, that dangled from the chain. The room swam upside-down.

Leoshine remembered Mother and her women wearing jeweled costumes when they collected her sisters for their Rites of Womanhood. She wrinkled her nose, unable to envision ao Kevath and Resham dancing or singing.

The drapes on the huge bed begged for her caress and she pulled the folds up to her cheeks. Nothing Mother ever wove equaled the blood-burgundy colour or the fur-like texture of the curtains. Wouldn't Father have slept well inside such a tent-like structure!

She knelt before a chest at the foot of the bed and listened. Her ears swept as far as she could hear as she lifted the lid. Books piled on top of each other all the way to the rim. Ever alert for footsteps and voices, she opened the topmost book.

A list of Myxolidian script met her eyes. Father had shown her a little as she grew older. There were also scratchings and swirls in a different colour and script. One by one she opened the other books. Lists and paragraphs filled the pages, all incomprehensible and maddening to her curiosity.

At the bottom she found loose-leafed pages with seals and swirls more ornate than any other in the chest. Tucked into a pocket at the back were several pages of very close, tiny writing with funny pictures in the margins. She thought she could make out a wild-haired woman sitting in a wheeled machine flashing a broad-toothed smile. After several more pages a detailed picture appeared, of the same wild-haired woman and a boy embracing with unidentifiable life forms all around them. Leoshine screwed up her eyes and tilted her head to see if another angle would bring meaning.

One by one she packed the books away. She had to rearrange them to get the lid to close properly.

The carpet did not cover the whole floor, only the area by the door and under her cot. Another lined the area by the cupboards and beside the bed. The table sat on the bare wooden boards.

She touched the hem of her sleeve to her lip. *When will I touch Mother's cloth again?* She covered her eyes with the folds in her elbow and held her breath.

A knock rang out at the door. Her heart stuttered. Dizziness overwhelmed her as the door swung open.

Her heart restarted with a gulp and warm blood surged to her fingertips and toes.

Father stepped in with his arms stretched wide. She ran around the table and fell at his feet. Her arms crossed behind his calves and her temples rested on the knobbles of his knees in the pose of respect Mother taught all Father's children.

Once they grew older, they no longer bowed this way. *I'm the only one left.* The faces of her siblings passed in front of her imagination. Georg—bearded like Father. Wol—also bearded, but thinner and slump-shouldered. Sharp-faced Giffshine. Round and soft Hillashine, haughty and aloof since her initiation.

She rubbed her nose on Father's kneecap. *Not Mother's cloth, but it smells like him.*

His hand reached down and cupped her chin. Her legs responded, and she rose, dangling from his clasp.

"Leotjie!" Her nickname caught in his throat. "You are well?" His eyes roved to the table. "You eat well? Your mother is worried." He searched her eyes for an answer deeper than her words.

Mother? "Is she with Giffshine and Hillashine?" She remembered the last time she saw Mother. Her mind flew around the room like a caged bird. *He won't want to talk about that.* "Oh, Father, oh, Daddy, they have such strange things." She danced to the water and dipped her fingertips in and motioned for him to do the same. "Look at this water, still warm with no fire. And the book! Can you tell me what it says? Look at the pictures. Where do the colours come from? I have hardly seen anything of, of …" She paused to collect her tongue muscles. "Of Ow, Kethff." Her tongue protruded between her lips. "Mostly it is that servant Resham. He is sour in his tongue. Is Georg really …?" She choked on sudden tears.

The laugh died in Father's eyes. His mouth became stern. "I came for a visit, just until your master comes." From behind his back, he took out a parcel wrapped in brown canvas. "Look, I have a present from your mother."

He laid the package on her outspread palms.

She tilted her head and looked through her lashes while she pulled at the paper. "Oh!" she gasped.

Mother's cloth the colour of raw fleece draped over her hands. *A woman's dress? Hillashine's? or Giffshine's? There's been no time to sew a new one.*

Father frowned at her cot, then at the chairs. He placed his hands on the top of a chair back and eased his weight. "She is safe. And your sisters too." His gaze meandered to the Mayoral emblems on the beams, the carved and curtained bed, and back to the table.

Leoshine lifted the fabric to her face. The natural fibers that would keep her warm felt stiff and spiky compared with Resham's shirt. The scent burrowed into the core of her soul. She held it against her body as if wearing it.

"Put it on. I'll step out." Father turned to the door and tapped.

The sentry opened.

"Be quick," he urged as he left. "Time is short."

Haste tangled her fingers as she unwound the red sash. She kicked the yellow blouse under her cot.

Loose sleeves flowed to cuffs at her wrists. The bodice sagged over her chest where the brace still restrained her maiden form and met the skirt at her hips. The hem reached nearly to the ground. Inside the pockets on either side, she found leather slippers which fit her feet perfectly.

"Ready." She danced on her toes.

Father entered and stopped. He mouthed an endearment and his eyes twinkled. Again, he spread his arms, and when she would have knelt, he held her to his chest.

Like he did Giffshine and Hillashine now that they were women.

She pushed away. "Come, oh come. Take me to Mother!"

"Didn't I tell you I am just visiting?" Father held her at arm's length and tilted his head. "I'll tell her how well you are and how you look in her present."

Leoshine loosed her hands and turned to the cot. Her shoulders sagged and her step dragged. She looked at the low mattress and wondered if she should sit. Where would he sit?

She narrowed her eyes at him. "Why can't I go to Mother? Why doesn't she come to me?" She tapped her shoulders with her right hand and held it to her chest.

"She is with your sisters. They stay in one room together. Mother stays to look after Hillashine."

"Why?"

"No, no." Father answered her unspoken fear. "She, well, it is good news. She is bearing the child of her man. Mother knew but didn't tell me and when she came back from the forest …" His voice trailed off. "Leotjie." He seemed to examine her again. "If you feel different, you know, if food doesn't taste …" He reached over and pulled at the ruffle on her shoulder. "Your mother wants to know."

Leoshine wrinkled her nose. "They eat strange."

She knew about pregnancy from the servants and women visitors to the palace. Mother would be furious and fretting over the threat of losing Hillashine's child. Giffshine had shown them that tragedy too often. Her first suitor had taken Giffshine through the initiation ceremony twice. Other men had tried after that with no success.

Leoshine glanced at her bed layered with blankets and pillows and thought of the desolation of her sleeping cupboard. "Where is her room? Is she comfortable?"

Father shrugged. He wouldn't know. She frowned and thought of the newcomers with perpetually warm water and beautiful books. They could make Hillashine comfortable.

With fierce tugs she stripped the bed sheets and blankets from the cot, pushed them into Father's arms, and gathered the pillows into her own.

"We go together." She commanded with her face half-smothered. In the background she heard the sound of heavy boots and the door closing. "I'll come back before …"

Suddenly the pillows pushed back and her breath knocked hard in her lungs. Over the pillows she looked up into clear blue, laughing eyes.

Liquid syllables rolled off ao Kevath's tongue. "Where?" he wondered in Myxolidian. Then he rumbled at Resham, gesturing with impatience.

Resham snapped the burden from Leoshine's arms and tossed it onto the cot. She held on a little long and staggered as though cuffed. The dagger in his eyes as they devoured her new outfit sent chills through her spine.

Father dropped the blankets on the mattress, bowing and cringing.

Instinct drew Leoshine toward the laughter. She knew the Overlord understood more words than he could wrap his tongue around. "My sister is ill. The shock. She is pregnant. She needs the bed more than me. You will let her have it?"

Father added more words mixed with many "ao Kevaths."

Resham growled and an argument brewed between the men. Several times he gestured toward her and the bed.

ao Kevath turned away to the table.

Resham gripped her arm and propelled her toward the cot. "You stay here. What were you going to sleep on? Don't tell me you will bring her vermin-infested sack-filled-with-straw in here because that is absurd and unacceptable."

Leoshine snapped back. "What do I need a bed for?"

Father stood by and watched. His cringing didn't change anything. She felt heat in her face.

"Dignity! ao Kevath's dignity. Nothing in his chamber will be less than perfect!"

Leoshine stood up on the cot. "What do I need three pillows for?" She dangled one from its corner. "There is enough for both of us."

ao Kevath spoke from the side of his bed.

"What does he say?" Leoshine demanded.

Resham swiped the pillow from her hand. "ao Kevath is impatient with your arguments. He is not against helping your sister if his dignity is preserved."

"Your dignity"—Leoshine stuck out her chin—"will not miss a blanket and a sheet and a few pillows."

Though ao Kevath struggled with the Myxolidian pronunciation, she heard the amusement in his voice. "She knows. Your sheets."

Resham placed the folded sheet, blanket and a pillow in Father's arms. "Wash your daughter before you put her in them!"

"Two!" Leoshine added a pillow to his burden. "She needs them more than me."

"Burn the other bedding!" Resham called as Father disappeared through the door.

Resham hurried to attend ao Kevath who had begun to struggle with his jacket. "You reorder that bed and sit on it until I have a moment to deal with you!"

Leoshine stepped down and remade the bed with one pillow. "I haven't seen them yet, Mother or anyone except Father." She climbed back up to watch her roommates.

Resham spoke a lengthy diatribe into the closet. ao Kevath, half-hidden by the curtains on his bed, answered too quietly for her to hear.

Leoshine murmured into her chest. "What are you saying?"

They conferred again. ao Kevath spoke at length, straining Leoshine's nerves.

Just as she opened her mouth to protest, Resham spoke in a weary Myxolidian drone. "ao Kevath says his mother is coming. You will learn how to be a gentlewoman from the ao Kenan Iliana and then you will forget your family." His eyes bored into her before he whipped his master's shirt off.

She staggered back against the wall, mouth agape.

ao Kevath stepped forward and flexed a tiny muscle in his chest. He lowered himself into a chair and leaned his head back. Resham spread white paste over his master's face and scraped it off with a short blade.

Leoshine dove face first into her remaining shelter. Unshed tears burned in her eyes. News of her family, expectations to forget them, Father's weakness, the sight of man-flesh all tumbled against each other in her mind. She grit her teeth, clenched her fists and eyes tight together, and listened to their voices bouncing back and forth.

A loud knock and tramping feet shot new pains through Leoshine. She sat with her back pushed hard against the wall.

Resham tossed a glance at her. "Eventually, you will fetch the meals." He directed other servants to place large trays on the table. "After a little schooling."

ao Kevath, fully clothed and seated at his usual place, rumbled something unknown. Changing into Myxolidian, he addressed Resham. "I give you new bedding from home, make your mother proud." He laughed.

Resham shot a questioning glance at his master who nodded. He continued in Myxolidian. "What other mother do I know, ao Kevath than the ao Kenan Iliana?" He uncovered the trays and the room filled with delectable odours. Selecting a sample from each onto a plate, he placed a meal before his master. "Eat a little, ao Kevath. The road may be long and late."

Leoshine's mouth watered. *If I 'fetched the meals,' I would leave this chamber. Who or what is 'The ao Kenan Iliana'?*

"You!" Resham rounded on her. "Sing something for your master."

Leoshine's scowl grew horns. She turned her back and crossed her arms on her chest. Resham stepped behind her, and she rocketed up on the bed to face him, her back and palms pressed into the wall.

"Now, what song do you know?"

Leoshine shot a pleading look at her master. He scratched at his plate with a fork and lifted one mouthful only to replace it un-eaten. He stared at his reflection in the tabletop.

Resham commanded again. "You want to be useful? Earn his approval? Sing!"

Sing what? His language reminded her of the softer syllables Myxolidian women invented for infants. A few tentative lullaby tones slipped past her open lips. She watched him lay the fork aside. Her stomach grumbled again.

Resham scowled. "He needs to eat, not dream."

Her brow furrowed. Her mind stalled. She could not find an eating song.

Resham nodded. "The Song of Golshore."

Her eyebrows shot up. She knew that play song with quick cracking sounds. The tune came quickly to mind.

ao Kevath looked up, his far away gaze searching for the source of the music. Leoshine made an eating motion though it had nothing to do with the song. He offered her a crust of bread. She flushed and looked down at her feet buried in the mattress.

The door rumbled and the song seized in her throat.

ao Kevath murmured, continuing to gaze at her.

Resham tended to the people at the door and then held the

top posts of his master's chair. As ao Kevath rose, Resham pulled the chair away.

One step before crossing the threshold, ao Kevath paused and spoke without turning, called out in a loud voice, and disappeared.

Resham's Story

Leoshine's stomach griped and her lower lip protruded and trembled. Sweet odours called her to the table. Her limbs refused to do more than watch Resham place the domed food dishes in the centre of the table and empty plates in front of two chairs.

Resham beckoned her to the table. "ao Kevath is pleased. You hungry?"

Leoshine looked up at him. "You eat first?"

"We eat together. But first you stand behind your chair and repeat what I say." Resham began a speech in the rolling vow-el-filled sounds.

A new test. She hung her head. A new torture, to set delicious food before a ravenous person and not allow her to eat.

"Just make the sounds. Later I will translate." Resham paused to gather her gaze and then repeated a few syllables.

Leoshine repeated in a flat tone. "Foor ot boo."

Resham corrected. "For what we are about."

Tears dribbled down her cheek. "Foor ot eee boo."

"For what we are about to receive."

"Foor ot weer boo ceeve.

"Make."

"Make."

"Us."

"Ows"

"Truly."

"Too-ee."

"Thankful."

Leoshine looked up at him, pleading.

"Go on. You can say 'thankful'." He leaned forward and moved his mouth slowly through the sounds. "Put your tongue between your teeth and blow, 'th'."

She produced the sound and felt pressure behind her eyes. Spots appeared.

"Blow and open, 'Tha'"

Drawing a deep breath Leoshine blurted, "Tha-kul. Please can we eat?"

His eyes softened. "Now you sit and eat. We will practice that until your tongue straightens out."

Leoshine dove into the chair and reached to uncover a dish. Inside she found familiar bite sized packages. She grabbed a handful for her plate and one for her mouth. The wrapping crunched between her teeth. Sweet salty onions with a hint of curried carrots soothed her tongue. In an instant she cleaned her plate and filled it again.

"Slowly, slowly, little stomach. Neatly with manners, for ao Kevath." When she paid no heed, he added, "There is no replacement if you vomit."

Leoshine looked out the corner of her eyes. His mouth corners had deep shadows under them.

She picked up a morsel of food from her plate and inhaled the rich scent of fried *qipgn* oil. *Did Mother make these?*

Her eyes popped open. Instead of the usual crunch under the wrapping, her teeth sank into something soft and bland. She spat out white grains like the ones ao Kevath ate in his sticky food.

Resham uncovered the other dishes and served himself. "What did your father say? What about your sister? You say she is pregnant? Already? I thought you said you were hiding only three days. Surely your people don't breed that quickly."

Leoshine emptied her mouth. "Her name is Hillashine and she bears the first child of her man. Why do you hate me? I didn't choose this!"

Resham's lip lifted in one corner. "Hate? I wouldn't waste my hatred on you. You are an unnecessary burden."

"You don't know what I am doing here!" Leoshine crowed. "I am a mystery beyond your cleverness!"

"I said I wasn't surprised you turned up again. If you prove useful you may win approval. If you are ornery, you will suffer."

Leoshine opened her mouth then closed it slowly.

"Why doesn't Father sleep here?"

Resham returned to the dishes. "Everyone recognises it as the seat of authority. Your father gave it to the new Commander."

"Did you bring any sages with you from your land?"

"We brought war surgeons. Your sister can whelp without them."

Leoshine leapt across the table, shoving her chair backwards. Food scattered onto the floor as her plate flew.

With claw-fingers she reached for his eyes.

He gripped her wrists. "Fiery vixen!" He snarled as he folded her limbs against her chest, lifted, and deposited her on the cot. His hand pressed her curled-up body into the mattress and his voice grated close to her ear. "I know your true colours, sister of Wol. Don't think you can ever do this to your master."

She buried her face to avoid breathing his air. *Wol? What has he done now?*

Women don't eat in front of men, she wailed in her heart. *Women don't enter men's chambers.*

"Whether you eat it or not, you will clean this mess. Now!"

Leoshine jumped to the floor with her head ducked between her shoulders.

"Every grain, Whisp-tarn." Resham sat down at the table. "And then you will remove that dress."

Leoshine pinched a white grain from the carpet and put it on the plate. *For Father, and one for Mother.* She repeated the action. And one for each of her siblings, even Georg because if she didn't see him dead, she could deny he was dead. *Everyone except Father is dead if I don't see them again.*

Other grains joined the pile—for her room, for her clothes and hair decorations and dolls. For the places she was free to go on her own in the palace and for the places she needed Father's escort, inside and outside. Even for her horse that ran away and the forest where she was captured and brought back to a town and palace she did not recognise, changed by a man who laughed and yodeled and bared his skin in the company of … what?

His slave? Why did she think she mattered enough to him that he would protect her from his flesh? He could do anything he wished. Father made that clear. She shivered and contemplated the grains on the plate and scattered across the floor.

Resham returned to eating with his back to her.

Scattered like the town people. Did Father convince them to accept the new Commander? Was everyone captive in a room with an Invader?

Maybe they are all dead. She finished picking the grains.

After placing the plate on the table, she held out her soiled hands.

Resham pointed to the bowl of perpetually warm water. "Over there." As she dried her hands, he said, "Take it off."

Leoshine stared at him. She felt the blood drain from her face.

"Put the blouse back on. You can't wear that."

"Why not?"

He enunciated as if she were an imbecile. "That is the dress of an initiate. You are not initiated. How much clearer do I need to be?"

"Mother gave it to me."

Resham's upper lip curled. "Your mother insinuates you are initiated. By whom, do you think?" His eyes blazed. "ao Kevath."

Leoshine's jaw dropped. Her blood seemed to drain down from her fingertips, out into the floor boards through her rooted feet. Her fist gripped her neckline.

Resham scraped the chair legs back. "Take off the dress or I will." His eyes never moved from her.

"No, no, please." Leoshine stammered and watched him walk around the table. "I'll not take it off in front of you!"

He picked up the blouse from under the cot. "I'll take the tray to the kitchen." He gathered the fabric and pushed the roll over her head, so it formed a necklace. "Dressed," he snapped, "when I return."

Leoshine stared at the door for a long moment after it closed. She wrapped her arms around her body and waist, fingering the mother-cloth.

No, no. Please. A picture of Resham overwhelmed her vision of Mother. He would strip her if she delayed.

His silky blouse slipped over her shoulders and covered her mother's dress. Two layers provided extra warmth, but he would see the bulk.

Mother's dress dropped around her feet.

She heard his voice bantering with the sentry. When the door opened, she sat on her cot with her hands stuffed under her thighs, and her muscles held tense to keep from shivering. She stared at the dress in her lap.

Resham whipped the cloth from her hands and strode to ao Kevath's cupboard without a word. From the corner of her eye, she saw him re-emerge and scrape at the carpet with a rectangular box on a stick where she had spilled the food. When he stopped, the carpet was restored to pristine beauty, as if nothing had happened.

Thundering on the door pierced Leoshine's heart, and she uttered a strangled squeak. The sentry called and Resham admitted a group of Aeolians, who moved the big bed and waved their hands in the air as they babbled. For a long time, they listened to Resham and discussed something involving the room. They stretched the same rope back and forth, up and down across the walls and floor.

When they left, the shadows had changed. Resham sat down to stare at the grey box.

Leoshine remained on her cot. Her thoughts stalled. Her heart ached until she felt nothing else.

"I went to see your sister."

Leoshine gripped the chair arms and growled through her food.

Resham had brought a tray after a night listening for ao Kevath, who hadn't come. He had forced the alien words from her mouth before nodding his head at a chair.

"Do you want to starve through the day as well as the night?" Resham placed a food ball in his mouth.

Leoshine swallowed a large lump. "You take the food away from me?"

"You look like you'll waste it again."

She sat back and chewed.

"The ao Kenan Iliana will be here by the time the baby comes. I will move them to a better chamber with good air."

"Why can't I see her? I could help her, you know." Leoshine tried to think of something she could do. "I could comfort her."

"Your duty is to your master. ao Kevath says you must learn."

Leoshine scowled. "Learn what?"

"To be Aeolian!" Resham grinned and popped another morsel.

"I don't want to be ..." The word seemed to slide around in her mouth, defying a hold.

Her companion only grunted, and they ate in silence.

Leoshine pointed to the jewel encrusted symbol at Resham's throat. "What does that mean?"

He grinned. "You want to learn about Aeolians?"

She ignored his slur. "I see it in this room. Over the bed, on his shirts, on papers, and on you."

Resham left the table and rummaged in a cupboard. He placed a thin, black board and writing stick between them as he sat. "Draw it."

Looking to see that he really meant what he said, Leoshine picked up the stick and moved the board nearer. Father had taught her how to hold the point onto paper and move it with some pressure. This one produced a mark with greater ease than Father's.

Resham fastened his paw over her comparatively tiny hand and traced the loops of the symbol. Under his command the image appeared as if by supernatural power.

Leoshine put the stick down and shied away when he released her hand.

He retraced a shape in the interlocking lines. "That symbol makes the Aah sound. It is the first sound of his name."

"ao keblaf?" Leoshine rolled out the Aeolian syllables Resham and Father used at the end of every sentence addressed to the Overlord.

"Kevath. That is a title. A reminder of my place and yours."

"My place is the same as yours?"

Resham boomed with his head held high. "No one anywhere has the same position as me!" He seemed to reconsider and relaxed his shoulders. "My fetters may look different, Obenici"—he reached for another plateful of food —"but they bind with the same power and permanence."

Leoshine shrank down in her chair.

"He has a name given by his mother, ao Kenan Iliana. You will meet her when she comes. Your mother called you Leoshine."

"Your mother called you Resham." She conformed the syllables to Myxolidian and received an intense flash of mortal agony from his soul.

Instantly, his eyes hooded. "His given name is Avram, hence the Ahh. This is Rhhhhhuh."

"For Resham!" She watched to see a hint of the mystery in his eyes again.

With a warmth and vulnerability that surprised her, he rumbled, "No. It stands for Regus, which means King." He followed the strange word with a Myxolidian translation.

Her lips twitched to imitate.

"Go on, say it."

Leoshine looked up in bewilderment, unaware of her movement.

The Resham she knew best returned. "Say it aloud. You can hardly wait to. Avram Regus."

Leoshine straightened in her chair, set her shoulders back, coquetted her eyes at him and repeated it.

"Avram Regus!" Resham snapped. "Memorise it! Brand it on your heart! Never turn away from it! A man chosen and trained by the High King to rescue this Dome from collapse. You will learn to be grateful, to appreciate what he is doing. From that you will learn to obey, to become what he wills of you."

Questions ricocheted off her skull walls. New Aeolian words flew in the air around her.

ao Kevath was chosen and trained. *Therefore, he was commanded?*

Resham rose and covered the food. "You can start by being grateful to me."

Leoshine wrinkled her nose. "You?"

"I didn't have to bring Myxolidian food, Tassanara."

Leoshine blinked. Resham used many words for her but Father had started speaking that one with warmth and affection. *After he returned from Aeolia.* She felt a chill.

She looked out the corner of her eye at Resham. *The last thing I want is endearment from him.*

He continued to clean up. "Just happens I like to be reminded. Help with loading the tray, then I shall let you out of your cage."

Leoshine jumped to obey. "Reminded of what?"

"Home food." He turned his back to her and tapped on the door. He returned and lifted the heavy tray.

"You're not ..." She examined his hairless face. "There's nothing Myxolidian about you."

"I'm an Oxikobh."

"You're too big to be an Oxikobh."

In one stride, he towered over her, one eye squinted and the other brow raised. "Dina your brothers tell o' Giant o' the forr'st?"

She leaned backward. Resham's tongue assumed the grating scrape of the forest people as perfectly as the town Myxolidian.

His eyes gleamed and his teeth shone yellow in the Domelight. "I's a he!"

Leoshine gripped the back of her chair and her throat spasmed. She eased the chair between them and swallowed hard. Giffshine's monster stories suddenly seemed more real.

Resham taunted from the door. "You can stay if you want."

Leoshine hesitated. Go with an Oxikobh? The councillors of Father's government told legends of tame Oxikobh. Town people had captured children and raised them to be slaves. One Oxikobh woman lived as a secondary wife to a famous hunter who had exchanged the life of another man for her. She gave him children. They bore the Oxikobh curse, not the curse of a second wife's children. One day she had escaped and taken them into the forest.

Leoshine slipped into Resham's shadow. Perhaps he was a descendant of one of those children. "You ..." her mind somersaulted. She had to run to catch up. "How did you ...?"

He reached the end of the hall and did not look back.

The mental tether of fear and intrigue tugged her forward and she slipped through the door to the outside courtyard before he closed her in.

They crossed the courtyard where a group of Aeolians marched up one side. They had turned and started on the other when Resham mounted some steps and marched through a covered passageway, into another building.

He never looked back. She slowed her steps. And he did not tie her wrist.

Loud laughing behind her propelled her forward. If she escaped, where would she go? Where were all the Myxolidians? Where were Father and his councillors?

He wears sandals. She observed Resham's heels. Aeolian in manufacture, built on an Oxikobh design.

She looked at the aliens lining the walls of this passage. They all wore boots. ao Kevath wore boots above his knees.

Oxikobh wore sandals.

She looked at her feet, covered in leather slippers she had salvaged from Mother's gift. Her toes curled. Father had caught the animal in the forest where the Oxikobh lived.

Two great doors opened and Leoshine stepped into Mother's kitchen. She glanced around and saw ten or twelve Aeolians chopping, washing, mixing, and laughing.

Resham set the tray on a counter. "Remember the way. You will fetch and carry trays when you are more trusted."

He walked around to another area and spoke to a man dressed in a flowing, red gown belted around his bulging waist.

A group stood around Mother's stove, shaking their heads. Two lifted an enormous pot full of steaming water from one burner to another.

Leoshine spoke before she thought. "They shouldn't do that."

Resham interrupted his conversation. "Why?"

"The stove tips a little with a weight like that. It won't burn as well."

He called out and burbled some smooth pebble words to them. They laughed but changed nothing.

The one in different clothes fetched a smaller tray and placed it on the counter for Resham to lift.

Leoshine leaned to see through the clear domes on the tray. "What's that?"

Resham picked up the tray and ducked out the door. "Your master's supper."

He marched on. Soon she realised they were taking a different way back to the prison. A tremour passed down her spine as Leoshine recognised the space where she and her sisters had played from the time they could walk. It was empty.

Gruff voices echoed around her. Animals in large numbers grumbled for their food. Wilder animals called in the distance. Restlessness reverberated in the air, calling her out. Above the murky grey Dome, she imagined patterns that twinkled and blinked at her. They hung so delicately in the fabric ceiling of her mind. There were other worlds out there, she had learned, where people ate and slept, loved and hated, planned and acted.

She sighed. Her jailer had slowed but never looked behind to make sure she kept up. He was disappearing through another doorway.

Another shiver danced through her body from scalp to toe.

"Wait for me!" She ran to follow. Father's chamber full of strange men was better than this deserted familiar place.

In the chamber Resham put the tray on the table. He set out clothes and refilled the bowl of perpetually warm water.

Leoshine stood by the door.

"Go to bed." Resham ordered from the other side of the room. "Sleep."

She sank onto the cot. "It's only the morning. I just woke up."

He crossed the room in three strides to place a cup in her hands.

"Why?" Her stomach growled as the steam filled her nose. *When I drink it, I'll grow weak and fall over.*

"You are hungry." He turned to the table. She thought she saw him touch the grey box.

"I ate enough."

"Your body is hungry for more. Your bones have holes in them. Your hair is thin. ao Kevath came to give you strength."

She sipped, passing the good taste over her tongue and the warmth down her throat.

Encouraged by his answers, though she didn't understand, she decided to ask until she lost consciousness.

"How did an Oxikobh come to serve ao Kevath?"

Resham stepped nearer, the bowl of water still in his hands. "His people took me, like they took your father. The ao Kenan Iliana took me into her home and taught me about the mission to rescue Myxolidia, about Ao Kevad and His choosing me to serve." He leaned back against the edge of the table.

Leoshine watched him gaze into the distance, remembering. She wondered that she did not yet sleep. He seemed to hover, waiting to cover her with blankets.

"After we grew to manhood, ao Kevath and I, we visited here. I guided parties of Aeolians, teaching about language and customs. We enjoyed ourselves until we were ordered to assemble and break the secrecy." He straightened and turned. "Don't fight against us, Leoshine. You are a small player in a very big game."

"I don't want to play."

Leoshine waited for unconsciousness, for his retort. She covered herself and snuggled into the pillow. Hillashine had two like it, she remembered and smiled in her heart.

ao Kevath in the Night

Avram allowed his personal servant to prepare the canopy bed for a restful night. He no longer dreaded the long hours of darkness. As a child he had wrestled night after night almost into a fever, trying to stop his brain from thinking. Now he pitied those who slept. "No sign of Wol?"

Resham shook his head. "She didn't reveal anything."

"Well?" Avram coaxed when Resham hesitated. "What did you talk about if not Wol?"

Resham rolled away the last of his brushes and ointments and stood with his feet apart, hands folded behind his back.

Avram imitated his shrug. "What is a girl raised in such a degrading culture fit for?"

"ao Kevath, she sleeps in your chamber."

Avram stood and set his feet on a path around the table. "I didn't ask for her. I don't want that kind of dependant."

"Give her back to her mother, ao Kevath."

"And forget why I came to Myxolidia?" Avram ground his fist into his palm. "What did those stinking men expect for her? If they did not seek my favour with her virginity, it would be no value to them. What do mothers do to their daughters here? How old is the girl?"

"Myxolidians don't measure age the way Aeolians do. There is no number quantification. First teeth and last teeth, when the hair reaches the shoulders, these are marks of age. For a female, of course, menstruation is the dividing line between childhood and adulthood. Leoshine is old enough to be initiated, but she hasn't been. Either her mother is hiding the information from her father, or her father is subverting tradition."

Avram pondered the Myxolidian initiation. "She reached this maturity after her father's return?" *From Aeolia.*

"Yes, ao Kevath."

"The father subverts tradition." Avram tried to imagine a Myxolidian going against time honoured protocol. In this, Curtstas had been loyal to the new mission and his daughter benefited in unforeseen ways. "A girl's mind in a woman's body?"

"A very young woman, ao Kevath."

"Are you suggesting I would stoop that low?"

"ao Kevath." Resham gestured with his palms up. His grin mingled humour and pathos. "Pity the priest who does not anticipate the temptations of his flock."

In the pre-dawn hours Avram, having decided the schedule of rotation for his generals for the duration of the mission and planned the location of the new crops, stirred in the blankets of his bed. "I'm hungry." He called out of habit. Food would be delivered. He had servants to spare him thought for the mundane.

He snorted. All Resham's oils and soaps would not disguise the unwashed man-scent of the former occupant.

The courtyard outside the window yielded snores and the regular tramp of a sentry. Inside the room he heard rustlings and bare feet combing through the carpet. The lamp on the table expanded its beam.

He opened his eyes. Leoshine stood beside the bed, ducking her head and wringing her hands. For cold or nerves? Both, he concluded.

His tongue limped over the Myxoldian, while his hands made eating motions. "Hungry. Fetch Resham."

She disappeared. He heard gentle rattling and saw her approach with a tray in her hands.

He groaned and punched at the pillows behind his back. Resham usually arranged them.

She stepped nearer and offered the tray. He took it with one hand and drew the air through his nose. *Womanstench!* He had heard the word from his father. He puffed air out his nostrils.

They weren't his usual company, though girl cousins and aunts and, in the last days in Aeolia, the parade of hopefuls lived in the background. He had memorised his mother's scent, made of flowers and sterilising agents and anointing oil.

He breathed again, comparing the memory with the present and looking at the slim figure beside him. All Resham's soaps and ointments would not disguise her scent, made of things he could not identify.

He placed the tray across his knees, folded his hands and closed his eyes.

Leoshine mouthed, like a baby gnawing its fist. "Fur outee boootoo ceeve."

Avram's eyes blinked open in surprise. "For what we are about to receive." He repeated slowly.

Leoshine tried again with better success, but could not finish.

"Make us truly thankful. Mmm ..." His low rumble cut off her attempt. "So, I'm right." He spoke aloud in his own language. *A bright mind will find its own whetstone.* He congratulated himself. He had left her lonely and bored and her starved mind had snapped up the first morsel that presented itself. *I thank Resham for that.*

He smiled. His servant knew the two things closest to his heart. First, blend the cultures through language. Get them speaking to each other and they would discover how very alike they were. The other was far subtler and more cherished.

The girl ducked her head and made symbolic motions with her hand across her chest. "What does this mean?" Her voice was sweet and breathy.

He silently screamed with frustration. She had reached across the divide and he wanted to seize her hand and pull her the rest of the way. "Food. Give thanks for food. Ao Kevad."

She nodded. "You're welcome."

He looked up from the tray. She seemed to vibrate as she repeated the supplicating motion and moved her lips without making sound. What did she want? He knew what her donors intended; perhaps she expected an invitation to climb into bed with him. He chewed a crust of bread until he could stand it no longer. "Stand still." He growled in her language.

She froze in mid tremble.

His frown deepened. He finished eating and motioned for her

to take the tray to the table. He lifted his arms, then realised he was waiting for Resham to sweep the blankets of crumbs and rearrange the pillows. He laughed aloud at himself. How had he grown so dependent on that rogue Resham? *I can fluff my own pillows!*

She danced from foot to foot at the table, gulping the remaining food, and then settled back in her bed against the wall.

Before the Domelight took hold of the shadows, he heard Resham's step, his growl to the sentry, and the scrape of the door.

Avram opened his eyes.

Resham hissed at the girl, pointing to the tray. "Did you eat this?"

"No! He woke up."

Avram smiled. *Fiery vixen.*

"I ate what he didn't finish."

Truth teller. Avram quietly enjoyed being pleased again.

Resham lifted the tray. "You remember the way to the kitchen? Take this and bring another that they give you. Speak to no one and come straight back."

Avram saw her shiver. "You trust her?" He swung his feet onto the floor.

Resham straightened the bed. "You are not poisoned or stabbed, ao Kevath. And where could she go?"

Avram removed his bed shirt and sat at the table. "She is strong enough for the tray?"

"Did she struggle last night, ao Kevath?"

"How did you know?"

Resham cocked his eye at his master and exaggerated his motion of sweeping crumbs off the sheets. "I ran the health protocol, ao Kevath. She is under-nourished and I have begun the remedy."

"Is that why she is so small?"

Resham retrieved his shaving tools and began lathering Avram's chin. "She is taller than the average Myxolidian female, ao Kevath."

"How old is she?"

"She is older than she looks, ao Kevath. Her father knew you were coming and kept her young ..."

"To preserve her from being destroyed by ritual rape and circumcision and handed off to a man who has no use for her except as a baby machine." Avram wondered why he was telling Resham this. "You know better than anyone."

"Give her back to her father, ao Kevath."

Avram stared at the mayoral medallions that still decorated the rafters. "What of Curtstas? You said the younger killed the older brother? You want me to give her to that kind of care?" He frowned. "You work to keep me safe here?"

Resham pulled himself up.

"Don't be offended, brother. Where I am is the safest place under this Dome. It is no more work for you if she is here."

"But ao Kevath, she could stab you or poison you in the night."

"She is not capable of that."

"She is a fiery vixen. ao Kevath. I nearly died at her hand yesterday."

"A likely tale!" Avram lifted an eyebrow. "And deserved it, too."

Resham bowed. "If I should comment upon matters to test a lady's heart ..." He cocked his eyebrow at his master.

"So she has proven her cunning! You said something to make her mad to see what she would do, and you learned? What?"

"That she is a fiery vixen, ao Kevath"

Avram laughed. "Vixens can serve our purpose."

"What purpose, ao Kevath?"

Avram smiled and sent his eyes into the distance. "Dress her as we wish them to dress. Amend her tongue and teach her worship. Show them by her good example. And keep her safe. Do you object to that?" Avram relaxed his lip though his brow remained creased.

"The debt is paid, ao Kevath."

The shave complete, Resham cleaned the blade.

The door opened and Leoshine entered.

"Careful!" Resham barked as the tray tipped forward. "Go. Sit." He relieved her of the burden and sent her to the cot.

Avram observed his roommate stumble to the foot of her cot and sit with her back to him. *She has moral intelligence.* Something Aeolians at home did not expect in her people. *Too much,* he decided as he stood and stretched and yawned loudly. He didn't want a prudish slave.

A bright green blouse soon covered him. Black trousers and his military jacket with the jeweled insignia at the throat completed his outfit for the upcoming audience.

He stretched his shoulders back, imagining the black, red, and silver casing in the cupboard and smiled.

Through the day of meetings, ao Kevath Avram listened to Myxolidian burghers who expressed their loyalty, Aeolian division leaders desiring answers to sticky cultural disagreements, quarter-masters tallying supplies. Councillors of the old order, robed in furs and medallions, declared an end to this and a start to that and bustled away to discuss his suggestions.

When her people were involved, he saw Leoshine lean forward, her face alive with curiosity. When the dialog slipped into Aeolian and she lost the thread of meaning, she screwed up her features and twisted her blanket in her hands. He never acknowledged her existence in the corner, and the audience followed his cue.

Resham took her out before her father's arrival.

Rasset the Scientist

ᴎ෴෴ ෴෴ ෴෴෴෴

Avram settled his left shoulder blade between a twig and a leaf carved in the post of his bed and eased his neck straight. Soon the workers would come to construct the higher ceiling. "These are your figures?"

Curtstas bowed to his new commander and the gaunt scientist sitting beside his assistants at the round table. "Yes, ao Kevath. And Sir Rasset."

"And you have kept record how long?"

Curtstas bowed his head again and shuffled his feet. "Thirty cycles, ao Kevath. I have always been interested in the Dome, since my father allowed me to join the inspections. He taught me to take measurements, but I invented the system to record them."

The scientist at the table picked up a thick, crudely-bound manuscript. "Remarkable. The guild of Dome-engineers congratulates and thanks you." He gestured to the two other men sitting at the table and spoke clipped Aeolian louder than necessary. "You say cycle. This environment was created to cycle in periods of light and dark and we count them in larger cycles of 300. This we refer to as a year. There are smaller cycles within: days, weeks and months, for the human is a time-limited creature."

Avram imagined rolling his eyes at the technical jargon.

"One thousand years ago this planet was chosen and established by the Dome of Aeolia for eventual settlement as per the mandate their ancestors received from the Dome that chose and established them. The biosphere built by your ancestors brought a perfect environment on an otherwise inhospitable planetine. They determined parameters for the lush vegetation, a perfect balance of light rays and a period of darkness, a constant temperature and a multitude of other thoughtful comforts of maximum benefit to human existence. Unfortunately, this did nothing to change the nature of the men and women and children who settled here. If the Dome had not been designed to operate independently, this beautiful utopia would have deteriorated back to the original state of the planet within four generations.

"In the minds of the 51st generation, which is yours, the Dome figures largely as a mythological beast, beneficial but having no immediate significance to ordinary life. Or so we thought until these records were delivered to us after you returned. Thus, we appreciate and recognise your diligence. As well, we appreciate the measurements you took upon your return with the instruments we provided. Data from inside the Dome, compared with data from our perspective, has given a complete picture of its decline."

Rasset cleared his throat. "The chemicals from which the Dome is made have been severely depleted causing drought, insufficient protection from gamma rays, breakdown of reproductive systems of all life, and the increase of disease as immune systems deteriorate. The yield from crops is poor in quality and quantity causing famine, stunted growth, high infant mortality and reduced life expectancy."

The man rose in his chair. His face flushed and his voice grew even louder, as if defending a favourite theory from vicious rivals. "All due to lack of diligence, intentional ignorance, and willful destruction of the vital elements. We have replenished the Dome's supplies from the outside; however, it became clear that only direct intervention to prevent further damage would obtain the two desired outcomes, that being the full restoration of the Dome and the settlers' compliance with the mandate of further settlement of the next planetary system.

"Do you realize"—he leaned forward and pointed at Curtstas with a long lumpy-boned finger—"the final consequences of full deterioration? A thousand years of work and a few thousand souls who had forgotten where they came from—up in smoke!" He forgot his jargon in his passion. "Even the size of the interdomary ships—the invasion force itself—was limited because of the fragility of the Dome. Our vehicles are extremely efficient and perfectly sustainable in a healthy situation; however, we are only able to have one, One! in this atmosphere, and that not until at least the imminent infusion. Perhaps the beasts you ride are comfortable to you, but ao Kevath is used to more civilised means of transport!"

Avram interrupted. "We are not blameless, Rasset." His left scapula ached, and he leaned forward to stretch his spine.

Rasset shook his jowls and dug his elbows deeper into the table top. "The nutrients for the Dome arrived with us and are now correctly and precisely combined. We request permission, ao Kevath, to proceed to the engine chambers and begin injecting the solution."

"What effect will this have on the inner atmosphere?"

"Immediately the light will diminish. The Dome will change colour to dark red or brown. This effect should gradually fade over two or three days." He condescended to speak ordinary words. "The temperature will rise gradually with the amount of atmospheric humidity until the final desired response: rain."

The other scientist shuffled his papers. "The average temperature for the past three generations has been 5 degrees below optimum. The rainfall non-existent. Water stored in the ground has sustained the vegetation and crops. However, this is diminishing at ..."

Avram picked out an inconsistent vagueness in the dry statistics. "What does 'rise gradually' mean?"

Rasset glanced at his colleague. "Five degrees is significant, ao Kevath. The mandate requires a half degree per cycle until the rain, ao Kevath."

"The people will notice."

"Yes, ao Kevath."

"What is the normal fluctuation of temperature?"

"No fluctuations were programmed, ao Kevath."

"Can you program this Dome to fluctuate?"

Rasset gulped and his eyes bulged. "ao Kevath, permit me to say it is in your interest to restore the Dome before tampering with it."

Avram smiled behind his folded hands which he tapped gently on his chin. "You have permission to proceed. Dorim and his squadron are your escorts. If you begin in the evening six days from now, the effect of the lack of light will be ameliorated for the people."

Rasset nodded. "I have calculated a 30 year curve toward full restoration, ao Kevath. Your permission, ao Kevath? Horses and wagons are an antiquated method of carrying volatile and delicately combined chemicals over long distances."

Avram stated rather than proposed. "You have a place for the mayor on your team."

Rasset opened his mouth, looked at his Commander and closed it again. "The mayor has skill with measurements and notation. His knowledge of the history of events is invaluable."

Curtstas bowed. "Seventy cycles have I lived, ao Kevath. Thirty of those have I been a student of the Dome, ao Kevath."

Avram waved his hand and Rasset and his assistant rose from their chairs, collected their papers and shuffled out.

Curtstas, Avram noticed, glanced at the cot but made no comment.

Ride Through Town

Leoshine watched Resham's sandaled heels pumping up and down. The outside air begged to be inhaled in deep swathes after days in the sweaty crowd of Father's bedchamber.

At the threshold of a round wooden hut, Resham grasped a handle on a door.

She turned to him with her mouth open and her eyebrows raised. *What have you done to the bathhouse?*

His lifted brow cast his eye into deep shadow. "Meet me here when you finish. In good time."

She turned with a lift of her chin and stepped through the new door.

Cupboards and benches lined the walls of a small vestibule. The bathing tub steamed on the other side of the old door. A light stick shone from the rafter and a thick towel lay on the benches Father built.

She shuddered and looked for the rock to secure the door. Instead, a satisfying click from the door-catch reassured her.

She stepped through the inner door, closed it, and stripped next to the bath. Her hair floated on the surface of the hot water until she ducked her head and washed with the soap Resham left for her. She knotted the brown strands to lift them off her neck. A branch of hyssop stung as she beat the last of the scabs off her skin. A tangy aroma drifted on the steam.

Leoshine's mind drifted over the scene she had witnessed in the "court"—as Resham called ao Kevath's meetings with Aeolian and Myxolidian citizens in Father's chamber. How could he keep track of the names and reasons and positions and requests? The only constants in the room were the Overlord in the throne-like arm chair, Resham by the door or glowering over her, and herself sitting on the edge of the cot. The shuffle of feet and the buzz of voices, broken occasionally by tense silences when every ear quivered to hear ao Kevath's judgment or advice, blurred on the edges of her mind.

The bathing room door caught her eye. How impatient was Resham today? At least he wasn't plunking stones and slandering her brothers.

Her eye trailed to the wooden boards of the floor. She blinked and wiped a drop of water from her eyes. Resham's blouse had disappeared.

Another drop ran down her forehead, around her nose and into her open mouth. She tried to remember undressing and couldn't imagine herself leaving Resham's blouse in the new vestibule.

Another drop fell off her jaw, slicing the water. The noise vibrated inside her like the blade of Father's axe ringing as he felled trees. Looking again, she saw the inner door had not closed completely.

Leoshine emerged from the clinging water and wrapped the towel around her body as quickly as possible. Her hands trembled as she rubbed her skin with a corner of the towel while trying to keep herself covered.

In the vestibule, a deep chill set in her stomach. A new clear-sided box filled with neatly folded cloth lay on the bench. Leaf brown cloth, heavy, like the Overlord's bed curtains, had been sculpted into clothing. She shook out every fold.

She checked under the bench. The chest brace had vanished.

The towel slipped and a draft chilled her legs and back.

She held up the heavy cloth. *Maybe it has a brace?*

She slipped her arms into the sleeves. The top clung tightly, providing support for her form, almost refusing to clasp. She looked down. Support did not mean flattening.

She thought of all the times she had complained to Gorphiline about the brace. How it squeezed her lungs. How it dug into her when she bent over.

Resham complained about the dress Mother gave her—that it declared she was joined to ao Kevath. She preferred that over what this one declared—that she was good for nothing except his bed.

"You coming?"

Fear rocketed down her spine to her fingertips and toes. Resham grew impatient.

Her hands shook as she fastened the jacket's jeweled collar that opened at her throat. *No initials.* She wondered why ao Kevath's slave would not wear his insignia.

Resham's voice thundered again through the walls. "You need help?"

She fumbled with the lower garment that consisted of tight-fitting leggings. There was also a short cape, or it might be a skirt. The lower edge was scalloped and the clasps down the middle (or back) were unknown to her. Cape or skirt? She draped it over her arm.

She paused and drew a deep breath. Immediately she deflated, blushing. How could she leave her desecrated sanctuary looking like this?

The door swung open.

"You are too long." Resham snatched the drape from her arm. "And you have that all wrong."

"Don't touch me!" Leoshine shrank back. "You …! Why did you come in?"

"They only just arrived. And I didn't come in. It was one of your own women who made these for you."

Maybe Mother made them. Leoshine stroked the collar.

Before she could object, his nimble fingers reordered her clothes. "There now. Ready?"

The drape covered her left leg. *What about the other one?* Leoshine shivered and crossed her arms over her chest.

Resham took hold of her shoulder and pushed her ahead. He swatted the air behind her head to hasten her steps back to the prison. As she entered, Resham pushed past her.

The feet of ao Kevath's chair screeched on the floor as he called out and straightened his arms above his head. *This is a common gesture,* she recognised. At least this time he wore clothes.

His eyes flared suddenly as they found her in Resham's shadow.

The blood swelled in her face and she felt hot, tingling and dizzy.

ao Kevath spoke again, a low, urgent rumble while his eyes roved over her body. When he jumped from his chair, she whimpered.

Resham disappeared through the door. She wanted to call out to him.

ao Kevath spoke again, curling his fingers around the back of the chair and leaning forward. He could continue to stare at her with impunity. He could do anything at all to her, and she could not object, and yet he gripped the chair with white knuckles, wrinkled his brow, and twisted his mouth into a wry smile.

"Sing!" He demanded in a language she could understand. "You sing!"

Oh to be a canary with one song and one mind to sing it! In the bath she might have yodeled and warbled happily at the top of her voice. Under ao Kevath's unbridled stare, she quailed to produce any sound. She gripped her wrist and shielded her chest with her fist under her chin.

He frowned, and she cowered away.

From his mouth came a stream of sounds, almost like singing. Did he want her to imitate him?

His brow stayed furrowed and she decided he was frustrated rather than aggressive. His tone seemed to plead and his eyes filled with a longing that didn't include her body.

They stared at each other across the table.

A ballad about a hunter and a squirrel began to hum in her head. When he stopped speaking and looked down at his hands, the words flowed very softly from her tongue.

She smiled and felt like a pleading donkey. He looked up and caught her gaze. She retreated with a hot blush.

"Come and catch me!" the squirrel chirped at the end of every verse. When the hunter finally caught the squirrel, all he got were nuts for his trouble. The words were a little sad and a little cheeky and her audience smiled through his frown and nodded.

The door rumbled. Resham entered, and Leoshine leapt on the cot. ao Kevath jumped toward his servant with an exclamation and dragged him toward the cupboards beside the red curtained bed.

Resham drew the curtains around the bed posts to block the view, and Leoshine's face filled with hot blood as clothes flew. She buried her head in her pillows to muffle the exclamations and scuffles. Muggy breath bounced back into her face.

A heavy hand swatted the blanket from her. "Come." Resham stood over her.

The door stood open and ao Kevath walked out, robed in colours her head ached to describe. Light danced around him, reflected off him, entwined about him.

She gasped, holding back. "Where?"

Resham flashed the tether coiled in his hand.

She shook her head and tried to draw breath without moving her chest.

Resham jerked his head out the door and she obeyed.

An erect and alert ao Kevath led his entourage past armoured soldiers lining the corridors. Resham eyed each faceless shell as Leoshine scurried behind him, trembling and cold, breathless with the pace and the scattered beating of her heart.

She stumbled through a double door into a high-ceilinged, open room. White stone walls reached two stories above them. Drapes hung beside ceiling-to-floor windows and colourful statues filled sconces on either side of the towering double door. Whole rooms seemed to have arrived with ao Kevath, like clothes.

Resham caught her elbow and clamped her jaw shut with his hand. "It isn't finished yet."

Leoshine gasped and shrank into Resham as a line of shelled aliens clattered their arms to their helmets. ao Kevath did not wear the shell this time, she observed and wondered why so many of them were gathered.

ao Kevath barked a command. The shelled-ones turned as one body and marched toward the far, carved doors. These opened, and she saw the street that fronted her father's palace.

Resham ushered her into the dimming evening light.

"Out?" Her lips moved as she looked up at her escort. Again, she stumbled, and Resham jerked her arm forward.

A wide landing led to a pyramid of gleaming white steps down to the street. Shelled aliens sat on huge muscular beasts. Flags fluttered up and down the line.

Resham's hands gripped her waist and deposited her into a shiny black, molded side-saddle. "I've seen you ride, Tassanara." He arranged her legs into an upper and lower hook on one side of the horse, like he would set the table with utensils. "I have a nice, gentle mare here. Try to model yourself after her." He twitched the drape over them. Now she knew why it only covered one leg when she walked.

Leoshine bristled at the implied sneer and looked down where the Myxolidian pommel would be. The hook for her upper leg was all she had to hang on to.

Resham reached for the upper hook. From it he extended a

thick black strip of metal all around her at waist level. She jumped and squeaked. Down from the wire, a curtain of undulating air popped over her legs, also supporting her on the side where her legs did not go. She felt pressed down into the seat.

She poked a fingertip into the curtain from the inside. Instantly she retracted. Her finger had gone all wavy too.

Resham patted her mare's neck. "Tesheddar. To support and shield. You'll be fine." He nodded at ao Kevath who held the reins of a giant beast.

Horse, she corrected herself. It nuzzled his hand and he smiled.

Resham watched their master exchange affection with his pet. "That's Paulos, ao Kevath's stallion. Birthed and trained by his own hand." Before mounting his own horse, he tethered her mare by a sturdy beribboned rope to ao Kevath's saddle.

She vibrated as her master gave the signal and the glittering cavalcade rose smartly to the trot. Her knuckles turned white gripping the upper leg hook. The undulating curtain did nothing to steady her against the rhythm of the stride. *People will see me. All of me.* Father kept her strictly secluded. No, that wasn't true. He was supposed to and Mother cursed him for taking her into his world.

Her people waved coloured cloth and cheered from the walkways, dressed in their finery. Prepared for a festival.

Shelled and unshelled aliens clumped on the street corners. They seemed to watch the Myxolidians more than the cavalcade.

ao Kevath waved back. A pack of boys ran beside them with unfamiliar flags and noisemakers. The crowd grew thicker, but they turned so many corners, Leoshine could not say how far they rode. Their clamour echoed off the two-story wooden buildings that fronted the streets.

At the great protective wall, the edge of the town, Leoshine shivered. The new clothes were no match for the chill in her heart as they rode under the soldiers looking down from the battlement towers. Immediately ao Kevath turned and the troop rode away from the gate, back into the centre of town.

She noticed a difference in the noise as they left bystanders behind. They pointed at her and their faces changed. They called to each other to look at her. News of her capture and ao Kevath's ownership of her soul and body must have been rife in the town.

Her throat somersaulted with her palour, pale and crimson in turn. She looked away, between her horse's ears where a feathery headdress tossed, down at her hands clenching the upper leg hook inside the curtain, back at the pointing spectators. Her cheeks flamed as her gaze dropped.

Her eye caught a lump of garbage floating in the irrigation channel Father had cut through the town.

How dare her people worship this impostor ruler! Did they forget Father so soon? How soon before they turned against the Invader? What form would their fight against this power take? Would her father's treaty be in vain after all?

A daze crept over her and the scene blurred. Her muscles complained and gave up holding her erect. She leaned against the leg hooks and the black metal Tesheddar. Stinging patches formed across her back, thighs, and calves. *What is that shielding me from?*

ao Kevath stood in his saddle, waved and called to someone ahead.

Her horse lurched forward and she fought for her hold. The Tesheddar clenched. Her legs went numb. Hooves rang on the hard pavement and echoed faster off the close-set buildings.

The buildings seemed to part. Leoshine gasped as they emerged into an open space, flanked by high wooden fences. Piles of rotten wood and debris cluttered the edges, and new-turned sod filled the air with a rich loamy smell.

The dirt compacted under ao Kevath's feet. He tossed the reins to a hastily arriving soldier. All around dismounting soldiers thumped to the ground, horses blew steam, harnesses jingled, and calls of revelers flooded into the field.

A man taller than ao Kevath stepped forward. Leoshine's eyes strained to bursting.

ao Kevath thumped the giant's armoured chest and shoulders and the two bellowed like oxen at each other. He wrapped his arm around the giant's shoulders and led him away from the cavalcade into the main dug-up area. They stepped high to gain traction.

ao Kevath halted in midstride, spoke back over his shoulder, and then marched on.

Resham appeared at her foot and waved his hand over the upper leg hook. The curtain disappeared and the black metal belt retracted into the hook.

She shrank away from him. Her forearms clutched across her

chest. "No." Her lips formed the word, but she lacked breath to pass the plea to Resham.

"ao Kevath commands." His huge hands gripped her waist, and she felt herself lifted like a doll. Her feet touched the ground. Immediately her legs collapsed. Resham chuckled in his throat and grasped her lapel. He propelled her to stand behind ao Kevath and the giant.

Leoshine held her breath until her ears thundered. With clenched fists and hunched shoulders, she willed her knees and legs to stiffen on the uneven and unstable footing. She lurched away from Resham, and he tentatively relaxed his grip. Her legs protested. She stumbled and regained her balance and glared at her helper.

ao Kevath continued to laugh and bellow at his companion. Soldiers brought flags from the horses and planted them in a square where ao Kevath stopped. He raised his voice and gestured, encompassing the open area.

The crowd hung back and Leoshine sensed more dour aliens than her people.

ao Kevath paused and the giant suddenly knelt in the dirt with his head bowed. Leoshine imagined his shoulders were as broad as her cot. She could lie across them more comfortably than riding in that side-saddle.

ao Kevath bent down and scooped a handful of brown, moist dirt. He spoke again. Soldiers and aliens joined the giant in bowing their heads.

ao Kevath lifted his closed eyes to the Dome, tilting his head until the curls that clustered on the back of his head touched between his shoulder blades. His voice took on a new quality, dreamy and reverent, chant-like and resonant.

Leoshine tensed her shoulders and flexed her unpredictable knees. She spied an opening in the fence and imagined herself jumping and running across the field. Resham's gleaming eye met hers from beneath his partially lifted lid.

Her throat spasmed and she looked down, blood rushing in her ears.

When he opened his eyes, ao Kevath set the clump of dirt on the top of the giant's head and rubbed the mess around. The stubble-blond hair turned dark brown. Sweat smeared and ran black down the giant's temples.

Leoshine's mouth dropped open and she forgot the plight of her legs. *What kind of ritual is this?* She swallowed as a bitter burn ate at the bottom of her throat.

A clear-sided box appeared in the dirt-smeared giant's hands. He bent forward and the cake of dirt fell into it from his head. Closing the lid, he offered it to ao Kevath who made another solemn speech as he accepted the treasure.

The giant leveraged an elbow on his upper thigh that seemed as thick as the irrigation canal that ran through the town, and rose to his feet. He laughed and wiped dirt across his forehead. ao Kevath punched his arm and laughed too. A soldier appeared with a bowl and towels. Leoshine observed that the giant attended to his own washing, but a servant poured water and rubbed the dirt from ao Kevath's hand. In the other he held the box flat on his palm.

The servant disappeared behind the wall of soldiers. ao Kevath paused, his head cocked at a curious angle. For a moment everyone held their breath, all eyes trained on their commander.

He smiled. His eyes glinted.

Leoshine's knees quivered as he stepped in front of her and bent to offer her the box.

She lost herself in his blue eyes. By their power, her hands lifted to receive the treasure. In his hand the treasure floated. In hers it collapsed downward.

"Hold tight!" Resham darted forward and fixed his fingers around the box, engulfing her limp, cold hands and upper arms.

She pulled the box closer to her stomach and twisted away from Resham. ao Kevath strode across the open field, pointing in all directions, arm around the giant's shoulders.

"Walk on." Resham fastened his hand around her elbow and pulled, but not ungently.

She looked behind and her heart sank to her boots. The horses were gone. Her hands lowered and Resham relieved her of the box.

"Why did he give it to me?" Half her mind followed ao Kevath as he moved farther and farther away.

"Shall I carry you?" Resham threatened. "Or you walk. Either way we follow."

"Leave me here!" Tears sprouted from her eyes. She didn't know where she was in the town and imagined lying down in the field. Her body began to shake and she could not feel her hands or lower limbs.

"Not likely." Resham replied and moved closer. He reached to grasp her lapel again.

She twisted away and tried to run. Her feet felt like they had iron shoes on, and her ankles turned over on the clods of soil. Tears blinded her. When Resham made no attempt to stop her, she halted and wiped her eyes and nose on her sleeve.

She had been running toward ao Kevath.

Resham walked past a few steps. "Don't stop now."

Once more she looked at the empty space where he might abandon her. *How long would I survive in the town? Dressed like this?*

The Domelight failed. A troop of soldiers shifted wooden boards, wreckage from whatever buildings had stood here in Father's time. Her feet seemed to grow roots deep into the ground, too heavy to lift, her heart too sore to beat.

Resham spoke from nearby. "Come, Tassanara." Then he spoke some Aeolian words into the air. He wrapped his arm around her shoulders but did not press her forward.

Sobs erupted from her broken heart. She shrugged against his touch but could not dislodge the weight of his arm.

A velvet nose thrust itself over her shoulder and into her face. She squeaked and jumped away.

Resham caught her and lifted her into the saddle. He didn't activate the shield-belt. "They hadn't untacked her yet. You can ride as far as the front door, but you have to carry this." Resham thrust the box into her hands and held it there while she realised his request.

She looked at the box through her tears. Soil from her home. Myxolidia. She was taking it to her new home. *Does it belong to me? What will ao Kevath do with it when I bring it home? Home?*

At a slow walk Resham led her across the field onto a paved road. He stopped before one of the buildings seen from the field. Broad white steps led up to a double door. Dirty footprints led up the stairs and through the entrance.

She felt Resham near, lifting her from the saddle to the top of the stairs, waiting for her legs to support her body. He steadied her by holding her elbow. The sentry obeyed his nod to open one half of the door.

She stumbled into the darkness, numb and burning with questions at the same time.

Ride into Oxikobh Territory

Avram scowled and paced between the bed and the table in his chambers. He shook Resham's hand off his wrist as he passed his servant standing by the door. His servant-physician had rebuked him before about rubbing his stinging eyebrow. "Did you see Wol?"

"No, though I believe he was there, ao Kevath."

"How are you going to catch him if you can't see him in the crowd?"

"He is good with disguise, ao Kevath. But he will leave a trail. My people will hear and report."

"Has he tried to kill his father yet?"

Resham smirked but did not answer.

"Go now." Avram growled and waved a dismissive hand. "Trap him in the town. We ride out again at first light."

Resham slowed his words. "I know, ao Kevath, that he is aware of his sister's presence with you and will be surprised that you exhibit her so freely. He will try to turn it to his advantage."

Avram raised his voice as he stopped in front of his chief of security. "I do not tailor my actions to suit his advantage! Your task is to see that he has none."

"He is more perverted than the Oxikobh, ao Kevath."

Avram lifted an eyebrow at Resham. "More than you?"

Resham jutted his chin forward. "When we were children …" The telltale pulsed behind his ear. "I have the scars to prove his superiority." He inclined his head and passed through the door.

Avram continued pacing around the table. Resham had given Leoshine the broth again and said she would benefit from the rest.

What did he care? He did not tailor his actions to suit her fear. He paced with heavier feet while a piece of his mind gnawed on her reaction to the ride. Proud, he decided. Prudish. Like her refusal to change into the night clothes she found on her cot when they returned.

Resham had quizzed her. "What kind of man would he be if he looked? What kind of man is he because he won't?"

Petulant, Avram concluded as he thought of her refusal to drink the broth and her declaration that she would not go out again in the morning. Resham ignored both refusals and left the broth on the table. Eventually she drank, hunger overcoming rebellion.

He admired Resham's patience with her, allowing her questions and giving a greater puzzle in reply. She made a grave mistake scrapping with him.

Avram set his feet in a path around the table to the cot again, bumping his head several times on the beams. He saw again the crowd cheering and the dilapidation of the buildings in the town. Through the night, plans to rebuild revolved in his head. *Especially*—he rubbed his bruised forehead—*the renovations to this chamber.*

Paulos whinnied and tossed his head at the bottom of the gleaming, torchlit white steps. Avram wrapped his arm around the corded neck and stroked the velvet nose. The scent of horse surrounded him, of comfort and companionship, overriding the tang of fear pervasive in the town.

He whispered in the twitching ear. "A foray into the wild. An inspection of new-claimed territory." He braced. Paulos swung his head round and whacked his teeth against his master's breastplate. The usual greeting. Avram grinned. If he wore one of his uniform jackets, Paulos would lip the buttons and bullions and snort.

Now the great stallion exhaled with an exultant rumble and tossed his head.

At Avram's nod, the soldier standing at the stallion's head stepped away. Paulos knew to keep his feet still while Avram swung himself into the saddle.

Avram pressed hard to assert his authority over the power which swelled under him. *Another greeting.* He smirked. *Later we'll gallop, when the girl wakes up. There might be a skirmish.*

He looked back at the cavalcade. Resham arrived at his stirrup, having secured the sleeping girl with the Tesheddar. It would keep her upright in her side-saddle until she woke up. Her head rested on a pillow tucked into the black metal brace that generated the shield.

Resham spoke under his breath from his master's stirrup. "Wol is not in the town, ao Kevath."

"You think he anticipates us?"

"Yes and no, ao Kevath."

Avram touched Paulos with his heel. He wasn't interested in Resham's subtlety today.

Beside the mayoral palace, he passed the open field where last night the city general, Gavin, was sworn into his post. Avram imagined the massive stone house they had cleared the mud flat to build, and the ceremonies Resham and Iliana and priests like them would perform there for generations to come.

Hoofbeats rattled on the fresh-paved street and echoed off the round edges of wooden buildings. Doors opened directly onto the street, without steps or porches. He drew the air over his palate, sensing a change in the mood since last evening. No waving. No cheering or boys joining the fun. Any faces they met turned away in the shadows.

An Overlord calculated, Avram reminded himself, calculated the time to harvest, the rations he needed to bring to satisfy the appetite of his army, the effect of every last footfall his people made in the new territory.

He called out in Myxolidian to the captain of his guard. "What you eat ... supper ... night before?"

The soldier saluted and shouted back. "Rations, ao Kevath!"

Avram nodded his approval. Perhaps when the abundant harvest filled their bellies and strengthened their children, the Myxolidians would smile without bribes. Would they ever appreciate how the Aeolians never strained the food supply?

The generals reported lingering shock in the territory they would explore today. Avram stretched again in his stirrups. The torches of the gate illuminated Gavin astride his diminutive horse.

His wife, Heien had pleaded with him to find a mount better suited to his physical and societal stature, but he remained loyal to his sturdy gelding.

Sentries saluted, and a flag hung as limp as the windless Dome over the two wooden towers of the gate. Without a word he ducked his head and added enlargement of the town entrance to the list of civic improvements. *One day a stone wall ... No,* he reconsidered. One day a wall would be unnecessary. All his kingdom would live in peace.

His senses exploded ahead into wide open territory where Curtstas had cleared a swath around the town as a good defensive strategy. The mayor had told them how the sacrifice of trees for building the wall had heightened the hatred between town dweller and Oxikobh and ensured fiercer attacks. *They love their trees.* Avram smirked at a memory of Resham as a prisoner in nearly treeless Aeolia.

He breathed the new smells and marveled. In training he could identify each species of tree and shrub because in Aeolia they were presented to him separately. Here they mingled with churned soil where his people created gardens outside the walls. Leaf mold, not the muskier scent of moss, drifted in from the forest. A team had been excavating a stream nearby.

To the left of the gate, the map showed three rows of stubby fruit trees that had defied the feuds between Townsman and Oxikobh. To the right a field of bushes propped up by poles testified to the efforts of Curtstas after his return. The old man tried, Avram acknowledged, like the tip of the arrow that gets crushed and discarded as the head and shaft follow through with the assault. *Now he must step aside for the real engine of change.*

Across the open plain, the hoofbeats puffed dust from the track. No pavement there. That would come when the town dwellers stopped fighting the Oxikobh, when all Myxolidians, and even the Aeolian settlers discovered they were all the same tribe after all.

Avram stretched the hearing of his town-clouded ears—full of the coughing of refugees in the streets, hooves ringing off cramped buildings, and rattling of crockery in his girl-slave's care—to the treeline to catch animated sound. One solitary warbler introduced the cavalcade to the idea of dawn as they crossed into leaf-giant territory. Hooves scuffled in the leaf bed. Saddle-creaks swam amid crusty round monoliths.

The soldiers fanned out among the trunks. The beginnings of light filtered through the damaged canopy. The Dome did not switch on or off like an artificial light, but dawn did not linger.

No rain. No surface moisture to nurture saplings. Only the trees that drilled their roots into the planet's core aquifer survived the prolonged deterioration of the Myxolidian Dome.

He called to Gavin who ranged up beside him. "Rasset's project."

"I thought we would meet with dead wood, ao Kevath, but the people have cleaned it all out with the undergrowth."

"They need fires, but they respect the living trees. Worse disaster would have befallen ..."

"We'd have come sooner, ao Kevath."

Avram coughed his derision. "Not a moment sooner. We are still barely prepared."

"After the rain, ao Kevath."

"After Rasset stops playing." Avram sat back on his seat and looked around and up. He imagined leaves blocking the Dome-light and vines, bushes choking the path, and the odour of life replacing the stench of fungus and decay. "We'll all get wet."

"Where first, ao Kevath?"

Avram heard the question, but counted thirty hoof falls before answering. "Alan. This is his quintile." He looked ahead where tree branches met over the path. "He is setting up his base closest to the town but will give us the furthest ride today."

He wanted to be alone to sort the overwhelming stimuli. The scurries in the shadows, the angles of twigs and trunks and flower stems cutting and interlacing above and beside him, the colours of the flowers themselves—all intoxicated him.

In man-made Aeolia, scurrying animals, mass plantings where the seeds grew up where they fell, and the unhindered mingling of flower species had been eradicated as the population swelled. Order ruled and chaos was overcome by intricate design. His home was never plain or uninteresting to look at; neither did lines and shadows dance with such complication as here.

Leoshine, too, unbound all his previous conceptions of humanness; lines and shadows danced in her soul that he wanted to quantify, as if that would tame her, place her. If he counted the pulses fluttering in her throat, or the times her swallowing made her eyes close? If he could describe her breathing—she must be dizzy from hyperventilating.

The way her mouth formed a perfect 'o' and her lashes splayed wide when she learned something new. He was impressed how she soaked up his language; at the same time the task seemed daunting. Resham spoke of the unexpected questions she asked. She wanted to know the exact moment they saw Myxolidia from the "giant birds"—the interdomary vessel.

If I could count and describe and explain ... I could know how flexible she is, how far I can take her away from her barbarian ways, and how fast.

The noises she made chasing the juice of the fruit down her arm made the hairs in his ears curl. The high-pitched abrupt scream she made when startled froze the nerves at the base of his skull.

Tame her? He laughed at himself. She didn't need taming. She needed freedom from devastating social constructs that maimed and devalued. As she grew into all she was—Woman as Ao Kevad made her—she would be more and more inexplicable.

What is woman? He had heard that the male soul would be intrigued, fascinated, enthralled, tantalised, and ... frustrated. He laughed again. The dancing sprite of woman eluded man in a primeval way. His instinct was to tame, but she would remain wild and free. The instant he succeeded, he lost the most precious interaction in Ao Kevad's palette.

In her presence, everything he counted as strength was weakness. Every talent, wisdom and skill he possessed met a stone wall in her elusiveness. He would run screaming into that wall. He would smash his sword against it and bruise himself, crush his talent and wisdom and skill. *Better to leave her very well provided—and distant!*

The forest disappeared. All sound ceased. *Who needs taming?*

"ao Kevath?"

Avram blinked and shook his head at himself.

"Avram?"

His name in his general's voice bent his heart like arriving in hyperdrive. Gavin. The general with a wife, Heien, niece of Iliana and granddaughter of one of Aeolia's Overlords. And daughters, tassanaras in their own right. He blinked and looked around. Paulos had halted in response to his involuntary jolt. The whole troop halted.

He nudged Paulos forward. The ambient sounds picked up where they left off.

Gavin hung near his stirrup.

"I was thinking of the *Talon.*" He didn't lie. "Full of women and children."

Gavin's face warped as if he went through extreme gravitational forces. "The homes will be ready, ao Kevath." Gavin's family would come on the *Talon,* giving him added incentive to prepare shelter for the new arrivals.

Ao Kevad! I am Your … in his mind he pronounced the word perfectly, *Rachnorgat. Tame me.*

"There he is, ao Kevath." Gavin broke from talking about how hard it was to build a palace for an absent wife.

Alan sat on his horse like a tree. He had the straightest back and the longest legs to match his long nose and pointed chin that jutted almost between his steed's ears. He waited in a clearing with his troop. "ao Kevath. Gavin."

Avram and Gavin landed on the ground with two feet together.

Avram glanced around. "This the spot?" When Alan nodded, he signaled the soldier standing behind Alan to bury his shovel in the ground at the general's feet.

The clod of soil revealed a world of worms and beetles. The smell of their fear reached Avram's nose.

"Bigger," he ordered. *Disturb the whole civilisation of the biome.* The scurry to escape him reminded him of the Myxolidians. "No sign of habitation?"

Alan swept his arm wide. "Compounds not far from here, ao Kevath." His eyes assumed a piercing light as he looked at Avram, then knelt down in the exposed dirt and bowed his head.

Avram accepted his general's questioning submission and stooped to gather a handful of the ground. Roots of tiny drought-resistant plants sprouted between his fingers.

He closed his eyes and tilted back his head. The forest seemed to close around them like the crowd yesterday. The trees were more reverent. *They know their creator better.*

"Ao Kevad." He boomed out his master's title. "You made Myxolidia to thrive. You charged us with renewal." He opened his eyes, lowered the clump onto Alan's long black waves of hair. On Gavin's balder head he had no trouble getting the symbolic anointing to stay in place. Alan had a point to the top of his head that made balancing his territory there a challenge.

Avram broke the soil into smaller clumps that ran down Alan's face and hair. "Your servant Alan is here, in this territory to win Your way. Guide and direct him in all he does." *We all need taming.* "Protect him to bring about Your purpose."

Gavin stepped forward with the box and Alan tipped forward to fill it. He stood and offered the box to Avram.

A shout rang out.

Alan swiveled on his feet. Avram and Gavin drew their swords and turned to watch the troop of guards coalesce around a tree about four men's lengths away. The captain of the guard called orders and dry leaves puffed up from the ground.

A young man's voice crackled from the midst of the troop. They stepped aside for Alan who grasped the youth by the scruff of his tunic neck and dragged him over to Avram. Every sword point threatened the huddled body.

The captain of the guard threw another, scrawnier youth beside the first. A barrage of grating sounds blazed from the young man.

Avram rocked back on his heels. He guessed that he listened to an explanation as well as an objection to being discovered.

Syllables, harsh and jarring yet no competition for the Oxiko-bh spewed from Alan. He gave back twice what he received then kicked the ground in front of the youths. They sprang to their feet faster than Avram could wince. Alan commanded the troop to part and the two youths dashed off into the forest.

Alan strolled to the edge of the dug-up dirt patch and sheathed his sword. "Pardon the interruption, ao Kevath. Just some locals come to watch."

"You know them?"

Alan half closed his eyes. "Yes. They belong to the compound by the stream."

Avram commended his general. "You come out here often? Not wasting time getting to know your province."

Alan only shrugged. "Be careful, ao Kevath. These were harmless. Others only need someone …"

Avram finished the thought. "To lead them. I know."

The straight lines of Alan's mouth showed his doubt in Avram's experience, not his knowledge.

Avram gestured for Paulos. He placed the dirt-box into the saddlebag. "I asked you to clear our path today."

"In my province, you have my guard. In Dorim's, his, ao Kevath."

"You coming to watch Dorim?"

"No, ao Kevath. I will plot out this base camp with your blessing."

"Fresh in your hair." The urge to jest swelled as he caught Gavin's eye. He held out his dirt-smeared hand. "You have water?"

Leoshine in the Wilderness

⟡⟡⟡⟡⟡⟡⟡ ⟡⟡ ⟡⟡⟡ ⟡⟡⟡⟡⟡⟡⟡

A loud noise burst nearby. Leoshine tried to blink. Her eyelids felt like huge wet woolen blankets and her ears seemed clogged with beeswax. Her heart thundered against her ribs and up her throat while her skin stung from the nerve needles piercing her arms, spine and legs. Yet she could not sense where she was or what the noise meant.

Her next wakening gave her time to realise the position of her body and the immovability of her limbs. She raised her head from something solid, though padded, and tried to arch her back. Domelight winked at her through a tangle of leafed branches. Her arms were wrapped across her front. Her legs were clamped in the position she remembered from the previous night. She trembled as the horse beneath her snorted. The nerve needles returned with an insufferable urge to twist and scream.

Armed soldiers sat on stamping horses. Bits jostled. Thick tree trunks surrounded them. Fluttery leaves, instead of banners and flags, gave the impression that the whole world vacillated.

Beside her horse and slightly ahead she heard ao Kevath laugh. He stood with the giant of last evening. The memory left her blinking. He had knelt in the dirt which ao Kevath had rubbed on his head.

The giant strolled over to her. He drawled soft-sided Myxolidian. "My name is Gavin." He unlocked something on the outside of her restraints. The undulating curtain, Tesheddar Resham called it, fell off her body.

Leoshine pitched forward. Her fingers gripped the upper leg hook until the blood drained away.

Gavin reached his dinner-plate-sized hands and took hold of her waist. "I have a wife and children. They are not hurt when I lift them. ao Kevath wants you."

Her mouth opened and closed as she neared the ground. She would touch Oxikobh soil, she realised, and bent her knees to prevent this sacrilege. Wol told her curses would seep into her feet if she left the safety of her horse.

She wrapped her arms around the giant's neck and looked down at the approaching forest floor. He bent lower and lower until she straightened her legs, rather than sit on the unclean ground and have the curse seep through her body. Her feet touched down. She sprang up and her forehead brushed his chin.

ao Kevath laughed again.

Gavin returned a comment with jesting in his voice.

She stood, stiff legged and vibrating.

"Come." Gavin gestured her forward. "Meet Dorim."

A new man stood with ao Kevath. They all wore red, black, and silver armour and thoughtfully cradled their beardless chins between forefinger and thumb. She guessed they must be the same age. The stranger had the highest cheek bones and bushiest eyebrows she had ever seen. His eyes seemed to lurk in their cavernous shadow and the rest of his face, though attractive, seemed withdrawn and insignificant.

He looked short next to ao Kevath and Gavin, though she had to gaze a long way up to see him.

With lips crushed between her teeth, she stepped forward. She gripped the cloth of her leggings drawn tight over her thighs.

ao Kevath turned to Dorim and motioned for him to kneel.

Dry leaves fluttered from the clod of dirt as ao Kevath plunked it on Dorim's head. A box transferred from Dorim's dirty hand to his commander's.

In the next instant, ao Kevath towered over her, holding the box out. Like the previous evening, she responded by instinct. This time she was prepared for the weight.

He smiled down at her. Staring into his eyes, she felt a jolt shudder down to her toes.

"Myxolidia for the Myxolidian." His tongue struggled but his eyes were earnest. "We keep in our chamber. We …" His face convulsed in anger and he barked some words at Gavin.

The blood drained from Leoshine's face down and out the soles of her feet, into the Oxikobh filth. Her knees collapsed when Gavin draped his hand over her shoulder. He grabbed her elbow and half carried her back to her horse.

She looked up into his face and almost coughed with the scorch in her chest. *What is your wife's name and where is she with your children? Where under Aeok'n are we and when are we going …?* Her mind stumbled over the word. Home was not home anymore.

She did not see him mount. A mass of brown and green trees blurred past. She closed her eyes and ignored the swaying motion. *Why didn't Gavin put the Tesheddar on?*

The other general, Dorim, rode beside ao Kevath and Gavin fell back toward her.

"Gavin." She called his name. A shiver teased her stomach. Speaking to a man without Father near promised punishment in the old times.

The giant slowed his horse. Her heart beat faster. He glanced toward ao Kevath and her eyes followed.

ao Kevath turned his head very slightly. Without a pause in his conversation with Dorim, he gave a short, curt reply to Gavin's silent query. Gavin resumed his position a horse's width from Paulos' rump and her horse's shoulder.

Leoshine blinked and her brows drew together. Her hands rested limp in her lap. "Where are we going?"

The sound died in the steady thumping of hooves. ao Kevath trotted on and Gavin joined Dorim in the conversation. Soldiers spread out around them, dodging tree trunks to keep their formation.

Her eyes scanned the bushes for the thousandth time. She imagined Oxikobh eyes under every leaf. Did they recognise the mayor's daughter? Her lips drew white between her teeth. How could they, in this …? What did Resham call this costume?

Oxikobh savaged town women. Georg promised protection when he had taken her out. Mother had spoken the truth: A curse is a curse. She had been too young for savaging then.

Georg held authority out here, she assured herself. Wol too. *Is he out here? Would he help me? Can those soldiers protect me?*

ao Kevath cried out and whipped Paulos into a trot. Leoshine's teeth rattled until she found the rhythm of the gait.

She missed Resham. As much as she detested him, he could speak properly, and he took care. *No, that's too strong,* she corrected. *He prepares for me. He provides what I don't think to ask for. He explains, sometimes.*

The branches above rustled and she ducked her head. An animal called. Her eyes ached from peering through the teasing angles of the tree branches.

Man voices recalled her from her daydream. Another armoured general stood beside a ditch. She heard gurgling and saw water moving through the snaking indent in the forest floor.

Father once took her into the dark, dank room in the middle of the palace, where water bubbled up from a deep hole and flowed in a protected bed under the buildings and out to supply the town. The ancestors provided the hole and the channels, and Father maintained and improved them throughout his tenure as mayor. Doing the chores of personal care and the household, Leoshine had learned to draw water from spigots in strategic places.

She looked around at the thickened foliage and lush green grass and bright flowers lining the ditch of water. Father had told her stories of underground streams. Her mouth watered at the memory of the sweet cress he brought back when he inspected the Dome Engines. She saw again the bright stones he had trickled into her hand one day, pebble jewels he picked out of the Core Rivers.

He never mentioned surface rivers.

On the other bank, Leoshine saw a table with a vase of flowers in the centre. Strange devices and tools lay around the vase. Her tongue felt even more parched when she saw a pitcher and goblets.

ao Kevath rode three circles around the new general, barking questions and frowning over each answer.

Sandy, wavy hair fell over the man's shoulders. His eyes danced with mischief though his hands played nervously with a clear-sided box. His thick brows and high cheek bones were familiar enough that Leoshine glanced toward Dorim where he waited with Gavin.

They all dismounted and Gavin came to her horse. "Come, meet Kirim, Dorim's brother. ao Kevath wants you."

"Does he get everything he wants?" Leoshine muttered.

Gavin lifted her up and deposited her on the green grass.

His smile broke wide open. The next moment, he frowned and cleared his throat. "No, no, he doesn't. That is why we obey him." He gestured for her to follow and walked to where the other men gathered.

Leoshine stalked after him, shoulders hunched. She halted a step further from the group than before, wondering what ao Kevath would do with the box if she was not near to receive it. She looked up. Kirim knelt in the water and ao Kevath stood ankle deep. The bank where she stood came above his knees.

Every part of the anointing ceremony was duplicated with water substituting for dirt.

Her eyes met ao Kevath's. He almost didn't have to bend. She blushed as he held the box out. She stepped to the edge of the bank. He did not speak, only stared with his brows drawn tight together. Her heart crumpled. His brows tilted slightly, and she wondered why she tested his authority.

The box of water transferred into her blindly obedient hands and ao Kevath nodded and jerked his head to Kirim, who stood and climbed up to her level. Dripping wet, he looked at Gavin with one eyebrow raised and a crooked twist to one corner of his mouth. Gavin raised both eyebrows and cocked his head at ao Kevath.

ao Kevath climbed onto the opposite bank, toward the table. "Take box to Paulos and come … table."

Leoshine tilted the box and watched the water slosh from side to side. Not a drop came out. Her hands were wet, but that was from the residue on the outer surface. *What will Oxikobh water do to me?*

The town stream collected refuse and carried it under the protecting wall. If this was the continuation of that water course then her hands were covered in things Father warned her to stay away from and her feet were covered in Oxikobh curse. She grimaced at ao Kevath at the table.

Kirim gestured for her to move ahead of him and kinked his knees to accommodate her lesser stride.

She held up the box to indicate the water. "Why did you?" Leoshine breathed the words, testing her ability to speak to a man.

Kirim cleared his throat and opened his mouth with his chin pointing forward. He closed it and coughed. "Yes, Tassanara."

The hair on the back of her neck stood on end. He used the word Father spoke in endearment and Resham sneered in derision.

Nothing, she decided, would ever induce her to like that sound in an Aeolian mouth.

She tried again as they stood in the shadow of the towering stallion. "What does it mean?"

Kirim took the box from her hands and deposited it far above her head. A drop of water fell onto her hand from his sandy hair and she tried to brush it off without his noticing.

He looked up and to the side, down at his sodden boots and then with soft wrinkles between his eyes, at his comrades gathering around the table.

Leoshine frowned and fought the urge to stamp her foot.

The wet one stuttered. "Er, yes." His teeth flashed and he motioned for her to move toward the group.

Does he not understand? Does he lack Myxolidian words?

She exhaled sharply through her nose, turned on her heel, and stalked toward ao Kevath. At the stream, she looked again into her master's face. Her hand crossed her chest and touched her lips in the most profound gesture of respect and pleading she knew. Her tongue melded with the roof of her mouth.

ao Kevath looked up from the conversation with Gavin and Dorim, over her head to Kirim. They exchanged a few words and suddenly Kirim lifted her over the stream. He left her to join the others.

He answered the wrong plea. He thinks I couldn't jump over a little trickle of water when all I want is to know why? Why does he play with dirt and water? Why are we out of the town? Why did he bring me?

Kirim received a cup from Dorim, and they exchanged glances. Dorim raised one mighty eyebrow above the other. Kirim tweaked one cheek higher, his mouth twisted and twitching.

He passed the cup into Leoshine's numb hands, received another from Dorim and cleared his throat. He looked at ao Kevath, tossed his chin out, up at the Dome, down at his feet, coughed, hum-hawed once.

Finally, he took a deep breath. "ao Kevath permits me to say"—he licked his lips and bounced his gaze off her eyes—"permits me to say that if you look"—he extended his arm and waved it out over the table—"you will see the town wall."

He speaks fine Myxolidian. Her eyes followed his gesture through a gap in the trees and registered the meaning of the brown smudge in the distance. She rose on her toes and strained to recognise a feature of her home. *Downhill. We are up higher.*

Gavin added. "You have perhaps not seen your home from here."

Her head shook slowly. She could see figures milling around, a group thickening and thinning, coming in and out of a hole in the wall. Had Father built that gate, or had ao Kevath brought it with him?

ao Kevath motioned to a thin sheet rolled out on the table. "Come see here."

Sidling up to the table edge, Leoshine leaned in to examine the squiggles and pictures covering the sheet. Her stomach grumbled.

Giant, warm bodies closed around her. Kirim tossed his hair in a towel beside Dorim and Gavin. ao Kevath stood on her other side and all directed their attention to the sheet.

ao Kevath mouthed the Myxolidian and pointed to the centre. "This is the town."

She blinked and squinted to examine the symbols where his finger landed. A blank space surrounded the representation of the town walls. From that ring, on all sides rose pictures of trees. Lines dissected the treed area into five sections, narrower near the town and broadening until … she followed ao Kevath's finger out to the edge of the sheet.

Until the edge of the Dome! She looked up and met ao Kevath's eyes. Again, he used no words, but she understood. He led her thought and seemed acutely attuned to how well she followed.

He invites. But what does he want? Her finger touched down on a box at the Dome Barrier, one of four around the perimeter of the treed space while her eyes returned his gaze. "This is a Dome Engine."

His eyes flashed and his teeth sparkled between wide stretched lips. "Yes." He searched her until she felt dizzy. "You understand maps."

Her face crumpled at the unknown word.

"Map," he repeated. "Picture of …" He looked at his generals.

Gavin provided the translation. "A 'map' is a picture of your home. Myxolidia." He placed his forefinger on the drawing of another dwelling near town. "This was our first stop." He traced a section of the bordered tree area that stretched from the town to the Dome Engine. "General Alan's territory."

Dorim traced the area beside it and grunted. "Mine."

"Mine." Kirim copied his tone.

Gavin put his finger on the territory beside Kirim's and

moved it to the next. "We will now ride to Lantro's." And the next. "And Uly's."

Leoshine saw on the sheet the circuit they had been following all day. *Would continue to follow,* she realised. *We circle the town and touch each territory and hold the ceremony for each of the generals.*

Gavin placed his finger on the picture of the town. "And finally, mine."

She frowned and leaned further over the table. "Father made pictures." She waved her hand over the map. He called them 'pictures' but she realised now that he probably knew the Aeolian word.

"Your father?" ao Kevath seemed surprised.

She raised her eyes and fell headlong into his. Thoughts swam, floated, darted without anchor.

You mock me?

You let me test you. She answered herself. *You let me search your mind. How?*

She glanced down, dizzy and still seeing unrecognisable thoughts, images. Her head filled with hot blood. *My people don't do that.*

Aeolian words pierced her daze. By his tone she guessed that ao Kevath questioned his generals. They answered back and used the devices on the map and away from it. Her eyes followed every motion.

ao Kevath barked and all the generals barked back and tossed their cups up to drain them in one gulp. Leoshine jumped and splashed some of the red liquid from her untasted cup.

In concert they thwacked their cups down on the table. ao Kevath spoke to Dorim and Kirim. Gavin rolled up the map.

The red liquid pulsed taste through Leoshine's memory. She drank until her lungs cried out for air. She coughed and spluttered red splashes on her clothes and Kirim removed her cup from her grasp.

She placed a hand on the table to anchor herself to the largest familiar object. One moment ao Kevath seemed utterly engrossed with her and the next, she watched the four expansive backs moving toward the horses. They had already crossed the stream.

I know where I am. I can run to the gate. Can I find a woman to take me to Mother? Father? Even Wol?

To be found by soldiers, by Oxikobh would be...? She looked at ao

Kevath collecting Paulos' reins and concluded she would not be on the other side of the table before he or one of his men mounted and thundered down on her.

The distance between her and her captors increased. ao Kevath mounted. Gavin turned and came back, and her breath hissed out through her flared nostrils.

Gavin offered his hand. "Need help?"

Leoshine looked down. If she lay flat her head would rest on one bank and her feet would at least touch the other. "No." She shook her head and looked at Gavin. His hands would bruise her ribs again if he lifted her over. Not that his hands bruised, but it was like the stream not being little. Nothing was as it seemed. "I can ..." She looked at ao Kevath conversing with Paulos. The horse stared directly at her and moved a half step forward, toward her before ao Kevath restrained him and looked up.

Words flowed from his mouth like the water.

Gavin translated. "ao Kevath asks if you mount alone."

Leoshine blushed and stared at her horse.

Gavin reached across. "Take my hand. You won't get wet."

She searched his face again. Immediately she lifted her hand, it was engulfed by warmth. She held her breath and leapt.

Before she could breathe again, hands fastened around her waist and she floated up. ao Kevath had brought the horses forward and she landed in the saddle before she knew she had crossed the stream. The general ran to his undersized horse.

They trotted out into the open. Her head lurched backward and she gripped the upper leg hook, almost wishing for the Tesheddar. The trees formed a solid wall on one side and the town flashed out of them on the other side, a brown smudge in the centre of the arc they would cover to arrive at Lantro's ceremony. Would it be dirt or water?

In town she could compare the subtle hues against known shades of stone and wood and flesh. Out here, surrounded by greens and browns and constantly undulating leaves and water, and a vastly greater quantity of Dome to measure, her eyes watered with the effort of telling time.

A voice called out of nowhere. ao Kevath and Gavin glanced around and shouted commands at the soldiers who bunched closer around them. The two brother generals broke off from the group. They vanished into the forest with some of the troop.

Leoshine's head lurched backward as the trot broke into a canter. She thought of calling out, but was too busy clutching, losing her grip and clutching again. Her head swam and the red liquid in her stomach came alive and threatened to reappear.

As suddenly, the rocking slowed. The Dome smiled down, and the town and the trees and the soldiers reappeared in her vision. Her stomach groaned, and her ears roared with untaken breaths.

ao Kevath and Gavin chatted, as if nothing happened, with a stranger wearing the same armour as ao Kevath.

Gavin had spoken of Lantro. From behind she saw long wavy hair sweeping past his shoulders that sloped and narrowed at his waist.

In a clearing, stood a table. See-through dish covers amid several vases of flowers, plates and utensils set her heart beating faster. *How long since I ate real food?* The gripe in her stomach answered. *Too long.*

The men dismounted.

Leoshine balanced on her single stirrup, swinging above the ground, judging the drop.

"ao Kevath says you anticipate him."

Leoshine jumped back into her saddle. She felt Gavin's bulk beside her and his breath on her neck.

"You must wait for him. Then I will bring you."

Gavin looked toward ao Kevath. From the corner of her eye, Leoshine saw him nod. Gavin wrapped his hands around her and plucked her off the side of the horse.

She landed with stiff legs and pulled her jacket down at the hem. Her body ached. Acid in her throat stung with the skin over her ribs and waist. She wanted to lean her forehead against the slow-heaving muscles of her horse's shoulder.

In the background, Lantro knelt. Vaguely she heard the intoned speech.

"Come."

The command sent needles down her spine. ao Kevath faced her and held the box out to her. *How will his eyes look now?*

She took a deep breath. *What would happen if I never moved? Would he come himself? No, he would send a general.*

The leaves shivered to a still point.

The table blazed in her memory. Food! She would receive the box and they would eat, and the blood would return thick in her veins. With a weak smile she stepped forward. The ground seemed more uneven and she placed her feet carefully.

ao Kevath grunted. "Ahead. Now behind."

Her hands fell further with the weight of the box. She missed Resham catching her as he did last night.

A hand touched her shoulder. She didn't know which general helped put the box in Paulos' saddlebag this time and she didn't want to look. Only their heads differed.

She followed the guidance back to her horse. ao Kevath approached, mounted and waved a dismissive hand.

Gavin bent down to lift her.

Tears broiled in Leoshine's tone. "But the food!"

Gavin averted his eyes. "Only one more stop." He hoisted her into her seat and fastened the Tesheddar.

Leoshine's pitch grew higher. "Why don't we eat?"

Gavin twitched his lips. "ao Kevath doesn't eat in the day."

ao Kevath spurred forward. Leoshine's head whipped back. Her mouth hung open and tears leaked from the corners of her eyes and trailed in the wind.

He stood up in his stirrups and leaned over Paulos' neck. Her horse lowered her head and stretched her stride.

"Stop!" Leoshine's open mouth filled with a gust of air.

Stop! Her heart cried out as her seat lost contact with her side-saddle and reconnected with a thump over and over again.

The red liquid came alive inside her. Every moment she expected to land with a crippling thud on the Oxikobh-cursed ground. Her body lurched forward, and the contents of her stomach gushed out her mouth into her lap and over her hands.

She swallowed and gulped the air to force down the bile.

At the first slackening of speed she strained against the Tesheddar. She gritted her teeth and wept and growled at her hands wrestling with the stubborn enemy. The ridges of the saddle jabbed her. If she stiffened and held herself upright, her back stabbed with pain.

The motion stopped. After an interminable interval she heard a voice nearby. *Myxolidian or Aeolian?* Gavin's slippery Myxolidian, she decided, but could make no immediate sense of the words.

Hot liquid warmed her throat. Firm hands folded her arms across her chest and wrapped her body tightly in a soft pillow.

Aeolians touch one another. Her head fell forward and her mind sank into oblivion.

Return to Town

"Uly!" Avram inhaled the fragrance of crushed greenery beneath his feet and flexed his shoulders. "How different this world is!" He whacked Uly on the back and received an equal thump on his.

Of all the generals, this one most closely mirrored his own physique. Broad shouldered, barrel chested, narrow in the waist and long in the leg. Avram remembered that his reach in boxing also matched his own.

"ao Kevath! It is!" Uly's bellow encompassed every living thing. "I haven't had a chance to really explore, but I know there are beasts and greens long missing from our diets as plentiful as the rocks here. I haven't chosen my headquarters in the province yet but there's a likely place a day and a half's ride …" Uly drew a deep breath. "ao Kevath, I know we trained for horses 'cus horses is all we're allowed but I do wish for a transport vehicle or two to cover the ground. Just a one-man Drake to get around."

"In time, Uly." Avram smiled and looked back at Gavin who seemed to be taking time with the girl. As soon as the pace had slowed, he smelled the vomit and knew she would not meet the last general. At least she had been told his name. *Would she remember?* "Pity him. He's been playing Resham all day."

Uly laughed. "And Resham's self? What's he up to today?"

"Collecting samples." Avram narrowed his eye at his general. "All ready?"

Uly's smile changed to glee. "Yes, ao Kevath! As you prescribed, shovel, dirt, box. A light refreshment."

Gavin strode up and exchanged greetings and sidelong glances with Uly. Avram had watched this through the day as his generals asked each other about the girl. Gavin correctly directed them to their leader for the explanation they all craved, and none dared require it of him.

"Kneel down and we'll anoint you." Avram stooped to gather a handful of the soil. "Not a good sample, is it?"

"Further out, ao Kevath. A day and a half ride there is a cliff and a plateau. Not sure but the water is closer to the surface up there, and the grass is thicker. Too far for today, without a transport, ao Kevath." Uly smiled innocence into his commander's face.

"Ao Kevad," Avram lifted his face to the Dome and called aloud. "Thank you for this man, Uly."

He paused. This would be the last time he enacted this ceremony and he wanted to savour the connection. The moment he smelled the vomit, he had questioned his wisdom, his creation of a land dedication and the girl's role. "Thank you for the strength, courage and wisdom you have provided, along with this fresh and bountiful land that he will govern in your name."

The clod of dirt broke apart and granules drizzled down Uly's head.

"Help the people to join the effort to restore your inheritance, Ao Kevad. Give to all the spirit of cooperation and mutual encouragement and inspire us with your peace."

Avram stretched his spirit out over everything under the Myxolidian Dome. He saw Gavin in the town and Alan at the cradle of his headquarters, Dorim in the forest and Kirim in the stream, and Lantro walking beside their diminutive Myxolidian representative.

He wondered at the heaviness in his heart and reached further, above the Dome, and deeper into his own will. Immediately he drew air and felt his spirit rising.

Uly's voice boomed from his humble place in the dirt. "Ao Kevad!"

Avram's heart jumped. None of the other generals dared invent a blessing.

Uly continued. "Please let my Aluecia know I am here. Tell her I'll work hard to win Your will under this Dome, to make her proud." As suddenly as he began, Uly stopped speaking.

Avram handed him the box and watched him fill it. "You believe she can see you?"

Uly's wife had died early in their marriage, but he continued to believe they were united in soul and their end would be as happy as their beginning.

The broad glow on the man's face spoke before his gusty words. "Yes, ao Kevath!" Tears spouted in Uly's eyes.

Avram's gaze softened. "Then she is proud of you already."

Why does my approval matter so much to these mighty warriors? Many nights while they slept, he had wrestled with the thought that it was only his regal birth that made them bow. He had begged Ao Kevad to endow him with something that would warrant their admiration. Ao Kevad seemed to refuse time and time again.

The box transferred back into his hands and Avram urged Uly to rise. "Light refreshment? Quick! The light fails."

Both generals laughed at his play on words. They drank together the health of the Dome. Avram and Gavin wished Uly well in his government of the province and mounted for town.

The diminishing light sent a creep into his soul as they walked the last arc toward the town gate. The countryside itched. He felt the fingers of discontent hovering in the tree canopy where the Oxikobh climbed to watch him ride by. He felt the rot and smelled the stench of degradation that he carried with him in the soil in the saddle bag, and on the girl that he dragged behind Paulos on the placid mare. *Resham will clean her.*

Dorim and Kirim hadn't reported yet. They had dashed off at Rasset's alarm with new zest to defend the mission. "Fresh in your hair," he remembered telling Alan.

Paulos picked up his feet and ears as soon as the new-laid pavement of the gate road came under his hooves. Avram patted his neck. *Too much town living is bad for man and horse.* As he passed through the streets, his soldiers crowded closer. Another troop, fresh from the barracks, joined the parade. Had Resham sent them? *Will he be at the palace, or has he found Wol?*

He spied his servant pacing on the landing.

Relief flooded Resham's greeting. "ao Kevath!"

Avram slid down onto the lowest step, slung the reins over Paulos' head, patted the sweaty neck. "You've earned a rest."

The great stallion turned to accept a treat and then followed the soldier who stood ready to lead him to the stable.

The girl's head popped up above the edge of the Tesheddar that kept her on the horse while she slept. Tousled and pink.

Resham's countenance fell when Avram tossed his head toward her. "ao Kevath, my place is at your feet, not hers."

Avram turned as he entered the hall. "I can use my feet. See to the one who can't."

The sentries opened the door to his chamber. A blast of plaster dust and paint fumes met him.

A step on the threshold alerted him to the girl entering of her own power.

She stopped just inside the door, face to the ceiling. He could now stand unimpeded, and half of another one of him on top of that. He smiled with relief. *No more beams or mayoral dregs to dent my forehead.* He resumed pacing back and forth before the bed.

Her mouth, still pink and moist from sleep, hung open as her eyes traveled over the brilliant white walls, the polished bed, table and chairs, the six tall windows high on the outside wall, and finally her cot. None of the furniture had changed position or size, but he had to admit they looked different in the new surroundings.

Avram paced deeper and hardly noticed Resham enter. For an unknown reason he found himself fighting the urge to take up the girl's hands and dance with her around the new floor. *Share my joy!* his spirit called.

Resham handed her a nightgown and directed her to the specially constructed screen hiding a section of the room between his bed and the new door in the water closet wall.

The girl moaned. "I don't want to change."

Avram paused and paced more gently to hear her.

"I want a bath and some real food." Her pitch ascended as her confidence grew. "I want my own room and my people, women from my own family who know what is decent and proper and..."

Avram waved a hand toward the screen. "I made for you."

Her mouth hung open, reminding Avram of a succulent fruit of his homeland. Her eyes widened, until he thought they might burst from their beds. The next instant they swam in tears.

Resham sneered at her. "Be grateful. ao Kevath took into account your need for 'decent and proper.' Go! Before you lose even that." He turned to undress his master.

Avram snapped his mouth shut. He had never seen a female dissolve before. She suddenly sprouted water from eyes and nose.

A small high-pitched wail grew to fill the room.

He turned and paced a tight circle and put his hands over his ears. "Make her stop!"

Resham's eyes blazed. His nostrils flared until he tossed his hands up from a half-unbuckled boot strap.

Avram caught Resham's arm and directed him to the cupboard. "No! Dress me so I can be gone! The white cotton shirt. The wool fleece."

"ao Kevath, the girl could leave."

Avram rubbed the corner of his eyebrow with his index finger. "Where would she go?"

The girl wiped her trailing fluid across her sleeve, and Avram compelled his jaw closed. Resham snorted and left off fetching his master's gloves to throw a towel at her.

"Use that, you norfinoof! Turn off the waterworks and get behind that curtain before I hurt you!"

The girl froze. The silence shuddered through the room. For a moment no one moved.

A sob broke the spell. The girl lifted the towel and the new gown to her face. While moaning into them, she collapsed onto the cot, folding her body over her legs and rocking back and forth. The wail was more bearable muffled.

"I eat in the barracks." Avram informed his servant. "I meet with the town councillors and ... and Gavin."

He strained against Resham's grip on his lapel. As he headed into the cold Myxolidian night, his servant grabbed his wrist and slapped some fine silk gloves into his palm.

He shivered as he crossed the threshold. *She can be taught. Mother will manage her. Resham will subdue her in the meanwhile.*

He liked the new room, he decided as he stalked through the halls, even if she brought mayhem to their introduction! And he had forgotten to ask Resham about Wol.

Language Lessons

Tasteless white paste stared back at Leoshine from a black food bowl. Her hand rested on the edge. She fingered the scoop handle with its head buried in the glutinous depths.

The red liquid she had drunk on the ride made all other food tasteless, she decided. *The curse has entered my bones.*

Every day—she couldn't remember how many passed since they rode in the wilderness—had begun in the dark with Resham commanding her to go behind the screen that stretched along the wall from the new door to where ao Kevath's bed began.

Every day a new outfit appeared on a stool there. Vibrant colours and luscious cloth with jeweled garnish bedazzled her eyes. Sometimes the design crossed her chest like the first costume, making her feel flaunted. Sometimes the material flowed in flounces and fluttery bits. The brace never returned.

Every day on a little table behind the screen, he left food which she ate while ao Kevath changed and ate. When summoned to the main room she sat on the cot while the room filled and emptied with men. When alone, she wept and slept.

Every night brought the same command: change into the cot clothes behind the screen, eat the food, lie down on the cot, sleep until woken and commanded to change and eat. Change and eat and wait, change and eat and wait.

Her eyes lifted from the white mush to the windows and the shelf below them. Six clear-sided boxes sat on that shelf. Every box but one contained Oxikobh filth, and she could not decide which one belonged to the ground outside the palace.

Her chest ached like she had eaten and drunk until their curse clogged her veins.

She wondered if they had returned from that ride to a different room in the palace. Maybe Father's room still existed somewhere.

Beside her, ao Kevath shuffled his bite-sized food around his plate with his back to the curtained bed.

This day began differently. She woke naturally with Domelight streaming all around her. Resham made no appearance. The little table behind the screen held no food, but a blue robe of thick warm cloth awaited her there. When she peeked round the screen, ao Kevath had summoned her with a vague wave to sit at the great round table in the centre of the room.

One of ao Kevath's giant hands leafed through the book that lived in the wooden box with the ornate, jeweled chain. She stole glances from the corner of her eye. He was always staring at her. If she looked at him, she would be pinioned by his ice and fire eyes.

Inhuman eyes. And yet more human than any she had seen before. Dancing, passionate, penetrating.

Her lids drooped. Her hand could not find strength to lift the scoop or lift away from the scoop handle.

"Leoshine."

Her lids shot open, stretched to their limit. She felt her soul lock down in his presence. Her identity and all he designed for her in his household trembled in those few syllables.

He held up the book to show her the picture she had wondered at. A fresh wave of horror swept through her face as she stared at his finger. Did he know she had looked at this book the first time they left her alone in the chamber?

He rolled a pebble word over his tongue, then the Myxolidian. "Mother."

He tapped the picture of the woman and repeated the sequence.

Leoshine's throat clenched. *The words in Myxolidian match the Aeolian sounds.* Very likely he wished her to copy the sounds, but her tongue was a stone in her mouth and her heart, finally beating again, pounded in her ears.

ao Kevath put the book down. He studied her, but she could not read the expression on his face. *Interest? Disappointment?*

His hand wandered to a piece of fruit on his plate. He held

the red succulent morsel between his fingers and looked through it. With an outstretched hand he offered it to her.

Without warning he reached out and grabbed the arm of her chair, dragging it, until it touched the arm of his chair.

Leoshine squeaked and jumped against the back of hers. Her body twisted. Her hands gripped the top edge and her toes locked into the bottom edge.

She heard him draw air into his mouth and saw him run his tongue over his lips, as though tasting the air above her head. Georg had laughed at Giffshine's stories of wild men who licked the skin off town children because it was sweet and tender.

He offered the fruit again.

She blinked and swallowed and gasped a shallow breath. *Should I take it?* She eased her feet down and her fingers from the back to the arms. She had now eaten at a man's table almost as a matter of course. Should she eat from a man's plate?

He crossed the divide. He behaved as though no divide existed and his claim, which he made by saying her name in the manner and tone that stopped her heart, gave his offer a quality of … She could accept, she told herself, because …

She wanted to accept. Fruit was a luxury before he had arrived. Father grew trees in the palace garden and made raids into the forest if he heard reports of a wild harvest. ao Kevath never seemed to lack supply for his table and she longed for the sweetness.

"Take. Eat." His mouth twisted and twitched.

Her mouth hung open and her eyes searched his. One part of her thought, *how dare he?* Another thought, *will he touch me, hurt me?*

She stretched out her hand and he placed the red morsel in her palm. She stared at it a moment, and then sank her teeth into the bristling flesh and sucked the juices between her tongue and her cheeks, knowing his unwavering gaze searched for her reaction.

She looked up as she chewed, and he smiled. There was a simplicity about him, she decided. Among the mysteries and unpredictable moods, he was pleased that his gift was accepted.

Next, he reached across her and pulled her bowl to sit in front of him. He used her scoop—the one she'd had in her mouth—to ferry white paste into his mouth.

Every muscle in her body ached from being wound tight. Her skin crawled with the intimacy of his gesture.

One more scoop entered his mouth. His throat stone bounded up and down. He laid the scoop down, sat back and looked at her with his head slightly tilted to one side. "You have questions." He smoothed the edges of the last word.

Leoshine blinked.

"Ask!" He popped a piece of food from his plate into his mouth. Pointing to the bowl, he wrinkled his nose and screwed up his eyes. "Taste bad."

"Why …?" Leoshine breathed.

He frowned and motioned for her to complete the question.

Leoshine pressed her spine against the hard wood. *I can do this*, she assured herself. She could engage with her master and win some answers. "Why do you eat my food and"—she gestured to his plate—"give yours to me?"

"I show we are same. I come to Myxolidia …" He looked up, pleading. A sound came from his lips. "To say that …" His mouth stayed open while his eyes squinted.

She remembered his deficiency with her language. Words he seemed to know stuck on his tongue. "Message?" She was rewarded with a flash of delight in his eyes. Her heart jumped toward that light.

"Message," ao Kevath grimaced and used the Aeolian in his next sentence. "You give Myxolidia the *message*. We are same."

Leoshine's mind whirled with proofs of how wrong he was. "When?"

He still smiled. His hands and shoulders were calm. "When we ride. See outside. You tell Aeolians also."

Leoshine furrowed her brow and tilted her head. "Tell them …?"

ao Kevath smiled more broadly and pulled his chin in while puffing out his chest a little. "We are same."

Her mouth went dry. "I can't speak to the … to your people."

ao Kevath tapped the table with his fingernails. "Say 'Aeolians.'" The light in his eyes pierced her like darts.

She mouthed the word, looking down at her hands twisting a piece of her blouse into a wet knot.

From beneath the book he drew a rigid board like Resham had drawn his initials on and held it for her to accept. "You speak Aeolian to Aeolians. I teach you."

Thick as perhaps a quarter of the book and stretching two spans of her hand in all directions, it showed no symbol or picture on its perfect black face.

"Speak!"

Leoshine opened and closed her mouth.

His eyes twinkled at her and his scabbed eyebrow quivered. He bent closer and spoke to the board. "Mother." He pronounced in Myxolidian.

A picture of a woman holding an infant blinked over the surface. The board spoke the Aeolian that was becoming familiar to Leoshine's ear.

"You! Speak Myxolidian word."

Leoshine gathered her breath and held it a moment. She shot a challenging glance at him and spoke. "ao Kevath."

A picture of a gaudily dressed ruler seated on a throne with gaudily dressed people bowing at his feet appeared and the board said, "My lord."

A clear loud laugh resounded from her companion. He said some words in Aeolian with his head tilted back. In Myxolidian, he stuttered. "Man who made picture doesn't know me!" He narrowed his eyes at her and said "ao Kenan" at the board.

The board responded with a picture of an equally gaudily dressed woman. "My lady."

He lifted the plate of food and tilted it toward her hand, offering the whole selection.

Offering, she realised. Sharing, rewarding, and gathering. She chose a white square. He took its mate and winked broadly.

"Same," he seemed to say.

A sound came from his chewing. A picture of a fruit appeared on the board, and he laughed at the sentence it spoke.

"No Myxolidian," he explained. "Myxolidia has no '*banana*.'"

He spoke, and a red fruit appeared with the same sentence. He made her speak the word several times and then taught her the phrase, "Please, may I have some …"

The tide of his enthusiasm swept Leoshine along. Her soul argued, *we are not the same.* Her grief complained. *Why should a slave ask for things?* But his approval and childlike pleasure at her success, and his sharp frown so easily erased by her earnest corrections overwhelmed her objections.

He picked up the board and offered it to her, holding on when her fingers curled around the glossy black surface. "For you. To learn my Aeolian."

Leoshine blinked at him. Tears spangled her lashes. "Thank you," she breathed.

Aeolian words answered her. He addressed the board. "Thank you."

The board responded with a picture of two people exchanging a bright package and a phrase she committed to memory.

The Domelight mellowed to late afternoon in ao Kevath's room. Leoshine had slept after the lesson and then day dreamed and watched her master. No one visited this day. ao Kevath did not stir from his chair but worked at the grey box. His thumb and forefinger stretched from cheek bone to cheek bone and his elbow rested on the table.

A soft crack on the door sent her heart pounding. She leapt to stand on the cot with her back and palms to the wall.

ao Kevath lifted an eyebrow at her. The sentry opened the door, and a servant delivered a tray with clear-domed plates.

A splendid aroma filled the room. Leoshine's mouth watered. The servant bowed and departed. Moments passed and ao Kevath remained motionless, staring at the grey box.

Leoshine blinked and her throat spasmed.

He looked up at her and waved his hand toward the tray. "Serve." He grunted and went back to staring at the box.

She crept to the table and lifted the domes. They were heavy, and she had to use both hands. The aroma doubled, and her stomach griped. Two different steaming foods stared back at her.

She looked at her master and back at the food. Her throat clenched.

"My lord?"

"ao Kevath."

"ao Kevath?"

"Yes?" He did not look up. After a pause he spoke again, still staring at the absorbing box. "We eat."

He pushed back in the chair. She jumped back and squeaked.

"No!" ao Kevath stood behind his chair. "No noise."

Leoshine covered her mouth. Her nerves felt like fire in her spine and scalp.

"Say it. 'No noise.'"

"No noise, ao Kevath."

"Stand. Speak. For what ..."

Leoshine tossed the words in her head and remembered Resham making her repeat them. Would her mouth remember the feeling of their shapes?

"For oot wee 'bout oo 'ceev," She stood behind her chair. "Maak os trooy thakfos." Not a perfect performance, she glanced at ao Kevath's bowed head and closed eyes. He seemed to enter a distant state of mind. She determined to speak the words into her new board the moment she was alone.

"Sit." ao Kevath looked up and nodded. "We eat. Same plate, same food."

One moment she looked at him. Her hunger overruled and quickly she sat on the opposite side of him from the morning meal and lifted the utensil.

The flavours cartwheeled through her nerves like the red liquid. ao Kevath ate a little and then went back to the box.

Leoshine stopped with her mouth full and looked at him with her brow creased.

He glanced up. "You finish. Eat what you want. Take tray to kitchen."

She ate every bite and bent to lick the sauce off both plates. Her taste buds cried for more, even though her middle swelled and threatened to burst if she moved in the wrong way. ao Kevath paid no attention to her as she replaced the covers, and loaded the tray.

Her arms strained under its weight. She edged to the door, glancing several times at him. "ao Kevath?"

He looked up, frowning and focusing his eyes.

She looked at the door, and back at him with a question in her eyes.

"Sentry!"

The dishes rattled as the shock of his command reached through her body. The door opened.

Freedom! She was outside. Her heart soared. The Dome above showed its last efforts at day before the rest period of dark.

The birdies rest, the squirrels rest, the Dome rests, the baby rests. She remembered a childhood rhyme.

The dishes continued to rattle. First, she planned, she would deposit the tray in the kitchen.

Huddled masses with rumbling boot-clad feet crowded some halls and courtyards and left others deserted and empty. *If I knew where Mother and Giffshine and Hillashine were ...*

No one disturbed or delayed her. The people at the kitchen window spoke no word, nor did they look surprised to see her.

I really am going back. She looked over her shoulder at the red, silver, and black figures lining the passageway. *I promise I'll go straight back to him.*

At the end of a corridor, a sizable window overlooked the field beside the palace where the general had filled the clear box that now sat on the shelf in ao Kevath's room. Torn-up buildings, half-built stone walls and piles of debris appeared in circles of light shed by mysterious Aeolian lanterns. Around the perimeter of the field, bare poles rose out of half walls like the skeletons of rotting carcasses. But these bones towered high above the surrounding wooden houses.

She sank down on the window ledge and leaned her head on the frame. The heaviness of the day's early hours crept back into her limbs. *Will he miss me? Where is Resham? How far can I go?*

He is changing the city like he changed Father's room. ao Kevath tore down and built up according to his ideas. He asked no one's opinion, waited for no one to get out of the way or save her treasures from his destruction. He lost no time nor left any space untouched, as far as a Myxolidian princess could see.

What had become of her world? Her land? Her family? Ominous masses seemed to move in all directions, hushed and sinister. Was even the air changed?

What did they intend? Resham called her slave, yet she ate at her "owner's" table. ao Kevath had every right to her body and she slept within his arm's reach, yet he made no move toward her. She shuddered and stopped herself thinking what if. No one would question it or defend her.

With plodding feet and slumped shoulders, she meandered back to their shared chamber. Cylindrical Aeolian lanterns shed honey-yellow pools of light in each corridor. She met no soldiers or servants except the sentry who held the door open as she approached. And closed it quickly behind her.

Utter darkness enclosed her. Placing her hand ahead, she took a step. Her bed, lying close to the door, caught her foot. She fell forward and cried out.

ao Kevath called out in Aeolian. She heard his chair clatter to the floor. A blacker shadow rose over her.

Breathing shallow and fast, she curled in a ball at his feet and cried out. "My Lord! No noise!"

He bellowed again, many words with a biting tone.

"ao Kevath! It is Leoshine!"

A shaft of light angled from the opening door. ao Kevath roared an angry speech at the sentry. Bright light returned to the room, as if the Dome suddenly blinked back on. The sentry ducked out.

Leoshine eased her face out of the floor boards. She saw his face, contorted, and his sword dangling in his hand. She slithered onto the cot and let out a little breath as her back touched the wall.

ao Kevath walked toward the door, turned, passed her cot, turned at the new door, circled the table where he tossed the sword, passed the curtained bed, and turned again at the door. Each time he passed her bed, she shrank down and held her breath. His face remained contorted, furrowed and glowering. He had torn the scab off the corner of his eyebrow. His finger came away bloody and returned to its worrying soon after.

A soft crack came from the door and it opened. A servant entered and ao Kevath gave a stream of commands with waves of his hand toward the cupboards. Another servant entered, and another, and they followed ao Kevath around the room.

Leoshine stared at his bare chest and back, his muscles rippling, his skin glistening. The blood pounding in her ears held her immobile until a shiny light blue blouse covered him. Breeches followed, and boots.

The sentry answered another summons, and suddenly the room was empty.

Tears welled in Leoshine's eyes. A laugh burbled in her chest. The image of ao Kevath pacing and rubbing his brow fixated in Leoshine's mind. *He is a mighty, helpless warrior-babe.*

Her lips were dry from breathing through her mouth. She buried her head in her hands and held her breath until she was too dizzy to see the darkness between her elbows.

Looking up, she exhaled noisily. Outside the windows, voices called and hoofbeats clopped in the distance.

She put her head on her pillow and stared at the ceiling far above. She sat up and looked at the table. The ornate box with the chain and the book sat beside the speaking board.

Rising, she retrieved the board. Huddled among her blankets and pillow, she ran her finger over its surface. If Resham came, he might order her to change. Until then she would revel in the luxury of her present outfit.

"For what we are about to receive." She mouthed the words and the board interpreted.

"Thankful. Full of gratitude. Receive with a glad heart."

Father had taught her to appreciate gifts. What gifts did ao Kevath give or receive with the food? Why did he stand behind his chair and wander away in his head while she spoke?

For a long while she spoke to the new device. The Aeolian sounds made no impression, but the pictures amused her.

Covering her head with a pillow to block the light, she slept.

A hand grasped Leoshine's shoulder and half her torso and whipped the pillow from her sleeping head. She leapt to climb the wall. The unstable footing of the mattress felt like Oxikobh filth to her dizzy, disoriented soul.

"Wake! Wake!" ao Kevath danced to the table and drew his precious picture book from the jeweled box. He stood with his back half turned toward her and glanced at her out the corner of his eye while he leafed through the book.

"Mother," he said in Aeolian as he pointed to the familiar picture of the woman with the child.

He wants to teach. Her heart steadied. *I want to learn. If he could be a little more ...* she wracked her brain for the word. *Like Georg.* She slithered from beneath the blankets to stand on the cot with her back to the wall, palms pressed against its frigid surface.

She mumbled, frowning through the fog in her head. "Mother."

ao Kevath smiled. He continued to repeat the word in her language and then his. She copied, gaining consciousness in the midst of his boisterous enthusiasm.

"Baby."

"Baby."

"Mother and baby."

"Mother and baby."

He pointed to the book and spoke the word.

"Book," she repeated. "Box. Chain. Table. Chair." As many words as he spoke, she spoke back to him.

He bounded around the room pointing and speaking and listening to her replies.

Eventually, Leoshine yawned behind her hand.

"Mother." ao Kevath drew her attention back to the book.

A noise outside turned both their heads to the windows. The light of the Dome would soon overpower the light in the room.

"Mother and baby." Leoshine smiled with her brows lifted.

ao Kevath laughed and placed the book open on the table.

"Hillashine and baby?" Leoshine dared. Her eyes pleaded.

His brow contracted and his eyes disappeared up under his lids.

In Myxolidian she said, "Resham says my sister will be a"—and she used the Aeolian—"mother and baby."

"Hmph." He blew through his nose and snapped the book closed. He opened it again. "This is Ao Kevad. Say that. Ao Kevad and mother."

Leoshine repeated the words in a flat tone. Later she planned to speak those syllables into the board to see what picture it gave them.

Dome Convulsions

Avram studied the circle of Myxolidian leaders, the old mayor's councillors, assembled in the traditional counsel chamber. To decide something, he was sure. He watched smoke curl up the chimney from the fire in the central pit. His sleeve had picked up a smudge from the soot on the wood-panelled walls when he entered the chamber through thick double doors, making work for Resham.

The Myxolidians wore fine-weave Aeolian blouses beneath their rough-hewn flax tunics. Animal skins draped their shoulders and covered their legs in breeches. Sandals and a mixture of wrappings swathed their feet. He scanned their bearded faces. *One day, they will wear only Aeolian cloth.* He would allow them a similar drape, but the animal skins must go.

He glanced up. His architects had raised the ceiling around the chimney and installed six Aeolian wall lights.

He sighed in his soul. Physical improvements would not prevent suffocation from the pomposity and endless drone of the Myxolidian councillors. They were talking about buildings. Town planning. His secretary would interpret later.

The crowd stirred and Avram felt a presence behind and slightly to his right. Their faces showed suspicion, distaste.

He felt the tension ease from his shoulders and he rocked back on his heels to welcome the newcomer. Resham would interpret for now. He sighed within. His secretary would arrive with his mother.

Into his hand he felt Resham place a coil. He fingered the metal. Toothed wire. He waited for Resham to solve the puzzle.

The speaking statesman slowed his pronouncement. They were glancing at each other and him. He nodded and lifted an eyebrow to indicate his attention remained with them.

When the speech continued, he inclined his head to hear the explanation.

Resham spoke in a low tone. "Found this in the hem of the girl's garment, ao Kevath,"

"She was supposed to kill me?"

"Or herself, ao Kevath."

"Bad for my reputation—girls dying in my custody."

The crowd grunted in unison, a Myxolidian form of group approval. Avram smiled. *Do they expect me to speak?* He looked around. *No.*

Another man plucked at his fur collar and began his speech.

Avram murmured the words to his right. "I've been unguarded in her company four days."

"Didn't find it."

"She wore that dress a day or two. Didn't expect it. Innocent babe." Avram tightened his grip until the metal teeth bit into his fingers. "Who put it there?"

"The mother sewed the dress. The father delivered it."

The blood rushed into his head and his breath caught deep in his lungs. At the next breath of the speaker he blurted a stream of Aeolian and marched off. He congratulated himself that he waited so long.

They could interpret his actions as they wished.

After the evening meal, Avram draped his limbs over his favourite chair at the great round table. The girl sat beside him, stealing glances at Resham and tucking bites into her mouth when she thought he wasn't looking.

He stared at the book with the pictures that he had left out for her on that first day. The symbols danced on the page. Resham fussed around the room folding clothes and righting the ruin that his absence caused. *Other servants.* Avram's lip curled at the thought.

He closed the book and his eyes. "Sing to me." He asked in his own language, and then repeated the phrase in hers. "Sing to me." Once more, softly in his.

Great round eyes turned slowly into throbbing orbs beside him. *How does she do that?* He rubbed his aching eyes with the nub at the base of his forefinger. *Perhaps with Resham home I'll sleep.* The newly washed and dressed girl beside him wasn't the only one to enjoy the break from routine, but now Resham would have to heal them of their waywardness.

The girl stirred.

He encouraged her with a nod. "Yes, stand."

She began to wriggle from the chair, like a baby animal. He pointed. "Stand on the chair." He used Aeolian for the last two words.

She unbent her knees while holding onto the arm and then the back. All the while her eyes studied his face.

Not shy. She lacks inhibiting self-awareness. But there is fear. He pursed his lips at the thought.

Her voice reminded him of his mother's garden in Aeolia. Bright colours. Lush and fresh. Her words evoked a scene of little green leaves in the forest withered in the drought, the light faded at the end of the day. The theme developed. A time would come and was coming when all things would pass clean away. New on the side of the morning, everything would be new and eternal. Nothing would ever die again.

He didn't understand every word, but he knew the hope of them. He knew that he deeply desired that day to dawn for these people.

Do Myxolidians know of Ao Kevad's plan to make everything new and eternal? How did she know to sing that song?

"You believe?" he asked softly when she finished.

"I thought about it a long time," she answered. "I have time to think now."

"What do you think?"

The girl's eyes widened. He watched her calculating, trying to decide if he was interested or just too tired to think clearly. He noticed Resham pause and turn to hear.

"I think about what you have done to my land. You are so strange, and your ways are so different. Why do you keep me separated from my family? Why do you read that book? What do you want with me?

"You call me a slave, but you treat me like a …? I don't know anyone who has ever been treated this way. Why does he call me

'Tassanara?' Or 'Obenshwimi'? What does that mean? What makes the lights go on? Is it the same as our Dome? And all the other things you have, the water warmer and the picture machine, how do they work and what do you have them for? What is happening on the outside? What are you building? Why are you here?"

"Resham!" Avram called as if he were on the other side of the compound. "Write down her questions and translate for me. Send a copy to …"

"The ao Kenan Iliana."

"Thank you. Put me to bed, I can't think anymore." Avram nodded to the girl and stood as Resham pulled his chair away. "You can answer her when she asks. She is ready."

Resham bowed and began unfastening Avram's boots. "Yes, ao Kevath."

"Why do you call her 'Tassanara'?"

Resham's eyes sparkled with mischief. "She is the daughter of the High King, whether she knows it or not. Why shouldn't I give her the exalted title He gives her?"

Before dawn Avram paced his room, fully armoured and waiting for a late report. He had not slept, even after Resham had purged his muscles of tension, warmed his blankets, and fluffed his pillows.

The girl ate at the table, clothed in her riding habit. Resham had completed the domestic chores and disappeared.

Avram swiveled on his heel as the door opened.

Resham stood to attention by the open door. "All clear, ao Kevath."

The sentries were in place, in other words. The path was cleared of the enemy and the Overlord could ride out.

He turned his head at the threshold. "Rasset?"

Resham repeated. "All clear, ao Kevath"

The atmosphere had rolled over like an ornery old codger, after much longer than the old scientist predicted. There would be significant darkness today. Rasset had not been able to be more specific and Avram heard the terror of uncertainty in his voice. Therefore, the Overlord's retinue would parade in ribbons and banners and costumes to demonstrate profound confidence in the work to restore the living environment. The Aeolians would follow his orders to actively pursue their roles without intereruption. They understood the temporary nature and the reasons behind the darkness.

The leader of the Myxolidian rebellion had shown his misshapen understanding of Rasset's role by attacking him the day of the generals' anointing. Dorim and Kirim, being soldiers and not spies, had swept the attackers aside without catching the leader. Resham regretted another lost opportunity to collect evidence he needed to convict Wol.

Paulos' teeth whacked Avram's breastplate and woke him to the shuffling feet and high-pitched whinnies around him. He slid his fingers under the headdress and rubbed Paulos' cheek. "Confused?" He murmured to reassure. "Armour and ribbons don't go together? Today they do." He patted his stallion's neck and placed his toe in the stirrup.

The cavalcade of hooves rang through the empty streets. Heralds had declared the event in the streets and in every Oxikobh compound, yet Avram felt the Myxolidians shivering in suspicion. Resham reported that Woltreaders, the mayor's second son's guerillas, found no difficulty in perverting the friendly warning and reassurances.

He called to a captain and ordered more lights in the streets.

It's not all dark, he thought at the gate. He could see the shadows of the trees forming the entrance to the forest. The Dome above looked grey, with touches of orange. The air pressed on his face, in his nostrils and on his eyeballs. He tasted the increase in moisture and rejoiced.

Would the burghers notice when their children's noses stop bleeding? Would the householders notice the water stayed in their buckets longer? Would they put it down to superstition?

The leaves hung limp on the forest trail to Alan's compound headquarters. Nothing stirred in the tree branches.

Resham rode by at a trot. He called to the guards and they changed their formation. His Myxolidian, forest-trained eye roved everywhere and his forehead wore a map of wrinkles.

Avram drew a deep breath. *Has the Dome air changed or do I smell fear?* Resham's fear, Oxikobh fear, Paulos and his kind's fear. *Soon the light will return,* he reassured everyone in his mind. *And the Dome will be better suited to human occupation.*

The girl's shivers passed into her mount and made Paulos fretful. "Is she dressed warmly enough?"

Resham rode up from tormenting the rearguard. "She does not share your confidence, ao Kevath."

Avram snorted. "Tell her! Explain so she *can* share my confidence!"

In the room, after the ride, Avram worked at the table. Reports, he scoffed, and discarded the majority. His servants provided better entertainment.

Resham and Leoshine bent their heads together over a set of cutlery on the other side of the table.

"Do you know the work your father has done measuring the Dome, Tassanara?" Resham glanced at his master and rolled his eyes.

She nodded, not looking up from her backwards reflection in the spoons.

"You understand that the Dome was dying?" Resham shook out a polishing cloth and lifted another knife.

Leoshine raised wide eyes. "No! Father never said that."

"We have helped it to survive this long, but repairs are necessary from inside. A few weeks ago, the scientific team, which includes your father, fed the generators.

"Particles of various chemicals protect us and make light and keep the air inside. These particles race back and forth between the engines to create the shield, the Dome. At first the particles will make a mess. That is why it is dark now. But in a few days order will be restored."

Avram saw the girl settle on her feet. She must have been standing on her toes.

"Is that all they have to do?" She shrugged and held a spoon at eye level.

"No."

Avram challenged Resham with his eye.

Resham returned the look with a straight mouth. Avram knew him well enough. He did not doubt the girl's cleverness. He mistrusted how the sister of Wol would use her cleverness.

"It will take a long time." Resham resumed. "The temperature must rise. Believe it or not this cold is not ideal. You've always lived like this. And the drought must end. Water must fall regularly from the Dome and the rivers and lakes must fill. Much of the new construction is to prepare the living quarters for the coming deluge."

Avram squinted up from wayward script on the communicator. "Tell her about the food." He understood Resham's Myxolidian better than the girl's, and he despaired of contorting his tongue to make their hideous syllables.

"ao Kevath wishes you to know of the improvement in the crops that we will grow." Resham continued in a removed, interpreter tone. "The nutrients ..." His mouth remained open while he searched for a word.

"I know what nutrients are."

Avram chuckled quietly. The girl perfectly imitated Resham's sneer.

Resham rolled his eyes. "They fall from the Dome in the water to enrich the soil. The crops that are grown now are poor in quality and the bodies of the population are poor too. Stunted and unresistant to disease. When properly maintained, the Dome can sustain fullness of life infinitely. We are here to ensure that happens."

The more patient Resham grew, Avram observed, the bigger his words grew.

Again, the girl used Resham's sneer. "Is that the only reason you came?"

"No. Your moral disintegration distressed Ao Kevad even more."

Cutlery scattered across the table and onto the floor. "What do you mean 'my dismorgistobin'? Why do you hate me?" Eyes blazing, the girl faced both Avram in his throne and Resham, standing a quarter round the table. "What have I ever done to you?"

Avram purred in Aeolian under his breath. "The fiery vixen speaks, brother Resham." To ease the tension, he lounged even deeper into his seat. The side of his forefinger rested equally lightly on his brow. Something within him thrilled to see her face up to Resham.

Resham's arms separated from his body and bent at the elbows. His knees bent, too. Though he was reluctant to touch her, Avram knew if she attacked her master Resham would kill her.

Thus they stayed until Avram purred again. "I do not wish my 'slave' to think we hate her, brother Resham."

"Yes, ao Kevath." Resham relaxed his stance, though his eye, if a spear, would have fixed the girl to the ground.

Avram turned a stylus in his fingers. "Does she know you are Myxolidian?"

"Yes, ao Kevath."

"Then her dilemma is even more disconcerting, brother Resham. In me she has all of Aeolia lined against her. And in you, all of Myxolidia."

"Yes, ao Kevath."

"Leoshine!"

She turned fractionally toward him and straightened to receive the command.

Avram watched the girl's thoughts fly across her face. Pride. Fear. Insatiable curiosity. "Pick up the spoons." Did she know enough Aeolian to obey?

She intoned in Aeolian, copying Resham exactly. "Yes, ao Kevath."

Avram's grin broke wide open and his eyes flashed. He jettisoned from his chair, palms slapping on the armrests.

Leoshine dove under the table.

Resham followed her with a shrug.

Amid the music of the cutlery, Avram heard her fierce-whispered demand. "What did he say?"

He paused his step to hear Resham's answer.

Just as Avram imagined the girl preparing to ask again, Resham spoke with care.

"He is Aeolian. I am Oxikobh. You are Townbred. Together we are ... together we work to fix the Dome and other ... disintegrations."

Duties

The pillow whipped off Leoshine's head and landed with a thump on her body. She dragged herself upright with a scowl.

"Up, Snorginund." Resham used a Myxolidian insult before continuing in Aeolian. "Shameful, ao Kevath, I looked for more from your 'slave.'" He bustled about with clothes and brushes and shaving tools. His hands slowed and his face softened as he replaced the special book and jeweled collar in their box.

ao Kevath yawned and stretched. Leoshine heard Resham's step around the room.

"They crowd the door already, ao Kevath."

I can understand them, Leoshine realised as she retreated behind the screen. *More every day.* When left alone she used the speaking board until her brain curled at the edges.

"I told them to be patient while ao Kevath ate."

The jingle of buckles and the scrape of the razor told Leoshine the story of their daily routine. Every day he lathered ao Kevath's face and scraped the paste off. Otherwise, Resham explained when asked, a beard would grow. Leoshine could not imagine ao Kevath with a beard.

Her stomach rumbled, impatient for the summons to eat from ao Kevath's plate.

When Resham called, she slipped into the chair beside her master. The fruit, cheese, and bread thrilled her taste buds as she watched her master pick up and replace a morsel.

Resham swung by the table and picked up a white square. "Will you not drink a little and taste this new cake, ao Kevath?

Cook is learning to do old things with new materials."

The door rumbled, and Resham snorted and threw down the new cake. ao Kevath signaled for the audience to begin.

Leoshine rose to take her place on the cot, but Resham's hand stayed her.

He slapped a piece of cheese into her hand. "Feed him." He cleared most of the dishes onto a tray, leaving one with bread and cheese, and passed it to a servant outside.

Leoshine drew her chin into her chest and frowned. *ao Kevath's spirit does not reside in his body.* She studied his lax eyelids. *What will they get from him today?*

Three of Father's town councillors, including one of Father's brothers, entered. Their eyes bulged when they saw her.

She imagined how she looked to them. The daughter of the mayor, dressed as an alien slattern, showing devotion to the new master of the dominion, the newly acclaimed warrior conqueror of the land. Her upper lip curled, and she kept her eyes trained on the plate.

"ao Kevath," the leader introduced. "We come to speak to your excellency about the impending crisis. The rebels are encroaching on our land so we cannot hunt anymore. Your soldiers do not supply our children with the meat they need to grow." The speech stretched on.

Rebels? Starving children? When did town folk ever hunt unimpeded by the Oxikobh who harassed all land outside the town walls?

The right-hand councillor bowed and halted a gesture across his chest when he saw her watching. "When, O ao Kevath? We only ask, when do the reinforcements you promised from your own Dome arrive here to secure the town?"

The square of cheese grew oily in her hand. *How am I going to get it into his hand without touching him?*

His eyes beneath the lids were bright and intent on her face. The blood rushed into her head and the room shrank. She had the impression he was vitally aware of every hair on every head in the room and also hearing music in an alternate dimension.

She offered the cheese. He cupped his hand. She deposited the cheese into this cup and sat back in her chair.

A sharp crack sounded at the door. A lone Aeolian entered. ao Kevath put the cheese in his mouth in the commotion.

The councillors stepped aside and ao Kevath heard the Aeolian report while staring at the wall.

Leoshine chose a piece of bread from the plate and waited. *At least it won't melt.*

ao Kevath cupped his hand. She looked at his face. He was not looking at her. The bread went into his hand and he ate as the Aeolian departed.

"O, ao Kevath," the third councillor's voice surprised Leoshine. "We don't know when the great birds are coming back and how they enter the Dome. How will the reinforcements find the town? Where will they stay? Within the walls? Who will feed them?"

Juices of the red fruit dripped down her fingers as she picked it off the plate. ao Kevath usually ate these first.

His eyes were again absorbed by hers. He nodded when she offered the morsel. Nodded toward her.

Her eyelids shot up. "Me?" she mouthed. *Eat from the Overlord's plate in men's company, in the presence of Father's councillors? Father's brother?* Her throat muscles contracted. Was he acknowledging that she also favoured this fruit, driving their 'sameness' home? More likely he displayed his differences to the Myxolidian men. He demonstrated her submission to the new ways.

"ao Kevath," she breathed, "I saved this for you."

The light in his eye narrowed to a concentrated beam. He grinned, leaned toward her and opened his mouth.

Leoshine gasped. He played a game. Challenged and counter challenged. Dared and counter dared.

He remained unmoving, eyes closed now, waiting for the fruit to touch his tongue from her hand.

The intimacy of the gesture stopped her heart. The Myxolidian men would not accept this from even the mothers of their children. *Does he intimate that I share his body?* She felt sicker by the moment. Would they see her bright red face and know he had never touched her in that way, that she lately had felt that threat less, until now?

Resham had moved to the door and opened it. The councillors began crowding each other toward it.

ao Kevath opened his eyes but did not close his mouth.

With a red face and shaking hand, Leoshine darted the fruit between his lips without touching them and whipped her hand into her lap. She rubbed her fingers and fought tears that assailed her throat.

Resham beckoned. "Come."

Leoshine rose and darted out the door to follow him through the halls.

"That was good." Resham approved. "We'll do that again."

"Why does he do that?" Leoshine rubbed the back of her fingers down her legs.

Resham did not slow down. "He is diverted. His mind requires a game."

They arrived at the bathhouse before Leoshine spoke again. She stood on the top step. Someone had carved the tall hedges into squared rows, and the bushes on either side of the step showed half open buds.

"But why?" She asked again, with brows drawn together and one eye slightly more closed. "Why does he do that there? With those men watching?"

Resham put his hands behind his back and spread his feet. He raised his eyes to the distance, an attitude she recognised from his talks with ao Kevath.

"He builds trust, Tassanara."

She shot him a scowl.

The muscles in his face relaxed, and his shoulders assumed a less guarded posture. "He takes you to your place of fear, to tell you that he knows what you fear, and to acknowledge his authority to make you experience your fear, the situation you fear. He plays there and invites you to join"—he leaned closer—"which you did." His eyebrows tilted without the usual creases. His jaw and temples relaxed from their habitual tension.

Is this how he smiles?

"He shows that he uses his authority to protect you from your fear. Neither he nor others"—he lifted an eyebrow at her—"will hurt you because you are his."

He means himself! Leoshine blinked. *ao Kevath will protect me, even from himself.*

Steam billowed around her in the vestibule and she breathed the moisture deep into her lungs. On the bench, she found a packet wrapped in brown paper. Her fingers trembled as she unwound the wrapping to discover mother-cloth. *This used to be the dress Father brought. Remade in the Aeolian style.* She buried her face and inhaled. Aeolian soap replaced the familiar smell, but the rough fibers rubbed comfort into her soul.

She stripped and submerged herself past her chin in the warm water. The ripple music lapped and stilled around her.

It's remade. She thought of the dress laid out on the bench. *Half Myxolidian, half Aeolian. We share some by losing some. I lose the binding but gain … what? Why do I get to wear it today?*

What does Resham mean, ao Kevath toys with me? He made light of life and death. She scowled and her lower lip lifted and rubbed against the upper.

What did the councillor men mean? Rebels and giant birds? Reinforcements? *They were playing with ao Kevath, and he ignored them, and played with me instead.* She tossed the hyssop branch against her arms.

Something had happened between the master and the servant when she spilled the eating tools. She turned her mind again. Something that involved her. Would Resham help her with the mess or explain ao Kevath or remodel Mother's dress if he really hated her? There was hate in him, no one would mistake him for a peaceful character. Perhaps he really was Oxikobh.

How long will he give me today? He threw no pebbles. Was he guarding? *I won't hurry.* The next moment she remembered the dress. *At least I know how to wear it.*

The towels soaked the water off her flushed skin in the miraculous, Aeolian way she was almost taking for granted. She laughed at herself and buried her face in the dress.

This is different. Leoshine thought of their route back to ao Kevath's room. She halted with her nose almost into Resham's back.

He had stopped at the window overlooking the bare field beside the palace. "Now, my pretty homespun Tassanara …" His fingertips pressed on both her shoulder blades as he turned her and held her facing out toward the new construction. "Are you going to tell me who you came to meet here that night?"

A chill ran through her body. He knew she came here! Her thoughts spun out of control. He suspected a lie!

She strained against his fettering hands and gnashed her teeth. The close atmosphere choked and suffocated.

"Do you know what they are building there?"

"You know I didn't meet anyone!" She bent away from him and lashed with her heels at his shins. He didn't even step aside to avoid her.

Resham lifted a finger at the closest jumble of metal and stone. "It is a place of worship. Have you ever worshiped, I wonder? Your master gives of his own treasure store a place for us all to gather for Ao Kevad."

Her one shoulder suffered a deeper bite of his fingers while the other felt complete release. Leoshine stilled and tensed. If she could see him perhaps she could anticipate his next action or learn something to help in the future. *One wrench might free me. One swipe would fell me.*

The tickle of draping, cold metal caressed her neck.

His fingers glanced off the tips of her neck hairs. "I want you to wear this. I have ao Kevath's approval."

Her body quivered as her intuition reached for him behind her. *He's clasping a chain.*

A low chuckle rumbled in his throat as he turned her to face him.

She raised her hand to touch the new weight at her throat. By lowering her chin, she could just see a clear, hard bauble, banded in gold, exactly like the chain in the box with the book but smaller. Her fingers explored the nubbles and holes in the intricate weave of the links.

"Why? What?" Her eyes flickered up to his, and met something she dared not receive. She blushed and lowered her gaze.

Leoshine stared at Resham's back as they tramped back to the chamber. *What does it mean?* Her hand again stroked the gift. *Why does he change so quickly?* He punished and rewarded, warned and encouraged, slapped and caressed, almost with the same gesture.

In his chamber, ao Kevath looked up. He measured the length of her body, down to her skin slippers and up to the pulsing in her throat that made the necklace tremble.

Her ears pounded, and her face flushed as bright as the red fruit. She sank onto the cot and fought the urge to scream or cry or run.

He hungers even if he restrains his urge.

He doesn't like me wearing the necklace. Her fingers ran over the lumps and gaps and the band about the bauble.

Iliana Arrives

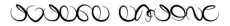

Slumped in her saddle, Leoshine pulled her leg out of the upper hook and touched her fingertip to the red welt striping her upper calf. She winced and bent to examine another welt just above her ankle on the inside of her other leg. She had watched Resham activate the Tesheddar before dawn and had deactivated it when she knew he wasn't accompanying them on this venture into the wilderness.

Long and hard, he had warned. ao Kevath would ride far from town, with as little reason as he had for the other rides.

She shifted her weight and ran her tongue around her dry mouth. Swollen, scratchy eyelids drifted closed.

Soldiers surrounded her. Trees, too, and she long ago gave up thinking about the Oxikobh that might be hiding in the foliage. ao Kevath chatted with Kirim as they rode. She had learned enough Aeolian to understand when they spoke directly to her, but, in her daze, this idle chatter melded into one stream.

A voice cackled to life. In the last while, the grey box had multiplied, throwing voices even when they rode in the wilderness, and now from ao Kevath's saddle. She lifted her gaze from the left side of Paulos' swaying rump to ao Kevath's back.

With an exultant whoop, he stood up in his saddle. Paulos gathered all his power. Leoshine gaped and clutched at her saddle as her horse's head snapped forward and the whole troop charged down the fresh-cut avenue in the trees.

One moment she felt muscles bunching beneath her and the next she felt air streaming upward. Her breath exploded from her lungs as her body hit the ground. Blood-tang singed her nose and mouth. She rolled and the bauble on her necklace hit one ear, then the other and then her teeth as the spinning slowed.

Instantly she gained her feet and tried to run. She ran for two steps before the vibration of heavy pursuit overtook her. She felt the mass of Paulos aligning with her under ao Kevath's command.

A force seized the back of her jacket. The collar strangled and choked her as her feet left the ground. She felt the air ricocheting in her lungs, seeking exit. The ground spun beneath her, farther and farther away.

High up she flew until her legs straddled Paulos' undulating neck. From behind, ao Kevath's arm clasped across her chest and over one hip.

Paulos swung around in mid-stride. She stared at the severed end of the beribboned rope lashing past. *My horse!* ao Kevath leaned forward, pressing her down with his chest, into the commotion and she felt him kick Paulos' withers.

She turned her face to lie beside the pumping neck. The whipping mane stung her cheeks. She willed her eyes to close. His body burned behind her. Sweat-stench enveloped her. Hooves beat drums in her chest.

ao Kevath stood up again. His yell burst her ears.

Alarm? She arched her back.

He settled back into his saddle. His body seemed to wrap around her. The pace whipped her ears with wind.

The trees rolled away and the land spread out before them, up and down, through gullies and over hillocks.

Yet again, ao Kevath stood and hollered and waved his rein hand.

An answering whoop sounded at a distance and a dust cloud rose to meet them. Without any relenting of speed, the two groups of thundering, grinning Aeolians altered direction and melded. Most wore the red, black, and silver shells, though Leoshine saw plain clothes among them.

She coughed from the dust and tried to cover her face. The iron bank of muscles held her arms tight to her body.

On either side the land rose up to hem them in. A dry gulch. The pace slackened. The whole army of Aeolians halted under some trees that overhung the bank.

She felt ao Kevath push her away. Other hands cradled the back of her skull and hips.

Resham! Her heart rippled with relief and fear at his touch.

Angry voices tangled over her head.

He carried her to the opposite side of Paulos from where ao Kevath dismounted and deposited her on a flat ledge in the bank.

Her hands quivered. Her teeth chattered. The whole world seemed to be in motion. ao Kevath appeared at Paulos' head and instantly at his tail, then back at his head. Resham and ao Kevath continued to exchange curt answers.

She held her breath and tensed all her muscles but the shaking increased. The taste of blood returned.

Buckles jingled all around. Horses blew and whinnied and stomped. Soldiers called to their comrades. Kirim and Gavin fretted in the background. After a moment of watching ao Kevath's ferocious track, they mounted and rode in different directions.

Aeolian formed in her mind. Some of the babble made an impression.

ao Kevath stammered. "I didn't … I thought …" He stopped just as he turned to walk another loop. "I was excited. I wanted to share it … Why couldn't she …?"

Behind closed eyelids, Leoshine imagined her master rubbing his brow.

"She doesn't know, ao Kevath." Resham's voice purred. "She has never met the ao Kenan."

ao Kevath's step hesitated. "That's exactly the trouble. If they knew. I hate ignorance!"

Resham towered over her, even though she sat high enough to not see under Paulos' belly. His hand rested on her head and his thumb drew aside her hair to see the scuff on her forehead. Her shivers froze while his fingers probed over her skull, neck, over her shoulders and down her vibrating spine. She winced as he touched the welted calf.

She kicked her leg and fought with her hands. She would not be disrobed in public! But her legs remained immovable in his grip and her body ground into the rock seat.

Resham lifted the other legging as if he knew what he would find. With a grunt he disappeared again.

Sobs wracked Leoshine and her tears burst their dam. She pushed her leggings back down to cover her skin. ao Kevath disappeared for greater intervals behind Paulos.

Resham returned, chewing something. She hated him! Why did he think to eat at a time like this?

He handed her a cup and jerked his head to indicate that she should drink. She refused, even though her mouth burned with thirst. He put the cup on the ledge.

Once more, he gripped her legs, and raised her leggings to expose her wounds. She fought. He turned and gripped her legs under his arm.

With balled fists, she pounded on his back and half screamed, half growled. "Leave me! Let me go!"

Her eyes widened, and the breath sucked from her lungs as he spat whatever was in his mouth onto her leg. Her fists pounded harder and she twisted with all her might. To no avail. No reaction.

Resham reached up and plucked some leaves from the overhead branch. Then he plucked her from her perch and carried her to a horse. Her horse. He replaced her in the saddle and spat again. This time she saw the white foamy ooze before he placed leaves over the welts. He drew down the leggings and amplified the force of the Tesheddar.

"No." Her heart turned to pleading. "Please, I don't want to ride anymore."

She stared at the Tesheddar. *It holds the poultice in place.*

Resham shot her a glance.

Rebuke. A warning chilled the pit of her stomach. *No.* She blinked. *I won't kill it again.*

Compassion. She turned away from the thought.

Humour, yes. She could accept mockery from him.

Her body swayed as he led her horse to its station behind Paulos and knotted the beribboned tether. "Where are we going? How much farther?"

ao Kevath stood by Paulos' head with a cup in his hand.

Resham lifted her cup. "Drink. You need strength."

"What is it?" Her eyes searched his face from over the rim.

She tasted. Warmth tingled down her throat, under her arms, down her spine and into her toes. Pain from the wounds on her legs flared briefly and disappeared.

"ao Kevath!" Resham studied a device in his hand. Leoshine felt the tingle of understanding. "She's here, down and out!"

Their master's face broke open in the widest delight she had ever seen in him.

"Who?" she demanded in Mxyolidian. Then she remembered the Aeolian. "Who is down and out?"

Suppressed mirth bubbled in Resham's eyes. "The ao Kenan Iliana. She has come under the Dome. We ride to meet her."

Leoshine scowled at the swaying knot in the tether from her horse to the Overlord. *I hate them.*

At the same time, the feeling of ao Kevath's power against her back, his forearm like an iron bar across her front, and Resham's ministry to her wounds drifted near.

She studied the six generals, the Overlord and his servant as they bantered together like little boys when their fathers gave them swords for the first time.

A dust cloud appeared. ao Kevath let out another blood-curdling whoop, and spurred Paulos. Leoshine squeaked and dug her fingernails into the saddle. Her seat held like the breath in her lungs.

A flickering blur of colour seemed to burn inside the dust cloud. An army of Aeolian soldiers and horses, wearing flags and banners, surrounded a silver, shiny ellipsoid about two horses high, with windows in the front.

The ellipsoid vehicle stopped and its escort parted. ao Kevath halted his army. A hole developed in the silver side.

Heavy breathing stirred tiny clouds around each horse. Leoshine watched ao Kevath and Resham lean forward.

Fluttery cloth flowed from the hole. Steps with handrails extended from the hole in the silver side to the ground like an insect lowering its leg.

"ao Kenan!" "Iliana!" A roaring cheer burst from the Aeolians on all sides.

ao Kevath held up his hand. Veteran Aeolian and newcomer held their peace with a space between. He dismounted and drew off his helmet. With echoing thumps and jingles, everyone followed his example.

Alone, Leoshine remained above the bared heads. Manes settled. The dust drifted on the breath of the men and beasts.

A slender figure emerged in the midst of the cloth flowing from the vehicle. Like a mobile tower of silver shapes that blinked and sparkled as if lit from within, it halted above the steps. A neck clearly narrowed above shoulders and a face glowed from beneath the crowning knot of purple-silver material. The bodice wrapped around a slender, feminine form like Leoshine had come to know without her brace.

More tower-like figures poured from the hole in the vehicle. Or the ao Kenan Iliana might be a being of many limbs. Leoshine could not be sure.

One of the parts drifted down the stairs. Leoshine saw the head swivel back and forth over the company. The shoulders heaved with breath.

ao Kevath stepped to the bottom of the stairs and bowed.

All around Leoshine, the soldiers bowed beside their horses.

The figure at the bottom of the stairs stretched to touch ao Kevath's bowed head. He remained utterly still, and Leoshine wondered if they would play with the dirt. She curled her nose.

She remembered her father bowing to ao Kevath, who never bowed to anyone. If this was his mother, he paid her rare honour.

The ao Kenan Iliana held out a hand to the side. One of the other fluttering figures placed a jar in her palm. Over ao Kevath's bowed head, into the newly freed curls, she poured the contents of the jar. Fragrance wafted over Leoshine like the heady red mead had overwhelmed her tongue. *Sweet*. She inhaled and digested the perfume. *Spicy*. Exotic and addictive.

ao Kevath's face tilted up and his broad smile met his mother's. Shiny streams of liquid ran down his cheeks and dripped off his chin.

He moved to stand but the tall figure held him down with a sharp wink of her eye. A thin band of gold appeared in her hand. She placed this among his curls and raised him with her hand in his. They embraced and touched cheeks. ao Kevath wiped some oil off her cheek with his sleeve.

Aeolians touch one another. They do things for each other's bodies. Mother used to touch me. She sobbed inside. *I used to sleep in the folded limbs of Giffshine and Hillashine.*

What if ao Kevath touches me? The darkest regions of her stomach twisted. She swallowed and tasted acid.

He takes you to your fear, Resham had explained. *He shows you he will protect you.*

Even from himself. Her blood ran cold in her arms and stomach.

ao Kevath's mouth and brow twisted. He grabbed at the ao Kenan's elbow. She shrugged him off, knelt down, and pressed the top of his hand to her forehead. Leoshine remembered her father urging her to do the same.

ao Kevath pulled at Iliana's elbow, urging her to rise. She laughed as he scolded. He gestured to the Dome and swung his arm wide. Leoshine imagined he told her something about Myxolidia.

He turned to the army. "Prepare yourselves!" Time passed. His body rotated to encompass all. The last echoes of his voice died in the distance.

His eyes stopped at Leoshine. Her face burned.

Why do you do this? She silently stared her question into his eyes. *Why do you make me the audience?*

Power streamed from him as he stared, shoulders back, chin thrust up and back, eyes burning. *You are witness,* he seemed to say. *You tell them. One people.*

"Prepare!" One second more he stared at her, then his eyes roved over the bowed heads. "In three days we feast!"

Heads popped up. The crowd convulsed to regain its feet.

ao Kevath touched the crown on his head. "Ao Kevad sent our noble mother with a gift confirming His mission here! We rejoice and humbly commit ourselves to knowing His will in Myxolidia."

The crowd roared. Leoshine jumped.

"Long live Avram! King of Myxolidia!"

"Long live Iliana, queen and mother to us all!"

"Praise to Ao Kevad, the High King!"

Leoshine watched the ao Kenan Iliana slip her arm into ao Kevath's and cuddle her face against him. They whispered together. ao Kevath's head bent at an odd angle. He made a wry face at his generals.

ao Kenan Iliana placed her hands on Resham's upper arms and examined his face, before disappearing in his embrace. Resham bent his face into her headdress, and Leoshine imagined him inhaling.

A murmur rose from the crowd. Leoshine looked around at the grins. Each clique talked together.

ao Kenan Iliana pushed away from Resham, and laughed up at him. Dorim stood beside them, and received her warmth and tenderness before relinquishing her to the other generals.

Gavin ran up the stairs, engulfed one of the fluttery figures in his arms, and dove through the hole in the silver vehicle.

ao Kevath waved his arm toward the ellipsoid. His mother laughed as he put his arm around her and walked toward the hole in its side.

Leoshine's mouth hung open. She thought of kicking against the Tesheddar that held her into the saddle. She thought of calling out.

The ao Kenan Iliana climbed the steps and merged into the vehicle. ao Kevath followed.

At the bottom of the step Resham turned and called. The soldier holding Paulos moved them forward, and Leoshine's heart leapt.

"What happened?" she hissed as her stirrup drew level with the top step, and Resham released her from the saddle.

Mischief danced across Resham's face. "The ao Kenan Iliana arrived."

"You know what I mean! Why? What does it mean for her to pour the perfume, and the crown, and the cheering?"

Resham reached up and, for a moment, seemed to offer his assistance. "They do that when they have been separated. It eases the pain of parting to know it will happen." He grasped her waist and swung her over the steps straight through the hole.

Soft hands took hold of her arms and body, even her hair. She felt the caresses as coming from one being, though now she knew there were many women besides ao Kenan Iliana and even some that might be children. The subdued light made all the fluttery cloth merge into one dulcet cushion upon which she seemed to be laid. She heard ao Kevath and Resham's voices in the din of the enclosed space. The Domelight vanished.

Strange forces pressed and weighed on her skin and her mind. Her stomach lurched, and her vision blurred.

Leoshine felt arms cradling her. She stared into blue eyes and knew where ao Kevath's came from.

Silver arches formed thin eyebrows. High, prominent cheekbones covered in fine wrinkles made the ao Kenan's skin look like a thousand downy pillows. "Poor darling!" The grand lady crooned. Her bright red lips rippled as they formed the Myxolidian words. "Feel how you tremble! Have those beasts mistreated you?"

Tears sprang up in Leoshine's suddenly wide-open eyes. The ao Kenan Iliana used a word only Myxolidian women knew. She searched the wrinkled face. *How did she know the word for what a woman felt when a man rumpled her by his boisterous nature?*

Bath with Iliana

Leoshine languished in the warm wrap of the water. Sweet notes of lapping accompanied her thoughts with new tenderness. Resham no longer accompanied her to the bathhouse, though he always seemed to know when she went there. His trust always balanced with his knowledge.

She tossed a hyssop branch across the skin of her arm, under the steamy surface. Dreams and insight played with each other, like the light-stick played with the rich greeny-blue of the water.

A startling form of womanhood arrived with the ao Kenan Iliana. Leoshine thought of the greeting in the wilderness and how the Aeolians worshiped at her feet.

How would Mother greet the newcomer? Leoshine watched the silvery bubbles rise from under the hairs on her arm. *Would she bow and squirm to gain approval?* She wrinkled her nose. *Would the two women ever meet?*

Father, like an open book, would probably fall at the elegantly shod feet. Had he met her in his travels to Aeolia? Giffshine would be jealous and spiteful; Hillashine would side with Giffshine for no real reason. Wol …

Leoshine shifted and froze.

The laughing of women in the distance grew louder until the outer vestibule to the bathhouse echoed with cheerful Aeolian words. In the water, Leoshine sank to her ears.

ao Kenan Iliana spoke backward as she entered the main bath chamber. "Now you may leave me, girls. I'll send for you later."

The blue-green dimness danced on and softly illuminated her tall nakedness in all its aged glory. As she stepped up over the rim of the large tub, unheard of suppleness and elegance sank beneath the water.

She is human. Leoshine stared in awe.

ao Kenan Iliana's eyes twinkled. Leoshine tucked her knees closer into her chest and dug her shoulder blades into the tub wall.

The older lady's long white hair floated on the surface of the water. Her head and shoulders seemed like an island surrounded by trailing vapour. When she finally spoke, she used Myxolydian in a hushed tone. "Hello, Leoshine. I am glad to see you this day." Then with an unnecessary repetition but overflowing sympathy, she added, "Hello, Leoshine. Are you well this morning?"

Leoshine blinked.

"I can't speak for long in your language, my dear." ao Kenan Iliana admitted. "It hurts my tongue. If I speak simply in mine, can you understand? Will you please stop me, and ask me to explain if you don't understand? I don't like to be misunderstood, you know."

A tiny glass bottle, concealed until brought to the surface, disgorged a small quantity of scented oil onto the surface of the water. ao Kenan Iliana stirred the slick with her long finger, breaking it into sections, and then encouraging them to meld together. All at once, she covered the oil with her hand, fingers closed tight, and pushed the oil deep into the water. She agitated with two hands, and the oil splintered and spread in tiny capsules. The burst of each bubble released a gasp of lavender-scented steam.

She smiled. "Never seen that before? Of course. Your daddy just built this bath. He wouldn't have been introduced to the oil. This is really very comfortable. Back home, we women book appointments and get our beauty treatments, and we set the whole world straight in an afternoon together."

She corralled bubbles and oil on the surface and spoke slowly in Aeolian. "Speaking of your father, you probably want to know what you should call me. Names are so important and we must get this right from the very start. Since you are going to be family, you must call me Iliana, clear and simple. I will call you Leoshine and we will get on very nicely together."

Leoshine fished through the stream of sounds for meaning. Father, family and, "call me Iliana" came through clearly. She sighed and her breathing slowed.

"We have the worship today. Then the banquet tonight. I think this is the first for you? Yes, a great occasion for me too. My first in the new kingdom. I brought along some supplies to be combined with some local food – should be interesting what cook can do. Avram has the soldiers setting up the tables in the green square outside with lights on strings and music boxes."

She sighed. "I will have to shake hands with every official and chancellor—how wearying—but I am sure there will be an interesting character or two to liven the proceedings. And speeches! Oh my, there will be so many, and I'll have to respond. I have been practicing. Would you like to hear?" Iliana lifted her slender fingers and allowed the water to drip off their tips.

Leoshine caught Iliana's coy side glance.

Iliana broadcast to the wooden walls in Myxolidian. "My fewow nountwymen, Wellnome to the celuaation that benins the reign of King Avram. Alloaf us totether are welnome at the tamle of His majest our High King. Peace be with you."

Leoshine's lips twitched. Iliana possessed a good vocabulary. Her tongue rounded the corners of all her words, but she was perfectly understandable.

Iliana grinned and cocked her head from side to side. "What do you think? How would you say it?"

Leoshine rose until her neck was above the water. Softly, shyly, with a shadow of the authority she observed in ao Kenan Iliana's voice, she rendered the speech. "My fellow countrymen. Welcome to the celebration that begins the reign of King Avram. All of us together are welcome at the table of His Majesty our High King. Peace be with you."

The water frothed with Iliana's applause. "Clever girl! Now repeat it word by word and teach me how to be perfect."

Rising a little further, Leoshine examined her student. The furrow between her eyes deepened.

"I think I can say 'my' fairly well, but what about 'fewow.'" Her voice drifted off as she frowned.

"Fellow." Leoshine remembered Resham teaching her the first words in Aeolian, and the constant struggle to produce the sounds of a new language. ao Kevath held back from the Myxolidian that seemed to sprain his tongue every time he spoke it.

One word at a time, Leoshine spoke the sounds and Iliana copied with sometimes comically distorted features. Tension ebbed from Leoshine's shoulders, and she stretched her legs out to the bottom of the bath.

With a jolt, Leoshine remembered her duties. Alarmed for Resham's reaction, she half rose, then sank down, glancing out the corner of her eye, wondering if Iliana saw.

Iliana continued to play with the oil droplets. "Don't worry, dear," she reassured in Myxolidian. "Sit back down. I made sure he won't miss you. Rayoon," she called to the door in Aeolian, "come in, please."

A tall woman, who had apparently been sitting in the outer room came forward. Leoshine shrank beneath the surface and crossed her arms over her body.

Iliana prattled on in Aeolian. She gestured with her hands. Then she turned to Leoshine. "I have seen you knot your hair, and it looks really lovely, but tonight is special and you want to look the part. Rayoon has exquisite skill. She has done my hair for many years, and I am sure you will be pleased with her work."

The maid moved behind and placed her hands on Leoshine's head. "Yes, ao Kenan." Her hands quickly twirled tendrils of hair and fastened them with metal clasps hidden in her pockets.

Leoshine's spine tingled at the feeling of a stranger's fingers in her hair. Submit? She held her shoulders with her hands and tried to sort through the sensations of threat and pleasure.

In less time than a bubble's pop, the servant moved over to her mistress, and Leoshine observed from a new vantage-point the technique of adept fingers, and the endless supply of clever little clasps.

"Mine is called the Quantril," Iliana explained. "The Shantil is used for young ones like you."

At last the maid's fingers stilled.

Iliana raised her chin. "Fetch the towels, please." Her eyebrow twitched toward the door.

Rayoon bowed and left the room.

"Rayoon and Keefa will dry us off and we'll get dressed. I have a few more surprises for you."

Leoshine sank to her chin in the water. Her eyes widened as

Iliana emerged from the water and climbed the steps. Rayoon appeared with towels and began drying her mistress. Another figure waited in the shadows with a towel.

Leoshine held her breath. *These people touch each other.*

"Come, dear. Bath time over." Iliana reached down.

Leoshine placed her hand in Iliana's and looked up.

Iliana smiled. "Come dear, you don't have anything I didn't, once upon a time." She paused a moment, then pulled.

As Leoshine's knees straightened, the water sloughed off her skin.

"Why darling! You're full of bruises!"

Leoshine only heard the horror in the Aeolian words. "I will die?" She shivered as she was turned by her examiner.

"On your shoulder and arm ... and on your hip ... You have fallen. No, dear." Belatedly she consoled in Myxolidian. "You won't die. I will ask Resham, and he will give you cream."

Leoshine had seen the cream he spat from his mouth. "No! No!"

Iliana frowned. "Why such fear? He is a ... what you call a body healer. Don't worry. I will help." She motioned for the new servant to step forward.

Leoshine sank into the warm water. "I don't understand. I am ao Kevath's slave."

Iliana held her arms out for Rayoon to dry her torso. "Is that what he said? I suppose for lack of a better term you are, a body he does with as he pleases. He pleases that I teach you and I please that you allow Keefa to dry and dress you. Are you an obedient slave?" She leaned down from her full height and squinted into Leoshine's eyes.

"I don't understand."

Perhaps I am Rellogat like Gorphiline. Leoshine considered her childhood companion who did the heavier labour. She didn't weave or sew but worked to allow Mother and the mayor's daughters time to do the skilled work. Father had influenced the choice of Gorphiline's man. *What else made her like I am now?*

Iliana continued speaking as Rayoon began to apply a soft paste to her back. "Understanding comes later. Do as I say and no harm will come to you."

The words struck a chill down Leoshine's spine. Resham said them with more ferocity. Harm came to Rachnorgats, the lowest order of slave.

Iliana reached again and helped Leoshine from the water. Keefa bowed and touched the corner of the towel to Leoshine's shoulder, who closed her eyes. Her arms hung limp and she felt them being lifted one by one. What did a Rellogat have to do with the deep pile of towels?

When she was dry, a sleeveless gown of fine weave drifted over her head and down to her knees. She inhaled a sweet fragrance. Keefa's hands twitched in all places at once, clasping and tying. Baggy pantaloons clothed her legs. A heavier robe with narrow sleeves followed the first. She sighed with relief when Keefa bent and helped her into slippers not too different from her own.

Keefa twitched a heavy cape over Leoshine's shoulders. A hood covered her hair, and she dared not turn her head.

Iliana inspected every fold before she tossed her hand. The two servants stepped aside, and she floated forward.

Leoshine stretched a tentative foot forward. Nothing impeded it. The skirt rustled like the noise of all the fluttery figures in the silver vessel Iliana arrived in.

Iliana spoke over her shoulder as they passed through the bathhouse hedge. "Come dear, no delay. Lots to do today. I imagine you have questions. Resham sent a sheaf of them to me at home and very good questions they are.

"If I were you, I'd wonder about how we got under the Dome, and what was that vessel we traveled in, and what the old lady did with the oil, and what the crown meant?" Iliana halted to turn and raise a thin eyebrow at her audience. "Tell me I'm clever!"

Her gown had hardly subsided before she began to float forward again. "I still know how to ask questions. I am wondering what you are thinking and how much of my prattle you are understanding and how you like your dress and"—she stopped again, and touched her fingertips to the end of her sharp nose —"of course, I wouldn't be woman if I didn't wonder if you could like me, just a little." Her eyelashes bounded up and down.

Leoshine watched, open-mouthed, straining to absorb every syllable and motion. Her mouth gathered in a tight, wrinkly 'o' and her own lashes bobbed twice in answer.

Iliana set her billowing skirts in motion again. "Let's start with your questions. The Dome has an entry point, they all do …"

Information flowed through Leoshine's ears. More than she knew to ask, more than she could find space for. How different from Resham's terse evasion. She skipped to keep up and ached because she could catch no more than fragments of Iliana's tumbling discourse.

"Now the oil is a personal expression. My boy is very precious to me …

"…the glorious palace he built me, almost a copy of my home in Aeolia …

"I can tell he is reluctant to wear it. He hasn't settled the land, yet, but sometimes Ao Kevad gives His approval to spur a greater outlay." Iliana paused for breath.

Leoshine tried to catch her breath. "Please? What is Ao Kevad?"

Iliana smiled, and arched her hands above her head. "The Great High King! Ruler of heaven and earth."

"What is earth?" Leoshine didn't hear the other word as clearly.

"Yes." Iliana's piercing eye once more examined her. "We have much schooling ahead of us. But not today. Today is for feasting. Come, my darling." Iliana motioned her forward. "I can explain a little, but we must keep moving."

They walked toward the silver ellipsoid until music began to play around them. Iliana reached into her gown and began speaking into her hand.

"Really? Are you certain? Can't I …? All right, if you insist." She touched her gown again, and turned to speak to Leoshine.

"He wants you back. In his room. He doesn't want you to get in my way as I organise the party. Oh, sweetheart!" She drew her long finger across Leoshine's brow, down her temple, and under her chin. "Why such furrows?"

Leoshine's eyes rolled back in her head and her body quivered. A thought tip-toed through her mind. *ao Kenan is all about touching.*

A sense of impending death seized her as Iliana moved away.

She brought her right fist, grasped with her left hand, under her chin. "I won't get in the way. I can … learn."

Iliana arched an eyebrow at her and smiled. She lifted her chin, and her chest forged the path. "Nay, sweetheart. ao Kevath has spoken! And you know we are all slaves of ao Kevath!" She made loose circles in the air with her hand. "Obeying to the least detail. But we shall see each other later, and I will give you something to learn while you wait."

Riding Lessons

Leoshine sat upright on the cot, balancing the hair construction that threatened to shift on her scalp with her every breath. The scent of Iliana lingered in the air of ao Kevath's chamber.

ao Kevath bounced to his feet from his seat at the table and busied himself with a cupboard. He spoke in Aeolian while stripping off his shirt. "We go to my Master's House."

Leoshine closed her eyes. Dizzy nausea washed over her. So far, she had puzzled out that ao Kevath's master was called Ao Kevad, that he lived in Aeolia, and could be a child with a mother.

"Wear that." He stood before her dressed in a bright green blouse and tunic, trimmed with gold braid. In his hand he held the box that protected the sacred book and heavy necklace. "We ride so put your cloak over."

Ride? She gulped and thought of the creation encasing her head.

"Cloak!"

Leoshine jumped and snatched the heavy garment that she had taken off when she entered. Her hair stayed in place.

At the door, ao Kevath paused. "You carry." He placed the box in her hands and ducked between the sentries.

She stepped through the door in time to see him turn right, down a hallway she had never noticed. She closed her mouth and hurried to catch up.

It wasn't a hallway, but a covered porch framing a courtyard on three sides. An empty fire pit occupied the middle. Six long windows pierced the fourth, and newly extended courtyard wall.

ao Kevath turned the corner and laid his hand on the handle of a door.

She called after him. "I want to stay in the room."

ao Kevath paused with his hand on the doorknob.

"What if I didn't follow?" Her fingers fretted the carvings on the box.

"I would have to kill you." He flicked something off his sleeve. "And"—he turned to open the door—"I know you, who detest killing, would do all in your power to prevent that."

Before the door closed, she ran through.

The air hung thick with manure and hay. She held her breath and buried her nose in her cloak. Warm, muscular equine haunches lined the walls, creating an aisle of swishing tails. Men, with their sleeves rolled up, shoveled hay and sloshed buckets over the cobbles. They brushed coats and greeted ao Kevath with casual waves as he passed by.

He disappeared through an open space in the wall. She followed and peeped through to an arena. Row after row of rafters stretched to a rough wooden wall far into the shadows. Hoof prints littered the sand.

Two soldiers held the bridles of Paulos and Leoshine's mare.

ao Kevath hurried to take Paulos' bridle, patting the handsome neck and running his hand down the bulging forelegs. He beckoned to Leoshine. "Come."

Paulos bent his head around and lipped ao Kevath's jacket.

As soon as she stood in reach, ao Kevath draped his hand over her shoulder and pulled her right under the stallion's nose.

She screwed up her eyes and hunched her shoulders. Gusts of breath flowed over her, ruffling the fine hairs on her forehead. The horse snuffled and nuzzled her ear and cheek with his cushiony lips. She raised the box and pushed against ao Kevath's hand to cover her face.

"Are you small?" She heard him wonder in Aeolian, as if he didn't know what small was.

He lifted the box from her hands and placed it in Paulos' saddle bag.

She looked up. His eyes seemed to radiate white light. She shook herself. *No, he is human. It's an impression. Resham also has this power with his eyes.*

"His head goes from the top of your head to below your waist and I'm sure it weighs more than you. And yet, Resham says you are larger than most Myxolidians."

Paulos lowered his head further and snuffled between her arms. She breathed warm, sweet air.

He tossed his head and her feet flew up. Her teeth slammed against each other as she hit the sand. Snatches of her scalp screamed with pain as the hair pins strained at their anchors.

ao Kevath exploded in a rare free laugh. "You trickster!" He rubbed the horse's offending nose.

Paulos stretched his head forward and snorted.

ao Kevath dropped the reins and gripped her hand. "You better get up. He's delicate on his feet, but he's unsettled."

Leoshine whimpered as she stood. "He hates me."

"No." ao Kevath rumbled with pride and mirth. "That was affection. Don't see it much."

He reached forward with both hands.

Leoshine felt her head engulfed. His palms pressed lightly on her ears, muffling the grinding sound of Paulos' teeth on his bit. Warmth seeped into her cheeks.

He fingered a stray lock of hair across her forehead. "That's better."

Again, she sank away from the present moment, hypnotised by his eyes.

"I have taught him to know you." His fingertips pressed on the base of her skull.

Is this how he killed Georg? A mere twitch would break my neck.

"I have given him your scent." ao Kevath's eyebrows twitched together. He seemed to speak to himself. "You are afraid. I can feel your pulse."

He's going to take me. Leoshine blinked up into his gaze. Her mouth fell open and his grip seemed to tighten as she shrank away. *He's going to do what the Oxikobh expected when they gave me to him. He will be cursed and I will be cursed.*

He blinked rapidly and tilted his head. "Haven't you lived with me long enough to know?"

The white light of his eyes seemed to throb as another loose strand of her hair trailed off his fingers to its end. She blinked and her throat spasmed. He turned and allowed Paulos to snuffle his fingers.

That horse will smell me on his palms. She shuddered.

He took me to my fear. She could hear Resham's explanation. *He played with me there.*

ao Kevath spoke in stronger tones. "He knows you have been on his back. Not many have. Resham can ride him almost as well as me, but the others make excuses when I offer."

Paulos now nuzzled his master and pushed at his chest. ao Kevath laughed again and held his hand flat with a treat. Paulos stretched his munching head toward Leoshine and shook his mane.

"Want to try?" ao Kevath motioned to the saddle. "That is his invitation."

Leoshine measured the distance up that mountain range of muscle.

"Come around." ao Kevath pulled her to stand with her back to his chest.

The warmth of him radiated through her cloak. They stood facing the same direction as Paulos, who lowered his head. The crook of his jaw and neck cradled her.

Leoshine reached up and stroked the smooth, hard muscle. *He is a giant. A giant's giant.*

"I caught him as he birthed from his dam." ao Kevath's voice boomed through her from behind. He reached around her and stroked Paulos' nose. "He saw only me and his dam for his first few days. That's how he is imprinted. He has known no other master. I want him to know you."

This is important. He wraps his body around mine. This is why they believe he has taken me.

This is why they are wrong. He has not touched me. I am still clean. He is not cursed. I am not cursed.

"Come." ao Kevath stepped away and beckoned to the attendants. "I'm going to teach you to get into this saddle."

One man led her mare forward while the other took Paulos to the outer wall. At a command, the first man left the mare's reins in ao Kevath's hand and brought forward a stepping stool.

"Mounting block." ao Kevath pointed. "We'll try with that, then straight from the ground. Eventually you should learn to mount from a run."

The mare hung her head, not even her ear moved.

Leoshine stepped up and allowed ao Kevath to place her hands on the upper and lower leg hooks. *Will you explain why my hair came down?* Why would he talk to his mother about his slave's hair? *The servant will just have to arrange it again.* She sighed and in-serted her foot into the cup he called a stirrup. His hand steadied the saddle on the upper hook as she sprang and transferred her weight to that foot. Her hair shifted.

She felt him reach out and then hesitate. *How will you kill me if you hesitate now? How will you take me if you hesitate now?*

"Try again, with more conviction," ao Kevath encouraged when she failed to arrive in the seat. "Hands here. Foot here. There!" he exclaimed when she succeeded. "Now hook this leg here and settle this leg lower down."

She gazed at the top of his head. *If he straightens, I could look him in the eye.* She shivered and dropped her gaze to his hand still covering hers.

"Leoshine." He waited until she looked up.

She felt herself sucked into a limitless pool in his eyes, icy up her back, and a blasting furnace in her middle.

His voice barely registered over the roar in her head. "Haven't you lived with me long enough to know I want peace for your people, but I will meet war where I find it."

She blinked and swallowed. Her hand felt cold when he re-moved his. The void he left made her ache and shiver.

He sprang onto Paulos' back. "Now we go."

Leoshine gripped the upper hook as her mare followed Paulos out a door to the main thoroughfare of the compound and into a side street of town. Citizens spotted them and followed as close as they dared.

For a few moments Leoshine blinked. Since the day the Dome darkened, she had grown insecure about its light.

She gazed at the bountiful tail of the war stallion. *No knot today. No tether today! No Tesheddar.* She straightened and darted glances from side to side. *Did he forget? I could escape.*

Around a corner, a colourful cohort of guards joined them. Sharp clattering of the hooves rang off the buildings crowding the lane.

She slumped in her saddle. *He tests me.*

ao Kevath dismounted beside a stone wall that reached to the Dome. The crowd kept on. The guards, Leoshine realised, had led the noisy citizens past while obscuring their Command-er's exit from the line.

Leoshine stalled, listening to their shouts.

Mayor's daughter.

Sister of Wol.

King's doxie.

Avram grunted, his head level with hers. "Didn't I teach you to dismount?"

She shook her head. He grasped her waist and dropped her on new-laid paving stones. Her ankles burned with the impact.

Resham is gentler.

He stopped briefly to retrieve the box containing the chain and book from Paulos' saddle bag and disappeared through an opening in the impossibly high wall.

She felt a tug like a tether on her heart and glanced at her horse, then the emptying street. With a gulp, she crossed under the lintel far above her head. The boom of the door closing exterminated the cries of the people, the bustle of the street, the clip clop of horses. She reached out with her ears into the thrumming silence of the stone-enclosed vestibule.

ao Kevath had already passed farther in. The light shone bright and natural upon him.

She stepped forward, her mouth open and her chin tilted up, up. Impossibly up.

A Dome within the Dome. She could not see if the lattice up there was filled with glass or open to the Dome. Pillars obscured a direct line of sight. Her ears sensed vastness, stupendous enormity that only an Aeolian could conceive.

Father's counsel chamber was the largest meeting space she knew. A low-ceilinged, smoke-filled hall with benches set round the central fire, she never saw it occupied. Scandalous enough that she saw it at all!

ao Kevath gestured with one arm. "A House for a King greater than I!" His boast echoed his deep reverence in every direction.

Leoshine swiveled her head to look full at her master. His master would be a king greater than him, she agreed, but this didn't seem like a comfortable place to live. *Are we really going to see this child?*

He smirked and the emotion of the parade, the jeering crowd returned to her mind.

"Follow. Further in." He turned and strode away.

The invisible tether pulled again. Leoshine glanced back at the door shadow and hurried forward.

Her thin slippers slapped on the shiny floor. *How does his smirk remind me of the way he flaunts me before the people?*

Their taunts—Mayor, Wol, King. Daughter, Sister, Doxie.

Her ears burned. Being a mayor's daughter was no slur. She was proud of Father. *Do the people change the meaning? Do they regard Father differently now?* She shuddered. *Does ao Kevath teach them lies?*

Wol's sister? If they had said, "Georg's sister," she would have breathed easier.

King's doxie, bedmate.

The smirk, she remembered. *He enjoys me. Takes pleasure in me. No. No. Not that,* she pleaded.

Pillars, thicker than the thickest trees in the forest divided their path from spaces on either side. Far beyond the pillars she could see the walls towering up and girded with twisted metal lace.

In the parade, she remembered, ao Kevath engineered and then fed off the people's reaction to her. Like a master stage builder, he posed the characters and props and devoured the outcome.

Here, as she entered his creation, he waited and watched and approved himself because of her awe.

They changed direction around a pillar. Four times more they swung around, and she realised he did not approach the centre of the House in any logical line. Did he intend to use any of the doors she had observed on the outside walls?

As he walked, ao Kevath passed the box with the chain and the book from one hand to the other. Sometimes it didn't even stay upright.

In one breath they revere and in the next breath they toss with ambiguity. Leoshine trailed him between benches that might hold all the town's people.

No effort of hers could hide her reactions from his razor perception. *He burrows, drills, channels deep and unhindered.* She crossed her arms over her chest and tucked her chin in. *When he looks at me, it's like he's feeding on me.* He seemed to grow on her helplessness, her amazement and wonder of all he taught, all he brought, all he was.

Around the next corner, a many-panelled fortress of clear and reflective material reached half way up to the open lattice work above their heads. This sparkling, iridescent tower reminded her of her first sight of ao Kenan alighting from the silver ellipsoid.

Again, they did not approach this bizarre, sparkling tower directly. Leoshine blinked and swallowed. *Does the child live there?*

When they finally drew near, and she thought they would stop, he led her past, into another wing of his Master's house.

She craned her neck, assessing and measuring as they wound through a fresh labyrinth. If Resham stood on ao Kevath's shoulders, they would need to do that at least twice to climb to the highest sparkling peak.

Waves lapped the steps at the edge of a pool of dancing water. *People swim there.* She imagined it would take five men of Resham's stature to stretch the whole width and length. Two crystal ramps, like arms embracing the pool on either side, lead up to a platform wide enough for Resham to turn around on.

As they completed the circuit of that second wing, and approached the other side of the crystal palace, Leoshine walked on her tiptoes and peered around her companion.

The colour of ao Kevath's shirt appeared in parallel and perpendicular rectangles up and down the panels. Triangles and other geometric shapes intersected in the colours of the benches and lights.

Did he stop? Did he pretend to arrive at a logical destination? No. Gaze trained down, head thrust forward, he marched by.

Leoshine slowed her steps. *If I wait here by the pool, he'll come back. He'll get the blisters, not me. He'll waste the effort.*

She imagined his view from the far corner of the house, of her reflected in the crystal. *He sees me. He's not looking, but he sees.*

He might leave. She ran to catch up, breathless and straining to see into the shadows around the pillars. *"I would have to kill you,"* he had said when she didn't want to follow him to the stable.

He isn't finding his Master. She sighed and tramped behind, watching his fingers rub the carving on the box that contained the chain and book behind his back. *It's all for nothing.*

Worship

Thoughts of his afternoon trundled behind Avram as his stride measured the new-lain flagstones.

Should she carry the box? How strong is she? We have a long way to go. Her arms will tire.

I must speak to Iliana about exercise for her. The muscles she developed helping her mother, because even a mayor's wife performed household chores. Avram's mind wandered. *Didn't her father speak of her gathering greens? Even he wasn't impressed by her skill.*

The muscles she developed helping her mother would atrophy, his mind returned to his original thought. *How did Mother stay strong?*

Ao Kevad! His spirit reached out into his expression of worship. His heart wept with longing to duplicate the Master's House in Aeolia. Centuries of history graced those walls and pillars back home. Every man who had died in the good fight, every feast, every famine, every King and Queen, all immortalised by beautiful creations that filled the halls. As well, the stories from Ao Kevad's life and death and resurrection blazed from art work on windows, floor, and furniture.

Only time could make this monument all he wished for. Blank iron lace work awaited coloured glass to create windows of glory. One day, tapestries, banners and plaques would cover the bare stone walls. Paintings and sculptures would join the few bare wooden benches and the commemorative inscription by the door recalling the dedication of this house to the glory of his Lord and Master by—one side of Avram's mouth twisted—the first king of Myxolidia.

He caught his reflection with its wraith-like shadow in the crystal panels. Her eyes were wide in disbelief, maybe even scorn. He appreciated the simple gown Iliana had her in, but the hair … he shrugged.

It's not an empty wandering, he wanted to tell her. *Ao Kevad! I seek You! I make myself available to You! I claim this space for You! I claim these people for You!*

One day, he imagined prophesying to his little oracle, *your people will return to their ancestors' true worship.* They would love their High King and bring gifts to His house to show their loyalty and thanksgiving. That history waited to be made.

On the perimeter wall, he planned for imaginative murals to teach the illiterate. The outer wall and the inner sanctuary would be plainly visible to each other. Successive layers of subtle differences in art work and decoration, progressively plainer and simpler to entice their thoughts beyond themselves, would lead the worshiper into the center, into the Inestimable Presence.

Sighing footsteps. Leoshine returned him to the present. Did she walk on tip toes, that the sound was so small? The print of her foot fit into the space his own toes covered. Resham called her 'little person,' but she wasn't little in age. Or Spirit! She fought Resham!

Give her a sword! Set her among the boys training with his veterans, that would build her up!

No. She must be a symbol of peace. She must be strong, but in a restful, gracious manner.

Peace. Peace. Ao Kevad! I am supposed to come here in peace, to find peace …

Too much turmoil. The people. The Myxolidian gift of hovering between realities held strong these many days. They would gain margin for an old way, while grasping every advantage of a foreign idea. Reinvent and reforge, wiggle and winkle, meld tradition with edict to everyone's joy and benefit.

The trouble would come when someone decided for the masses, when a rival tipped the balance and convinced them to go his way. The Aeolian masters had studied the odds and thrust their man, their chosen son into the fray to defeat all rebellion.

The Aeolian chosen son halted between the front-most benches, directly before the pool. He heard the girl gasp.

Like a majestic bird of prey with its pinions stretched abroad, Resham lay prostrate on the stone floor, dressed in resplendent white robes—ceremonially washed like the body they clothed—dedicating himself anew to his priesthood.

The water lapped at the steps. The lights below the surface scribed patterns on the crystal walls.

Avram recalled the last time he had seen his priest wear the white under-tunic, the riotously colourful over-tunic, the white robe and white coat of his order. A few days before they departed Aeolia they had gathered in the old cathedral.

It was the first time anyone would lead worship in this house, thus he lay in holy paralysis. Resham's heart had made a long journey and needed cleansing and purification before he could lead others.

When he gained his feet, he stepped up and took hold of Avram's wrists. They stared at each other, asking the questions they were taught by their masters, testing the spirit for purity of devotion, dedication, force of purpose.

With a nod, Resham bowed his knee and lifted Avram's fingertips to his forehead.

The deep heart of Avram trembled, and he expected the same from Resham. There had been many firsts in the five months they had lived under the Myxolidian Dome. Mother's arrival and this dedication and first worship in this House hammered something down, made the transplant a little more permanent.

From the jeweled box, he brought forth the heavy gold collar and allowed the links to trickle over his fingers. *Now,* he decided, and motioned for the girl. She inched forward, primed, he hoped, by all those other boxes he had placed in her hands. This box, still containing the sacred book, weighed her hands even further.

With two hands, and a practiced eye, he arranged the worship collar around Resham's neck and laid it on his shoulders.

A blur of white appeared on the periphery. Iliana knelt to show her dedication to her Overlord, in robes identical to Resham's. They rose together.

She smiled, anointing her surroundings with approval. "Magnificent." Her exclamation reverberated intriguing music amid the columns. "Heralds have proclaimed to Aeolian and Myxolidian alike an invitation to worship! Our people are preparing with joy, and the Myxolidians … well, I suppose they mingle curiosity and suspicion."

Resham wrapped his arm around her shoulders. "Don't carry yourself too far, ao Kenan Mother."

She turned and melded into his embrace, snuggling her face under his chin. He had to stretch his neck to avoid being suffocated by her headdress. After a time, they turned together and disappeared behind the crystal altar.

Avram strolled to the square, low-backed chair brought from home. He dared not lift his gaze.

He called from his soul. *Ao Kevad!* Words defied him. Tears bathed the innermost well of his heart.

He heard the four doors scrape open and the first footfalls, soon smothered by murmurs and echoes.

Faces peeked from behind the pillars as the crowd of worshipers seeped to the benches. They had been warned not to speak as they entered.

Five months to achieve this. Avram exalted and praised the artisans and craftsmen before Ao Kevad. Five months of secrecy and the House still lacked windows and a roof, among other important accoutrements.

A thin melody, played on a solo reed instrument, snaked between the pillars, and he remembered the foundation of the worship house in Aeolia resounding with anthems. A muted scuffle reminded him of the little slave and he turned toward her. Her impossibly round eyes sought his. He nodded to the bench behind him and again, she impressed him by slipping onto it without a word. He wondered what she would do with the box.

She had so much to learn, and no one lived in Iliana's shadow long before the spirit of worship was kindled.

The noise of humanity swelled and began to hurt his ears. They disobeyed his stricture for silence. Myxolidian heads swiveled in every direction. Their voices babbled. He clasped his hands between his knees to prevent himself digging his fingernails into the chair arms. *Why can't they be like ...?* His spirit diffused as he glanced over the five rows of Aeolians to the right.

One by one, other reeds joined and enriched the melody with counter-themes and rhythms. A stringed instrument punctuated all with the last glittering highlights before a hidden Iliana opened her long, mellow, throbbing call and he looked to the base of the balcony arms. *Forget the Myxolidians for a time*, he scolded himself, *and bind the ceremony around the bloody wound.*

my wound?

The pit of Avram's stomach cramped at the whisper in his mind. *Ao Kevad! Here I am preparing to worship, and I'm caught in prejudice.*

A blaze of music lifted his gaze to where Resham and Iliana finally emerged, climbing on either side of the crystal altar to their positions on the highest and centremost point above the Crystal Pool.

Avram pressed himself deeply into his seat, settling his middle vertebrae into the carved knobs of the chair back and closing his eyes. His arms hung slack from his shoulders, his forearms along the arms of the chair.

Mournful and longing, in high Aeolian, Resham called and invited. Iliana's soprano split the air and hushed the audience. Her part wended back and forth in passionate acceptance and bitter rebellion to Resham's invitation.

The worship duet never failed to lift Avram into a sphere beyond. He knew his own rebellion, and the compelling call of the High King. At last, he believed Ao Kevad, that he had the strength to complete the mission of the todays until the next Worship Day.

The Aeolians in the crowd spontaneously rose to their feet and burst out with the performers in jubilant chorus. Avram heard voices catch like his. *As one! As one we lift our eyes and consider the One behind the whole endeavour, and all the work that has been done and still awaits us.*

He answered the compelling urge by stepping forward. He knelt at the lowest point of the rail, in front of the water. Singing from his deepest being, with his head tilted upward and his eyes closed, he lost all concept of time.

Where did the booming silence meet the dying reverberations? At what point did the spell of the music subside? Experienced worshipers waited for the Spirit to signal the time to move. The Myxolidians murmured and babbled, and eventually giving up the hope of seeing more spectacle, they shuffled home.

Iliana rushed down the ramp to embrace Avram. "Thank you, thank you, my son. This is a magnificent space to worship. You have done well." Her eyes urged him to accept the strength her praise offered. "We'll see you this evening! Come!" She wrapped her arm around Leoshine and hurried away.

Banquet

Leoshine stood, receiving the different sections of her party gown. Each sleeve came in six pieces, fastened separately, and that paled in comparison to the skirt. "Why does ao Kevath keep Resham's jeweled collar in the box with the book?"

Iliana threw back her head and laughed. "No, Avram is not a priest. Resham is not a king." She reached out to straighten a strap. "You know we are ruled by Ao Kevad, the High King. He is head of our government as well as our worship. High King and High Priest. He is perfect and easily fills the duties, but He knows that Avram and Resham are not. Therefore, He does not expect either one to fulfill both roles while representing Him. The little ceremony they go through is a reminder to them both."

"But why did Resham bow to ao Kevath? ao Kevath does not bow to Resham."

"Avram did bow, later. Didn't you see him?"

"But that wasn't to Resham." Leoshine twisted her eyebrows in puzzlement. That was the only part of her body she felt free to move.

"You could say Resham didn't bow to Avram. Didn't receive his collar from him." Iliana ran her hands from Leoshine's neck to her shoulders, smoothing her gown. "It bothers you, this bowing?"

Leoshine straightened as proudly as her encumbered position allowed. "It is a matter of life and death to us." She lifted her chin. "Even my father, the mayor doesn't expect his councillors to bow. The only time that happens …"

"They bow to Avram."

"They fear him, and don't know how to please him. But they don't mean it."

"Has Avram asked you to bow to him?"

Leoshine's eyes darted to the flowers on the mantle. "My father asked me to bow with him."

"Did you mean it?"

Leoshine blushed. Father told ao Kevath she had known no master. Obedience and bowing came from Father's gentleness. She never wondered at it.

"When …?" Aeolian failed Leoshine. "This afternoon. When we went …"

"Worship." Iliana supplied the Aeolian.

"You and Resham wore …" Leoshine scribed filigree in the air with her hands.

This time the Aeolian did not meet recognition. "Fancy clothes." Iliana tried Myxolidian.

"Yes. And ao Kevath wore … ordinary. And I just wore what I left the bath in."

"Avram wore that blouse at our farewell, his last worship in Aeolia." A low purr emanated from Iliana's chest. "You are right, we do make a distinction. And you are right to note the difference. When we go to worship, we are not trying to impress anyone. We cannot impress Ao Kevad. But tonight is a party! We will show each other who we are and how we feel about what we have done."

Iliana floated out of the room. When Leoshine moved to follow, a serving woman held her arm and indicated a cloth-draped chair in front of a wall covered in a mirror. The illusion of looking forward and seeing behind added to her confusion.

"Please sit, ao Kenan."

Leoshine placed her hand on her chest. More absurdities fought in her mind: sitting on a contraption she would call a chair, in a contraption they called fancy clothes, and being called 'my lady.' "I am not ao Kenan."

Iliana floated into the room. "What are you then, my dear?"

Rayoon followed and placed a large wooden box, painted with flowers and gold filigree, on the table. As she opened it for Iliana to study, Leoshine saw lights and sparkles dancing within.

Leoshine's lower lip drooped. "I am ao Kevath's slave."

Iliana gazed a long time at "ao Kevath's slave." Her one eye squinted closed. "And he will be pleased that you are so proud of it"—she lifted a small cloth bag from the box—"but you can't expect the girls to call you that." From the bag she dribbled gems into the palm of the serving woman. "Sit dear. Clara will put these in your hair." She diverted her attention to the box and waved her hand. "Rayoon."

Her personal maid stepped forward.

"Tell the girls to call her 'Tassanara.'"

"Yes, ao Kenan." Rayoon stepped back.

Leoshine's heart jumped. "My father used that word. To me."

Iliana looked up from the box. "Your father is a very clever man, but we can hardly suppose he knew it meant 'ao Kevath's slave.' Ao Kevad alone knew ao Kevath would have a slave!" She placed her hands on Leoshine's shoulders and guided her to the chair. With gentle force, she made her sit.

"And Resham uses it." Leoshine continued her interrupted thought. "Who are the girls?"

Clara danced around, re-touching Leoshine's sculpted hair, seeming everywhere at once. Iliana leaned back and studied the effect. Her face brightened at the mention of Resham.

"Ah!" She leaned forward with a stick. "You see! That confirms it. The girls? They are my Omaeuli. You will see them in my house, at the party serving, everywhere I am. Some who don't have families come to live with me, and when I asked who would like to come with me here, why, there were so many to choose from!"

Leoshine felt soft tickling on her face. "You could call me Omaeuli."

Iliana pulled in her chin and frowned. "It is not a title of address, darling! And you are singular, not plural. You don't hear me call them 'Omaeulenen'! Besides, men don't have Omaeuli. Isn't proper."

"You use their names. They could call me Leoshine."

"No, dear, you don't understand. In Aeolia we use titles of address. Ao Kevad, ao Kevath, ao Kenan, Tassanara."

"What is Resham?"

Iliana's eyebrows twitched together. The flesh under her chin shuddered. She finished tickling Leoshine's face and gave Rayoon the stick.

"You will hear him called ao Kevath by some. Now, you have a necklace and you have no place for earrings yet." She lifted Leoshine's fingers one by one.

"What is 'Earth'?"

Iliana looked up from the box and tilted her head at Leoshine's reflection. "You know that we are under the Myxolidian Dome."

"Aeok'n." Leoshine corrected.

"Exactly! How clever you are! You hear the similarity between Aeolian and Aeok'n. Your fathers' fathers and my fathers' fathers are the same."

There were other words about Domes creating Domes and Earth being the first Dome in a long line stretching across space, but Leoshine's mind stalled on the two phrases that her father and ao Kevath used. "Fathers' fathers" and "The Same."

Father believed ao Kevath. They worked together. How much "same" from their fathers' fathers did they expect to recreate?

"We speak different languages." Leoshine spoke aloud before she realised.

Iliana's hands hovered over the jewelry box. "Pardon, dear?"

"Myxolidia is not the same as Aeolia. We speak differently. We have different clothes and customs."

"Those evolved from the Schism, dear. Your people thought they could do it all on their own, without the community of the other Domes. They worked very hard to be different but they failed. Your Dome needs replenishing and there are practices that deeply displease Ao Kevad."

Leoshine clamped her unusually slippery lips together. She spoke the truth to Father. She didn't mind learning new ways. ao Kevath and his mother were fascinating and full of surprises.

She made a note to make a list of the good things in Myxolidia. Father would know, if only she could speak with him about it.

Iliana continued. "I learned your language and you are making marvelous progress learning mine. Myxolidia is unique in the chain of Domes and Avram and I feel greatly privileged to be here. We acknowledge our part in the Schism and must do as Ao Kevad wills to restore His Myxolidia. You, Beloved, are uniquely placed to help us. I know you will do your part beautifully.

"I don't think we'll try rings tonight. How do you feel? Are you ready for your debut? I can't wait to show you off to Heien! She's very busy with her little ones, such a sweet mother, but as soon as they are settled we'll have a bath with her. Rise up, now, and follow me."

From the top of a long, tunneled flight of stairs, Leoshine stared at the bottom. ao Kevath and Resham waited on either side of the door in the hovering silver ellipsoid vehicle that had brought Iliana under the Dome. Eight serving maids floated down the steps in their finery. Resham took each one's hand to balance her entry.

Down the stairs, Iliana floated in a fantastic gown of purple and silver. Each layer of cloth built up on the last, yet, by some trick of light, each was visible.

Leoshine heard both men exclaim and saw them embrace and touch Iliana's cheeks with theirs.

A tiny squeak sounded in Leoshine's throat. *They're staring at me. How do I ...?* She thought of managing all those steps in a box-like gown with a mind of its own. *If I turn one way, it goes the other. I can't feel the ground through these shoes!* Her eyes stared at the steps. Her blood turned to ice.

Iliana floated back up beside her. "I remember the first time I wore fancy dress. At least I had the example of other women before me. Would it help if they weren't watching?"

Leoshine's tight-clamped lips numbed.

"Avram!" Iliana called down. "Resham! I left something in the house. May I trouble you ...?"

Instantly, both men stood on the top step.

"I wrote a speech and just thought it would be nice to have the copy with me. Resham, could you look on the mantle and Avram in the desk?" She spoke gently to Leoshine as the two dashed to find the speech. "What obliging boys! Now let's get you down before they return. Steady now." She gathered up the skirt to expose her legs up to the knees. "Watch my feet. Roll up your gown so you can see your feet too. No, it isn't elegant, but it is safer for your first try. That's the way. There. That took no time at all. And here are the boys each with a copy. What a lot of speeches I shall have to make!"

Iliana grasped ao Kevath's hand and seemed to float into the vehicle like a pillow of smoke.

Leoshine took hold of Resham's hand and looked into his eyes. The muscles twitched in the corners of his mouth. Lights danced in his eyes, under drawn brows.

She swallowed hard and raised her foot. His strong hands fastened around her waist.

Leoshine collapsed into the nearest seat. She clenched her eyes, lips, and fists and held her breath as long as possible. Her stomach lurched.

Where are we going? This is normal, even pleasant to them.

ao Kevath, Iliana and Resham lounged and chatted on the journey. *They play a game. They know all the rules.*

She eased one eye open. Resham glanced in her direction and smiled to himself so smugly that Leoshine growled. He sat with his one leg crossed over the other, one arm draped over the back of the long, padded couch where Iliana perched. Her light, dappled flow of musical words filled the chamber, bounced off the walls, and tingled the nerves.

She is pleased. She likes parties and her son is behaving, or will behave, in a lordly manner.

ao Kevath glanced at her. A row of creases tormented the space between his eyebrows. He seemed puzzled, shifting in his seat, standing and pacing to one end, back, sitting down, twitching his cuffs. When he sat down, he resumed his stare.

She looked down. Somewhere beneath all those folds, her feet crushed against the walls of hard-sided shoes. Her eyes rolled and her tongue seemed to be swelling. She swallowed.

Leoshine reconsidered as ao Kevath paced past and the cushion exhaled as he sat down again. *He has the opportunity and trappings to behave as his mother designs.*

Down a long aisle of bowed heads, Leoshine followed Iliana. Her gown tugged and nudged her limbs and torso in all directions. By concentrating on her feet, imagining the floor through the stiffening and loosening of her shoes, she narrowed her fear, and arrived at a platform at the far end of the glittering room.

The aisle collapsed behind her. Everything seemed to convulse and undulate and her eyes ached in the swarm. Lights and sounds pummeled her senses.

"Like this, dear."

She heard Iliana repeat this phrase and arrived beside her patroness, viewing the throng from above.

A firm object touched behind her knees from within her dress. Her heart jumped. Omaeuli grabbed her elbows and upper arms and eased her backward into an unseen seat. A backrest rose out of the floor and clamped around her, supporting her arms and spine from the outside of her gown.

Iliana seemed to whisper from far away. "Specially designed for these dresses, but we only have two. Don't be afraid. Perfectly secure." She turned to ease herself into a similar seat, as the guests waited to greet her.

Leoshine wriggled and pressed her back into the cushions. Her eyes were at the same level as the standing crowd. *Otherwise, I would be buried in the flood of skirts and trampled under the boots of the men.*

The pageant of Aeolians paraded by, exchanging hand touches and pleasantries with Iliana. The giant general came past with his very small wife. At least that is how she appeared next to him. Iliana gushed Aeolian words as she brought her to touch hands with Leoshine, who blinked.

Beyond this, the scene throbbed and swelled in a blur. Gradually, Leoshine discerned that the mass flowed in concert. When a new guest entered, a man's voice called out and all heads turned. One half of the room or the other would advance, and she realised a difference in attire.

The Myxolidian women wore their beribboned hair in a solid braid down their backs. Leoshine immediately appreciated their logical and practical style.

When Aeolian guests arrived, their own kind would surge forward and gather them into their half of the party. Their women wore gowns and hair creations that looked like ao Kevath's new town architecture: shiny objects nestled in curls and swirls high on their heads. The men looked like their leader, clean-shaven in coats and boots.

An Aeolian face bent over her, shining with joy. "Leotjie!" The man stood on the platform holding Iliana's hand, which he released as he stepped nearer.

"Fa ...?" Leoshine gazed into the warm crinkled eyes that transported her back to her childhood.

"I wouldn't have recognised you either if the ao ..."

"Father! Your beard!" Leoshine reached out to him. Her heart bounded in its cage. Then she blushed and covered her chest.

Father rubbed his chin. His eyes slid out the sides of their sockets to glimpse Iliana. "Yes. It will grow back. It's just to welcome ao Kenan Iliana." His jacket, breeches, and boots might have come from ao Kevath's closet. None of the other Myxolidian men achieved such an imitation.

"ao Kenan Iliana brought this suit with her. They were made for me when I visited her court. She promised I would wear them again." He bowed from his waist with her fingers lined against his forefinger.

Leoshine pulled back her hand. Before she could protest his Aeolian manners, the party vanished. Against her face, almost up her nose, a familiar bosom suffocated her breath.

Mother's voice wailed in Leoshine's ear. "My baby! The last of my womb! Captive among the heathens!"

Leoshine pushed away and tried to rise. Off balance, and gripped by the arm rests, she gasped and whimpered.

"Woman!" Father scowled and caught Mother's shoulders. The next moment they were jostled off the platform.

Leoshine's mouth hung open.

"Don't cry, child!" Iliana exclaimed.

Leoshine felt cloth touching her face. She put out her hands to push Iliana away and tried to rise. A many-armed beast seemed to attack her. She grabbed two wrists, but the others continued to dab her face with pointed sticks.

"You just can't cry with paint on!" Iliana admonished. "Your mother didn't mean what she said. It was just the surprise of seeing you."

"Please!" Leoshine cried out. "I want to see them. Let me up!" She struggled against the chair and adamant hands.

Iliana grasped her wrist. "Out of the question, dear. We are having such a happy party. Isn't your father a fine gentleman? He is so proud of you."

A sharp pain like the point of a thorn pressed into Leoshine's wrist. She frowned and jerked away, but Iliana held on with a gleam in her eye.

Why is she hurting me? Leoshine felt the seat rising up to cradle her suddenly too heavy body. Iliana's face faded. *Where is Resham?* Leoshine blinked and the party vanished.

Failed Traps

For the forty-seventh time, Avram passed the cot where Leoshine lay flat on her back with her bloodless face peeping above the blanket.

He scowled, then skewered the door with a glance. Nothing moved there either.

Forty-eight, forty-nine. The pageant paraded across his mind.

Iliana had created a little piece of home for herself and reminded the Aeolians of what they had given up to join this mission. *When will she realize, we have to leave Aeolia behind?*

He glanced at the cot and answered himself. *When the Myxolidians come out of hiding.*

For now, the two peoples segregated themselves on opposite sides of the party, and only the generals mingled. *If only I could get them speaking to each other.*

My people speak Myxolidian, generally. He thought about his own struggles with their harsh consonants. Not one of the Myxolidian burghers had taken up his offer of Aeolian lessons. He kicked the corner of carpet that had flipped up at his last pass.

More than Iliana's ceremonial costuming of the girl had bothered him. While he had dragged Resham and ornamental sleeves and socks and boots behind him, dressing for the banquet, an empty place had hung in the room. *An ache? I won't chastise Iliana for her party. We're all clutching, trying to manufacture replacements for our losses. That's how we'll create a blend.*

The generals played their part, laughing and imbibing and crossing the room to invigorate conversation wherever it died, following their commander's cues according to their character. Kirim and Lantro wrapped their attention around the women, Alan and Dorim and Uly cultivated the men, and Gavin ... Avram stopped to smile.

Gavin had his wife, Heien, back. As a cousin to the royal family, she had come with Iliana, with all their brood, the first Aeolian children in Myxolidia. Gavin would be distracted for a while.

Avram twisted his hands behind his back and bent deeper into his stride. *I am further along than them.* He glanced again at the still face in the cot. *I missed something from my Myxolidian life.*

At first, the girl's terror had puzzled him; the shock and vitality of her wide eyes sucking clues to her situation from the rich tapestry, the sharp rise and fall as she breathed with her shoulders, the constant swallowing.

She had followed Iliana into the room, down the long aisle of leading citizens, without a squeak. She had fussed at the new apparatus and then sat blinking at the lights and colours, swallowing, and gasping tiny puffs of air through her nose.

Soon after the buffet opened, Resham, ever the servant, had brought her refreshment and clasped her wrist, measuring her pulse, ever the physician. He had arranged the table attached to her chair and encouraged her to drink. When he had placed himself at the bottom of the steps, at a discreet distance, the girl's breathing slowed. She leaned surreptitiously one way and another to peer around him.

The Myxolidians refused to eat. Even the beardless Curtstas, who knew his role and otherwise mixed with both peoples, never approached the sumptuous feast from Iliana's kitchen. His woman had trailed in his shadow.

A new aspect of the drama suddenly occurred to Avram. The woman had recognised the glittering confection on the dais as her daughter. She had hovered in the shadows while Resham sat at his station and had pushed Curtstas toward Leoshine the instant Resham disappeared.

Avram frowned. His step stalled by the door, listening for Resham's approach.

The soldier's quiet message, in the midst of the roaring party, had chilled his heart. "Wol, ao Kevath."

He had called Resham to hear the report. Wol had fallen into one of many traps set to grind him into the dirt.

That cursed murderer needed to die, immediately. His ragged band of rebels had tormented the Aeolian mission too long and prevented expansion in some key areas. Avram ground his feet deeper into the floor and dug his fingernails into his palms. Resham had slipped out to catch the mayor's son and when he next looked, Avram had been shocked by the profound change in the girl.

When Iliana had begged leave to take Leoshine away from the party to her palace, he remembered snapping at her.

"To my room! Remove the paint. And the gown. And never drug her again!"

He picked up a stylus from the table. It snapped between his fingers like a chicken bone. Iliana took her medical powers too far with that syringe ring. The scene Leoshine might have made when her parents ambushed her on the dais was no justification for using it.

"She is under Resham's medical authority. He knows her better than you, knows when she will make a disruption."

"Yes, ao Kevath." Iliana had bowed.

"Don't 'ao Kevath' me!" He had dismissed her with a sneer.

Drugged! Iliana had passed an edict that her son never fall under the influence of mind-numbing chemicals, yet she splattered them far and wide to the rest of his entourage. *I will pass a similar edict for Leoshine. She needs Resham to wake her. And I need Resham to catch her brother.*

Near dawn the sentry tapped to signal Resham's arrival. Avram spun round on his ever-pacing heel to face the opening door.

One glance at Resham's stooped shoulders told all.

Avram leaned on the table and roared. "You missed him?"

Resham's eyes darted to the cot. He squared his stance and looked up through hooded eyes.

"ao Kevath." Resham might as well have continued aloud. *I will not report until you are ready to hear.*

Avram's title shot fire through his veins and his palms flared. The rebuke was aimed at the man failing to live up to the responsibility of a multifaceted mission.

He picked up a vessel full of beverage intended for his breakfast and, with a loud snarl, hurled it past Resham's shoulder. As the liquid dripped down the wall, he turned and ground his steps again, around and around the table.

"How could you miss him? You said the trap was secure. The mission cannot proceed without you doing your part to secure our safety from his kind." He rounded on his servant and pushed his face into Resham's. "Is this too much?"

Resham's purr rumbled with menace. "Do you wish my resignation, ao Kevath?"

Avram snapped his teeth together and flung himself around the room. "You told us there would be no resistance. Now we have a sniveling upstart rebellion that gathers momentum every day. Especially when you make a fool of yourself trying to close traps on a vapour! We can't afford any failure at any time. Do I have to remind you?"

Resham closed and reopened his eyes very slowly.

Who's the fool?

Avram shut his mouth and paced the opposite way around the table. The girl had rolled over. The noise reached her dreams.

After pacing around the table fourteen times, Avram waved a hand in the air. "Report!"

Resham spoke in his usual, calm voice, though his eyes tilted downward at the outer corners. "He was in the town, ao Kevath. He attended the event that mirrored ao Kenan's fete as we anticipated. The ring of surveillance around the building was not breeched."

"Then how?"

"Decoys, ao Kevath. Or a disguise. Or the tunnels known to be under the key buildings of the town, though we scouted with our equipment and found none."

"Is he...?

Resham's tone dripped with scorn. "If he remained inside the town walls I would not be reporting, ao Kevath. I would be hunting."

"Why don't you follow him out?"

Resham's eyes narrowed. "Is this ao Kevath's command?"

"No." Avram strolled around the table to his seat. "Go to bed. Keep setting traps in town. When the generals assume their territory, we will expand the hunt into the wilderness. We are yet too insecure in the town."

He sank, loose-limbed, into his chair. "Go!" He tossed his hand. "I can feed myself. No, wait, check the girl. Iliana drugged her."

Resham's brow twitched as he bent over the girl. He lifted her eyelid. "She will wake normally, ao Kevath."

Avram nodded and picked up a morsel from the plate. "Why does she do that?" *Tell me something I'm missing.*

"Medicine to control behaviour is second nature to the ao Kenan Mother, ao Kevath."

Avram watched the memories of Iliana's behaviour control flash across Resham's eyes.

"I can't catch Wol, Brother." He dismissed his servant, and the memory. "That is your first duty."

"Yes, ao Kevath." Resham bowed. At the door he stooped, retrieved the dented vessel, and took it with him.

Morning Haze

Deep blue met Leoshine's opened eyes. Her head rested on something very soft that was made of this iridescent colour. She could not hear her sisters snoring. Men were calling to each other far away. *Father's Rellogat*, she concluded.

She turned in the blankets and stared with rounder eyes at the ceiling. How had it moved so far away? In her sleeping closet, she should be able to reach out a finger to touch it.

She sat up suddenly, an action that would have bumped her head in the old life.

ao Kevath's room! She glanced at the table. He slouched well down in the chair, with his brows furrowed ominously. His hand supported his head, and his finger rubbed at the tortured brow.

The lamp still burned, even though the light streamed through the six long windows.

Leoshine slipped out of bed, one eye wary to his reaction, and disappeared behind the dressing curtain. No food awaited her. Nothing to wear. She skipped to the closet where Resham had hung her wardrobe. *I can choose for myself!*

In the deepest corner, she reached to touch the dress she had worn into the woods, the dress she'd worn when she came to ao Kevath. Resham had mended the tears and washed the stains.

The remodeled dress Mother had sent with Father, shortly after she arrived in this room, snuggled against the other. She glanced at the curtain and chose a simple brown tunic to slip over her head.

She peeked around the curtain opening. He didn't look like he would move today. She approached the table, bobbing her head and screwing her hands together under her chin.

"I will fetch food, ao Kevath?" She lisped the Aeolian words.

He squinted his eyes but did not turn his head. She knew to wait. His mind arrived from far away or, like a traveling emperor, sent a viceroy to consider her request.

At the listless wave of his hand, she trotted off. They had had enough mornings like this. She knew what to do.

There was no tray of empty dishes for her to carry to the kitchen. *He didn't eat. What happened last night?*

She stopped at the window overlooking the Worship house. Shadowy dreams of a grand lady and a sparkling assembly of fanciful people hovered in the corners of her mind.

She ducked her head and scurried past the red, black, and silver-shelled figures that forever lined the porches and hallways. They never moved to block her or speak to her, though sometimes they spoke to each other. Their hands moved and they shifted on their feet.

She kept her head tucked down as she slipped into the kitchen. There seemed to be less smoke than usual in the blackened rafters. Pots and metal utensils hung over-head. The Aeolians had brought an army of cooks and tools. The cacophony and bustle of bodies always confused her. She was grateful that the counter, where she collected the tray, divided the small area by the door from the main food workshop.

She stopped and stared at a long braid that fell down the back of a woman who stood beside the stove that didn't work unless the pots were properly balanced. The woman's chin seemed to rest on her shoulder and her hand fluttered in her long skirt. Her thumb and little finger were extended. They drummed against her thigh.

She wards off a curse. She must be afraid of the Aeolians.

Leoshine looked closer. *Gorphiline!* Her hand rose to cover her chest.

"Gorphiline." She called and reached over the counter.

The woman's shoulders hunched and her hand drummed faster.

"Gorphiline! It's me, Leoshine."

An Aeolian rattled loose Myxolidian. "Move on now." He placed ao Kevath's tray on the counter, blocking Leoshine's view. "No talking."

Leoshine gaped at the man. *You don't understand. I know her. She is the first woman I've seen in*—she corrected herself—*the first Myxolidian woman.*

She stepped to the side and reached around the blocking sentry. "Why … I talk …?" Leoshine stuttered in Aeolian. "What harm … do?" She bit her tongue in frustration. "I know her." She raised her voice in Myxolidian. "I need to talk to her."

The Aeolian had turned away. Turning back, he spoke in a harsh tone. "Tray. Take ao Kevath his food."

Leoshine bobbed her head back and forth to see around him. *Where did Gorphiline go?*

The sentry scowled. "You need I call Resham?"

Leoshine shook her head and grasped the handles of the tray. She peered behind the bubbling pots and strained her ears above the crash of crockery in the sink.

The stove is working well; they must have brought her to fix it. At the door, Leoshine paused and looked back. In the shadows a small round face with wide unfriendly eyes popped out.

She's seen me.

The woman raised her hand and shook it at Leoshine, thumb and little finger extended.

The curse. Leoshine recognised the gesture. *She thinks I'm cursed.*

Leoshine stared at her reflection in the dish covers on the tray. Dark shadows ringed her eyes.

She thinks I'm cursed. Her feet shuffled forward, drawn by the familiar tether.

Half-way to ao Kevath's chamber, she rested the tray on a railing. Mother's words to the Oxikobh in the cave rang in her ears.

"A curse is a curse."

I am uninitiated. I sleep in ao Kevath's room. I don't wear the brace. How do I tell her they took it away?

A curse is a curse. If ao Kevath is cursed for taking me, I am cursed for being taken.

All strength drained from Leoshine's arms. She propped the tray with her body. Her knees wobbled.

A hand touched her shoulder. The dishes rattled as she jumped.

"Are you ill?" a faceless shell asked.

She stared at the shiny smooth covering.

"Take to ao Kevath?" the shell asked in Myxolidian, indicating the tray.

Leoshine handed the tray to the soldier and drew the first deep breath since she saw her compatriot. "Yes. You take." She turned to go back to the kitchen and talk to Gorphiline.

The shell walked forward, away from her.

Another hand grasped her shoulder. All her body turned to ice.

"Hurry on," a muffled voice commanded.

She turned and looked into her own eyes reflected in a black and silver face shield. At least it wasn't Resham. He wouldn't wait for her to recover. She set her jaw and clenched her fists. Gorphiline might not be in the kitchen the next time she fetched ao Kevath's tray.

The grip on her shoulder pushed her forward, toward ao Kevath's chamber. She had to move her feet to keep her balance. She arrived at ao Kevath's door as the shell carrying the tray handed it to the sentry.

Leoshine gestured to herself and reassumed the tray. Later, she would find Gorphiline. She just had to.

The sentry tapped and opened the door.

A bell struck somewhere outside. The Domelight had changed while Leoshine studied on her cot. The thin black reading board showed a number that meant the middle of the afternoon. She had discovered the divisions of time in one of the screens.

"Sing!"

Leoshine's heart imploded. Her skin flashed to ice.

ao Kevath had pushed away his work and leveled his burning, red-rimmed eyes on her. "Leoshine." He drawled her name, conjuring an essence of nobility and power she dared not own. One eyebrow lifted and his eye burned like a star outside the Dome. "Sing."

Leoshine stood from the cot and shuffled nearer the table. She slumped around herself and thought of her new clothes. She had seen him like this before, starved of sleep and companionship, fretting over his own nobility and power. Did he disown it as she did? Release came when he slept and had what Resham called "a meeting."

Resham had shown her how the board could make music and she had studied an Aeolian song for an occasion like this. She forced the notes from her throat as she maintained her gaze on the back of the grey box.

He exclaimed with a repressed energy. "Again!"

"The same …?"

He narrowed his eyes at her. "The same."

She understood. He never missed an opportunity to emphasize his dogma, *we are the same,* even when asking for an encore.

She tried to run the recording from the board through her head, to imitate it. Her body relaxed with the rhythm and cadence.

"Again!" ao Kevath slumped a little less and the smoldering tragedy in his eyes softened.

She filled her lungs and blew the air through her nose. *How many times will he ask for this song? Did I find his favourite on my first try?*

Her throat spasmed and her eyes wandered to the flagon of water kept ready for her master. Of course, he shared that with her as well.

After the last note, silence hung between them.

ao Kevath lifted his eyes as if listening behind him, one long finger pointed upward. "The men. They hear you."

A chill ran down into Leoshine's fingers. The voices outside had stilled.

"Thank you," ao Kevath rumbled, still wallowing in lassitude, but calmer. "I was sitting here not hearing my Master. He spoke in your singing."

Leoshine felt her eyes widening. Her mouth formed an 'o'. Her thoughts fled to the Worship house. "Where is your Master, ao Kevath?"

His lip curled. "Ask Iliana. She's the priestess."

With the name came a blazing recollection of the lady. The impossible clothes suddenly tugged again at Leoshine's mind, along with the flash and roar of the party.

Had Mother sent Gorphiline to the kitchen to meet me?

"Where is she?"

"In the house I built for her. You should be with her. She is going to teach you."

"Where is Resham?"

He would explain. *He must explain and take me to Father,* whose clean-shaven face danced before her.

She blinked, and fought off the feeling of Mother's caress, and the scent of her embrace.

"Out." ao Kevath replied as he reached for a small device, touched it lightly and spoke to it. "Resham."

A few moments passed before Resham's voice sounded among them. "ao Kevath?"

"You return tonight?"

"The quarry is hot, ao Kevath. I would remain."

A broad grin covered ao Kevath's face in a flash. His eyes sparkled with mischief. "Need help?"

"Not yet. I will bring him to you for the killing."

Leoshine frowned, pressed her lips together, and stepped backward.

ao Kevath cocked an eye at her. "Leoshine! Speak!"

Her mind shrieked correction at him. *Slaves don't speak. In my world slaves don't have minds to speak from.* She looked into his eyes. He was waiting, and would not speak again until she presented a plausible, relevant thought. She knew from past experience. "I do not like the killing, ao Kevath." Her chin lifted as the words left her mouth.

"You would nurture my enemy?" He thrust his face forward over the table. His eyes blazed with challenge. "Resham?"

"ao Kevath."

"When the time comes"—ao Kevath narrowed his eyes at her—"I will come to you for the killing."

Leoshine's face flushed. A weight unfathomed gripped her chest.

He enjoyed killing Georg. Wol, Father, Mother, Giffshine and Hillashine. He will kill them soon.

She squeezed the question from her constricting throat. "Where is Father?" Her shoulders straightened. *He wants my thought?* She defied his lunacy. *He can have it!* "Where is Mother? Why do you keep me from her? Why do you keep me here in this room when I could be with my sisters? I could learn normal household things that a normal girl learns." Sobs intruded among the words. "Instead of figures and symbols and ... and things." Her appeal reached a desperate pitch. "When are you going to let me go? You can't hold me here forever!"

Silence and a steady stare met her.

"I can't think past the end of today, Leoshine," ao Kevath drawled. "Leave forever to itself."

She shrieked out her tears, and ran, throwing herself onto the cot, sobbing into her pillow.

ao Kevath spoke and Leoshine stilled to hear. "I would have dealt with her family last night. If Iliana had not interfered."

Resham's disembodied voice responded. "Yes, ao Kevath."

"Would you have drugged her?"

Leoshine's heart suspended as she waited Resham's answer.

"I would not have exposed her to the threat, ao Kevath."

"The father made an effort, but the mother ..." ao Kevath paused.

Silence outlasted Leoshine's ability to hold her breath. The hot pillow stuck to her face as she stifled her sobs.

Father!

Looms

Iliana and her dazzling promise of woman company had evaporated. For the last three days, Leoshine had alternated between loneliness in the chamber and buoyant language lessons with ao Kevath. At any time, day or night, he demanded her attention and her tongue. Days of the week, colours, counting, he demanded that she repeat and repeat until fuzzy dots appeared before her eyes. He had read simple stories and shown her pictures on the board.

After the ceremony of standing behind his chair, ao Kevath sat down to devour the sticky, white and yellow mass.

He will eat it all. Leoshine's lower lip rose up. A nauseous hunger ate at her inside like a traitor.

At last he pushed the plate to sit in front of her. One small pile remained.

He will stare at me until I eat, she knew from experience. She picked up her fork and plunged it in. The sauce oozed up around the clean metal like pus from a festering wound. Her upper lip arched around her lower lip which was pressed far back against her teeth. She plunged her hands into her lap and closed one eye to hold back her bile.

ao Kevath reached for the grey box. "Cover it if you won't eat now. It's best hot. Rice. A new crop we'll grow when the rains come. And milk. Iliana brought a fresh supply. One day we'll have dairy cows."

Leoshine sighed with relief. With the plate covered the odour would subside.

She sat on her cot, unoccupied, forcing away memories of her family and how she lived before the Aeolians came, until ao Kevath dressed and left.

Immediately, she leapt to the table. She imagined herself gliding past the shelled figures in the dark, placing the tray on the counter quietly so none of the workers noticed. Then she saw herself ducking under the counter and sneaking up behind her servant. She would scream at the impudent woman like Mother did when the servants annoyed her.

I am not cursed.

She stood up, peeked at the congealed mass and hastily re-covered the plate. She tipped the flagon and sucked the red nectar to the last drop.

The dishes rattled as she passed through the chamber door. For a long moment, she felt her heartbeat in her chest. When she had worn the brace, she never felt that throb in her ears.

She forced her feet over the wooden floors.

In a dark space between buildings a voice hissed her name.

The tray seemed to develop wings to fly away.

"Don't look at me," the voice hissed.

That's Gorphiline. If I look at her she'll be cursed. Leoshine narrowed her eyes. *I'll also give you away to the Aeolians.* She glanced around the square ahead. "Where's Mother?"

"Wait." Gorphiline drew the word out. "Wait for Wol."

Wol. Leoshine's mouth went dry. Again, the tray seemed to writhe in her hands.

"What's he going to do?" She didn't want a man's help. She wanted the society of her own kind who had her best interests at heart. "I want to see Mother."

Silence. Leoshine stepped deeper into the shadows.

Nothing. No one. Gorphiline had vanished.

Leoshine shivered. In her mind she searched the compound. Gorphiline didn't matter if she could find her mother.

Sobs poked, piercing the walls of her throat. She glanced around the square. A door on the other side beckoned and she ran to get rid of the tray.

From behind pillars and in the shadows of doorways, she dashed in short spurts. The weave-shop door opened without a sigh and she slipped into the still, twilit room. Curtains covered the windows. Dust and lint stirred as she slunk in the shadows of the looms, sleeping like stallions against the far wall.

The tables lining the near wall were still covered with half-sewn garments and Mother's tools. Under each loom, a pile of cloth waited for the weaver to complete the yardage. Leoshine tunneled into the pile nearest the door and cocooned herself in the brownish red heap. Boiled onion skin mixed with the smell of the fibre.

I didn't want to lose my brace, she told the absent Gorphiline. *They took it from me. I would still be obeying Father and wearing it. I feel naked without it, like they can see the curse in me. They see right through me anyway. They see things I don't see. Was Father trying to hide the curse in me by making me wear it?*

I'm not cursed. Vicious sobs wracked her through and through. The mother-cloth she rubbed on her lower lip abraded her skin. At last, she succumbed to exhaustion.

She woke to footsteps padding away from her, down the line of looms. Her shoulders rose to meet her ears. Through the legs of the loom, she saw Aeolian boot toes returning toward her, turning, and at last stomping out the door.

Her sudden exhale stirred a cloud of dust. Her nose tickled.

The door opened again. Two Aeolians now paced back and forth. They chatted and laughed. They picked up Mother's tools and cleared off her tables into tubs. Leoshine crouched in the yardage to watch them.

What are they doing? The room looked like no one had touched it since ao Kevath arrived. *Why are they here today?*

Two more Aeolians entered. The group stood for a long time around the second last loom at the far end of the room. Their voices echoed and boomed. Leoshine rubbed her nose, and breathed through the cloth to keep from sneezing.

Two more Aeolians entered.

"You know the workings?"

Myxolidian, Leoshine perked her ears to hear her own language.

A diminutive figure nodded. Leoshine could not see who it was. *One of Mother's weavers,* she reasoned. A sudden clattering noise broke off the chatter of the group. Pins and needles danced from Leoshine's skull to the tips of her fingers. She wiggled to place her feet under her. From under the folds she saw four Aeolians at the corners of the loom. They twisted and yanked at it. One corner after another lifted, and slammed back down. She felt the floor boards jump beneath her.

"Break it down!" yelled one of the Aeolians.

"What will you do with the cloth?" the Myxolidian asked.

The Aeolian yanked a bolt from under the loom. "Burn it. No use to us."

Leoshine's mouth tasted ashes. *Burn Mother's cloth?*

Her body unbent. The folds of the cloth dribbled off her shoulders.

In that instant a hand closed over her shoulder. She looked up. Resham.

The world went black for a moment. She swayed against his grip. When she twisted, he held tight.

"No," she breathed.

Resham placed a steaming cup in her limp hands. "I thought you'd be thirsty."

She stuttered and stared at the liquid. "For sleep?"

"No. You'll walk out of here."

She stared at her fingers agitating against each other around the cup.

Resham motioned to the Aeolians, who walked out the door without a word. Leoshine never saw the weaver servant leave.

Resham softened his broad grin. "Did you like my little game?"

"Game?" Leoshine mouthed.

"Your mother has a new home. She asked for her looms, and I was going to send them to her. When word came that you were hiding in here, I pretended we were going to destroy them."

"You knew? You expected me ..."

Resham cupped her chin in his palm. "You would give your life to save them." He stared into her eyes.

She felt reality slipping. Vast worlds opened, very like what happened when ao Kevath looked into her eyes. *Is it a magic they have?*

"Where were you going, Sassnigor?" Resham crooned a snatch of an Aeolian sounding tun e, though the mocking name was Myxolidian.

Leoshine snapped her brows together and broke his spell. "To my mother."

"How were you going to find her? You know there is nowhere under the Dome you can hide from me."

"I want to go to Mother."

"Yes." Resham's mouth twisted up on one side, and his brows lowered. "Maybe I should."

Leoshine leaned forward. "Should take me to her."

"Drink." He touched the bottom of the cup. "Your mother"—he drew a breath and glanced around the room—"Your mother was using the looms to get into ao Kevath's headquarters. She wants to see …"

Leoshine's eyes brightened.

"Whether you bear ao Kevath's child." Resham's tone was grim. "You know what she wants to do with such a child, Tassanara?"

"No." Leoshine drew her shoulders up. Her jaw clenched.

Resham smoothed her hair down to her shoulders where his hands remained. "She is of two minds. Shows your father's influence. But the Myxolidian will win out." Resham's voice dropped. "It would be a blood sacrifice."

Leoshine felt the world fade again. *She has cursed me. She believes that ao Kevath has taken me. Without the initiation. Because I'm exposed.*

"I bear no child."

"Neither did Giffshine, ao Tassanara."

Leoshine's mouth opened and closed. Her eyes saw ao Kevath's wide, innocent grin. "He has not …"

Resham took the cup that she did not remember emptying. "Nor will he. But you will never convince your mother of that."

"I'm not old enough."

His eyes radiated pity and mocking. "ao Kevath came to free you from that lie."

Her mouth snapped closed and she twisted from his hold.

"Come. ao Kevath thinks you are with the ao Kenan Iliana and"—he pressed his face in her direction—"you will keep him thinking you were there all day."

"Why?"

Resham spat a laugh and motioned for her to follow. "There are things he doesn't need to think about."

Me. Leoshine answered herself. *ao Kevath does not need to think about his slave.* Her lower lip pushed up. *Who can't even run away.*

She thought of Resham's words, *'nowhere under the Dome'.*

And Mother's curse.

"Resham!" ao Kevath leapt from his chair at the table as they entered the chamber. "Leoshine! What are the days of the week? Show Resham how clever you are."

Leoshine shuffled toward her cot.

"Sunday." Resham prompted with his head in the cupboard. He peeped round the open door to prod her when she remained silent.

"Sunday, Monday …"

"Now the months." ao Kevath prompted when she finished. "Now count. Now the colours."

This isn't happening. Her lips moved. The correct syllables floated forth.

"Isn't she clever?" ao Kevath asked Resham. "What is the fitting reward?"

"Life." Resham raised his eyebrows at Leoshine.

Her head flooded. Her face burned.

"With you, ao Kevath." Resham bowed to his master.

Leoshine stared. ao Kevath's ears had turned red.

Giffshine's Visit

A cold bony hand covered Leoshine's mouth in the dark.

"Leo." A tall dark figure whispered over her bed. "Leotjie, wake up softly. Don't be afraid. It's me, Giffshine."

Leoshine's body stiffened and broke into a cold sweat. Just steps away in the canopy bed ao Kevath might be sleeping. What was she thinking? He never slept. If he was there, he was wide awake and ready to kill them all.

The hand released her. The next instant Leoshine leapt into her sister's arms, clinging, burying her face in her neck.

The back of Giffshine's fingers stroked the tears away. "Leo, Leotjie, don't cry. You are safe, I am safe. We are all safe. But listen. I can't stay long."

"But how did you …?" Leoshine looked at the canopy bed. The curtains were open. The blankets lay unrumpled. She snuggled her shoulder deeper into Giffshine's side.

"I got in easily. The window isn't high as long as you have a step up." Giffshine giggled and covered her mouth. "See this little bird's egg? Isn't it precious?" She tipped the tiny egg into Leoshine's palm.

"How is Mother?" Leoshine drew away. "How is Hillashine? Does Resham come to look after you? Does he give you everything you need?"

"Mother is so anxious for you, she wishes so much to see you. She has been offered a great honour in the new regime, but we don't want her to take it. Sometimes we see her getting soft and wanting things she shouldn't have."

Leoshine opened her mouth.

Giffshine placed her finger on her lips. She placed her other hand's thumb between Leoshine's eyes, and drew it down the bridge of her nose. "Is Resham that creepy catlike creature? He is so high and mighty with us. I hate him. He comes to see Hillashine, but I don't want him near her. Oh, Leotjie, she is still so pale and weak, and does not move from her bed. She is anxious for her man. No one can find him. But I must go. I'll scramble up the wall, no problem."

"No, wait." Leoshine clutched at Giffshine's sleeve. "I saw Gorphiline. She made the sign at me." Leoshine imitated the gesture.

Giffshine bared her teeth. "Gorphiline. That witch. I'll deal with her. Wait for Wol, my ephitide. Wait for your big brother. Don't talk to her. You know the problems she caused Mother when she stole the hatchlings. Don't talk to her. Wait for Wol."

"What will Wol do?"

Giffshine jumped. "I hear a noise." She scurried up the wall.

Leoshine's mouth dropped open as her sister wriggled through the narrow window. "Not much space, but if I can do it, you can too. Not yet though. Wait, and be a good girl. Father wants you to be a good girl." Her instructions came down in short gasps. "I'll come again … Don't tell anyone … Be a good girl."

Leoshine stared at the blank wall. When she drew breath, it seemed like the first, ever.

She looked down at the egg. Without it, she would not have believed the last few moments.

Everyone safe. Giffshine in ao Kevath's hideout. Hillashine's man. The call to return to her family.

She raised her eyes. The memory of Giffshine's embrace still felt warm on her back. *He doesn't take me*, her heart called to the window. *I don't sleep in his bed.* She glanced at the empty canopy. *He doesn't sleep in his bed.*

Is Hillashine's man with Wol? Do they think I am so isolated that I don't know he steals from the Aeolians and leads the Oxikohb to burn the new buildings?

ao Kevath. Her eyes pulsed almost beyond their sockets. *ao Kevath must not know.* She plucked the sheet back and tunneled into her mattress to hide the egg.

Before the light strengthened through the windows, Resham came with the tray and ordered her to dress behind the curtain.

She moved like a device that obeyed his command, without thought.

"Come out, Tassanara!" Resham sounded annoyed. He burst in behind the curtain to check her progress. "You didn't eat." He picked up her plate and marched to the big round table, where he slapped the meal down. "Eat here. ao Kevath won't be in until later."

Leoshine stood by the huge carved chair, while Resham bustled about his duties. She knew he observed her paralysis and wondered why he did not rebuke her for being inattentive. After a while, she wandered to her cot, and sank onto its edge.

ao Kevath came in with an arguing horde that didn't leave until nightfall.

Leoshine sighed. When she denied to herself that Giffshine had ever been there, she would catch thought of the egg hidden in the bedding.

ao Kevath sat at the table in the warm glow of his lamp. She saw him look up. His lips moved and she knew he called her name but distracting thoughts clouded her hearing. And froze her limbs from moving.

He glanced at Resham. They murmured together.

Resham stomped over and grasped her head in his one hand. Her face tilted up and she blinked and swallowed.

"She'll live, ao Kevath."

Resham stayed in the room that night while Leoshine lay with her face to the wall. He dozed in the chair and nothing stirred until the darkest hour.

"Leoshine." Resham purred in deep velvet tones. "Leoshine, Wol wants you. Even at this moment I fear his hand reaches out of the darkness to draw you to him."

The sheets rustled as she sat up. She saw his form brace in the shadows.

He continued. "Only you and I keep watch for the trouble that comes in the night. You have been ill today. I fear it is the sickness of Wol's hand." He paused. "Will you be a pawn in his hand?"

"You lie," Leoshine hissed.

"You are brave. You are learning so much here. Your master has come to depend on you. You won't take away the pleasant times he has in teaching you. You will stay."

"I have to stay! I'm a ... a slave."

"You will stay because you know it is right. Wol has plans for you. The plans your true lord and master has for you are greater."

Her hands shook. She buried them beneath her thighs.

Resham rose and departed without another sound.

The Egg

"See the shape, dear? This makes the 'zz' sound."

Leoshine heard Aeolian words from an Aeolian matron who sat beside her at the Aeolian table in the Aeolian drawing room that replicated the distant world, where everyone scrawled symbols that made sounds on lighted boards, sounds of their slippery, fat-tongued language.

Leoshine did not see an Aeolian sound. The row of shapes forming under Iliana's gifted stylus brought Giffshine's egg gift too dangerously to mind.

"Leoshine?"

Her tutor had been repeating the same phrase until, at her name, Leoshine looked up. Not a syllable of reply formed in her mind.

Iliana placed her hand over her student's icy fingers. "What's the matter, dear? Poor sweet! I understand. You don't cry with those two burly men, but here"—Iliana placed her arm around Leoshine's shoulders and folded a scented square of lace into a tear catcher—"here, we can be women."

Leoshine felt her head pressed toward the padded shoulder of her comfortress. Side by side was not an acceptable position for weeping. Mother would have faced her and held her head between her palms.

Mother. Hillashine. Giffshine.

Her body trembled. What would this alien know of Myxolidian birds?

It's just an egg. What if I tell her? Will she tell ao Kevath? What difference would an egg make to him? Resham would recognise the bird. A shiver ran over her neck and across her shoulders.

"I am lonely." She admitted in Myxolidian.

Iliana replied in the same. "Of course you are, Babim."

"The ..." Leoshine touched the tablet to indicate the symbol. "Reminds me of ... times." She paused, fabricating a scene innocent enough to pass beneath ao Kevath or Resham's notice. "My sisters and mother and I ... and Mother's sisters and their daughters in the garden. We collected birds' eggs to eat. Mother kept fowl, and other birds came to nest in the vines. We would compete to climb the vines and collect the eggs and I was the smallest and could climb the highest."

Iliana lighted the screen and Leoshine began tracing the shapes.

"I can see." The tutor agreed. "A sweet memory."

"I kept one in secret. I kept it a long time. I didn't know what kind of bird made it."

At Iliana's touch, the screen displayed true life pictures of eggs. "Do you see it here?"

Leoshine scanned them quickly. "No, I don't see it."

Iliana commanded with the tip of her finger, and a new slate of candidates flourished before Leoshine's astounded eyes.

Including a perfect image of her treasure.

She pointed to the specimen next to hers. "Is this one very small?"

"Not really." Iliana considered. "This one is smaller." She pointed to the correct egg.

Iliana smiled and conjured the image of the bird. "This is from a Gallalla, very rare where I come from. Do you have them here? They are very tiny, not too colourful, but their heads have a broad black stripe down the middle. You would have to be very clever to get this, because they are so careful to hide their nests, and then they defend it so fiercely for all that they are so small. Now the one you pointed to ..."

Wol! Leoshine's heart sank into the floor and rose to her throat at the same time. Only Wol would be clever enough to know the bird's habits and steal an egg.

He sent it as a message—a gift with a message that he remembers me. If he can steal an egg from a nest, he can lift me from captivity.

Her gaze darted out the window to the green trees in the distance. *Where is he?* All her hair stood on end. Her mysterious brother, unreliable and confident, arrogant and charming.

Where is he? Close? Near enough to know her condition. She gasped a tiny expiring breath. *Near enough to be in contact with Giffshine! He gave her the egg. She lied about its origin.*

Iliana went over to the window and peered out. "What do you see dear?"

Leoshine tightly pursed her lips, looked up, blushed, and looked down again. What could she say? Her fingers tangled in the necklace at her throat.

Iliana's eyes burned into her, as if they knew her every thought.

The room shrank again. Iliana brought her chair beside Leoshine, and sat down. She reached out to grasp her hands and caress them.

Iliana's eyes flickered to the ornament. "That was mine once, you know. I see you have learned to love some things I love." Iliana rose and tugged Leoshine's trembling hand. "Come into my room. I want to show you …" Her voice trailed off as she entered the next room.

Leoshine's feet dragged in the carpet.

A yellow and white pattern swirled over the walls in the room they entered. Yellow cushions graced white sofas and padded chairs. Dark wooden furniture lined the walls. The Domelight streamed through a large window, curtained with billowy material.

Iliana seated Leoshine on a sofa and went to a cupboard. She returned with the box, painted with gold filigree and flowers, that Leoshine recognised from the preparations for the banquet. She sat close and opened the box to display her treasure. Leoshine's fingers trembled as Iliana laid glorious gold chains and jeweled bracelets, sparkling diamonds and faceted rubies in her hands.

"This is just a sample, things I couldn't do without. I have more at home. Do you like them?"

Leoshine blinked and swallowed. Iliana clasped necklaces and bracelets, placed rings on her, and leaned back to admire her work.

Leoshine lifted the hem of her gown and laid a richly jeweled pendant beside its corresponding symbol. "What does this mean?"

"Aren't you a clever girl to pick it out! Have you seen it elsewhere?"

"Everywhere." *In the book in the box. On the chain that ao Kevath lays on Resham's shoulders. In the jewel that they wear to clasp their jackets.*

"Ao Kevad died on this tree," Iliana explained. "Eons before our time. A cruel death, painful. But He loves us so much. He knows you, Leoshine, and He loves you. He wanted to do whatever was necessary to draw you close. And He knew He would live again soon after. No, we don't understand either, but one day you will stand in His presence, and He will explain everything."

"How can He? I ..." Leoshine's voice dropped. "I don't understand."

Iliana reached out and drew Leoshine's body to lie against her own. "He loves you, dear. He knows you, and He sees your tears."

Leoshine wrapped her arms around herself. *This is wrong.* Her knees drew up toward her chest.

"Shhh, dear. You don't need to explain. But will you remember that Ao Kevad loves you, and wants the best for you?"

Leoshine lurched for the door. *All wrong! Wrong!* Chains and jewels splashed across the floor.

At the same moment ao Kevath and Resham burst through the door in full armour with ruffled hair and dirt-smeared cheeks.

ao Kevath scoured the room. "We received your message, Mother. You have her here?"

Leoshine choked on her bile. *What message? What do they know?*

Resham's fingers dug deep into her shoulder and collar bones. "What's the meaning of this?" He blurted in Myxolidian. "Where are you going?"

Leoshine thrust her shoulders back and twisted free. *Hide.* Her heart screamed. *Keep the secret.*

Iliana's face and hands replaced Resham's. She smiled with a gleam. "I'm sorry I worried you. Really, we have been having a lovely morning. I didn't think you would respond in person, and so suddenly."

I've seen that look before, Leoshine searched her memory. *When she made me forget Father and Mother at the banquet.* Black patches appeared in her vision. *I must go back to ao Kevath's room. I must wait for Wol.*

ao Kevath bowed and spoke formal Aeolian. Leoshine strained to understand the last sentence.

"Come, Resham, bring the girl. Yes, Mother, it is necessary. The battle draws ever nearer."

In the evening, Resham dropped to his knees at Iliana's feet. For a moment, he held her hand to his forehead, and breathed her scent deep into his soul.

She settled like an owl into her wing-backed perch. Her fingers massaged his scalp and rubbed his ears until his thought drained to a puddle.

Iliana turned her hand over to indicate a chair opposite her own. "What would I do without my boy?" With Resham seated, she continued. "She'd hardly crossed the threshold when I knew trouble brewed. I wanted your insight and look what I caused."

Resham sank into the cushions. "We are delighted to come whenever you call, ao Kenan Mother. It is our privilege to serve you. Something has happened." He tossed his hand. "You've seen how stubborn and proud she is."

Iliana smiled and looked through her lashes at him. "I have known the same in others."

Resham returned her smile. "I continually marvel at your patience, ao Kenan. How did you manage me?"

"Very differently from the way I have to manage Leoshine." Iliana sighed. "I was trying to explain Ao Kevad and His grace this morning. With Avram it was easy, Ao Kevad was in the house continually for my poor fatherless boy to imitate and love. You had only to see His face to recognise your place at His feet. But the girl"—Iliana traced a design on her knee—"I am learning how to make Ao Kevad known without all the pictures and books, and the example of others. His presence is here, so close. How can He be so hidden to her?"

Resham's lips curled, and his eyes grew soft. He reached out and draped her fingers over his palm. "You learn new ways, ao Kenan?"

"She has an egg, Resham." She squeezed his forefinger and released it. "A Gallalla egg. When I talked about it, her agitation multiplied. Something outside the window frightened her, and I didn't want to pursue it without knowing your side of the tale."

Resham burst from his seat to pace the room. An egg! Small enough to hide, significant enough to change her whole aspect.

Heat pressed on his face. "Thank you, ao Kenan." Once more, Resham knelt with Iliana's hand to his forehead. "I go now, by your leave. I must know."

"Go in peace." She touched her fore finger to her lips and nodded.

Resham moved a device laterally over Leoshine's mattress and blankets.

He removed the covers, shook them out, scanned them separately, and discarded them. He set his teeth and scanned the bare mattress. The device hovered over the farthest corner. His mouth twisted and his eyes gleamed.

He rifled with his fingers, until they found a small hole. Inside, buried into the stuffing, nestled deep, he touched something hard. Delicately he tickled the Gallalla egg out.

Resham placed the egg in a small box of another device, and inserted it into a c-shaped cavity. A green light flickered over the mottled surface. A row of numbers appeared in the display. He compared those numbers with a table. Clearly Leoshine handled the egg frequently.

A yellow light caressed the egg's shell and a new row of numbers displayed themselves. Giffshine, the messenger. Resham's smile grew malicious.

Lastly, he ran an invisible scan to detect the minutest particles. Wol's reading matched exactly.

He carefully replaced the egg in its nest and rearranged the stuffing to appear undisturbed. After a glance at the heap of bed clothes on the floor, he decided to change them and be present when Leoshine entered the room. From a spacious cupboard came fresh linens.

"Good evening, ao Kevath." He greeted his master when Avram brought Leoshine in from his mother's house.

A tiny movement of Leoshine's lips betrayed her. Otherwise, she gave no outward sign that she suspected her treasure had been disturbed. A warmth encouraged itself in Resham's soul toward such circumspect control. What a mighty tide of turmoil there must be in her mind when they *could* see her distress.

Ambush

From her cot, Leoshine strained to sift the Aeolian words of one of the generals coming from the speaking box.

"ao Kevath, that will require a whole cohort. Wol's taken all our guard posts between the Gorge and that village."

ao Kevath sat straight in his chair. He tapped a staccato message with a stylus on the table. "A show of force, Alan. Give them a look at us. You come too."

The general continued. "Ambush, setting fire to machinery, stolen food aid …"

"Road crews disrupted, building delayed for lack of material." ao Kevath half crossed his eyes. "His power grows unwieldy. Time we trimmed it."

"Yes, ao Kevath."

A hammer pounded in Leoshine's head. *He knows. He knows.* Each time she dozed, she woke with a jolt.

He can't know, countered a sharp pain in her temple. *You would be dead, you would be dead.*

Her jaw ached. Her teeth ached. Her tongue adhered to the roof of her parched mouth. *Wol. He makes more trouble for ao Kevath than he did for Father. Where is Father? Why doesn't he stop him?* Father never stopped Wol from anything.

Not long after ao Kevath turned out the light, he lay down on his bed. The new door at the back of the room eased its hinges. A blacker bulk glided across Leoshine's vision. Footsteps sighed past in the carpet.

She sank far down into her pillow and peeped over the blanket. *He can see in the dark.*

ao Kevath grumbled. "Use the light."

Resham's shape emerged, lit from behind by a warm glow. "Yes, ao Kevath. I did not mean …"

"You do anyway." ao Kevath snapped.

Resham opened a cupboard and rummaged, hidden from Leoshine's view by the doors. He carried something behind the screen.

Setting out my food, Leoshine thought. *Setting out the clothes for the day. Soon he will wake me.*

He knows. He knows. The hammer resounded with the heavier beating of her heart.

I would be dead. I would be dead. The pain throbbed, and she closed her eyes.

The next moment a giant hand gripped her shoulder. She screamed, and her jaw was hastily clamped shut by a fleshy finger.

"Peace, child," Resham murmured. "Time to rise, greet the day." He leaned his face close to hers and examined her with a crease between his eyes.

She wondered at the absence of rancour. *Maybe he doesn't know. If I could pretend that nothing happened, he might never know.*

She imagined her hand slipping into the hidden nest and her fingertip touching the hard egg. *If I even look in that direction he will know.* She gained her feet and disappeared behind the curtain.

A cup of steaming soup awaited her on the table, behind the screen, not the usual paste and fruit. She picked up a blouse of satin from the chair. Blue, green, and yellow flaps decorated the long, full-pleated sleeves and chest-crossing supports. The leggings were plain blue, but the drape for her legs copied the colours of the blouse.

In the other part of the room, she heard ao Kevath pacing as Resham dressed him. Neither spoke. Once ao Kevath made a deep noise in his throat.

She sipped and the hot liquid warmed her warring emptiness. Half of her demanded and devoured the nourishment, the other half rioted and rejected the invading substance. She put the cup down and squeezed into the new clothes. Usually ao Kevath wore the colours and flaps. *What else will they change today?*

She sat on the small, hard chair, wrapped her arms around her shins, and rested her chin on her knees, awaiting the summons.

Resham broke the silence. "Your sword, ao Kevath."

"I didn't take it before."

He lies. He cut the tether when I fell off my horse.

"Strap it to the saddle." She heard him slap his hand over the metal scabbard. The buckles jingled. The door opened, and his boots stomped out.

Resham heaved a weary breath. "Your girl, ao Kevath."

Leoshine half rose, expecting the call. ao Kevath's stomping receded down the hallway.

She sat back on the chair, her hands limp in her lap. Her mouth snapped closed as Resham parted the curtain.

He held out a pair of high boots. "Put these on."

She looked up to search his face. "He doesn't want me."

Resham was already busy at the cupboard.

She slid her feet into the boots. She wished she had the courage to speak. In her mind she saw ao Kevath and Wol fighting. *ao Kevath would die.* She felt chilled. *ao Kevath would kill Wol.* This was worse than the dilemma of betraying her master if she kept silent about the egg or betraying her family if she told him.

Resham stepped forward and examined the cup. He turned to examine her, one brow raised, and the other crushing the eye under it. "What are you afraid of?"

Immediately Leoshine straightened and clenched her fists beside her legs. She looked up again and met his all-knowing eye.

"March!" He drove her out of the room all the way to the landing.

A hot, gluey mass of air assaulted her face. Her lungs struggled to inflate against an unseen force and her hair hung limp on her forehead. She looked up at the Dome. A film seemed to obscure the ceiling of her world. A deep, soft vagueness replaced the usual pale grey.

Soldiers lined the steps like statues. Armoured shell figures sat on horses up and down the street. Headdresses and covering blankets danced and waved at Leoshine. Flags awaited the motion of the riders to unfurl.

ao Kevath laughed and adjusted his seat on Paulos.

He wears a costume as ridiculous as mine.

His piebald outer cape matched her leg drape. Superfluous flags of satin peeped from his sleeves and knees, under the cloak. The last thing she saw, before Resham propelled her toward her mare, was the bright metal scabbard buckled to the saddle, within reach of his right hand.

Resham lifted her into the saddle. She twisted and scowled. *I don't need you. I can get on the horse by myself.* The Tesheddar fell like a veil over her saddle.

She whispered to the top of Resham's head. "What's the matter with the Dome?"

His gaze snapped up. "Questions, Tassanara?" The all-knowing glint pierced her again.

He knows, the hammer renewed its chant as her face flushed. *My questions have been missing like my eating and he notices.* She suddenly realised that he wore his tunic and blouse without the coat, and his sandals built of Aeolian material on an Oxikobh design, not riding boots.

Resham glanced sideways at ao Kevath, up to the Dome, and back to his hands. "Rasset, playing. Making rain."

He's not coming. The hair on the back of her neck stood on end. "What is rain?"

She remembered ao Kevath using the word at the meal of sticky white grains.

"Water falling from the Dome." Resham patted her mare's neck and moved away. "Aeok'n is sick. Needs a washing. Rasset sends the water to scrub the sickness away."

He seemed to study her a moment and she met his stare with a pleading message.

Wol won't attack if you are with us.

Another part of her mind hated herself for wanting him. ao Kevath had scoffed at the general who thought all these soldiers were not enough. As if one more man would change Wol's mind. She watched Resham climb the steps and wondered that he did not confer with ao Kevath.

She put her hand over her eyes and rubbed her forehead. *Wol won't attack if he sees Resham, the fierce and nasty, uncompromising and vicious. Why did he call the Dome by the Myxolidian fable name? He knows I understand about the engines.*

And he knows. He knows.

You would be dead.

The next moment, she lurched forward. The clatter of many hooves rang off the high stone wall of the Worship house. Cheers rang out between the buildings.

Leoshine's knuckles turned white, gripping the upper leg hook. She squinted her eyes and flinched as the gate flashed overhead. The air burned her lungs. When she drew it through her mouth, she tasted murky, clinging, fatty soot like the servants scraped off Mother's stove.

Leoshine glanced quickly from right to left. The empty space between town and Oxikobh territory was crowded with tents and cook fires. People in Aeolian clothes waved flags and banners and sang songs as their leader passed along the paved road.

"ao Kevath, the road is unpassable." The long-nosed, pole-limbed general met the cavalcade a short ride into the forest. "Gravel on tar. They're spreading it now."

"Tell them I have come to inspect." ao Kevath dismounted, and motioned everyone else to stay up.

Leoshine watched him dash over ditches and heaps of crushed rock. Men in jump suits pushed hand tools over smoking ground. She curled her nose at the stench. A giant box, twice ao Kevath's height, roared and hissed behind them.

ao Kevath grabbed a shovel and made an imprint of his initials in the road surface. By the time he remounted, the general had disappeared.

Leoshine rubbed her eyes. The constant rippling of the leaves created confusing angles, patterns, and shapes in the forest.

A new costume, broth instead of porridge, the sword, ao Kevath and Resham not speaking. What does it mean? What of the soft notes in Resham's speaking?

Shouts ahead! She straightened in her seat. They rode up to a wagon surrounded by fresh vegetables. The general shouted at soldiers, who were flinging leafy heads of cabbage back into the cart.

"Not your usual diversion!" ao Kevath teased them.

The general reined in beside ao Kevath. "This is not an accident."

"Most entertaining, Alan." ao Kevath laughed. "What is your next surprise?" He called out to the wagon owner. "Did you grow all these?"

The answer had to be translated. No, he collected them from the Oxikobh compounds.

Leoshine wrinkled her nose.

ao Kevath called to a soldier. "Here! Throw one this way!"

As the cabbage head sailed at him, he unsheathed his sword, and divided the missile perfectly in half. The pieces burst as they landed, exposing a rotten core.

Leoshine's mouth twisted. *That wagonmaster collected those from a refuse heap.*

The road cleared. They rode on.

Not an accident? She glanced at ao Kevath. Her heart swelled. He and Paulos cut a mighty figure. *Why is he pretending nothing is wrong?* A new terror seized her and she shrank down in her seat.

What if he is pretending Giffshine never came? What if he knows, and makes no immediate change in his approach?

The general's stirrup almost touched ao Kevath's. "ao Kevath, can you feel it? There is something in the air."

Leoshine leaned forward to hear. *Wol! Wol is out here.* She glanced around. *Wol is watching. Wol planned the cabbage disaster.* Her eyes darted from one tree trunk and branch to the next, lingering in the shadows to catch a movement.

What if I see him? She shivered and swallowed and stared at her hands. A flash in her peripheral vision lured her gaze out of hiding. *Would I cry out? What if Wol rushed up, cut the tether and ran away, leading my horse into the forest! ao Kevath would send all the soldiers after me.*

Or ... She remembered his cavalier attitude to her that morning. *He might let me go.*

What if I stood between them? Would they kill me as they tried to kill each other? What if Wol cried out to ao Kevath that Giffshine had been in his room?

"Yes." ao Kevath's reply sheared her terror, and brought her back to the present. "We are near the village."

Village? Leoshine mulled over the word. As far as she knew, the Oxikobh lived in compounds, separated from each other, independent, and even at war with each other.

A house, with closed door and shuttered windows, appeared amid the trees. The design did not seem Oxikobh to Leoshine, but she doubted her expertise. The wooden walls and roofs showed signs of recent building.

Soon houses appeared on both sides of the road. Many voices gathered together ahead.

A crowd of well-dressed children met them and ran before ao Kevath, waving flags and cheering. On the front landing of a building larger than the houses, a crowd of adults stood shoulder to shoulder.

An Aeolian called out and bowed to touch a dismounting ao Kevath's hand to his forehead. He introduced others and some women brought trays of cups and plates. ao Kevath and his general drank and ate, but everyone else in the cavalcade remained on their horses.

Children surrounded them to gawk at the horses. Some of the soldiers brought out picture takers and the children squealed when they saw their own images. The general tried to stop them.

ao Kevath held him back with a laugh. "They can't see the Dome." He pointed up at the tree canopy. "They can only feel the change in the air, which isn't so much under these trees." He walked to Paulos and assumed the reins. "On a day like this at home, we'd see rain. Rasset almost has the balance."

They mounted, and the general rode off.

On the outskirts of the village, almost too late, Leoshine turned toward a craggy face whispering doom. "Watch for him, my darling. Wol is coming."

Leoshine's eyes had only a moment to widen before a commotion plunged Paulos forward. The lead rope snapped and dragged her horse's head.

Wol. Coming. He wants me to join him. He sent Giffshine with a message. Her head seemed pierced by a thousand swords.

She sagged and swayed against the Tesheddar. Her heart thudded a dull rhythm now. ao Kevath never spared her a single glance. He only laughed and called out to the soldiers. He played a guessing game with them, and Leoshine wondered that his tongue never grew dry.

Had they paraded Father behind them when he visited Aeolia? Did he appear as a captive, a trophy, a freak, as his daughter continually felt? No, Father always implied his undying affection for his captors. Leoshine now strongly suspected they had bedazzled him with gadgets and fantastic displays. Iliana's palace gave a small sample. What must a whole world of such finery do to a simple soul?

They cantered. Leoshine clung to the saddle and fought back an urge to weep. *On and on, without any purpose,* she mourned as they sped through the forest.

The general thundered toward them. "This is not the road, ao Kevath."

"What do you mean? There is only one road."

The general studied a device in his hand. "Out this far, there are paths, not roads, ao Kevath. I think we have missed the main path to the new road." He rode forward.

ao Kevath called all to a halt.

In a few moments, the general returned. "Unless this is lying"—he indicated the device—"we need to make a detour to the right. The navigator agrees."

"The navigator can be demoted," ao Kevath snarled.

"We've been decoyed, ao Kevath. The light is failing."

ao Kevath tossed his hand in the air. "Turn us around then! Another gallop with you leading!"

Leoshine woke from her daze and squinted her eyes to see ahead. She could hear soldiers rustling through the undergrowth. Every muscle in her body ached. Every sinew tensed as ao Kevath plunged forward again.

The sound of dry leaves underfoot drowned everything else out.

Out in the dark? She shivered. *Lost in Oxikobh territory after nightfall?* Every legend of what forest savages did to town people danced before her eyes.

The Tesheddar held her upright. She poked her finger in and out of the curtain of air surrounding her. Would it protect against the horrors of the night?

She eased her hand down inside her boot. *No welts.* Her legs felt numb, from being in the same position too long.

She imagined her words. *ao Kevath! I can't anymore. I have eaten nothing, and drunk nothing, since before the light. You are a mighty warrior*—the lament developed—*you may ride forever and never falter, but we are not the same!*

What if I slipped off into the night? He paid no notice all day, why would that change?

A bath! She imagined not just a quick lather, timed by her jailer, but a long soaking. Steam and hyssop and maybe some of those oils Iliana brought. She drew a deep breath, inhaling an imaginary anointing. A good meal, honest food from mother's kitchen, fresh water from Father's well, her sisters and mother and aunts and cousins talking together, teasing and teaching.

Undisturbed sleep! She would take the bedding from her new cot into the private sleeping closet of her childhood and release all her fears. No one would watch. No one would rustle the carpet in the dark. No one would grab her shoulder or have the freedom to touch any other part of her on a whim.

The pace increased. Her heart quickened with a sharper pain. She was going back to town, back to safety and ancestral familiarity. And she was going back to captivity, back to living with an unpredictable and pretentious man, who, she expected, would discover her secret, and punish her with death.

ao Kevath had taken out his sword, and aimlessly whacked off leaves and branches as they passed. Leoshine had to duck the falling litter.

The general returned to trot beside his commander.

ao Kevath shot him a sour glance. "How much farther?"

The general named a distance Leoshine did not recognise. "Lights, ao Kevath?"

ao Kevath shook his head. "Spoil our vision. Where's Gavin?"

"Awaits orders, ao Kevath."

"Send him out." ao Kevath sounded brighter. In a louder voice, he announced, "We'll practice …"

He named something that, again, did not belong to Leoshine's lexicon. The general sped away.

ao Kevath called in a hearty, jovial voice, "And tell Resham to prepare my bath!"

He's pretending.

The next instant a face loomed beside her. Angry screams and heavy thuds resounded through the forest on all sides.

She screamed. Her saddle slithered to the right. Her horse lurched forward.

ao Kevath's roar drowned all sound and hot sticky liquid splashed on her face and blouse. The neckline of her coat wrenched tight. Her neck stretched as she flew upward, while her boots tugged down, caught in the Tesheddar. It vanished in a flash.

"Alan! To me!" ao Kevath bellowed again.

Leoshine screamed, dizzied by a sudden twist and the shock of landing in his saddle against his taut body. He kicked viciously. Paulos swerved, left and right. A heart not her own pounded in her ear. Hot breath burst in the other. Her chest and arms felt a bruising, crushing hold. Her skirt tore away in a grasping hand.

Wild-eyed riderless horses ran in every direction. Swords flashed and bulks wrestled in every shadow.

A rider thundered alongside. *Many riders.* Leoshine's senses revived. Thundering, pounding. ao Kevath in the lead, with her before him in his saddle. He hawed at the top of his voice to force more speed from Paulos.

"Sister of Wol." The phrase echoed in her ears. She had heard it before, from Resham, from a hag on her first parade behind ao Kevath. Sister of Wol. Sister of Wol. One of the attackers had renewed the cadence in her heart.

ao Kevath roared again, splitting her ear drum. Lights ahead! A pounding noise and suddenly a rush of riders in the opposite direction swerving to avoid them. Tents. The clearing before the town!

ao Kevath stood up in his stirrups, lessening the pressure on her chest. Leoshine squirmed to the side. Cold air rushed past her one bare foot.

He settled back in the saddle and pressed her down into Paulos' neck with his chest. A vicious kick at the heaving flanks launched Paulos faster than ever through the forest.

The trees fell away. The town wall lay ahead. ao Kevath swerved. Paulos' shoulder collided with another horse. "Take Paulos!"

The gate towered above. Armoured statues looked down from the wall.

Suddenly, Leoshine felt free. ao Kevath had leapt away.

In the next instant Resham breathed in her ear and clamped her tight in his arms.

ao Kevath bellowed from the back of another horse. "Guard her!"

Resham bellowed back with equal fury. "ao Kevath!"

Leoshine fought back.

He caught at her legs and arms and gathered her into his cradling hold, far more secure than straddling the pumping neck.

"In my room!" ao Kevath cut all opposition. "With your life! Nothing else matters!"

For a moment all went still. She felt Resham gazing after his master. Then he spurred Paulos. The iron-shod hooves rang the alarm through the town. They careened from side to side, navigating the twisted streets.

Leoshine sank her teeth into Resham's forearm.

"Don't fight me!" Resham snarled and brought his elbows sharply inward.

Leoshine gasped. Lights blurred. Noise faded into a dream.

Resham landed with both feet on the ground. Leoshine's teeth jarred against each other.

She wrenched her shoulders and his grip tightened. "I don't need you!"

Resham snapped back. "I don't need you either. ao Kevath needs me and I cannot go to him because of you! Why were you out so long? Where did they stop you? How many attackers?"

She twisted again and won free, or he allowed her feet to touch the ground. They collapsed under her. She shook violently.

He picked her up and marched forward.

Resham looked down at her, while waiting for the sentry to open the door to ao Kevath's room. "Want to try standing again?"

She peered into his face in the artificial light. Did he mock, cruel fiend?

His eyes were soft. His mouth was grim, but curved to resignation.

Her bare foot touched down on the wood boards. She staggered two steps and collapsed on the cot, face down in the pillow.

Once begun, the tears gushed forth. Her chest ached, and her head throbbed.

Resham's hand touched down on her head and caressed her hair. Leoshine froze. His grip squeezed gently on her shoulder, signaling her to sit up. Her body continued to shake and her breath came in shudders. He held her shoulder for support and she wondered again.

Sometimes he seems so gentle.

A steaming cup slipped between her hands. Heat radiated through the towel and from his hand wrapped around hers. The odour of the broth stirred memories of other cups.

For sleep. The steam clung to the surface of the brown liquid and then drifted to the rim.

Resham hovered in the low lamp light. He didn't speak. The steam disappeared from her cup as it cooled untouched. He touched the bottom of the cup to lift and hold it while the liquid slid down the girl's throat. She stared into the middle distance for another moment and then melted. He imagined her dribbling through his fingers, she was so limp.

Immediately he stripped her dirty clothes off, smelling the raw fear-soaked sweat of her. His mind darted to the door. *No fear of Avram coming. I'll have to bring him in for a feed and wash.*

She lay still as he fetched water and ointments. When he raised her to sponge and anoint her back, her eyelids twitched. He held still and watched first one eye and then the other blink. He smiled.

Still fighting, Obenici? He longed to ask, but she must not hear his voice in her vulnerable state. It was bad enough that she felt his touch. The look she gave him when he had set her down on the threshold made him grin again.

Yes, Tassanara, I know. I have seen the egg.

He laughed at himself as he bathed and anointed her arms and face. *I am the royal physician. I serve you as though you were Iliana herself.* When he laid her back, her eyes were closed.

No wounds. He almost sighed with relief. When they had come charging through the gate, splattered with blood, the royal physician had greatly feared. *And was not afraid to admit it,* he told himself as he bathed her legs and rubbed in Iliana's healing oil. The ache would be much alleviated. The air she breathed would benefit from the ao Kenan's artful potion.

He drew a long straight gown, with Iliana's lace at the throat and cuffs, over her head. This time, sitting her up stirred no sign in her. He swaddled her in a blanket, wrapping her arms across her chest.

He stood looking down at her. She had ridden all day in a foreign saddle, through the most frightening territory a town woman could know, unfed and unwatered, in the company of a grouchy master. And still she kicked and bit as he rode through the town to this sanctuary.

Did she fight Avram? No! And thus, showed her wisdom. *And what more could a man wish for than mettle and wisdom?* Resham sent his spirit out in search of an answer.

"Poor little pawn." He turned off the lantern and opened the screen under the windows. "They won't get another chance at you."

He looked up at the recently completed section of cathedral roof. His hunt had proven that Giffshine visited there. He had a long list of devices she had stolen from the careless Aeolians. She would not miss an opportunity to see into ao Kevath's sacred chamber.

He lifted the whole cot, careful to keep Leoshine perfectly level, and carried her behind the screen. He castigated himself for his fear of her waking. Sleep was still her best medicine.

From the adjacent room, he brought his cot and quickly arranged blankets and pillows as if she were sleeping there in full view of the windows.

Back behind the curtains, he held a device over her chest, and watched the graph of her heartbeat leap into sight. Hard work and fatigue, he saw. Also, spikes of the terror lingered. He hoped the sleep would dull them. The broad low wave of anger would remain until she accepted her place in ao Kevath's mission.

You might know before Avram what your place is in his mission.

Resham felt his knees weaken and he sank down onto the little stool. He rested his elbows on his knees and clasped his fingers together. With closed eyes and uplifted chin, he sent his spirit out, beyond his frame, beyond the room, feeling his way through a light too brilliant and welcoming the familiar infilling fire.

Ao Kevad!

The words suspended in the air and shattered as he had once seen Aeolian diphidious crystals vaporise at high frequency.

I see Your work here. He bowed his head and his hands opened before him, finger tips still laced.

Aftermath

Hoofbeats thundered through Avram's heart as he galloped away from Resham and the girl. His fresh horse sped past abandoned tents in the open space between town and forest. *Nothing else matters. Nothing else matters.*

Fool! He scolded himself. The flood light from the wall illuminated soldiers forming the guard at the perimeter and herding citizens toward safety.

A mounted figure saluted as he arrived where the road entered the forest.

"Dorim!" Avram returned the salute and reined in beside his general. "Report!"

Dorim responded from the perspective of his post. "All quiet, ao Kevath. Kirim on the other side." With a straight arm he indicated his blood brother's position, opposite his own. "Uly and Lantro at the quarters under the wall." With two arms spread, he indicated the other positions on opposite sides of the town.

"We practice Bertrae, Gavin practices Cortransa." Avram named the maneuver for defending the town and for the meeting of two friendly forces that he had flippantly ordered moments before the ambush.

"Gavin with Alan, ao Kevath."

"I'll take their report when they come in." Avram turned his horse and galloped back to the gate. He didn't begrudge Gavin the battle aftermath. Once the other generals assumed their territories, he would be rooted in town where assassins ruled, not open war. Meanwhile, his assigned post required a commander.

Though he wore full armour under his gaudy costume, Avram felt the air cool the sweat where the girl had pressed against him. *Did Rasset win another degree?*

He glanced to see if the Dome had changed colour. He had predicted to the village people that everything would be covered in a fine film of water in the morning. Dew! The first step toward atmospheric purity. Rasset had heated the air and now cooled it. "With sufficient temperature fluctuations and radiation effect, one might be able to actualize condensation ..." He heard his chief scientist's vocabulary run through his mind and grimaced.

The gate loomed.

"Bellepherone!" The sentry challenged with the day's password.

"Alexander!" Avram replied. "Report!"

"All quiet, ao Kevath."

A face looked down from the parapet.

"Zolous! What do you see?"

Gavin's second in command swung his arms to point along the roads to the forest. "General Dorim, General Kirim." He changed his position to point at 90 degrees to the roads and down under his position. "General Uly, General Lantro, ao Kevath. All quiet, ao Kevath."

A buzzing tumult grew within the gate.

"You lie!" Avram bellowed.

"No enemy, ao Kevath," Zolous corrected.

"Open!" Avram commanded the sentry and entered the town.

Voices hailed him from all sides within the crowded square. Angry Myxolidians pressed against his legs and grabbed at his bridle. *Paulos would have bitten their hands off.* But Paulos deserved his rest.

"Silence!" he bellowed.

The men closest to him quieted. The rabble on the edges continued to heckle.

He waved an arm toward the gate. "We were ambushed! In the forest. The Bertrae Guard is in place. The town is protected. There is no risk to your personal safety. You can all go home and sleep soundly in your own beds."

A bearded, red-cheeked man pumped his fist. "The town's filled up!"

A grey-beard croaked. "Strangers among us!"

Avram replied to these accusations. "The vulnerable from the tents came inside the wall. They will go back outside in the morning. This has been a good exercise. We have proven our worth as defenders. Soon we shall move to crush the Woltreaders!"

A tall man, hung with furs, stepped forward. "How far away was the attack?"

"A good distance." Avram turned to single out the questioner. He cast his mind over the geography of the forest. "Near Gaugheli's farm, where the road will divide." One fork to Uly's quintile, one fork to Dorim's.

His tongue ached and his throat rasped from shouting Myxolidian. He had exaggerated the mispronunciation of the place name to obscure the distance. *Does the average citizen know about the Aeolian farms in every clearing of the forest, working to feed the masses, to stockpile supplies before the rain?*

The cacophony rose again, at a lesser pitch.

"The town is secure," he declared, pressing his horse forward. "Go to your beds!"

"We would fight the Woltreaders!"

"Enemies of our town!"

"Traitors!"

"Well spoken!" Avram bellowed back. "We fight to quell a rebellion. We fight to secure the forest food supply for the town. In the morning, we will take the names of brave volunteers."

"We defend our town!"

"We fight now!"

Avram sighed in his mind. "Half of you stay here. Half of you go to the back gate. But I tell you, this is only an exercise. The ambush was small and is already defeated. General Alan and General Gavin have disarmed the Woltreader attack. The town is secure."

He gave a low groan. *I don't want Myxolidians in my army.* Town folk fighting against forest folk only perpetuated the ancient, brutal feud. The Oxikobh were as much under his protection as the town folk. Some town-bred men were out among the rebels, who were led by a town-bred villain. *The morning's volunteers will be assigned to town defense far from the battlefield.*

None of the rabble had moved to the back gate, he noticed. Consolation and assurance ranked more important in their plump little minds than defending the city.

An Aeolian cried from above. "ao Kevath!"

"Zolous!" Avram replied. "Report!"

"All quiet, ao Kevath. General Alan reports taking prisoners to the jail. General Gavin requests the transport vehicle for the wounded."

"Send coordinates to the pilot! Auxiliary 1450."

This would be the vehicle's first flight outside the walls since Iliana arrived, using the code to leap the walls and descend directly into any clearing near the ambush site.

As chief of security, Resham would question the prisoners in the newly-built detention facility. Avram grinned. Even incomplete, the building would serve Resham's methods.

"I killed today." Avram strode through the door to his chamber and continued around the table. "Paulos bit him on the shoulder as he tried to cut the cinch. I plunged my sword down his throat as his mouth opened to scream." He continued past the cot and around the table.

Resham stood by the bedpost, taking confession and military secrets in the same calm stance.

"Another cut the girl's cinch. I grabbed her and thrust through another gullet as she went down. They just melted out of the trees. One moment we were riding. They decoyed us and we were trying to get back onto the road."

Resham nodded. His mouth wore the patient, angry twist of old.

"Well?" Avram snapped. He rounded on the cot, kicked it over, and marched through the curtain to where Leoshine slept.

His inner soul smiled to hear Resham, not a step behind.

The smile twisted further inward as he gazed on the face, white as snow, on the vivid blue pillow. *Will she ever know snow?*

he follows the instincts of his master.

Ao Kevad? Avram's brows twitched together. The words formed in his spirit, but he knew they did not belong to his thought.

"I understand the screen," he heard himself ask Resham, "but not the decoy cot."

"ao Kevath, I have reason to suspect …"

He prepares me. Avram's hand rose and his finger settled on the nubble of bone at the corner of his eyebrow.

Resham finished his thought. "They see into this room."

Avram stalked out of the partitioned shelter and resumed pacing. "How?"

The sentry knocked. The door opened.

"Alan! Gavin! Tell Resham what you know so he can be away."

Gavin opened. "Eleven dead, ao Kevath, two of them ours."

"They are all ours!" Avram corrected.

Alan resumed the report. "Two soldiers dead, ao Kevath. Three wounded. Fourteen prisoners. Eighteen cinches cut, fifteen horses recovered."

"Three lost?"

Alan stared past his commander as he answered. "Booty for the enemy, ao Kevath."

"Estimated force of ambush party?"

"Thirty, ao Kevath."

"One moment there were only trees, next there were men, silent as the wind. Next there were men falling off horses."

Alan addressed Resham. "I was near ao Kevath."

"I should have sent the transport." Gavin mourned.

Avram cut him off. "We don't play 'should,' Gavin. We were delayed and decoyed." He turned to Resham. "Do you have what you need? Go now. Round up numbers one through four. In the dawn, four hours from now, the others will stand down. Rest, all of you. I'll call orders in the afternoon."

They answered in one voice. "Yes, ao Kevath."

The sentry hammered the door all morning. Citizens of all statures brought vehement assurances of loyalty, pleadings for protection, demands for settlement. Avram listened with half an ear.

The town filled with refugees escaping Wol's forced recruitment among the Oxikobh. They would sleep in the streets until Gavin lodged them in the new buildings and fed them from the Aeolian stores. Conflicts between the Oxikobh and the city folk inevitably overflowed into the Overlord's chamber.

Would it be siege? Would the Overlord pledge his soldiers? Would he crush the rebellion quickly?

At midday Avram yawned, stretched, and called for his soldiers to clear the room. After a bath and change of clothes, he summoned his generals.

The sentry knocked as Avram paced past the decoy cot for the sixty-seventh time. In two strides he dove into his chair and leaned back, his elbows on the chair arms, one finger placed as though supporting his lower lip.

He watched his comrades-in-arms cross the threshold and recognize the scene. Many times, they had gathered around this table to discern a battle plan with their leader, even before invading Myxolidia.

Once their chairs ceased shuffling around the great old table, Uly leaned forward. "The traitor Wol holds all the country north of the Kaaipit Mountains, ao Kevath."

An exalted name for some rugged hills, Avram thought.

Gavin added. "He foments trouble with lies and tortures the citizens into joining him."

"How did this happen? Did we underestimate the enemy? Did he know of us before we came?"

Alan spat. "No, ao Kevath. He is as cunning and devious and ruthless as you reckoned him from the first. He was his father's enemy, now he is yours."

Uly continued. "The people are hard to measure, ao Kevath. They are like shifting sand."

Lantro reported next. "They compromise and justify until they work in opposite directions, labouring on road building crews in the day and feasting in Wol's company at night. He has a reputation and safe hiding among them that he exploits. He has powers of disguise that baffle us, so we can't lay hands on him."

Avram waved a casual hand to dismiss their stale news. "What is different that we didn't see?"

An uncomfortable pause gripped them.

Uly glanced around the table. "It's the girl, ao Kevath."

Avram frowned and tapped his lower lip with his finger. A bubble had burst. They had finally dared to speak of her.

He had broken all the rules by accepting her, and by keeping her in his room. He had waited for them to object and observed occasions when they might have mentioned her to test his reaction. Their reticence amused him. They didn't usually hesitate in pointing out his faults. He couldn't help being relieved at the delay. He hesitated to explain to himself why the girl remained.

"Out with it!" he commanded. "I'm ready."

"ao Kevath ..." Dorim coughed and glanced at Uly who leaned forward and interlaced his fingers.

Uly raised his eyes, blinking. "He, the traitor, uses her presence here. In shameful lies, he turns the minds of the weak. She is the difference, ao Kevath. We did not see her in our plans. We did not make a space for her in our strategy."

Kirim looked down at his hands, up at the bed post behind Avram's shoulder. "We are unable, ao Kevath, to counter his strategy. Un—until we know yours, ao Kevath."

"If it were a boy, ao Kevath," Lantro interposed, "who might be trained to war, ao Kevath ..."

"It won't always be war, Lantro." Avram opened his hands, palm up. "We have plied diplomacy and negotiation for a generation already. And shall ply them long after this glorious military brilliance is achieved." He relaxed back in his seat. "Seeing that she is a she, one sees no need to"—he swung his hand palm up, idly bidding the idea to coalesce. Manipulate was too strong a word— "to influence the male soul under this Dome. It is wise to engage the other, the female of the Myxolidian species, and this one is our ..." *Broadcast device?* He wondered how to call her. "She will speak our mind to them. They will adopt clothes and customs because they see her adopt them."

Alan leaned to his neighbour and murmured, "And who shall speak our mind to the winsome lass?"

Gavin glanced at Avram. "Iliana."

In Avram's memory, he heard Leoshine call Gavin's name when they rode in the wilderness. At the time he had justified stopping Gavin from replying by telling himself her culture forbade women from speaking with men, notwithstanding Gavin had attended her the whole day. Now he wondered, did he fear what Gavin might discover?

The rest of the generals nodded in relief.

Avram remembered another interchange, with Resham this time, after the honourable Mother's arrival.

The girl goes to Iliana, ao Kevath? Resham's tone had only hinted at a question.

"Iliana has earned her disgrace." He had seen the telltale behind Resham's ear. Iliana's drugging of Leoshine angered him too. "Which will end at my convenience."

Resham had leaned closer, hovering for further disclosure.

"When we go to battle." Avram had allowed before closing the conversation.

The generals sat in silence.

Avram waited too. *Should I laugh to make them comfortable, or should I enjoy their unease, and even increase it with a mock display of outrage?* He weighed which would give him the greatest interval to formulate a reply.

He rejected both courses. "Friends." He peered into each face. "Admitting the girl to my presence has strained propriety. I accept full responsibility for my actions. When she was delivered here, my first instinct was to protect her from the obvious harm. Women continue to suffer gross indecency in this culture and I am sworn to do my utmost to change that. I took the earliest opportunity. When I realised her family connections, I used her to secure the loyalty of the old mayor."

He watched his words smooth their brows. "I have gained insight from her into the subtleties of the culture I believe would not have been available to me otherwise, and she has been, in my opinion, invaluable in translating our culture to the common Myxolidian. The bathhouses we build are full every day because she took up the custom before we arrived. Their own hands fashion the cloth we make available into a style imitating hers. Other things are at least not rejected because she is seen associated with them."

He held out his index finger to emphasize his point. "I can tell from one look at her whether the merchant or informer is lying. How would we have ever caught out that scoundrel selling parasite-devastated lumber? What a disaster it would have been if Leoshine weren't such an open book. Or that guide who wanted to lead us into new territory. Did any of us know that the North Gorge is uncrossable at that point? You thought I was so clever to turn their ambush into a rout for us. You never saw the little face in the corner."

Just behind that screen …

"I freely admit, I have become accustomed, no, even dependent, on her presence. Resham finds her useful in looking after me. I wish he were here to add his voice to our discussion. Ask him when you meet him out there. She could be sent home, but we don't expect any contact for another month. She could be placed in Iliana's custody; however, I fear for her safety." He nodded at Alan. "With good reason. Have you forgotten that we still have the Overlord of Aeolia's expectations to maintain? He needs concrete proof that our military strategy against the rebels is absolutely necessary. This latest ambush proved the savages would attack a peaceful expedition with females in the train."

Avram looked around the circle. Some stared at suddenly torn fingernails, others at the papers and tools that would soon plan the battle.

They wanted a ruthless commander, who spared no sentiment and put all lives at the mercy of the mission. He felt them relax when he spoke of manipulating Aeolian expectations by placing the girl in danger. At the same time, he trusted they would die ensuring any female arrived home safely.

"Do you know when I first ...?" His throat closed over. *What am I saying?* His face tingled and pulsed. Heat spread up from his constricted diaphragm.

He forced himself to look into each set of eyes before him and swallowed his overlarge Adam's apple. "Two or three days after she, er, arrived ..." He blocked his ears from betraying his heart. "I had slept." They would know the significance of that. "I woke and called out." They would know he called for Resham. "She came with the tray. The air vibrated around her, how could I not ... my senses aligned to her presence." They knew of his hypersensitivity. Had he not seen them align, however less acutely, to her presence? "Yet, despite her fear, gentlemen, she performed her duty. She served me despite everything in her telling her not to." He looked around the circle again. "Gentlemen, she deserves a place here, among you. Among us."

He drew a deep breath and met each answering gaze. "Where is Wol now?" He shifted a device into position.

Lantro laid down his fork. "Which comes first, ao Kevath? Rebel surrender or rain?"

Avram laughed. "Rasset promised a long wait. Things looked promising, but he made a false prophet of me among the villagers."

"We'll say the forest prevented the dew, ao Kevath."

Alan chimed in. "They didn't understand a word you said."

Avram pulled himself up in his seat. "I have improved! I know all the words!"

"Doesn't guarantee a tongue to pronounce them."

Avram laughed with the others. In the contented lapse

in conversation, they filled their mouths with meat and root vegetables.

A sigh, like the waking mew of an infant, alerted him to imminent company.

The sheets rustled behind the screen. Drinking noises. He heard her eating the food he ordered the servant to place behind the screen. Would she come out, he wondered, or stay hidden until the room emptied?

She knew the generals by name. She would hear their voices. She would understand, at least, the topic of their easy banter.

The moment her fingers appeared, clutching the curtain opening, he called. "Leoshine!"

The generals stopped and followed his gaze. Gavin and Uly turned in their seats.

"Come forward."

She seemed to coalesce around the curtain, holding it until the last possible moment. Her fingers twisted at her throat and he realised she half strangled herself with the necklace.

The nightgown covered her from throat to toe and still, he knew, was not what she would wish to appear in before men. Her overdeveloped sense of propriety matched his, for once.

He rose from his seat at the table. Leoshine shrank but remained with her feet bedded in the pile of the carpet. From the clothes cupboard, he took his uniform jacket. Draping it over her shoulders, he buckled his insignia jewel under her chin, nearly at her chest.

He inclined his head toward her. Something about the insignia … *I'll make you a new one. L. T. Leoshine Tassanara.* "Are you hungry?"

Her eyes swelled. Her throat spasmed. She shook her head with tight, brief movements.

He imagined her thought. *Don't ask me to eat from your plate!*

He lifted his eyebrows at her. "The only thing to improve the evening would be a song."

Yes, she had learned to sing at his command. Again, he read her mind as she frowned. Under the engulfing jacket with sleeves almost touching the floor, he knew she clenched stiff arms beside her body, her fists balled in the cloth of her nightgown. She swallowed again and took a deep, shuddering breath. He had taught her to obey by outwaiting her disobedience. Nothing would happen until she sang.

In a small throaty whisper, she began. A Myxolidian song, he noted with interest.

The birds call at dawn when the hero sleeps. He is weary, but the birds call him to defend what he loves. The maiden hears the farm beasts groaning. She remembers her hero and longs for his safe return. The song ended with a question that echoed the deep yearning in all their hearts.

Dorim surprised them by replying in Aeolian. His home, he sang, lay far away beyond a river. He would only arrive late after a weary battle. His longing sometimes overwhelmed him, but he soldiered on because of the beauty and peace and the presence there of the one he loved.

When he finished, he beckoned Leoshine to his chair.

Avram watched. She counted the steps forward, away from the screen. She looked up at him and he smiled his pleasure. She ducked her head and shuffled to stand between them.

Dorim laid his hand over her head. His fingers ran down to the base of her skull and over her ears like thick candle wax drippings. "Child, you must keep your gift of singing. And you must learn to sing the best song of all." He placed a round thin gold disk in her hand.

Avram called for her to show him the disk, the size of her thumb nail, engraved with a picture. He held it up for all to see. "The High King!"

Chairs scraped back. They all stood with their cups held out toward the centre of the table. The jacket lay huddled around the girl's footprints in the carpet, as if she had evapourated from its midst.

Avram bowed his head. "Lord, grant to us the success over the enemy we seek. Set your people free from the errors of their ways. Bless us as we go out into the battle."

Six bass voices thundered and rolled with emotion. "The High King! Ao Kevad!"

They drank.

One by one they knelt before their commander and touched their foreheads to his hand before drinking from his cup. He remained standing long after the door closed behind them.

Paulos whinnied and Avram's step picked up. After the ambush, the grooms would have inspected the stallion for wounds and given him a thorough rub down and a special meal, then he would have waited.

The rider's hand flowed over the supreme lines of wither, hock, and rump on its own tour of inspection. No wounds, no swelling. The beast pushed out to take full advantage of the caress and swung his head back to nuzzle Avram's breast pocket. Sweetness? A treat?

In the darkness Avram guided the saddle and bridle into place.

Paulos was like his sword, built and honed to respond to Avram, and Avram alone, to fight and destroy his enemy. The only difference? Paulos' training and skill directed the blow. Avram merely asked for his stallion's skill and power to be delivered.

Avram's forehead rested on the warm, firm shoulder. "What do you think of her, my friend? You have carried her now, twice. You have guided her often."

Resham could ride Paulos. Of the generals only Uly had tried and had dismounted in shivers, exclaiming it was too much power for one man to command.

You are born to be commanded. He slid his hand over Paulos' sleek neck before he mounted. *To trust and endure whatever I ask of you.*

He rode into the middle of the darkened arena and made Paulos stand while he mentally reviewed every move of the battle. At the twitch of Avram's calf-muscle, Paulos leapt to begin the re-enactment.

With his eyes closed and body poised, Avram commanded the swerve to better front the attack, the half rear to lash out with the front hooves, the leap to kick the slippery vermin that came between him and his rear guard. That was a special maneuver since the mount's back had to remain perfectly level. *Leoshine probably did not know it happened.*

After each move, Avram praised Paulos and reinforced the dance of sublime connection and refinement.

In all his life, Avram had never been connected to anyone more than Resham.

Resham chose to obey. Very rarely he came out from his servant mask. Sometimes Avram had to put him back, though he hated doing so. Only in those peerless moments when Resham acted as a brother did the Overlord come close to having one. But Resham chose to obey. And Avram could not force him into ... what? Equality?

Ao Kevad did not permit an equal.

Resham had said something about service to the High King. "It may not be slavery." He'd said something about "mutual." A togetherness.

"Don't think you achieve anything as Ao Kevad's slave." That was another of Resham's sayings. "Ao Kevad works in you, through you."

Mutuality made more sense like that.

The sleepy groom opened the arena door to free them. Sentries at the town gate bowed to their supreme commander. Paulos tossed his heels and begged for the wind.

Wol.

Assembling his troops in the west, far from Aeolian eyes.
Darkness.

Avram stood and leaned along Paulos' neck, putting his mouth beside the horse's ear. "Do you know the road?"

The stallion surged forward settling him deep in the saddle. Mane hair flogged his face. His curls straightened in the wind.

He inhaled the fresh Myxolidian cold and laughed at himself for missing it while Rasset played with heating the atmosphere. In his ears, the hoofbeats tore the road. Beneath his legs, the power surged.

Iliana had instructed her people to call Leoshine "Tassanara."

"Does she know what it means?" he had asked, remembering that Resham also used that exalted title for her.

"She thinks it means, 'ao Kevath's slave'." Iliana replied.

"Don't tell her any different." *It isn't time yet.*

Suddenly he knew why the girl intrigued him, why he studied her features until they swam in his eyes when he closed them, why his flesh sang when she lifted her voice in melody, why the tiny creases in her brow influenced kingdom building decisions.

He had told the generals of her courage in serving when everything in her screamed for her to run. Did they understand? Within that tiny mite of humanity dwelt the greatest spirit any of them had ever known.

Her position was precarious, deadly. Her cultural perspective insisted on death and dismembering rituals. She expected them every moment, waking or sleeping. She knew nothing else.

When he came with a different perspective, honouring her gender and person, she mistook him for a fool. And still she served.

Her dedication, in the face of such ground sweeping danger … *I feel it too.*

Mutuality.

Ao Kevad might permit her to be my … He paused and turned the supposition into a plea.

Equal!

He stood in his stirrups. The branches of the unseen trees trembled as they passed his head. Paulos stretched out with even more speed and recklessness. Joy quivered and sang through them, indistinguishable who gave and who received.

As he bade his friend goodnight, Avram tied a cloth over the halter nose band. "This is hers. Leoshine. She wasn't afraid when you pushed her over. You must know her better.

"It is time now. She must know she is not my slave."

Curtstas Captured

A small dent in the plastered wall focused Leoshine's attention.

A different dent, she remembered, *on a different wall.* Even the light fell at a different angle from the long windows.

She twisted her shoulders to look up. The curtain rod framed the ceiling. The shelves holding the five boxes of Oxikobh curse and one of clean dirt hung over her head.

Her fingers wriggled beneath her pillow, into the far corner of the mattress. Last night, when she woke in a strange position, her heart had stopped, until she proved that whoever moved her, Resham of course, had moved the mattress too. The egg remained. Her fingertip caressed it a moment more, glanced upon the metal disk, and then crept back to the bauble at her throat.

She swallowed and dropped out of bed, slinking to the chair at the little table. Resham did not come this morning. She would have to fetch ao Kevath's plate and share his food. *Is he there?* She listened.

Silence, she knew, did not mean his absence.

The open closet against the wall gave her a choice of outfits. *How long since I chose my own clothes?* She wriggled out of her nightgown that Iliana made and pulled the dress remodeled from her mother's gift over her head.

The struggle surprised her.

I've grown! Did she remember incorrectly? Had it really been changed to accommodate not having the hard plate on her chest? The sleeves didn't reach her wrists, unlike ao Kevath's jacket that he put on her last night—*Why did he do that?*—and her shoulders were squeezed together.

She struggled out and lifted the first dress Resham gave her. The sleeves were too short when she stretched them in front of her arms. Then she took the most recent arrival to the collection and passed her head through the neck. It fit.

He sees. She crossed her arms over her chest, her hands resting on her shoulders. *He adjusts for me growing so I don't even notice.*

She passed the brush through her hair. *I have been here long enough to outgrow clothes. If I was with Father …* She stood up and shook her head. *No sense in thinking about what might have been.* She knotted her hair behind her neck and peeked between the folds of the curtain door.

ao Kevath slouched in his chair with his legs stretched beside the table, not under it. His finger rested on his eyebrow. She could see the scab from previous rubbing flaking off.

He faces me. He has changed his position to stare at my new place in the room. She gulped and touched the curtain to her lower lip. *Before I woke up, he was staring at this opening.*

What if I crept under another side of the curtain? Looking again, she saw the tray with the clear dome already before him.

She stepped forward and whispered. "You did eat, ao Kevath?" She stepped again and bobbed her head. Her fingers entwined with the necklace at her throat.

Grey light from the speaking box washed his face, leaving fierce dark shadows under his brows.

Does he stare at me or the curtain? She could not distinguish if he focused as she moved toward him. *Does he live?*

She dug her fingernails into the crevasses in the carved chair back.

She didn't see his lips move. "For what we are about to receive."

"Make us truly thankful," she returned with relief.

"Make haste," he murmured again. "They are waiting." He held up his finger and tilted his head the minutest amount.

Leoshine poised on her toes and listened. Voices clamoured outside the door. Not a dull rumble, as she usually heard if ao Kevath held audience in his chamber. Men were shouting at each other.

She looked at her master with great round eyes.

His finger tapped his lower lip. "I make them wait for you. Eat. Then go back." He pointed to the curtain.

"I could ..." Her words choked in her throat as he held up a cautioning finger.

She slid into her chair and lifted the cover. *If he wants his slave to eat at his table, if he wants to hold the entire kingdom at bay for it, if he wants to watch it eat ...*

Why did I forget? She stared at the colourful squares of sustenance. Now she would have to eat something to appease him. Again, her body cried out and hunger gnawed, like last night when she found the plate behind the curtain. The plate had been empty before she had realised she felt sick.

She took a red square. She gulped juices that exploded in her mouth.

ao Kevath stretched his hand out, palm up. She lifted a white square. His brow twitched. He wanted the red one, she knew, not only because it was his favourite. He asked for the same one she took. If she never touched the red, neither would he. If she did not eat first, the square would rest in his hand, on the table, until she did.

Something thumped against the door and Leoshine's spine tingled. *I should go. I should finish.* She shot a glance at ao Kevath, but he stared at the speaking box, his hand resting, palm up on the table.

She placed a red square in the cup of his hand and took a white one into her mouth. This was more like cake, very moist, pasty, maybe even half-cooked dough. When he put his hand out again, she put a white square into it.

"Leoshine."

She swallowed. She pleaded with her eyes. Singing, speaking, learning, all seemed as impossible as eating the third square that she had been staring at.

He did not sound angry. A tremour of hatred, a harsh bitterness edged his tone. "I want to teach you." His brows contracted.

There had been a lull in the rancour outside. Suddenly blows rang out. The sentry tapped.

"Behind the screen." He gestured with his head. "I will teach you later."

Leoshine covered the food, and walked back to the curtain, glancing once at ao Kevath. He had not moved. His legs still extended beside the table. His elbows still rested on the arms of his chair. One finger rubbed at his brow.

The fabric rippled as she slipped through the gap.

"Sentry!"

Her back was turned, and ao Kevath's bellow caught her unaware. She jumped and staggered to the cot.

The noise swelled as the door opened.

"One by one," ao Kevath commanded wearily.

She stared at the curtain. In her mind she saw a Myxolidian shuffle in, speak a few words, pause for effect, pause again for a reaction, and shuffle out. One by one. Some dared to raise their voices. She lowered her head into her shoulders. ao Kevath returned no bellow. She sighed and relaxed a little.

She remembered his words last night with the generals around the table, planning a battle against Wol.

"Lord, grant to us ..." How could it be a gift? Who would give her people away like that? What did he mean, the errors of their ways? Who was in error?

Wol committed a grave error but why should her people suffer while two men struggled for supremacy?

Who would win and rule the aftermath?

The door opened. Loud voices and tramping Aeolian boots rumbled through the door.

"Gentlemen!" ao Kevath greeted the arrivals with renewed vigour. "Uly! Lantro! Dorim! Kirim! Alan! Gavin! Seat yourselves. Report!"

Leoshine heard many words amid laughter. Military words, she guessed, and worked hard to piece together their ideas. Wol held a high place on a ridge. The Aeolians held a secret weapon, and ao Kevath commanded very sternly that it not be used.

One of the generals complained. "Then why drag them all that way, ao Kevath?"

"We show them what can be done. Fear wins. Lives are saved."

Someone prophesied. "Years of our lives will be lost hauling those monsters."

Suddenly the noise outside clarified. The door had opened again and amid the cacophony more Aeolian boots stormed in.

"ao Kevath!" Resham sounded triumphant.

Scuffling noises puzzled Leoshine. She crept forward and peeked past the curtain. Her breath caught to see her father fall to his knees between the soldiers. Chains rattled on his wrists.

"Found him with number three, ao Kevath. Found this too." Resham placed a paper in front of ao Kevath.

Silence collected like congealed blood. ao Kevath sat up straighter. His elbows remained on the chair arms.

His chair legs scraped the floor. Like a tree unfurling, he pulled his legs and back straight, and inflated his chest. Purple, white, and red spots fought for holding on his face. "Read it." He ordered between clenched teeth. His eyes skewered Father, who cringed and whimpered.

Resham cocked an eyebrow at his commander, twisted his mouth and read. "'My son. I am frequently at the house. Your sister remains a prisoner and, after the failed attack, the guard has been doubled ...'"

"You wrote this?" ao Kevath's roar might have blistered the paint on the plaster.

Leoshine's heart burst from her chest. She dashed out and fell at her master's feet. Her head tucked down between her clenched hands. "ao Kevath!"

"Back!" ao Kevath pointed to the screen.

Hard fingers gripped her waist and she was hoisted through the air.

She fought back and cried out, but Resham pinned her arms to her sides, and clamped her jaw shut with his other hand.

In her ear, he whispered, "Is this who you really are, Leoshine? Do you side with the traitors?"

She gasped as though stabbed with a searing knife. *Giffshine's visit made me a traitor! Hiding the egg makes me a traitor! I don't have to side with them, I am one! I didn't ask for the secret!*

Father!

"You can do nothing here." Resham purred. "You have been so good for so long. Don't spoil it now." He tightened his hold until her brain reeled. "Are you going to sit?"

The least release in pressure allowed the humblest of nods under his bruising grip. As he let her go, she flung herself into the corner as far away from him as possible. She wept and screamed into the pillow.

"Listen!" Resham whispered.

Both froze. *Will Father ask for mercy?* Even the possibility of the words chased a chill through her bones.

"You foul traitor!" ao Kevath's chair clattered to the floor as he fought free. "You might have been a hero for our combined history. Instead you choose to grovel at the cesspool. Is this how you repay our benevolence? Shall we execute you or leave you free and wait for the dagger between our shoulder blades? No! You will rot in the new prison! You will be forgotten! The victory shall go on without any mention of you. Take him away! And his wife and daughters, too!"

Leoshine sat up. *That's me.*

Resham held out his hand in warning.

Uly's stern voice spoke out, "ao Kevath it does no honour to deprive a pregnant woman …"

Leoshine's ears roared with sobbing blood.

"May it please ao Kevath to keep the woman safe until she delivers."

ao Kevath growled and hurled the fallen chair at the door. "Make it so."

All the chairs skidded backward. Boots tramped out.

Resham strode toward the curtain. Leoshine jumped to her feet. *Do I go to prison?*

"Stay!" Resham growled, narrowing his eyes along his pointed finger.

She shrank back and hated herself for cringing. *Brave his violence!* She commanded herself. Her legs shook, and her spine crumpled.

Alone! I am alone. Giffshine never returned. Wol never rescued me. Even if he did, where would I be? On the ridge? In the battle?

She wrapped her head in a blanket, wrapped another blanket around her shoulders, and wrapped her arms around her knees. ao Kevath and Resham spat words at each other. Tears burned in her throat and eyes. Her heart seemed to wobble in its cage.

She had hoped for news of her family. Now she knew. She had hoped they were safe and well provided for. Instead they were in a cold, isolated prison cell. *I am in a different cell, no less captive.*

Nausea crept into her throat. *What will Mother do?* The fret and worry for Hillashine and her baby would kill her. And now Giffshine would never come back to visit.

How faithfully does Father follow Wol? How trustworthy can Father's second son be?

Forgotten Slave

Leoshine sat up and strained her ears and eyes. The Dome-light filtered through the windows above. Footsteps sighed in the room. Not Resham. Not ao Kevath.

She leaned forward, ready to stand. Ready to run.

A hand fumbled for the curtain opening. "Leoshine?" Iliana whispered.

"ao …!" Leoshine's mouth formed the syllable.

"Sweetheart!"

Leoshine felt warm arms gather her close. A sob choked her.

"Sweetheart!" Iliana crooned and guided them to sit on the cot.

Leoshine buried her face in the folds of Iliana's robe. For a long time, she could not control the shuddering gasps.

Eventually, she noticed the cool hand stroking her hair and raised her swollen, sodden face.

Iliana lifted a painted eyebrow. "Hungry?"

Leoshine turned her head back into the crook between Iliana's neck and shoulder.

Iliana eased them back against the wall. With one hand she covered them with a blanket.

"I wish I could take you out."

After a quick glance, Leoshine sank back.

"This time is a strain on everyone, my pet. Everything is upside down. I have never been so close to a battle before. But Avram is doing his best." She turned to force Leoshine to sit up face to face. "You must believe that, sweetness. He bears the very hardest burden. Can you see it?"

Leoshine could not sustain her gaze into Iliana's eyes.

The raw mark on her master's brow blazed on unhealed. *But the hardest burden? He wouldn't suffer if he stayed away from Myxolidia.*

Iliana reached out again. "Can you tell me the worst thing that worries you? Is it your family?"

Leoshine tilted her head to tuck her chin in. *Family? What else is there to worry me?*

"It is only a short time, I promise. I will ask Avram to make them more comfortable as soon as the troubles are settled. And we all expect it to be soon, very soon. Hillashine is with me, you know."

Leoshine sat up.

"She has a lovely time with my girls. I will ask Avram if you may see her and maybe you can bathe with her too, when her baby comes. Time is not still, sweetness. It moves in an organised way. My Master controls all. Very soon things will change, really, and you will see how happy we are all together."

Leoshine sank back. All her strength seeped away as Iliana spoke. Hillashine lived with Iliana. Hillashine enjoyed "the girls." *The Omaeuli.* She thought of the floating, fluttery beings that accompanied the ao Kenan wherever she went ... *except here.* Leoshine's lower lip swelled and quivered.

They sat in silence a long while. Leoshine rubbed her cheek and lips on the silky fabric of Iliana's shoulder. Her fingers traced a delicate pattern on the sleeve that rested across her lap. Across her cheek, the long thin finger stroked her tears when they flowed. The Domelight slowly changed, whispering of the end of day.

"I'm hungry," Iliana extracted a shiny black box from her gown. "What did you intend to feed us?" She asked in her most imperious voice.

A noise came from the box in the rhythm of Aeolian speech.

"Well, who can be trusted?" Iliana sounded angry. After another pause she rolled her eyes. "Thank you. Just as I thought."

She folded the little box, and turned back to Leoshine. "The girls will be along soon, and we'll have a nice meal together. How long has it been since you ate in civilised company? They will bring food from my very own kitchen and we'll have a scrumptious time together."

Leoshine pressed her body tighter into the embrace. One of Iliana's bones prodded into her ribs. *How dare you?* She accused herself. *How can I enjoy this, wish for this, long for this never to end?*

Her mind stretched back to her childhood when Mother would run her thumb along her daughter's nose, the times she climbed into bed with Mother and lay deathly still. To wake Mother was to be evicted back to her own cold sleeping closet. Giffshine and Hillashine allowed her to come more often and stay longer, their bodies warm and comforting.

Like this. These people touch each other, she reminded herself. Especially Iliana. ao Kevath slapped backs and grasped hands and put his arm around shoulders of his closest companions. *I am becoming Aeolian.*

Iliana looked up at the shelf. "I haven't been in Avram's room before. I wouldn't come except I knew they would be busy and you might be lonely." After a lengthy pause she commented, "When the girls come we'll draw away the curtain, don't you think?"

Leoshine stiffened. *How many girls are coming? Where are Resham and ao Kevath? When will they return? Never,* she decided. She never wanted to see them again. She sank deeper, burying her eyes in Iliana's arm.

She smells like a flower. She drew tiny puffs of breath through her nose. *I can imagine I am cradled in petals.*

The sentry tapped. Leoshine bit her tongue.

The door opened to the pleasant, easygoing laughter of the Omaeuli.

Iliana disentangled her limbs and sat on the edge of the cot. "Here, girls! Draw back that curtain. Set the food on the table." She rose and helped Leoshine up.

The room opened up. In the next instant, a pretty cloth covered the solemn old table that had been a war desk. Dish after dish covered the centre. Flowers touched every place setting with charm and grace. Three Omaeuli stood before ao Kevath's bed and three before Leoshine's cot, and the remaining six stood behind chairs at the table with Iliana and Leoshine.

Iliana closed her eyes and trained her chin upward. "Ao Kevad!"

All the other faces were tilted up in the same absorbed silence.

For what we are about to receive, Leoshine spoke in her head. *What does eating have to do with the High King?* She wondered again, time without number.

"Thank You, Ao Kevad."

The Omaeuli repeated in unison. "Thank You, Ao Kevad."

They all sat down and started chatting.

"If Avram or Resham come, they'll run straight out!" Iliana giggled. "Come, dear, eat a little something?"

An Omaeulenen held a dish of white grains mixed with green balls beside Leoshine's plate.

My own plate! She realised with a start. *No sharing, no expectations.*

No appetite, she thought with the next heartbeat. She scooped a small pile of grains onto her plate and nodded.

The murmur of Omaeuli laughing and chatting together changes the whole room. Why can't I slip away with them, become one of them? I could serve Iliana. If the invaders are here to stay, I could learn to serve. Why do I have to stay useless, alone?

Other plates were offered, but Leoshine noticed that Iliana ate very little. She felt no guilt in turning them away.

Iliana leaned toward Leoshine. "You must be wondering where they all come from. Back home we are very crowded. There isn't enough housing. Sometimes a family will have more children than house space and, though it is strictly forbidden, they abandon the baby. Our High King rules, but men's hearts still find ways to hurt Him, especially where children and other helpless ones are concerned."

Her voice took a reflective tone. "I have a home full of abandoned ones. Especially the girls, though Dorim and Kirim came to me that way." Her eyes closed and her mouth dragged down at the corners. "I chose these to come here." She looked up and smiled at the assembly. "Well, I asked who wanted to come and chose these from many. Such adventurous spirits! I love them all."

Leoshine stared at the half-covered design on her plate. Her hands rested in her lap.

They all came from Aeolia, knew the code of conduct, the secret code that admitted them to some glorious presence. She merely existed under this scorned Dome with no code. Not a surviving one, anyway.

After the meal, the Omaeuli took every scrap of femininity with them.

Iliana sat back on the cot and held her arms out in wide appeal. Leoshine nestled down. She wondered if Iliana intended to stay through the night. One lamp on the table glowed warmer. The Dome slipped into darkness.

"Leoshine." Iliana swallowed, her breath shallow and rapid. "Do you have anything to say to me? I haven't heard you say a word."

Say? Leoshine opened her mouth. A thousand thoughts sprang to life and crowded for utterance. "Thank you for ... coming." She lisped the gentle syllables with her eyes downcast.

Iliana's face beamed. "There!" She settled down against the wall and twitched the blanket into place.

"You know there is a battle coming, my dearest? And there is a part for you to play. You will be alone here. Avram and Resham are both responsible for"—she paused—"divisions, maneuvers. Do you understand what they are about? They must organise their men, to make the land safe. I will come often, but when I am away you must remember that I am helping Hillashine and don't get angry with me. Don't get angry with Avram, beloved. He is trying his best to make you comfortable."

Comfortable? Leoshine knew he spared her no thought. *Why should he spare thought for a slave?*

Comfort? He knows nothing but his own! She despised him from the distance he imposed on her!

Iliana spoke after another long pause. "Resham believes Wol has given you a message."

Leoshine sprang up and twisted to face Iliana. Her ears rang and her tingling lips parted. Food lurched into her throat and she felt hands steadying her shoulders.

"It has been twenty-one days since you mentioned the Gallalla egg, beloved."

Leoshine's eyes flicked briefly to the corner of her mattress, where the egg lay in its nest. Iliana followed her gaze, and she recognised her mistake. Colours floated across her vision. Blue, green, red. Nausea too. Only Iliana's face hovered crystal clear in the middle of the fog. Threatening? Accusing? Calling? Inviting? *To what?*

Iliana kept her gaze locked and reached for Leoshine's hand. "You don't know about confession, do you? Nor repentance, nor forgiveness."

Leoshine drew her hand away.

"But please believe me, the sickness you feel is because you hold a secret. You feel that releasing it will bring punishment, the end of what little good you find here."

Acid bubbled in Leoshine's throat. She failed at swallowing.

"Please, please believe me, my dearest and most precious Leoshine, that releasing it will bring peace." Iliana sighed and her shoulders slumped. "You don't believe me. But beloved, you and I have enjoyed lessons together. You are so clever and you understand so much.

"When that secret came it broke our fellowship. I tell you on my oath as my Master's servant, the happiness will be restored when the secret is released." Iliana leaned in and grasped Leoshine's chin in her hand. "We already know that Wol gave you the egg. Have we punished you? Have we treated you any differently?"

Tears forced themselves through Leoshine's sickness. She twisted out of Iliana's caress and bowed her head into her hands.

They know. They knew.

How long? Was it ever a secret? How did they know? Why did Resham say nothing? Of course, this connected with Father's arrest! Father must have spoken of Wol's message under torture.

Resham had bruised her to keep her from defending Father. He wanted to do more, and now she knew where his violence sprang from.

No, Iliana said a number. Father taught her to measure the Dome cycles. Iliana, and ao Kevath before her, taught her how to number in Aeolian. Leoshine could not correlate the systems. She remembered days and days.

She felt Iliana relax.

Why did Iliana not see the bruises? Leoshine touched her jaw. *Because she has spoken to Resham and expects them.*

"My love for you has not changed. You believe I love you?"

Love? The word came often to Iliana's lips.

"We don't know what Wol told you, beloved. Please, we need to know in order to protect you."

Will she never stop? Leoshine shuddered.

"How can I be happy until you know you are loved and secure from all harm."

She is like her son. Many times ao Kevath had waited silently for her to obey. *They are good at waiting. They always win.*

"May I see the egg, sweetheart?"

Leoshine's body shrank into itself.

"It is very small, I remember. I promise I won't hurt it."

I could wait. The blood pounded in her ears. What would happen? They knew. They had known. Nothing would change their knowing. *Yes,* she decided, *the egg can come out of darkness.*

Would Iliana believe that she had no message from Wol?

She dug deep into the mattress while Iliana watched. The egg and the coin emerged together from their nest, into Leoshine's quivering palm.

Iliana gasped and reached to grasp the delicate egg. Leoshine closed her hand.

"Ahhh!" Iliana's hand came up to her throat and she sat back with her eyes closed. She cradled Leoshine's hand in her own and pressed gently until the fingers unfurled. "Where did that come from?" She pointed to the disk.

"The man gave it to me." Leoshine formed the Aeolian words slowly. "ao Kevath's …" *What did he call them?* "Will he want me to give it back?"

"Beloved!" Iliana exclaimed. "You talk well! I mean, I love to hear you. You should speak more, and more often!

"We use these in trade. This symbol is to remind us of our High King even in everyday dealings. I am reminded He is at work here! My Master arrived before me, and His plan is in motion. Keep it. If my Master wants it, He will come Himself to claim it."

Leoshine glanced around the room. "Where is He?"

"Oh," sighed Iliana with a contented smile. "He is here, there, and everywhere. We cannot see Him, but we can see His work and when He visits, it's like nothing else. The feeling of joy! One phrase we have is, 'My cup runneth over.' Can you imagine your heart running over like a cup?"

Leoshine shook her head. What was there to understand about an invisible being that traveled unpredictably and ran over the heart, as if it were a cup? Did they run over cups in Aeolia? What with, transport vehicles? Feet? Love?

"You know the story of His work, don't you, Love? His work covers everything. He is with every one of us." The old lady yawned prodigiously. "I'm tired. But will you remember this?" Iliana straightened and prepared to rise. "'Because of His great might, not one of them is missing.' Not one of them is missing, dearest, not even you."

With wide, pleading eyes Leoshine reached out to grasp Iliana's forearm.

Iliana smiled her comfort. "No, it would be unwise for me to leave now. Avram would be upset if I wandered outside in the dark. I'll sleep in his bed. I expect it is comfortable enough, though I dare say he doesn't know." She embraced Leoshine briefly and then rose to turn down the covers on the great chiseled poster bed. "It belonged to my father. But Avram would not use it until now. Funny the whims the boy has. Could you bring me that bag, darling? The girls brought my gown, and one for you too."

Leoshine stared at her treasures. *Should I put them in the nest?* They seemed to spiral downward. Her eyes ached.

She heard her voice urge Iliana. "He didn't tell me anything."

"Be patient, sweetheart," Iliana began to say, but stopped. "Oh, you mean Wol." This more seriously: "I'm glad."

The air tautened as Leoshine awaited more interrogation. The pressure before she had brought forth the egg still gave her chills. Now her mentor appeared to have lost interest. "He is …."

With a pettish look and a wave of her finger toward the bag, Iliana silenced further explanations.

Leoshine opened the flap, and shook out two white, frilly nightgowns.

"Do you like it?"

Leoshine felt like a ragdoll as Iliana loosed the ties of her dress for her and pulled the nightgown over her head. Her skin shivered as the bony fingers dug into her shoulder muscles, and then guided her to lie down.

I'm not here.

Iliana draped the blankets, and touched her lips to Leoshine's cheek.

No thought broke the misty calm. *In the morning,* she promised herself. *I'll ask questions.*

When morning came, she found herself alone. Iliana had left a slip of paper on the table. She could read her name, 'Leoshine,' but the rest remained undecipherable. She tucked it in with the egg and the disk, a meagre hoard for a forgotten slave.

Three days. Three days in a cage with no company, no faces to break the monotony, to inform of the shattering events changing the world outside the plastered walls.

Leoshine flung herself into ao Kevath's chair and surveyed the food Iliana had sent via an intensely stupid or sworn-to-secrecy Omaeulenen. All the girl could say was that the ao Kenan was busy with Hillashine and please be patient one more day.

When Leoshine pleaded for information about her sister, the girl shrugged and squirmed out the door.

On the first day, Leoshine had dug out her treasures and placed them on the table in a bowl. If they knew, there was no point hiding anymore.

She hoped Iliana would return and cuddle more. Or did she only do that when her "love" demanded secrets? Leoshine's lower lip protruded and her brows drew together.

Hillashine lived with Iliana now. Leoshine tried to imagine her sister sinking into the sweet-scented embrace. Her lower lip pushed further and further out. Short, fat Hillashine. Giffshine had whispered that she was pale and thin with the pregnancy.

Hillashine with a swollen middle. A baby. No matter how hard Leoshine imagined, she could not see her sister with a baby.

Mother, Hillashine, cross, baby. The Aeolian words echoed from a long-ago lesson. *What did he know of mothers or sisters or babies?* She scoffed. Cross? A figure of filigree. A symbol representing a sound that she didn't know, even after all this time.

On the second day, Leoshine opened the door. The guards turned to block her way, grim-faced and frightened. She scoffed and wondered how she knew of their fear. Perhaps because they looked at each other from the corners of their eyes, as if they confronted a Myxolidian savage. *Ao Kevad forbid!* She rolled her eyes at them.

What if they had to wrestle me if I tried to run? She slammed the door in their faces.

How did ao Kevath survive for three days without food? Resham might bring the tray somewhere else, but what about fresh clothes? Did his hair not need the brush or his nails need shortening and rubbing? What about shaving? Did he cover his throat stones with hair now? Or his shoes, did they not cake with dust? Did Resham find polish elsewhere? Or did he neglect his duty? Did he not mend, repair, replace buttons on the royal garments and uniform? Did he abandon this room for another? Did they have another set of furniture and personal effects? Another slave?

The black board device and writing instruments lying beside the food tray caught her eye. Earlier in the day, she had thought about writing to Iliana, sending a message with an Omaeulenen. But the symbols she had traced to please the ao Kenan meant little at the time, and nothing now. She mourned her failure. *If only ...*

The Domelight faded and Leoshine lit the table lamp. *At least I know how to do that! I can take care of myself. I just want to go out. Just let me see what is happening.*

She stood away from the chair, and surveyed the room. ao Kevath's bed called to her. She had watched from her cot as suave, dexterous servants dusted and polished the edifice. She climbed up and sat cross-legged in the center. The mattress sprang under her and she bounced until she was breathless.

She lay down and stared at the ceiling of the canopy. *Deep red.* Dark like the blood on ao Kevath's hands after he had killed with his sword as he had lifted her onto Paulos. She shuddered and rolled off the bed.

The carved post called to her toes. *Climb!* That story she told Iliana was true! She had climbed the vines to collect eggs. She had climbed trees, and walls, and Father's watch tower, to gaze outside the walls to the carpet of trees where the Oxikobh lived.

The massive carved pillars of the bed gave splendid holds to her fingers and toes. In an instant she sat atop the canopy, in the center, away from the edges. The cupboards on one side of the bed touched the wall with the windows.

Windows! In the light of tomorrow, she might see the courtyard below, or further, across to the next building. Voices reached her. Murmurs nearby and bellows and summons and cries of every human expression. Horses! She drew air through her nostrils and tasted the warmth from the nearby beasts.

She rose, half crouching, and leaned against the wall. If she put forth a sturdy effort, she might climb from the top of the canopy onto the cupboard and from there the shelf with the Oxikobh filth boxes.

What if I knocked the boxes off? Leoshine's spine tingled.

Giffshine came this way. If Resham came ...

Every moment she expected him or her master. The longer they stayed away, the sooner they might burst through the door. If Resham came and found the room empty, he would not rest until he found her. There existed no place under the Dome he would not search, and not a place that she knew of anywhere she could hide. Who among ao Kevath's servants would fail to recognize her and not replace her, or take her to Father in the jail? What change would that be? She did not expect to share a cell with him. Life would be worse there.

But three days? Three days of desertion? The night stretched empty. The meal sat on the table untouched. The walls of the dungeon closed in.

She slithered down the bedpost, clenched her fists, and raised her shoulders near her ears. Her breath hissed through her flared nostrils.

She hurled herself against the other door in the room. Resham came from there in the mornings.

The shock of impact rattled her teeth.

Had he foreseen this moment? Had he built it strong to crush her bones as they collided with its impenetrable mightiness?

She stormed a few steps to the screen around her cot and filled her fists with fabric. The frame collapsed with one tug. She stumbled forward into the tangle of curtains and poles, and wrestled the mattress and pillows onto the floor. After a moment to catch her breath, she heaved again, and the mattress somersaulted. The bed frame clattered onto its side.

Heat swelled in her arms and face. She stomped over to the carved wooden box at the foot of ao Kevath's bed. The lid snapped back to reveal books and boxes. One by one, she flung them over her shoulders to land where they willed.

Facing the bed, she remembered Iliana's words. "It was my father's bed."

This was my father's room, she hurled back in her mind.

She swarmed up the canopy and swatted a box of Oxikobh filth across the room. The dirt scattered by Resham's door.

Perfect. She reveled. *Oxikobh filth!*

She stretched. Her toes clung to the canopy edge. She swatted two more boxes onto the floor. One smashed on the edge of the table, and the other near her old cot.

Father's room, desecrated. Desecrated by aliens.

This is Father's room. She slithered down the bedpost. *I'll purge the Invader's curse.*

Sheets and blankets and pillows on the offending foreign bed writhed and twisted in her fists. Her arms strained, and her spine complained until they lay in the gathering mountain on the floor. The curtains laughed at her first efforts to tear them down and then one yielded and buried her with a thump.

The cupboards vomited their contents. Devices, garments, tools that Resham used to polish or trim or mend or smooth his master; all flew from their containers. No jacket though. ao Kevath took his jacket and his armour with him, wherever that was.

When no object remained where Resham expected to find it, she bruised her toes on the heap of debris. She hurled herself into the mayhem and whaled upon it with her fists, screaming, weeping until her throat dried and her eyes swelled.

Her arms failed. Her body succumbed to heaviness.

Mother ... A warm embrace. *Iliana.*

Did Hillashine imagine herself cradled in petals? Bossy, grumpy Hillashine who treated little sisters like Rellogat and Rellogat like Rachnorgat and Rachnorgat ... Father hadn't owned Rachnorgat since—her mind caught in a side trail—since he went to Aeolia.

If Hillashine owned Rellogat, they would die from neglect. Like ao Kevath's Rellogat. *Why?* she asked herself with her face smothered in wet fabric, *do I expect anything different?*

She changed, Leoshine thought of her sister again, *like Giffshine changed after the Rite of Womanhood that gave her to a man.* Giffshine's change had drawn the younger sisters closer. Hillashine's change left the youngest lonely. *Did Father take me away from Mother more often because he knew this?*

Leoshine remembered the bruise on her leg from the last time she climbed into bed with Hillashine. *No,* she concluded, *Hillashine did not snuggle with Iliana. She hated Father's new ideas. Why would she adopt them now?*

Escape

∿⌇∽⌇∿

Leoshine's eyes opened before her dream ended. A sharp noise shattered her nerves in complete darkness.

She raised her face off the folds of curtains and blankets from ao Kevath's bed that she vaguely remembered heaving onto the floor and burrowing into. She stretched her stiff neck to listen.

Something hard rattled across the table, hit the edge of the food tray, and rattled to the floor. She tore a blanket away from her head and strained to hear.

"Leoshine." A hoarse whisper pierced her heart. "Come to the window. Climb like Giff did."

Wol! Shivering beset her bones as she waited to hear him again.

"Come to the window, Leotjie. I have to talk to you!"

She clambered up to the canopy and measured the distance before she leapt onto the cupboard top. Her lithe body scrambled to the shelf.

Below the window, in the courtyard, Wol peeped up at her from beneath a large brimmed, floppy, and dented hat. "Come to me, I'll catch you."

Many times as a child she had leapt from garden walls and tree branches into his arms.

Lights shone in the stable windows on the opposite wall. Muffled noises of nighttime chores reached her from all around. "How did you get in here?"

"I'll tell you when you come down. I can't stay long."

"I …" She glanced back at the room. *ao Kevath is coming. I have to clean up.* "I can't go with you, you know. You'll have to help me up again."

*Wol. S*he hovered on the lintel. The chill air kissed her cheeks. "I need a shawl." She half turned into the room.

"Sure, anything for you. Leo. Quickly though. I can't stay long."

He can't stay long. She turned back. *Maybe* ... She wriggled through the window and launched herself.

Her body collided with her brother's arms. She looked up into his face. Her heart imploded the instant she recognised triumph.

A course rope strangled her tongue and all went black. Coarse material scratched her cheek. A cold sweat exploded on her neck and arms. She kicked against pinching arms. *Oxikobh,* she remembered. *Oxikobh, who brought me to ao Kevath, held me like this.*

Not savages, but Wol hissed near her ear. "Quiet, Leotjie, don't you want to play?"

Play? The gag he used to "play" bit into her lip corners and strangled her breath. Raw rope scratched at her bound wrists. His shoulder bones jabbed into her ribs. Her body twisted at all angles until she fell heavily and the wind knocked its way out of her lungs.

Wol laughed. "What a sack of cabbages! Come on, we're late."

The last she knew, she was picked up and flung across hard protrusions.

<p>

Leoshine felt herself tumble out of a sack. Immediately, hard fingers grasped her limbs and swung her into Wol's arms astride a horse.

Reviving new air came in sobs through her nose. The gag clamped her tongue.

Hoofbeats rustled in the dry forest debris. The darkness pressed on her eyeballs. *The forest! Oxikobh territory!*

Wol laughed nearby. "Play with me?"

She gnawed at the gag. *Let me go!* She screamed without syllables. *He will kill you!*

Wol whipped his horse. Other hoofbeats pounded in her ears. At times, she heard voices near and far, warning of Aeolian activity and pointing out the road.

ao Kevath said he had a camp. A ridge. Wol camped on high ground and waited for the Aeolians to come to him.

Hands gripped her again. Her head lolled over, and her hair fell across her face as she landed on a straw mattress. Wol's face swam in a blur. His eyebrows knit together in the middle of his forehead.

He undid the gag and the wrist bonds. Fresh air, colder than the town, stirred her exposed skin. "Sorry about the ride, Leo. We couldn't take any risks." The late light shone red on his mud-splattered face and bright grinning teeth. "Here, eat a little, then you can sleep. I've got it all under control."

Leoshine rolled away.

"What's the matter?" Wol stood up and dusted his hands. "Been spoiled by that new stuff they call food? Remember how Mother made this?" He slurped a mouthful. "No, I admit this isn't as good, but don't get all high-nosed about it."

"You eat it." She groaned. "Leave me alone."

He held up his hands in mock surrender. "Okay, okay. Anything for you, Leotjie. We'll talk in the morning."

"Open! Open!" Resham bellowed as he approached Avram's chamber.

The sentry stepped backwards. Resham threw the door back on its hinges.

Inside all lay as still as death. *Black death arrives when the heart stops.* He flared his nostrils and sensed tears. Fear. Weeping. He tore through the debris. Horror gripped his spine with cold fingers.

Violence? Did they offer the little one harm?

His foot scuffed in dirt near the door. Empty shelves. At the table he examined the uneaten food and lifted the egg. Between his fingers, the tiny messenger could be crushed in a twinkling.

She caused this. One agony replaced another. *She escaped.*

Beside the egg he found a slip of paper. *Iliana's scrawl.* "'Because of His great might, not one is missing.'"

"Are you joking?" He asked aloud. *SHE is missing.*

"Send to the barracks for ao Kevath." He commanded the

sentry as he whipped past. "Tell him nothing except … he must come immediately."

A few strides brought him to the courtyard under the chamber windows. The body of the sentry lay over the abandoned fire pit in the centre of the square. A trickle of blood still oozed from his throat.

Two soldiers arrived on the covered porch. Resham bent down and scratched in the dirt between the flagstones. One man had come. *Only Wol himself could lure her out.* He could not have come through the palace or the stable. A gash and hand prints in the ancient ash showed how the villain climbed from the tunnels beneath the palace.

Resham heaved the lid off the fire pit and lowered his head as far as possible. The walls were newly scraped. Wol had dug a new tunnel to this place.

"Trackers!" he ordered while marching back to Avram's chamber. "Follow with 100 men. Take pictures of the body. Sweep the area with the scanners." He dove through the door. *Avram will arrive soon.*

In that instant, Avram filled the doorframe. He rested his head on arms raised to lean on the lintel. Resham tensed all his muscles.

Avram's jaw dropped as he surveyed his scattered possessions.

Resham watched the blood play in his face.

"The sentry …?" Avram pointed toward the wall with the windows.

Until last night, a soldier had guarded beneath them.

"Murdered, ao Kevath."

"The girl, Leoshine …?"

"She climbed out, ao Kevath. Yes." Resham surveyed the rubble. "She did this."

Wol will murder her! The thought flashed between them as their eyes met. He had killed the other brother and delivered their father to be slaughtered by Aeolians.

"Too important to him." Resham answered.

Avram's chest heaved. His nostrils flared and his teeth clenched. "Search party!"

"Trackers sent with 100 men."

"Double it." Avram kicked wildly at the objects littering his path and waved his fists to accent his speech. "Treble it! I will lead them!"

"ao Kevath, the battle. Can we spare the men?"

Avram picked up a metal cup from the tray of her untouched evening meal and hurled it against the door frame. The liquid splashed red on the wall and dribbled down the plaster. A plate followed, then another, and then the whole tray. He stepped forward and crushed something under his boot. Every stride brought further destruction.

He fought his way to the clear space by the main door and hovered on his toes. "Leave me." He groaned and swatted his hand at Resham. "Find her."

Resham picked the egg off the table. He gripped Avram's wrist and placed the egg in his palm.

Avram writhed free of the touch and twisted toward the door.

"Find her!" A noise wheezed from Avram's lungs as he ran down the hall.

At dusk Resham returned from his reconnaissance. The council chamber sentry's expression told him Avram was not inside. The jumble of sheets and curtains and books remained untouched, and Resham considered what evidence he could collect. Wol had not entered the room. The girl took nothing with her.

As he left, he nodded to the hovering chief steward, giving permission to return the room to usable condition.

He marched through the deserted courtyard to the stables. Avram had turned his communicator off, silencing the locater, a vain attempt to hide from one who knew his habits.

Paulos' stall was empty. Sometimes a sulking Avram could be found lying in the straw. The tack hook hung empty.

A soldier cocked his head to the arena door, and Resham followed the cue.

He paused to listen and sniff the air. The warm bulk of Paulos rumbled to the right.

A rustle of cloth and a breath alerted him to a presence against the left wall.

Resham announced to the thrumming silence: "As commander of the sentries I tender my resignation."

"Denied." Avram replied in a flat bark. "Report!"

Resham dug his feet into the arena sand. "Wol outwitted me." He copied Avram's blank, disinterested tone. "It is uncharacteristic of him to employ the same device twice, yet both his sisters climbed the wall and exited through the window. If I resign you can appoint ...'"

"Someone more capable?" Avram snapped. "Where is your second in command, Burg? Let's promote him."

"Dead, ao Kevath."

The heavy breathing included a snort.

Resham studied the dark patch where Avram's voice came from. Paulos' hooves crunched in the sand beside him.

"Won't let me ride him." Avram scowled.

"You've never approached him in your anger."

"You think I am angry?"

Resham braced his shoulders and bent his knees. Sometimes a fist or a tackle followed such a wicked rumble out of the darkness.

The breath sighed out of Avram's bulk. Resham now could see him sitting on the ground with his arm swung over his knees and his head turned away.

"Where is she?"

"Wol's camp."

"You didn't bring her home?"

"The battle, ao Kevath. You have finally forced Wol to fight by your parameters. Fetching the girl would set him back to his."

Resham remained braced. Paulos shook his head and snorted.

Avram gave a bitter laugh. "I tendered my resignation to Ao Kevad. I, too, was denied. There is no resignation in this campaign, unless we go the way of Burg, because if there is no Resham, there is no Avram." He jumped to his feet and rammed his left shoulder against Resham's right, an acknowledgment of their childhood when they fought in hatred and of their late teens when Iliana's heir learned to express his anger and his servant learned to fight back in a way that took the anger to Ao Kevad.

"A priest is a warrior." Resham remembered Iliana teaching him. "A priest fights before, beside, behind"—she had looked at him with these same piercing, frank eyes—"and against." He rolled onto the balls of his feet and pushed back.

"If the city is full of assassins, why am I still alive?" Avram sneered.

Silence.

He answered his own question. "Because no one is your equal. In the next few days, I will be on the battlefield, and you will agree that is a much safer place for me than this traitor-riddled town. Leoshine escaped because we left her alone. You expected me to return here. I neglected, no, I purposely stayed away. The responsibility is mine, but"—he reached out his hand—"it is you who must retrieve her.

"The generals were right. We anticipated organized resistance and are dealing with it. Maybe back in Aeolia we underestimated Wol, but a little extra effort and"—Avram snapped his fingers—"and to spread enlightenment further and deeper"—he looked away—"one must expect sacrifices."

The hair on Resham's neck rose up. "I will ..."

Avram cocked his eyebrows to repeat the question. "You think I'm angry? It doesn't feel like before."

Resham filled his chest and grabbed Avram's forearm. "The loss will be avenged! And restored!"

Avram's eyes blazed. Resham blinked. His instinct bristled.

Avram relaxed and held Resham's elbow. "We were to dine with Iliana. She will bless me. Leoshine was to stay with her for the battle."

The corner of Resham's lip curled upward and he felt relief to see the spark of humour at Leoshine escaping the honourable Mother's tender custody.

He turned and collected Paulos' reins, offering them to their master. "Still time to ride."

"Iliana knows?"

"Gavin told her."

Avram raised his hand. "She'll wait."

Paulos stepped between the men and flicked his head against Avram's chest. A grin crept onto Avram's face as he rocked back on his feet. "He forgives my anger. Do you, brother?"

Resham gripped Avram's wrists and stared into his bloodshot eyes. "The debt is paid, ao Kevath."

Paulos' gesture brought Leoshine's tumble in the arena sand to Avram's mind. *Where did I go wrong?* He puzzled during the ride, grooming, and march to Iliana's palace.

Iliana sat alone in a darkened room with a book open on her

lap. She did not rise as he entered and could only muster a weak smile to greet him.

Paint and dust and construction glue hung too recently in this room. Only by burying his face in her lap could he evoke her private parlour in Aeolia.

He shivered as her fingers stroked his hair. He lifted his head to speak. "Why did she go? Didn't she trust me? How could she go with that … that …?"

Iliana touched his lips, warning him not to dishonour himself with slander, even if it sounded like truth at the moment.

His soul writhed at her rebuke. The question pounded with his heart as it had with Paulos' hoofbeats. *How could she? How could she?*

Iliana tilted her head to one side. "My son, you don't know how she went. Do not judge her until you know that, and then do not judge her at all. Be content that you have always done honourably by her." She kept her head tilted as she held his clenched jaw in the palm of her hand. "Leoshine is a woman worthy of you."

He sprang to his feet and paced. Spots obscured the room and he screamed between clenched teeth when his shin collided with the short-legged table in the middle of the room. The radius of his steps opened to include the sofa opposite his mother. Blood smeared his fingers from the raw skin above his eye. The intolerable pain in his chest constricted his breath, and he pulled at the fabric of his blouse.

Iliana settled into her chair. "My poor quaint son. You think your love for her is your secret. Do you remember how you longed for your father when he left us? You thought he could do no wrong. You worshiped him. Then he returned and you found that he was a man full of anger and bitterness and your heart turned against him.

"You have isolated that girl so that her family has grown in virtue and stature in her mind. Her brother would be a hero from her babyhood. If he came to offer her his company, she would not think twice. He could tell her any lie. He could offer her the humblest path and she would not hesitate to take it.

"Can you trust her to stay and watch your enemy? Do you believe in her intelligence and wisdom as much as you want her to believe in yours? Surely she will see the truth and she will freely give her heart to you instead of your coercing it from her."

"You set Father free. It nearly killed you!"

Iliana straightened in her chair. "He nearly killed me."

Avram cursed and paced faster. Both hands squeezed his blazing purple temples. His breath snorted through flared nostrils.

Iliana murmured in a lilting voice. "You are angry."

"Yes!"

"You want to kill."

All motion ceased. "No!" He cast himself at her feet. *Father killed in his anger.* In her tone she warned him that he reminded her of that cruelty and insensitivity to life. No! If he killed anything in his anger he would be killing her and all she had taught him.

Leoshine didn't like the killing.

He leapt up, crossed the room, and stared at the wall. He paced behind her sofa and held his breath until her song reached his heart. By increments, he came to stand in front of her and sank to his knees, lowering his head into her lap.

Avram felt his mother soften. He could not understand the words, but her melody curled in his ear.

Solemn stillness followed. Calm settled and neither moved to break it. Avram subsided and he sent his spirit out. He knew Iliana's was ahead, already convening with Ao Kevad.

Quaint, she had called him.

Iliana curled his hair around her fingers. "She has distracted you from your first purpose."

"No, don't say that. You don't know how many times I have cried out, 'This is too much for me!'" Avram swallowed hard. "I would have broken under the yoke if there hadn't been a little face in the corner reminding me, urging me toward the redemption of her people. She is a gift. Now she is gone, and I'd rather have my heart torn from my chest."

Iliana's tears splashed on his hand. "What did you come here for?"

His tears soaked her skirt. "To regenerate the Dome and renew Ao Kevad's presence here. She was an example to her people."

"Now she is an example *of* her people?"

"No!" Rebellious? Contradictory? Leoshine had tried harder than her father to accept new ways. Now she put herself in danger. Why? *What am I missing?*

He rose again and paced for another long stretch. *What is she teaching me? What do You want from me?*

He finally looked up, frowning. He imagined running his sword through the rebel leader. "So to battle?"

"Throw yourself into it. She is waiting for you on the other side."

Acknowledgements

Colleen McCubbin – who charges forth through epic thunderstorms, cuts to the chase and inspires her community to heights they never imagined! (But that she did all along.) Human connection is her superpower, and she doesn't mind if everybody else has that one too.

Marcia Laycock – the renowned author of *One Smooth Stone* (among other novels) applied her unerring instinct for story to smelt the gold of Leoshine out of the dross of my words. What a privilege to have her vision with me!

Christina Pitre – who shaped the smelted gold with intricate details and profound concepts. Her heart beats for freedom and specificity and Leoshine leaps off the page into readers' hearts as a result.

Pauline Miller – an exceptional writer, my first writing buddy who read early drafts, took me to conferences, introduced me to behind-the-scenes Drumheller Passion Play, and waits patiently for her own debut.

Claire Mose – who taught me grace by giving it. She doesn't want me to tell you about the box of chocolates, but this is an example of the heights she will go for Leoshine.

Corrine Vooys – who asks questions that I don't have answers to (which I love to just know about). She probes deeper, quests for greater insight, and doesn't mind if I answer with flights of fantasy because she knows how to put my feet back on terra firma.

Katie Gerke – who gives more than she has in listening to my sob stories and solving my problems. Also a brilliant writer, artist and advocate, she doesn't stop at the finish line. Her patience would be a lesson for Job.

Cindy Homer – who has ancient (printed) drafts of Leoshine and has believed in her story from the very first. Practical and down-to-earth, Cindy gave me the glass ball pendant that inspired the one Leoshine wears, and catalogued the many and various pronunciations of Leoshine's name.

My fellow Nestbuilders – Connie, Marcia, Robert, Travis, Lisa, Charity, and Fred have blazed the way before me, solved challenges, and celebrated like true artists. Our spirit of community and collaboration in the Nestbuilders author cohort at Siretona Creative is unmatched!

My family – father, husband, sisters, brother and daughter who have listened to my stories and lifted me with all manner of encouragements, material and skillful. "Without family there is no home."

ATB BoostR Shout Out

Charity Mongrain – who puts her heart into her work for others. You gathered my rough edges, sweetened my gruffness, and put your energy behind my grand leaps of fantasy. Your efforts will live on in the hearts and minds of many generations.

Faye Hleuka – who uses a high voltage wire to connect her people together.

ATBBoostRs – C. Reimer, D. Bentley, E. Lombard, G. Sherman, I. Cassidy, J. Dinsdale-Perryman, J. Bosch, K. Beasley, K. Matiko, K, Templeton. L. Davies, M. Attridge, P. Lester, T. Lust, M. Renton, D. Henrichsen.

Thank you for your support of my crowdfunding efforts through the ATB BoostR!

Tassanara Font

Every fantasy world needs its own alphabet and font. The Leoshine Series is the only world with Travis Williams and his magical piece of spring. He kept that coil of metal for at least ten years before his imagination recognised that Leoshine was the perfect home at last.

You can watch his interview on MicAndPen. https://go.micandpen.com/youtube The glyphs he created are beyond beautiful. I squealed with joy when I saw them.

Travis didn't stop there. He taught me all kinds of ways to use them. On the book cover, in Internet Treasure Hunts, on the map, as chapter titles, on the Leoshine merchandise at https://www.tassanara.com/shop/

Visit https://www.tassanara.com/ to find the font legend and use it it translate any Tassanara text you may find, such as the following words from the map border.

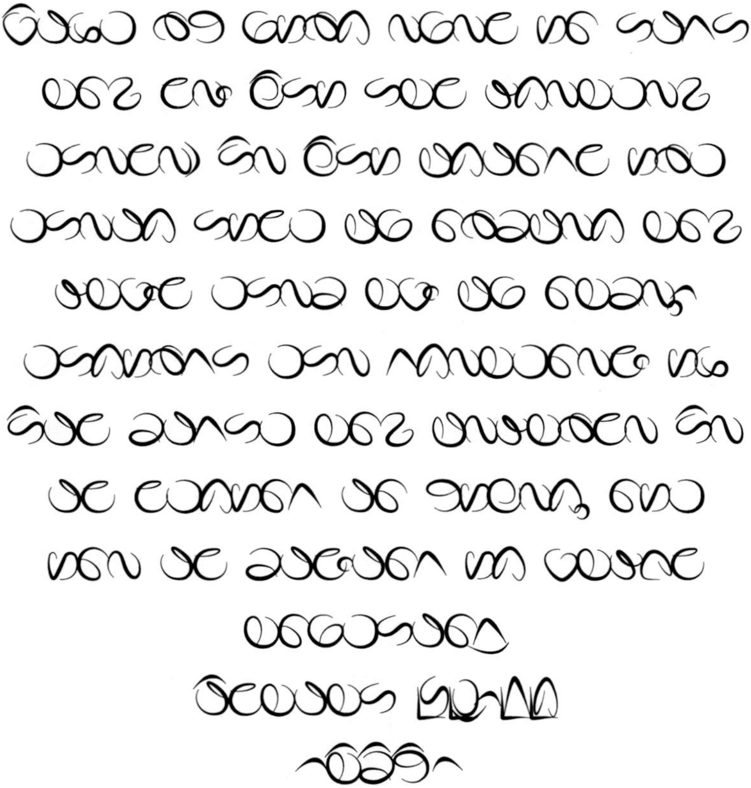

Excerpt from
Leoshine, Princess Quarry, **Book Two**

A chill breeze ruffled Leoshine's hair. The shivering of the trees continued in the path of ao Kevath's monsters. The black mark was a line now, edging ever longer, ever toward her.

Will ao Kevath notice the band of attackers? His force would brush them off like mother brushed flour off her apron. Leoshine sighed and twisted her fingers in her chain.

A sound like weeping drifted in the air.

Leoshine placed her hand over her chest. The sound like weeping ceased, and then began again. Leoshine stood and listened behind her. *Is it me?*

She climbed over the ridge. The weeping grew louder. In a hollow, where the rock ridge plunged under looser ground, she found a huddled boy wearing coarse, dirty and torn clothes. His feet were soiled enough that Leoshine had to look twice to see he wore no coverings on them.

He started and seemed to wince. One eye stared at her through long, matted hair.

He straightened and extended a purple, green, and black hand toward her. The skin distended so far that his fingers blended together.

Leoshine crouched down beside him, her hands tucked in her lap. "How did that happen?"

The boy lifted his face. Tears welled up and ran over the eye that peeked through the hair. His lip trembled.

"You're no older than me! You need help. Is there anyone? No!" Leoshine considered Wol's people. "A healer? Oh, what's to be done?" She bit her lip and her brows met together high on her forehead.

She touched the other arm of the boy. "Come. Can you walk? If you come, I might be able to help you." She tugged on his sleeve. "If you don't come, well, I can't." She shrugged and scrounged her resources. Resham would know what to do.

The boy pulled away, then cried out.

"See?" Leoshine urged. "That hurts." The next time he moved, she winced too.

The boy stared at her, his brows knotted, the tears spilling.

Leoshine continued to ask and tug on his sleeve. "How old are you? Are you going to fight in the battle? Not with that arm! Did you fight? Did you fall?" At last he yielded and struggled to his feet.

Step by step, tug by tug, she guided him along the path to the circle of tents. At the perimeter, he dug in his heels and made inarticulate mewings and moanings.

Leoshine put her arm around his shoulders. "You need to come to the fire. Why don't you want to come? Trust me!" She called out to a passing man with an ax on his shoulder. "Hey, you! Go tell the cook that I need hot water!"

Instantly the man turned and disappeared between the tents.

Leoshine called to two other men. "I'll need you. You must help me." Her tone commanded. She tried to imitate Wol and even Resham, demanding obedience of herself as well.

Hot water might cleanse the wound. But the rottenness seemed to be inside the arm.

The men turned toward her.

Photo by Elizabeth Summerley

Nicola MacCameron thrives between hard-won earthy wisdom and flights of spectacular fantasy. She is proud of her Third Culture Kid identity, having lived on three continents and now settled on the Canadian Prairie. She worships the one God, is wife to one man, mother to one child, and piano teacher to many. Through authoring and narrating books, she hopes to bestow to you "treasure through story."

Looking forward to Book Two?
Stay in touch @ http://www.tassanara.com/